STRANGERS BEHIND CLOSED DOORS

Catherine Adel West

Recycling programs for this product may not exist in your area.

ISBN-13: 978-0-7783-6006-3

Strangers Behind Closed Doors

Park Row Books
22 Adelaide St. West, 41st Floor
Toronto, Ontario M5H 4E3, Canada
ParkRowBooks.com

HarperCollins Publishers
Macken House, 39/40 Mayor Street Upper,
Dublin 1, D01 C9W8, Ireland
www.HarperCollins.com

Printed in U.S.A.

26 27 28 29 30 LBC 5 4 3 2 1

Praise for *Saving Ruby King*

"*Saving Ruby King* is a stunning force of a novel that has everything anyone could want in a family saga—honey-dipped prose, strikingly human characters, and a satisfying, soul-stirring conclusion that will stay with me for a long, long time."

—Zakiya Dalila Harris, *New York Times* bestselling author of *The Other Black Girl*

"Told with teeth and tenderness, *Saving Ruby King* is a surprising, pedal-down debut that explores what happens when the fabrics of family, faith, and friendship snag on violent machinations of the heart."

—Leesa Cross-Smith, author of *Whiskey & Ribbons* and *So We Can Glow*

"Catherine Adel West breathes life into violence and mayhem like a poet on a new day. These are the stories we need to hear: voices of hope in a wilderness of pain."

—Rene Denfeld, bestselling author of *The Child Finder* and *The Butterfly Girl*

"[An] ambitious, keenly observant debut . . . West's tale of grace, redemption, and hope would translate handily to the screen."

—Publishers Weekly

"A multilayered love letter to South Side Chicago's African American faith-based community."

—Kirkus Reviews

"A story of intrigue and heartbreaking family secrets . . . A fresh look into the church community of Chicago's South Side with a bold female perspective."

—Library Journal

Praise for *The Two Lives of Sara*

"West writes with charming precision and intention. Every character is a beautiful, relatable complication . . . *The Two Lives of Sara* solidifies West as a literary force."

—*Booklist*, starred review

"In this utterly absorbing and dazzling novel about the stories we tell to stay alive and the secrets we keep to protect ourselves, Catherine Adel West explores the intricacies of family and community . . . I couldn't put this exquisite book down."

—Nancy Jooyoun Kim, *New York Times* bestselling author of *The Last Story of Mina Lee*

"This heartfelt novel about a survivor trying to build a new life among a found family cuts deep. Catherine Adel West has woven a rich story filled with warmth, faith, and hope while also incisively exploring the limits of resilience."

—Maisy Card, author of *These Ghosts Are Family*

"A wondrous journey that combines everything I adore in a story—resilient Black women, hope, and love!"

—Jamise Harper, coauthor of *Bibliophile: Diverse Spines* and founder of the Diverse Spines book community

"A stunning journey of a mother's love and sacrifice."

—Nancy Johnson, author of *The Kindest Lie* and *People of Means*

"Catherine Adel West's beautiful writing is truly a gift—a poetic treasure that engages the heart and the mind."

—Wanda M. Morris, Lefty Award–winning author of *All Her Little Secrets*

For Mable Jean and Ursula

We Wear the Mask

We wear the mask that grins and lies,
It hides our cheeks and shades our eyes,—
This debt we pay to human guile;
With torn and bleeding hearts we smile,
And mouth with myriad subtleties.

Why should the world be over-wise,
In counting all our tears and sighs?
Nay, let them only see us, while
    We wear the mask.

We smile, but, O great Christ, our cries
To thee from tortured souls arise.
We sing, but oh the clay is vile
Beneath our feet, and long the mile;
But let the world dream otherwise,
    We wear the mask!

—Paul Laurence Dunbar

PROLOGUE

Nivea Dugrave

December 22, 2023

Someone is following me.

I know this like I know the emergency room is gonna be down at least two nurses on Christmas. I know this like I know Ava is gonna ask me to read her two bedtime stories tonight because it's a Friday. And I will because no matter how bone-tired I am from a double shift, my baby girl deserves a good book and pretty dreams.

Inflatable Santas, reindeer, and elves bend to the wind's mercy. Twinkling electric lights frame the windows of houses.

Green to blue to gold to magenta, then red.

A dirty white Oldsmobile cruises past, slightly swerving to avoid the craters passing for potholes. Tinted windows slowly lower, a hand juts from the opening.

Gripping the chain link fence to my right, I steady myself as I turn to run but all the outstretched hand holds is the butt of a cigarette. The driver tosses it in the street, then speeds up and turns the corner.

I jump at my buzzing cell phone.

Mom: save u a plate?

Me: Can make my own. thx.

Mom: U close?

Chicago wind hisses and shrieks, the pressure from the air shoves me forward, encouraging me to stay alert, move faster, but the black ice in my city is a particular type of sinister. My phone buzzes again.

Mom: U ok?

The lights twinkle. *Green to blue to gold to magenta, then red.*

I'm not okay, but Momma taught me to be strong. To fight. And when she didn't think I was watching, she taught me how to hide things you don't want people to see, to protect them. To protect yourself.

Me: Fine. Ava awake?

Mom: got her books picked. lol

Mom sends a picture of Ava clutching Pinksy, her best friend and stuffed unicorn. Bright smile with two missing teeth. One at the top. One at the bottom.

I type: Be home in 5 min. 😊

Behind me, there's a light crunch of dead leaves under someone else's feet. Their shadow expands and contracts, slithers closer. I pick up my pace down Wentworth Avenue as the busy blare of car horns recedes from 111th Street. Searching for my house keys, my fingers graze the small aluminum canister of pepper spray. A gift from the hospital to all the nurses last week, since carjackings are on the rise.

Merry Christmas.

My mouth is sour. I can barely swallow. I'm being paranoid. The world isn't completely evil. Not everyone is out to get me. Not everyone is Cormac. Some people are still nice. Like the person who sent flowers the other day. An orchid. No name. That was sweet. Momma calls this a random act of kindness.

There are also random acts of violence.

Voices rise from behind the door of Divine Hope Christian Church as I pass the one-story brown brick storefront. The soulful, softly blended notes of "O Come, Emmanuel" should comfort me but only unearth fear. The footsteps are louder. The shadow grows, a monstrous blob of a thing. A hand clutches my shoulder.

"Ma'am, *ma'am*. Please, if you could spare anything. A nickel, quarter? I'm just tryin' to get me somethin' to eat tonight," says a man in a dirty brown jacket. He focuses on the ground.

I clutch my chest and take a few deep breaths. "You gotta be careful out here, dude." I exhale again. "I thought you were someone else."

"Ain't mean no harm. But you been the only person I seen on this block for a while and it's cold and my leg—" The lights play off his umber skin. *Green to blue to gold to magenta, then red.*

"Okay, okay. I got you. What's your name?"

"Marcus," he answers in a raspy whisper, not meeting my eyes. His slumped shoulders do little to camouflage his towering height and wide muscular frame.

Releasing the keys and pepper spray in my pocket, I surf around for loose change. "Nivea." I pull a lone, wrinkled dollar bill from my pocket. "It's all I got, Marcus. But if you hustle toward Wentworth and go two blocks north, Eden Mission might have a bed for you. It's almost seven o' clock. Might be able to get a meal, too."

"Nivea Dugrave. Pretty name. Pretty name for a pretty girl."

"Excuse me?"

Marcus grabs the dollar and lowers his face to meet mine. His fingers graze my palm. He has manicured nails. His strong jawline is clean-shaven. He gestures to my coat. "Your badge."

"Hmm." My badge sticks out from my coat. I look down. Only my first name and the *D* in *Dugrave* are visible. This man doesn't have X-ray vision. I put my hand back in my coat pocket and grip my pepper spray. An ungodly heat spreads through my body. Puffs of frozen air burst from my lungs.

"I appreciate you helping me, Nivea. Not too many people left like you in this world." Marcus closes the space between us. His jacket is dirty, but I don't smell anything. Body odor. Beer. Urine. I smell . . . cologne. A faint scent of sandalwood.

"I—uh. Thanks." I point east. "Wentworth is that way."

Green to blue to gold to magenta, then red.

I wait for Marcus to leave. But he stands there. I step back. My fingers search for the tab to open my pepper spray so I can blind the hell outta this creep and run home to my momma. To my Ava. I reach for the fence, but miss the post. I prepare to fall, to hurt, but Marcus grabs my arm and steadies me. The keys and pepper spray fall out of my hand and into the grass.

I don't feel physical pain, but staring into the abyss of Marcus's gaze, I feel something much worse. I try and free myself from his grasp, but he doesn't let go. I open my mouth to scream.

"Your address is 252 W. 117th Street. Your momma, Charlotte, makes bomb-ass mac 'n' cheese. Ava's favorite color is orange." Marcus laughs, a sick, deep sound from his throat. "What kind of little girl likes the color orange?"

He jerks me to him and squeezes my right bicep. Pain shoots down my arm. "I'll start with Ava first. Make you and your mom watch. Or you can come with me."

My phone buzzes again. Marcus takes it from my pocket, his sharklike eyes scanning the screen. "Mom unlocked the door. Shall we go pay them a visit?"

Bile rises in my throat. I swallow it. "N-no. Please."

A needle pierces the flesh of my neck.

Green to blue to gold to magenta, then red.

Now black.

CHAPTER 1

Giovanni Mason

June 12, 2025

Hospitality is a call to service. It's a game of observation. It requires a self-destructive level of persistence. It's crazy-ass problem-solving skills like finding an animal skull for a group of maxillofacial surgeons who have a medical demonstration in less than two hours. It's about knowing how to tastefully rebuff a request to source two dalmatians as greeters for a lavish wedding. Or drugs. There's always a guest who asks if I can get them drugs.

And I can, but I won't.

Working at The Chicago Ivory Hotel and Resort has taught me many things, mostly about self-control. That's why I'm trying to remain calm; listen to the measured trickle of the thirty-foot crescent-shaped sable water feature fixed in the middle of a lobby twice the size of the entire first floor of my apartment building. But his voice is getting progressively louder.

Front desk agent Evon Canders straightens her back. "Sir,

at The Chicago Ivory Hotel and Resort, we strive to give our guests—"

"I don't want canned answers. I want the room I paid for!" He slams his fist down on the desk.

I almost expect it to break. The lively chatter of the other guests in line morphs into low murmurs and turning heads. What he's not gonna do is yell at Ms. Evon, a woman old enough to be his mom, pixie short with graying hair, one of my de facto aunts at The Ivory. Who raised you, dude?

"You turn small battles into wars, Gio." Momma reties the patterned scarf around her head.

"I let a lot more go than you think." Keeping my head down, I give her privacy and scroll through my phone.

"And that's the stuff you should fight about. You gotta love yourself enough to figure out your priorities, little girl."

I put down my phone and look at her. "You. You're my priority."

Click. Click. Click.

Yesterday's conversation with Momma plays in my head as I stride across the alabaster floor tiles with stark onyx veins reminiscent of lightning strikes. Momma would say this is the Aries in me. The hotheaded, impulsive force of movement first and the cool, intellectual rationalization second.

I squeeze between the guest and Ms. Evon. My three-inch Manolo Blahnik lava-colored heels toe-to-toe with his chestnut-shaded Tom Ford shoes. "Why don't we step this way, sir." I slide my eyes side to side. I need him to pick up on my vibes:

You are big and Black and you're drawing the wrong kind of attention.

I usher the guest to a desk four feet away. Each station a technologically advanced teak and marble fiefdom, but out of five, only two are occupied.

"I'm Giovanni Mason, chief concierge at The Ivory." I offer a business card from the left pocket of my ember-colored pinstripe suit. "Sounds like you're having a tough day, Mr. . . ."

"Bale," he mutters. He doesn't move to take my card.

I tuck the card back in my pocket. "Okay, Mr. Bale. Let me see what I can do."

Bale slides his long fingers down his stubbled jaw. "I asked for a room with a view of Michigan Avenue *not* the Chicago River." There's a tan line on his left ring finger. People whose lives are thrown into chaos want control over every little thing.

I open our hotel management software, NexusLuxury, and log in. Employee PTO; Meetings; Quarterly Reviews. I click onto the General tab. Rooms; Guests; Guests (Special); Events. I didn't forget how to check in guests. Ms. Evon wouldn't let me. Like converting from Baptist to Methodist, she'd never allow me to become a complete apostate.

"On vacation, Mr. Bale?"

"No." He stares down at me, but not with the anger and frustration he directed at Ms. Evon. His face is full of . . . disdain. Maybe I remind him of an ex-girlfriend. A critical mother. He can take it up with his therapist.

"Visiting family?" I type. Muted clacking, the only conversation between us. I click on Rooms.

"I—uh . . . something like that."

"Would you like me to make a dinner reservation? Tickets for a show?"

The rooms are labeled Low, Mid, and High. There are dozens: facing the pool, facing the river, facing brick walls, or a view of a roof on a shorter building.

He shakes his head and slides his driver's license across the desk. Full name Ronan Bale.

"Why don't you enjoy some fresh lemonade. I'll call you

over soon. Okay, Mr. Bale?" I keep my voice pleasant. I smile though it's the last thing I want to do. I'll solve his problem though it's the last thing he deserves.

Bale scans the immediate area aware that eyes still linger on him at the desk. He has nowhere to turn his anger, so it's fizzled out. For now. He slinks off to a rust orange Barcelona chair with a brass mid-mod overhanging lamp and pretends to look at his phone.

Ms. Evon tends to another guest. All's well. I survey my little kingdom. The place where Momma and the rest of the housekeeping department practically raised me, where the valets would give me candy she forbade me to eat, where Teddy in Security taught me how to throw my first punch, where front desk agents babysat me while Momma cleaned rooms to pay for a home where we spent little time and an education that led me back to the place she wanted me to escape, not for my sake, but for hers. I remember the tepid smile and the two-pat hug she gave me when I told her I was hired as a front desk agent.

"Good for you, my Gio."

There are questions I want to ask her, sharp and spiky inquisitions that a body riddled with cancer and a heavily medicated mind can't clearly answer. Or in Momma's case, doesn't answer. Not out of malice. Out of protection. But she is wrong about me.

Most people are.

I'm stronger than I look.

"The only rooms matchin' what he's looking for are on the Mid Floors or High Floors," says Evon, sneaking up behind me like the Force ghost of Obi-Wan Kenobi.

"I'm close to finding something."

My stomach gurgles as I smoothly clack away on the computer built into the desk. "We got a lot of R&Rs this morning."

Ms. Evon's eyes sweep over the lobby. "Yeah, a lotta rooms that still need cleaning."

There's a Mid room overlooking Michigan Avenue. 2204. But the room number is highlighted in red. Still needs to be turned over, but it has the view Bale wants and is only $30 more per night. That'll do.

"This room should make him happy, but I need it cleaned before he blows his top again."

Ms. Evon taps my shoulder and points to my right. Near the bank of six elevators that go to the High Floors, Mecca Cordray, the housekeeping manager and another de facto aunt, hurries to the second elevator as the first one has just closed in her face.

I power walk and swerve my body in front of Mecca. "Need a favor."

Mecca's head gently swings from left to right. Her perfectly coiffed silver French braid slashing along her shoulders like an irritated viper. "A favor implies that I'd get something in return for my service, *Ms.* Chief Concierge."

"That's quid pro quo. I'm asking you to perform an act of kindness for a . . . beleaguered guest."

"You mean a difficult guest." Mecca presses the up button. Her walkie chirps. One of the housekeepers needs extra time for a turnover. A guest vomited behind the dresser. Mecca acknowledges the request, then clips the walkie back onto the belt of her black and red uniform. Her dominating six-foot frame could scare me if I thought she was capable of anything other than giving me a hard time and still loving me despite hating me sometimes, too.

"I bumped a guest from a Low Floor to a Mid Floor, but it's an R&R." I hold Mecca's mildly indignant hazel glare.

Low Floor. Mid Floor. High Floor. R&R. It's a secret language steeped in service, based on the categorization of wealth and influence. And though everyone at The Ivory is valued (it says so on our website), there's the reality that some guests have more value than others.

Yes, because they are wealthy and powerful.

No, I don't like hierarchies based on wealth and privilege.

But we live in a world that worships capitalism and I don't have the means or the time to dismantle a system that rewards greed and overlooks generosity, because rent is due in a week.

The elevator doors begin to close without a squeak or groan. Mecca waves her hand to stop them. "How much of a tantrum he throw to get *that* bump in status?"

"On a scale of one to Whitlock, a six." I glance over at Bale, his head is tilted back either looking at the six-ring glass chandelier above him, counting down to his next outburst, or praying. "Can you help?"

"I've got 307 rooms, 56 floors, and 29 housekeepers. Five of which are out sick. I look like I have anyone to spare, Giovanni?"

"I'll owe you. Okay? Quid pro quo."

Mecca shakes her head. "You know he won't appreciate all the hoop-jumpin' you doin'."

I shrug. "It's not about him. If you're gonna do anything, give it your all."

"That's Diedre talking." Mecca's face becomes an uneven mix of annoyance and concern. "I'm gonna head on up there tomorrow."

"That a yes?"

"What's the room number?" asks Mecca.

"2204."

Mecca lets the door close and walks to the left elevator bank of six elevators, three for the Low Floors and three for the Mid Floors. I follow.

"I'll throw in dinner at Tootchie's, your favorite. Sound good?"

"I don't want dinner." Mecca presses the elevator button and swipes her badge clipped to her black uniform shirt trimmed in scarlet. "Send him up in half an hour."

"Thank—"

The elevator doors shut.

". . . you."

My phone buzzes with a text.

Willa: Forwarding calls to you for the next hour. In a meeting.

I retreat to my secluded perch in this lavishly decorated cage of wealth as Head Chef Aidyn Ledger leaves The Ivory's three-starred Michelin restaurant, The Cathedral. He saunters toward the elevator bank meant for High Floor rooms. Three minutes later, Willa Vanacore, the general manager, my boss, and the serrated-knife-edge pain in my ass, emerges from the Low Floor elevators and follows Aidyn. Her three-carat diamond wedding ring glittering on her slender finger. She doesn't look in my direction.

One crisis solved and it's only 9:30 a.m. My time, devoured by entitlement and begging and negotiating, feels both like a few hours and a few seconds. Time flows differently at The Ivory. Guests' demands shift like Chicago summertime weather. My motivations and memories are fluid, healing me and cutting me. But I'm adaptable.

I don't give myself a choice to be anything else.

CHAPTER 2

Redding Stark

June 12, 2025

> Holding a rally for Nivea on the 17th @ 6:00pm. Hasan Park. 68th & Oglesby. Hope you can make it.

I stare at Charlotte Dugrave's text. In my soul, there's a rancid hope that if I don't answer her, my guilt will disappear. I stare at the five manilla folders lying next to a vase of blooming yellow roses.

Nivea, Stacey, Annette, Olivia, and Mia.

There was a time I loved flowers. Lilies. Daisies. I even liked dandelions. They reminded me of Dad. He transformed wilting flowers into lush gardens. It was akin to magic. I miss that magic. I miss Dad. I miss peace.

Emmett kisses me on the cheek. His full lips produce a tight, quick dry thing. "Morning, Redding." He moves past me to the pantry and grabs a bottle of water. His muscled arm reaching for the bottom shelf. "Get any sleep? Heard your phone ringing."

I go to the refrigerator. The yellowed paper of Hudson's drawings lightly flutters as I place a cold bottle of water on the countertop. "Surprised you can hear anything from the guest bedroom."

Emmett's sienna-tinged eyes narrow. He returns the warm water to the last shelf in the pantry. He's careful as he rises so he doesn't bump his head on the door frame. "You need your space. I'm giving it to you."

"I never said I needed space." Feeling every bit of my forty-two years, I flex my right shoulder, hoping to loosen it up.

"The files you leave in our bed say otherwise," retorts Emmett, his sharp tone etched with a little bit of pride.

He's learned to give as good as he gets. He used to be softer. I've turned him hard. My peripheral vision catches a spider slowly creeping its way toward the edge of the counter, beyond the flowers to my files. I smash the bug with my hand, twisting my wrist the slightest bit to the left, making sure it's gone to that great, intricate web in the sky.

"They're not in our bed now." I wash my hands at the sink and dry them with a paper towel. "I was lucky to get copies of those files before—"

Emmett mumbles to himself and takes a few sips from the bottle.

If you're going to fight with me, don't be a pussy about it. Go for it!

"I didn't catch that."

Emmett shakes his head. "*I said* I'm not doing this with you, Redding."

"Mmph. You must really be mad the way you're saying my first name."

"For a detective you're slow at noticing details."

"I clocked you a week ago when I returned to work. It's the way you said 'Redding' this time. Like it's damn near a curse word."

"Now you care how I say your name? All you do is obsess over what you can't change, and you don't give a damn about what you can!"

Emmett looks up. So do I. There isn't any creak or groan above to indicate movement from Hudson's room. Maybe he didn't hear us.

"We're having a fight we should've had a week ago." I massage my temples.

"We should've had this fight *months* ago." Emmett wearily peeks over at the files then back to me. "Wouldn't've made a difference anyway."

"I'm not gonna justify what I do and who I am to you. You knew who I was, and you once loved me for it." I caress a rose petal. I focus on the softness and remind myself not to say something I'm unable to come back from.

I glance at our son's old sketches as they silently accuse Emmett and me of the absence and distance that we're both guilty of maintaining. Emmett stares at the refrigerator, too. The tense line of his wide shoulders relaxes. We love Hudson and don't want to damage him in some irreparable way. Though, as parents, we should be long past the fantasy that we haven't somehow deeply screwed up our kid despite our best efforts not to.

Emmett takes a deep, shaky breath. "It's Violent Crimes, Red. Markham is gonna be fine as long as you clear cases and keep him looking good."

He called me "Red." Emmett still loving me should grant me comfort, but finding those women, what happened to them, is my chance to restore some version of the woman I was and regain the peace I long for. The peace we all deserve. Nivea, Stacey, Annette, Olivia, and Mia.

Orchids left in homes or workspaces. Poetry. Typed on laptops. Scribbled on stationery left on top of a bedroom desk. In Nivea's case, a sticky note on the back of a smashed phone.

Stacey Atwater—Open minds in tortured bloom. Marked memories and bled potential from open wounds.

Annette Hawkins—Elevated in onyx. Shaped in amber. I am created to be golden for you.

Olivia Madden—I make You and unmake You. I make Me and unmake Me.

Mia Curran—In long lines and lost connections, I have been here. Hidden by your dark excess.

"You think anyone kept looking for them while I was gone?"

Emmett opens his mouth, but I answer before he can utter a syllable.

"No! And now, they won't even let me touch that case—"

"Let Missing Persons handle it," interrupts Emmett. "I don't want the news vans back out here. Phone calls from reporters. We had to switch Hudson's school 'cause the kids wouldn't leave him alone about his cop mom. You were wrong and someone almost died. *You* almost died."

"And they're still missing! Yes, I could've died, but it was worth that to try and bring them home when everyone else wanted to look the other way. There are coincidences and then there are patterns. I see a pattern. A violent pattern." I massage my right shoulder. "Each victim had someone deliver an orchid the day before they went missing, then left a line of poetry from the place they disappeared? Come on, man."

Emmett shakes his head. "It's . . . thin. You want me to lie? That doesn't help you."

I don't want help. I want validation. The man out there snatching these women covets what they have. Their talent, their bravery, their determination. He craves their love. And he wants what all men want.

To possess.

He wants someone he can no longer have. Each of these women is a reminder of that loss. A symbol of what he can reclaim. And the silence helps him. The silence engulfing their vanishings keeps him able to disappear us. Again and again.

There were no national news stories, no documentaries; there was no longing to know what happened, no hunger for justice. Only apathy remains when Black women go missing. So, we try and save ourselves, put up flyers, post on social media and plead for information on our missing, pray. Or some measure of all three.

We are not searched for. We are not missed. We are not protected.

My throat burns. "Finding them is one less haunting, one less atrocity we bear."

Cormac Lennon left sketches for Nivea in the nurses' station. He worked as a lab technician. He'd write her poems. Sing to her in the breakroom. Asked her out. Two medical professionals. The perfect meet-cute. Nivea declined the offer. Then Cormac started following her home. For safety, he said. Friends told Nivea to get a protective order. But Nivea believed she could wait him out. Then she disappeared. I followed Cormac to a café in Bronzeville. I wanted to talk. That's all. I wanted to know what he knew about Nivea.

"Red, what you're looking to do is . . . it's impossible."

"I'm gonna find—"

Emmett holds up his hand. "I'm not saying finding those women is impossible. It's improbable, not impossible. But you're fighting some desperate battle to fix the past by finding these women. What you're doing is self-delusional, at best. Self-destructive at worst."

"I have to stand in that gap, Emmett. No one else will."

"Is it safe?" asks Hudson at the bottom of the stairs. His voice is deeper, that little squeak vanished, replaced with a light baritone lilt, like Emmett. His father's twin in every way except the eyes. Hudson has my eyes. His grandfather's eyes. Wide set, amber, and always watching.

I turn on the stove and grab a frying pan. "Want a cheeseburger?"

Hudson looks past me to Emmett. "No." He remains near the stairs in a black-and-white Nike T-shirt, black shorts and running shoes, all gangly limbs he'll grow into in a few years.

"Come on, you love my burgers! You always talk about 'em."

By always, I mean over a year or more ago. I remember Hudson hugging me, smiling, and laughing, like it was yesterday rather than . . . when was the last time I've seen my son smile?

"He's gotta eat healthier if he wants to make junior varsity at Walter Payton in the fall," says Emmett.

"Junior varsity what?"

"Basketball," says Hudson.

"What about your art? You used to paint downstairs. Let me watch you." I walk to Hudson, placing my hands on his tense shoulders. "Now you stay in your room. Barely say anything anymore."

Hudson scoffs and rolls his eyes. "Learned from the best."

It takes everything in my power to not pop my son on the side of his head. When I was Hudson's age, I wouldn't dare mouth off to Dad.

Hudson grabs his backpack near the breakfast bar. He pulls out a notebook and opens it. Sketches in muted colors. Landscapes. Our block in Bronzeville, East 48th Street. The hundred-plus-year-old greystones melded against redbrick townhomes. Dunbar Park. The Light of Truth Monument on 37th and Langley Avenue.

"I have time for both. You weren't . . . around enough to mention basketball."

I flip the pages. Marveling. Simmering. I look over my shoulder to Emmett. "You knew about this?"

Emmett fingers the collar of his T-shirt. "You can come with us. A nice evening jog can clear your head."

A miles-long jog in humid air isn't my idea of fun but spending time with Emmett and Hudson and not talking could become my idea of heaven. It could be a step to something that binds the wounds that scarred us.

"I—" My cell phone buzzes. It's French Webb, my partner, my babysitter, Dad's best friend.

Good tip says perp @ 7747 S Drexel Ave. Tactical going in 15. Coming?

"Go do what you do, Red." Emmett holds up his hand in temporary truce. "You ready, son?"

Hudson nods and strides past me as if I'm a nonentity. I want to grab him and hug him. Shake him a little bit but mostly hug him. There's an unsteady dial of emotion parenting teenagers.

"Hey!" Emmett puts some bass in his voice, a moderate amount when he wants to get Hudson's attention. "Don't be a jacka— . . . kiss mom, Hudson. No one likes a jerk." Emmett meets my eyes when he says this.

Hudson begrudgingly pecks me on the cheek, an even drier smooch than the one Emmett gave me earlier. "See ya later," he mutters in a resigned tone, flat and fading from me, perhaps along with any hope he harbored that I'd choose him over my job. The large windowpane on the back door rattles as Emmett closes the door.

I want to tell my son in a way, I'm choosing him. I'm trying to find people that look like him, like us. Because it will keep him marginally safer in a world built to destroy everything he is. It is a torturous kind of calling when doing the right thing requires the sacrifice of everything I am and will ever be. Hudson's mom. My father's daughter. Emmett's wife. A detective.

But this is about more than love. This is about survival.

Our survival.

I text French. Be there in 7.

I snatch the yellow roses out of the vase. As my garage door squeaks and groans its way open, I lift the black lid of the garbage, tossing the flowers inside.

CHAPTER 3

Giovanni

June 12, 2025

I ignore Julien Whitlock's black eye, the surrounding skin shades of eggplant purple, egg-yolk yellow, and sewer-water green. He tugs at the cuff of his floral-print dress shirt. Cerulean, small snow-white blooms with emerald leaves covering his lean chest and forearms. He smells of wealth. Bergamot and cedarwood.

Julien gestures to the puffy right eye on his pale fawn-tinged face. "You're probably wondering about this."

Not my monkeys. Not my circus.

Julien takes my silence as a desire to listen. "So, I'm playing tennis. The game went to deuce. Uh, that means we were tied."

I know what it means, Julien.

He puts his elbow on the counter and leans over. "My buddy serves and the ball smacks me—*bam*—right in the face. Almost jumped over the net and kicked his ass, but, you know, I picked myself back up and won."

After a tennis ball to the eye? Sure, you did.

I don't care enough to call Governor Whitlock's son on his

lies. I do care about how well I do my job. One cross word from this man and The Ivory's first Black chief concierge can kiss it all goodbye. And it will be another hundred years before they consider having one again.

"She's gonna love this." He sneaks a peek over his shoulder to his wife.

Victoria Andersen-Whitlock sits in the lobby across from Mr. Bale, flanked by uniformed officers from their security detail. Two brown-haired men whose necks constantly rotate from left to right. She hasn't looked up once, reading a book.

Julien redirects his attention from Victoria to a girl at least twenty years younger. I've seen more welcoming looks on a hyena closing in on a lame gazelle.

I cloak my lips with a bright smile and nod. "The strawberry and lime cupcakes from Sucré will be delivered to your room within half an hour. You can pick up your tickets for *Macbeth* at Goodman Theatre's will call."

"She's gotta forgive me with all I'm doing, Gio." Julien hands me two crisp hundred-dollar bills from his wallet. He slides the money to me across the desk.

I swallow and take it. "Thank you, Mr. Whitlock. We appreciate your patronage at The Ivory. And it's Giovanni."

Julien laughs, his obscenely white teeth morph into a humanlike smile. "Okay, Gio." He walks away.

I allow few people to call me "Gio." It's either Giovanni or . . . Giovanni. Gio is intimate. It is three letters with which I allow myself to be free without The Ivory looming over me, without the guests' expectations or my constant fear of failing them. Or of failing myself. Gio is my safe place.

Julien's security detail follows him and Victoria to their three-bedroom suite. Room 5163. The only suite above him rests on our top floor. That monstrosity of overindulging opulence is reserved for the VIP of VIPs—his father.

"Room's ready," says Mecca from behind me.

I bite my tongue. "Thank you." I swallow traces of blood as my flesh pulses in pain. Did Mecca and Ms. Evon go to the same ninja school, or did they make a pact to terrorize me today for the hell of it?

Mecca mumbles something resembling, "You're welcome."

Outside a woman in a sleeveless sky-blue dress takes pictures with a crowd. The flashes of cameras produce a temporary strobe-like effect, transforming my space with its deceiving calm elegance into a rowdy and transient nightclub. I can't see the woman, only her sable-hued skin, lithe frame, and her black hair, a thick braid wrapped in a bun atop her head.

Murmurs of conversations ebb and flow like ravenous tides. I gesture to Bale in the lobby. He stalks up and takes the key to his room, his head turns to the entrance where a crowd gathers and grows.

"Is there anything else I can do for you today?"

"No," says Bale. He skulks off, waving away a porter offering to help him with his luggage. Not even a "Thank you." Mecca was right, but I still did my job. I find solace in that.

My tongue throbs. I grab a bottle of water from the built-in refrigerator mimicking a set of drawers. We normally offer them to VIPs. Today, I'm making myself a VIP.

The painting above me is slightly crooked. Two haphazard vertical brush strokes of steely gray stain the middle of the canvas with a midnight-black horizontal line beset on each side and random patches of gold bleeding into the gray. I set down my water and adjust the frame.

"Excuse me," says a soft voice from behind.

Blood whooshes through my ears. Both my arms ache from reaching, but I manage to straighten the painting. I turn around. "It's a lovely day at The Ivory! My name is Giovanni. How may I be of—?"

Is this some sort of cosmic joke? A miracle? A punishment?

Natalie Moore, beautiful, loving, regal, cruel, manipulative—these virtues and vices barely encapsulate the woman standing before me. What does Natalie feel? How does Natalie feel? She could cock an eyebrow, and I knew the words she'd say before she uttered them. Now I can only get those answers if I open my damn mouth and speak.

"N-Natalie. I . . . umm . . . it's lovely to see you."

"You too, Gio." Not a hint of anger or resentment in the easy upturn of her dimpled cheeks.

I retrieve another water. "It's been what, five years?"

Natalie nods and sets her purse on the desk. "Went to LA after . . . everything."

"Yeah, um, well, judging from the crowd outside, looks like you've made it."

"Looks like it, but people are always looking for what they can tear down and . . ." Natalie's round cinnamon-colored eyes widen. "Not that I was saying anything about you. I—"

I wave my hand in dismissal and give her the water. "You're good. It's fine."

It's about appearances at The Ivory. Clean rooms. Stellar service. Bright smiles. Even if you're slapped in the face with your past. Even if you're overstressed and understaffed. Even if your mother has Stage 4 ovarian cancer and is dying less than a mile away at Dovemire Memorial Hospital. Smile. Just smile!

"So, influencer, huh? Okay. I see you."

"Yeah, my following has picked up the last three years. I travel a lot for events now," she says and leans forward. "You run this place?"

"Chief concierge. I'm only filling in at the front desk. Taking care of a customer issue."

"Still trying to make sure everybody is happy." This sounds more like an accusation than a compliment.

I pray for a sinkhole to swallow me. "Hope your flight was smooth."

"It was. Thanks." Natalie fidgets with the gold hoop earring in her left ear.

There's a gloom in our silences and a stiltedness of conversation that would've once been alien to us. It should be a relief that perhaps old sins appear to be forgiven or at least set aside. It's more of a relief that Natalie won't make a scene, ask for another concierge, or yell at me for ruining her life.

A tall, slender, older man strolls up beside Natalie. The sharp lines of his fade enhance the graying edges around his otherwise raven-black hair. The ombré of his trimmed mustache and thick beard go from black at the top to white at the bottom.

"Hello, sir. I'll be with you as soon as I finish checking in this guest."

"I'm with her," he says, pulling a credit card from the inside pocket of his tailored burgundy plaid suit.

F.T. Winstead.

I steal a glance at Natalie. She plays with the cap of her water bottle. Is she waiting for me to render judgment through my words or my face?

I wear a mask. One I show to all guests. One that prevents me from saying what I really think of them or their requests. But unlike other guests, Natalie and I have history. A bond. A love. And possibly lingering hatred.

I still want to hug her. Shake her. Yell at her: *Really? You remember the last time you were mixed up with an older man? You remember what it cost you?*

What it cost us?

I type in Natalie's name in NexusLuxury. She's on one of the High Floors along with her . . . friend, Winstead. I swipe his credit card, which is unsurprisingly accepted. He bends over, whispering something to Natalie I strain to hear, but can't. High Floors are only for VIPs, celebrities (under aliases), and politicians.

As popular an influencer Natalie is or claims to be, she'd get a Mid Floor at best. Who is Natalie, really? Who has she become? Who is Mr. Winstead?

"Are we celebrating any anniversaries? Birthdays? Special occasions?"

"No," says Mr. Winstead.

"Business?"

"Yeah, Gio. bellezza2025. It's *the* beauty influencer convention."

Natalie offers nothing more on the matter. I finish programming the room keys and hand two of them to Natalie who gives one to Winstead.

"Your room is 4329. If you want to take advantage of our Wi-Fi—"

"Thank you, Ms. . . ." Winstead reads my nametag ". . . Mason." He gives a curt nod and strides off. He trips over his feet a few steps away. So much for a smooth exit. A valet rushes to assist, but he brushes him off and enters an elevator, leaving Natalie at the desk with me.

I grab the attention of a porter who immediately and neatly stores Natalie's luggage on his cart. "Your manager?"

"Same ole Gio. Always gotta have all the details. Hey, do you get to stay here for free when you want?"

That's not what I asked, Natalie.

"We get a discount, but who is the gentle—"

"What time you get off work?" Natalie begins rifling through her purse.

"Why?"

"We should catch up. Grab dinner." She finally finds her prize, a pen and a scrap of paper. "It'll be nice." Natalie leans in close, the light mint on her breath refreshing. She lowers her voice. "I bet you no one's got you outta that business suit in a minute. I'll be more than happy to play my part in getting you laid."

There's the Natalie I remember. Naughty. Able to get me to follow her lead no matter what she asked me. And funny as hell! I press my lips together tighter. I can't laugh out loud here. Giggle. That boisterous sound, freeing my body and my mind from guests and high heels and "I'm sorrys" and "How can I helps."

Nah, not at The Ivory. I gotta keep it together.

"Come on. What're you doing tonight?" asks Natalie.

"Working. Then going to see Mom."

Natalie leans back and avoids my eyes for the first time in our conversation. "I, umm, yeah, someone told me about Ms. Diedre. I'm sorry."

"She's fine." There's more edge in my voice than I intended, but I don't want to think about how Momma is far from fine; how people saying *sorry* constantly reminds me of this. All she had to do was go to the doctor when her stomach started hurting and she lost fifteen pounds in two months. But Momma had shifts she couldn't miss. No one could get those rooms as clean as she could, as quick as she could. By the time I made her go to a doctor, it was Stage 3. I should've pressed harder. I should've prioritized her instead of gunning for the chief concierge job.

I should've done a lot of things differently.

"Come on, we should have dinner, Gio. Catch up."

"That's not a good idea."

"Some of the best times start with a bad idea." Natalie winks. Her masterfully mascaraed eyelashes resemble a fan. A mischievous grin tugs at her lips, painted in nude pink gloss.

"No," I say. "The last time we were together—"

"It's in the past."

"Is it?" I ask.

I wait for a beat or two. So does Natalie.

"It's done." Natalie makes the motion of crossing her heart. "You go see Ms. Diedre today. We'll have dinner tomorrow." She scribbles her cell number in angled, sharp writing, and draws a heart above her name.

"I choose the place," I counter.

Natalie nods, smooches the air twice in my direction, and saunters away, all eyes following her to the elevators to the right of the lobby. In adoration. In jealousy. In lust.

"The last time we were together . . ." I say to myself.

I let the sentence trail off, but the memory completes itself without prompting and without mercy. I remember the shouting, how fallen branches felt like glass shards on the hard earth. I remember the blood I drew from Natalie's flesh and the blood she drew from mine. I can feel the stickiness of it and the uncommon heat of that evening.

The last time Natalie and I were together, we almost killed each other.

But, yeah, dinner is a great idea.

CHAPTER 4

Giovanni

June 13, 2025

"You're a grown-ass woman, Gio. You wanna see her or not?" Momma readjusts her pillows, then leans back.

I bob my head side to side. "I shouldn't go tonight."

"Girl, watching you go back and forth is making me more nauseated than this chemo, good God." Momma weakly chuckles.

"Natalie and I . . . it's messy."

"What made it so messy?" asks Momma.

"Does it matter?" I pick up a pamphlet boasting about the new Hartwell and Julianna Whitlock Oncology wing at Dovemire Memorial Hospital. They have state-of-the-art everything here, but not a cure for Stage 4 ovarian cancer.

"Matters to you. Else you wouldn't be here on your lunch break talking to me when you're normally doing your job and someone else's."

"I'm not arguing about The Ivory today."

"There's no argument, Gio. It's not the right move. You don't agree. Didn't need my counsel on that decision."

"It keeps food on my table. And your medication at a decent price. Still got a problem with where I work?"

"Watch it, little girl. Don't let your temper get your ass into something you can't get out of. Teddy taught you how to fight. But I taught Teddy."

I close my eyes so I don't roll them, then think carefully about my next words because it doesn't matter how sick Diedre Anais Mason is, she'll rise from that hospital bed and whip my ass like the time I was seven and thought I could throw a tantrum about strawberry ice cream.

The perpetual commotion of beeping medical equipment, hallway conversations, and background television noise do not a damn thing to drown out the voices inside my head nor blunt the memories that linger years later.

Breathing deeply, I utter, "I just wanted your opinion."

"Humph, such an Aries." Momma tightens the scarf on her head. "And you don't want my opinion, you just want me to make the decision for you, 'cause you don't want responsibility for whatever happens next."

Stepping closer to the bed, I say, "So you're saying I should meet with her?"

"You made your decision. You just want me to . . . what's it y'all say now . . ." Momma waves her hand about her body ". . . cosign! You want me to cosign on it," says Momma.

"Been reading *Urban Dictionary*?"

"Been listening to some of these nurses," she says, then looks out of the window. "When I get outta here, we're gonna go see *Christmas Around the World* at the Museum of Science and Industry."

Momma talks about what she's going to do when she leaves

the hospital, like a soldier making plans to return home after war. And though I'm probably selfish for talking to Momma about my problems, who else do I have?

Who else can I trust?

I pull up a chair next to her bed and lay my head on her lap. "I think about Nat a lot. I wanna see if she thinks about me. If I meant something to her."

I want to know she loved me like I loved her. If I was important to her. Has she learned to give more of herself to others than she did to me?

"Natalie can't . . . umm, live rent-free in your head, Gio. It doesn't matter if she made you sad and angry or if you did the same to her. You should leave her in the past. Let it go," says Momma.

"Maybe." I chuckle. "Rent-free, huh? Something else you learned from the nurses?"

"No, watching television when I got the energy." She yawns. "Oh, can you pick up my ticket for tonight? Jackpot's up to $264 million."

"Yes ma'am."

Momma pinches my cheeks in response. Her hands are warm. She strokes my face and hums a song. "Precious Lord."

I'm relieved as I shake her hand. "Thought it was just me on this floor."

We study the ceaseless movement of white bodies roaming our university residence hall. She lifts a box from my dolly, putting it on my side of the room. Her side is already decorated, bed already made.

"I heard Omega Psi Phi's having a party tonight, celebrating the start to a new year." A mischievous grin on her face.

I start making my bed. "Sounds cool, but I don't know you like that."

"Natalie. Call me 'Nat.'" She unfurls my comforter, folding it neatly in thirds.

"Giovanni," I answer.

"Well, Gio. Looks like you can use some fun, loosening up, and I'm that girl."

Smoothing out my fitted sheets, I meet her eyes. "Are you now?"

Natalie smiles. So do I.

CHAPTER 5

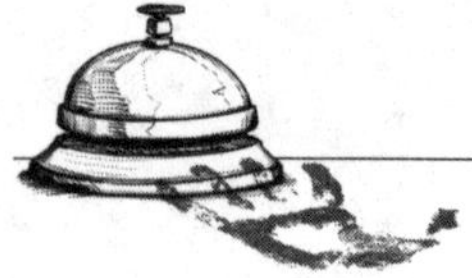

Giovanni

June 13, 2025

It's either irony or karma that I'm sitting across from Natalie on Friday the 13th. This evening could turn into a horror movie so consumingly dark that Jason Voorhees might drop his machete and retire. Or maybe not. Maybe Natalie and I will talk about the good times, the edges of memories we pull close to cover us like a favorite quilt on a cold night.

The Michelin-starred wonder of The Cathedral isn't a place where you eat a nice meal. You can do that at a run-of-the-mill steakhouse. The Cathedral is an experience! Elevated seven stories within The Ivory amid the cadmium-tinged allure of the evening skyline, high timber-loft ceilings and sultry candlelight keep others to the shadows, providing enough light for interest but leaving enough darkness for intrigue.

Momma lies back in her hospital bed, smiling as she listens to dueting, then dueling violins of Sonata No. 2 in A Major begin in bright nimble fashion at first then intensely build into a sacred, pulsing momentum of strings and brilliance.

I smile because she smiles. And she doesn't seem to be in pain.

"Joseph Bologne, Chevalier de Saint-Georges was a genius," she says. "People don't appreciate genius until someone dies."

Guests surround us near tables forming larger circles on the outside of Natalie and me. Booths on each side are anchored against the exposed brick walls painted a shy shade of alabaster.

I don't know if I feel safe or trapped. But in my flamingo-colored long-sleeved chiffon dress, with my hair shining and my makeup expertly applied, I blend in well. I requested the best seat in the house. Dead center with a view of East Wacker Drive and the Chicago River winding through the city like a black cottonmouth snake. And it wasn't a request, more like a low-key order.

There's a slight tremor to the table and I stop bouncing my knee and nurse my mocktail of passion fruit and soda.

"That all you're drinking, Gio?"

"Got work tomorrow. You know how it is." I smile, reaching back to adjust the tag on the brand new $400 dress I bought on my nearly maxed-out credit card.

Natalie finishes her second watermelon-lime mocktail, a vixenish *Mmmm* escapes her lips. "I've seen this place all over my socials. I hear it's like at least a four-month waitlist."

I grin. "Six, actually."

"Then how did you—"

"A chief concierge never reveals her secrets." I finish my mocktail, the tartness satisfyingly squeezing my tastebuds.

Actually, a chief concierge never reveals Head Chef Aidyn Ledger's secrets. Namely, that he sleeps with Willa at least three times a week. He also has proclivities for snorting coke after dinner rush. Not that I'm judging. Give people the gift of discretion. Don't outwardly acknowledge you're seeing what you're seeing unless it saves your ass. Or someone else's. I got two more of these *favors* left according to Aidyn. Why not use one of them for Natalie? Hell, why not treat myself to a day of dressing up and forgetting about my problems?

Our server silently reappears, removing the empty glasses. "Would our honored guests enjoy some of our top-tier libations instead? Or something else perhaps? The Cathedral's cellar holds some of the finest wine put to lips. Our sommelier would be happy to make recommendations." He bows down. "And Chef Ledger asked we take *extra special* care of you tonight, Ms. Mason. Dinner is gratis, of course."

Natalie cocks her head to the side, her lips open, a "well lookie here now" expression etches itself onto her face.

Yes, I got pull around here. Never mind how I got it. Just know I got it, girl.

"Why thank you, but I'll stick with my mocktail for now. Natalie?"

"I'll stick with my drink, too. Thanks," she says.

"Very well. Our first course will be before you shortly." Our server gracefully backs away from our table and glides toward the open kitchen. A rectangular window separates patrons and the staff.

"Who was that?"

"No one." Natalie puts her phone down and rests her head on my shoulder. "You should enter the talent show."

I ignore Natalie's lie. You don't spend three minutes texting "No one." "I don't like attention."

"People need to hear you sing, Gio. Don't be scared."

"I'm not scared."

"You are scared. And that's fine. That's why you have me. To see the 'you' that you can't see."

"So, why do you have me?"

Natalie lifts her head from my shoulder and smiles. "Same thing."

Faint laughter floats past the custom imported Italian olive wood bar, with golden brown and black striations. Julien sits in a corner booth drinking a martini. His black eye still the main attraction on his otherwise shallowly handsome face. On his left, Victoria browses the menu tucked in a corner booth. Next to Victoria sits another woman with dreadlocks pulled back into an intricate braid that stops at her mid-back.

Natalie whips out a rose-gold cell phone from her purse and begins taking pictures of The Cathedral. The bottom of her saffron-yellow, off-the-shoulder dress billows out from under the table.

I hear a raised voice close to us and turn my head. Bale stands briefly at the hostess station. The woman looks at her tablet and shakes her head. At least he doesn't make a scene and walks away.

The server returns with our drinks and again disappears. Natalie picks up her phone again and takes a picture.

"If you wanna drink, drink, Gio." She clacks away on her keyboard for a minute, then puts the phone back on the table. "Remember when you drank that defensive lineman under the table at Donny's Bar. Freshman year?"

"You charmed the bouncer, like you do everyone, and we got in sans identification."

Natalie unwraps her silverware. "I made over $300 betting on you!"

"I didn't see any of that money."

"I bought dinner," she says.

"We got White Castle that night, Nat."

"Still spent some of it on you."

We laugh. Our laughter turns heads in our direction. I quiet myself and lay my napkin across my lap. I glance around. Everyone has gone back to their conversations, eating their meals. Ignoring us.

"Stop that," she orders.

"What?"

Natalie leans back in her chair. "You wanna laugh? Laugh. It's not that serious and it's not their business."

"And you don't have to work here, Nat. I do."

"You're not meant to blend in, Gio," says Natalie. "What was the name of that song? The one from the talent show."

"'Whatever I Am, You Made Me.' KoKo Taylor."

"Everyone was on their feet!"

A woman at the table to the left clears her throat, the specific kind of throat-clearing asking you to lower your voice without having the courage to demand it out loud. Natalie ignores her.

I focus on my plate, envying Natalie's IDGAF mastery. I try and imitate her disregard for others' opinions, keeping myself from turning to see who's looking at us, who's judging us. But I'm conditioned to care. I say conditioned, Natalie would say brainwashed.

The mystery that is our server reappears with someone else in tow. Both men are synchronized in placing our first course on the table—vol au vent stuffed with lobster and crab in a citrus beurre blanc, garnished with fennel. Natalie again clutches her phone and snaps pictures for her followers. She's surrounded by servers and delicious food and an incredible view of the river, but she refuses to live in this moment.

To share it with me.

"It's the way I pay my bills." Natalie takes her phone and shoves it back into her purse.

I relax the muscles in my cheeks and my forehead. After work, my poker face takes some much-needed time off. I pick up my fork and taste the first bite of the vol au vent. *Glorious!* I almost feel guilty eating here for free.

Almost.

Natalie does a little dance in her gold-trimmed high-back

chair. Her arms slightly raised, fork in her left hand, moving her body from side to side.

I giggle. "I take it you like the food."

The evening pushes itself toward completion, toward that point of night hovering between *this was fun* and *I'm getting too old for this*, but our past lurks underneath the full bellies and joyful memories with each carefully chosen word, each avoidance of a subject. Nat and I don't talk about the man who checked in with her.

Who is he? How long have they been dating?

She picks our topics. I pick my battles.

"You like being a concierge?" she asks.

"*Chief* concierge. And yes. Well, I like being able to solve people's problems."

"Oh, well excuse me." Natalie leans back in her chair and places her hand on her chest in pretend offense.

"No, it's just . . . I worked hard to earn that title. And a lot comes with it. Some power, but more sacrifices than I'd thought," I explain.

"Like what?"

"Late nights. Lots of moving parts." My stomach churns with the thoughts of the sacrifices that don't come along with overtime and paperwork. "You like being an influencer?"

Natalie reminds me of Lupita Nyong'o in all her flawless, beautifully deep, melanated glory. She reaches for my hand, which I give her, and says, "Ah, no!"

No, this heffa didn't just mess with me like that! I shake my head and cackle.

Natalie swallows a bite of suckling pig. "It's work for pennies before you get a following. Then when you build one up, you gotta evolve, stay up on trends, controversies. Or dabble in a bit of drama yourself."

"So, what's the latest drama in the beauty influencer world?"

"Well, it's me and this chick, Phoenix. We've been having a . . . disagreement."

"What disagreement?"

She puts her fork down. The bright smile moments ago collapses into a resigned frown, then something darker. "Failed business venture. I just . . . I don't want to do it anymore and she doesn't wanna take no for an answer."

I've learned when a guest needs to vent. Let them vent. Natalie is no different.

She continues, "You can't trust anyone. Influencers. Brands. People say they wanna help you, but they don't. They want something from you and if you won't give it to them, then they'll try and take it."

I smooth the back of my hair. I wait for that beat in the conversation welcoming my input. Natalie takes a few more bites of food, but without the gusto of a few minutes ago.

"Is Phoenix gonna be at your conference?"

"bellezza2025? Yeah," she says.

"It'll be okay. Plus, her name's Phoenix. You know she can't fight a damn with a name like that." I laugh. It's not genuine but it gets a small smile from Natalie.

"It's . . . scary out there, Gio. I love what I do . . . or I did."

"No matter what's going on, I know your mom and dad would be so proud of you."

Nat nods and bites her bottom lip.

A busser grabs our plates, effortlessly balancing them and our empty glasses in his hands as he retreats to the kitchen. Our server sets down a dessert. A red sauce is drizzled across the plate's canvas, the detail worthy of a Jackson Pollock painting. A flaky tower of pastry sits in the middle with ice cream on top.

"Deconstructed cherry pie with a lemon buttermilk gelato.

Enjoy," he says and again fades into a crowd of everlasting demands and plastered-on smiles.

Natalie's hand reaches for her damn phone again. The flashes of her camera burst in front of my eyes.

I squeeze them shut. "Thought you just did makeup, stuff like that."

"I do a little of everything, Gio."

"Regardless, can we just savor this without documenting everything?"

Natalie shoves the phone in her purse. "It's a few pictures. Let it go."

"Been more than a few pictures," I mutter.

We eat our dessert in silence. Each of us sizing up the other. What are the safe topics? What can get us back on track to laughing and smiling and pretending like nothing was ever wrong between us?

"This gelato melts in your mouth, doesn't it?"

Of course gelato melts in your mouth. It's gelato! God, help me.

Natalie licks her lips, devouring the bit of lingering cherry sauce at the bottom. "So . . . anyone special in your life?"

"Not really."

Dating is a pipe dream. I use an app to scratch that itch when it resurfaces. Monastic living with a little bit of screwing here and there suits me right now. Just like older men seem to suit Natalie. If she's not happy with the influencer life, then maybe the suave older guy she was with brings her that bit of joy she craves.

"The guy I saw you with, he's handsome. You dating him?"

Natalie looks past me to Julien and Victoria's booth. "That the governor's son?"

"Yeah, he's a frequent guest. He and his wife." I quickly glance and return my attention to Natalie. "You didn't answer my question."

"Let it go," she says wearily.

"You asked me. I wanna know about you. That's why we're here, right? Catch up on our lives."

Natalie sucks her teeth. Her eyes drill into mine. "Let. It. Go."

I lean forward and lower my voice above a whisper. "You just told me you were struggling to be happy. That you were scared. If that man you're with is scaring you, then leave. I'll help. You deserve more than that."

I extend my hand to Natalie who snatches hers away.

"You judgmental bitch!"

The servers, well versed in the art of discretion, stare at us for a few seconds before regaining their composure and returning to their jobs.

"Jesus, Nat! Lower your voice." I whip my head around to gauge who's heard us.

"You're always sticking your nose in business that doesn't concern you," accuses Natalie.

My heart slams against my ribs like a prisoner trying to escape his cell. "You always turn my concern into something ugly."

"It's not concern. It's control. You just lie to yourself and call it something else like help. Or love."

"And who comes crawling back asking for that help? 'Cause I sure as hell didn't drive myself to the—" I stop before I finish the sentence.

Natalie rests her chin on her interlaced fingers. "What else do you have in your life besides that?"

"A job where I don't use my looks for attention . . . or nice hotel rooms."

The screech of Natalie's chair disturbs the rarified air around us. She stands up and starts toward the exit. The easy conversation and light chatter surrounding us has ceased.

I grab Natalie's arm. Our bodies barely an inch apart. "Sit back down."

"Get your hands off me or we're gonna have a problem," she growls as she snatches her arm from my grasp. "Don't let my makeup and nice clothes fool you. I'm still the same girl from the Wild 100s."

"And I'm still the same chick from Englewood."

"That same chick who has no friends."

"I got—"

"Employees. They're nice to you 'cause they have to be. They feel sorry for you. Like I did." Natalie brings her lips to my ear. "You're alone. Always have been. Always will be."

I don't see me slapping her. I *feel* it. As I wind back. The momentum. The connection. My left hand burns. Natalie spoke my fears out loud and this was the only way I knew to stop her.

Chef Aidyn peeks through the open-windowed kitchen. Again, I am center stage, a piece of entertainment, and again it's Natalie who has pushed me toward the spotlight.

I don't look at anyone as I leave. A scream sticks in my throat, but I swallow it along with the hope I had for us to become like sisters again.

Outside of The Ivory, I dial Momma's phone. It rings. Her voicemail. I dial her room phone. It's a little past nine, but she might be awake. There's a click and open air. My words tumble out. "I shouldn't have seen Nat, Ma. All I wanted was, like, what we had, but she can't forget what happened, and I can't either, I guess, and . . ."

"Whoa, hey, hey, umm . . . who's this?" a voice asks.

"Who's this? Where's my mom?"

"Ah, uh, Ms. Mason. I'm an overnight nurse. Ms. Diedre just fell asleep," she says.

"I, oh, sorry." I hang up. Heat rushing to my face. I didn't stop talking long enough to recognize I was telling a stranger about arguably the worst night of my life.

If there's a cure to make me forget the past twenty-four hours, I'd take it.

A bell tinkles across the street. A small liquor store with a blazing red neon sign blinks *OPEN* in the picture window.

That'll do.

A bus stop stands a few feet off the side for those patrons who need an alternate way to get home with their libations. The southbound 6 Jackson Park Express runs along this route and can take me home.

Lucky me.

The cashier doesn't acknowledge me. His head is bowed as if in prayer, eyes worshiping whatever streams across his phone. The cameras in the corners of the store will do the watching for him. They'll witness my selection—two bottles of rosé and a large bag of Flamin' Hot Doritos three days before its sell-by date.

The cashier, with a curly mess of auburn hair and flat green eyes, swipes my credit card. I don't hear that long beep.

He bags my wine and chips and goes back to his phone.

Tonight was a horror movie. And just like those girls who traipse off into the dark woods to search for their missing friends with nothing to protect them, I ask myself, "*Why did you go in there?*"

Why the hell did I go see Natalie?

CHAPTER 6

Redding

June 14, 2025

The mustard-yellow and ketchup-red shack of Jim's Original isn't a grandly built parlor of high cuisine, but people still line up on Union Avenue at barely nine o'clock in the morning. I stifle a yawn and a craving for a pork chop sandwich with hot peppers and a bag of French fries. Cars on the Dan Ryan Expressway zoom north and south, a metal and gasoline lullaby.

Holding a rally for Nivea on the 17th @ 6:00pm. Hasan Park. 68th & Oglesby. Hope you can make it.

I let my failure float between the space of my fingers and Charlotte's message. French drones on about mundane things. He doesn't mention the raid or almost getting shot by the perp. He only complains about the paperwork. Maybe talking about the boring helps him process his trauma. I should try that instead of stealing files and alienating my family.

"You even listening, Red?" he asks with his mouth full of a polish sausage, stinking up the department-issued three-year-old black Ford Explorer.

"Mmm-hmm," I lie.

He smirks and continues his story. ". . . then Steve just looks at me all guilty-like with my left shoe in his mouth." He doubles over laughing; prickly blond stubble covers his cleft chin.

"I don't understand why you named your dog Steve. That's a human name. Why not Odin or Mustache or Rover?"

"Odin is a human name." He takes another bite of his polish.

"Frenchie, I don't know a person named Moustache or Rover."

He looks down at a glob of mustard that's stained his white shirt. His cheap gold-framed glasses slide down his aquiline nose. "I don't know a person named Frenchie."

I smile. It's the first time today. "I'm not breaking a thirty-something-year tradition."

Frenchie leans forward. His knees barely touch the glove compartment as he reaches for one of the napkins bunched near the windshield. "So, how's Picasso?"

"You didn't look at it." Hudson stuffs his sketchbook into his backpack.

"Son, I said it looked great." I rotate my shoulder.

"You stopped reading those files or whatever, looked at it for, like, ten seconds and said it was nice. Not 'great.' Nice."

"Let me see it again," I say.

"No." Hudson leaves the living room and retreats upstairs.

"He only wants your time, Red," says Emmett from the kitchen.

"And the sooner I can find them, the ones who look like us. The safer he is. And I know he can't see that now, but he will."

Emmett emerges from the kitchen. "But he won't. At least not in enough time before he stops talking to you."

"Hudson is . . . well, he showed me some new sketches of the neighborhood."

The truth was that he showed me the sketches under duress, before he left with his father for an evening jog, and Emmett had to force him to say goodbye to me. But I don't wanna tell Frenchie that. He'd be concerned, and that's sweet, but it also might mean he overshares to one of his buddies at Area Three, or worse Commander Markham. No one taught Frenchie the old adage "what goes on in your house, stays in your house."

Frenchie finishes cleaning off the mustard, then sips coffee from a thermos with a koala bear head and the word *Koalafied* at the bottom.

His phone plays a pingy, annoying tune, breaking my self-destructive train of thought.

He picks up and puts the call on speaker. "Detective Webb."

"French, it's Sergeant Adams. We have a scene at The Ivory Hotel and Resort. There's blood but no apparent weapons. No suspects on scene."

Turning on the car, I check my mirrors and proceed to the expressway. I flick the cold metal switch in the middle panel. Sirens on. Vehicles move aside as I part traffic like the Red Sea.

"Crime scene at The Ivory? They normally try to keep those kinds of things quiet."

"Obviously, they can't make this go away." I glance at French, an unreadable look in his muddy-brown eyes.

"Doesn't stop people from trying," he says.

As I approach Officer Danzinger, I pull out my pen, moss-green notepad, and a general progress report. The rookie patrolman takes special care to observe the people floating up and down the hall, making sure no one slips past him.

I put the GPR under my notepad, then jump right into my questions. "First on scene?"

"Yes, Detective."

I flip past the pages and pages of notes from other cases. Solved and unsolved. "Witnesses?"

"Theodore Upchurch." Danzinger points to a wide berth of

a man in a black uniform with a sharply lined fade; dark, round eyes; and a heavy brow. "Got here around six in the morning, but didn't enter once he observed blood at the entrance. He's also head of Security."

I write fast, using abbreviations that only I can decipher. We should have tablets or something other than my green notepad and this 8" x 10" white sheet of paper that I have to go back and hand type into my computer at Area Three. Theodore lingers in the hallway. His walkie chirps, but he doesn't move to pick it up.

I flex my shoulders to relieve the growing ache between them, then walk to the security guard. "Here to keep an eye on us, Mr. Upchurch?"

He straightens his back; his over-six-foot frame appears even larger. "Call me Teddy. Everyone 'round here does."

"Detective Stark." I hand him my card. "You're head of Security here?"

"*Interim* head of Security. I'll probably get the job."

"Congrats," says Frenchie, his breath drop-kicking me in the face.

"Yeah, congrats." I dig in my pocket, find my Altoids and offer one to Frenchie.

Teddy scoffs. "They'll just pay me once to do twice the work."

Some of us tell ourselves that our job is a calling, a skill we're meant to do. People like Teddy are more pragmatic about work.

The world is a wheel. We're the cogs.

"Why were you up here? Noise complaint?" I ask.

"Security tends to patrol the High Floors. Makes the VIPs feel . . . safer," says Teddy. "I announced myself. Knocked on the door. And . . . saw what I saw."

Frenchie finally pops the mint into his mouth. "You found

the blood coming underneath the door around six this morning? Why didn't we get a call 'til after 9:00 a.m.?"

Teddy looks down at his shoes, then scratches his ear. "You were contacted. Can't tell you why there's a gap. You should talk to our general manager, Willa."

I point to the room's entrance. "You know who was staying here?"

Teddy pulls his phone from his pocket and quickly scrolls through it. "Fleur Winstead. Natalie Moore."

"Stay here in case we have any more questions," I order.

"Okay." Teddy puts his phone away.

I enter room 4329, with French close behind, sidestepping the small pool of blood amid the otherwise stark white marble entryway laid in a diagonal pattern. Sparkling gold grout draws my eye to the living room. The two-bedroom suite would be top-tier if not for the slashed, low-sitting, pearl-colored sectional and the broken glass vase in front of a narrow soft-edged table. Autographed headshots and stems of lavender are strewn about the floor. The room smells of dying flowers, expensive perfume, and drying blood.

A trail of destroyed electronics leads to the first bedroom. A stomped-on rose-gold cell phone lies next to the blood-stained cream fur rug. Unsalvageable, but maybe we can still pull data from it. A ring light camera mount is smashed. Shards of plastic are scattered. Strangely, a glow remains from the broken stand. A sleek-looking camera, however, doesn't appear to be so lucky. It's almost severed in two separate pieces.

I turn and study the entrance. "Door wasn't kicked in."

Frenchie puts on a pair of blue latex gloves. "Yeah, I saw that."

"Electronic lock was still tight on the door," he adds, handing me a pair of gloves from his pocket. "See, I can be useful, too." He chuckles. "Anyway, doesn't look like anyone messed with the lock, but we can't tell for sure, yet. Maybe we're looking at a DV."

"Normally, someone always stays to talk about what happened in those situations."

"Eh, you got a point, Red."

"I know." I walk into the bedroom on the left.

Hanging in the open double closet are dresses, blouses, skinny jeans, flats, and heels. Where's Fleur's clothes, his luggage?

French warily treads around the evidence markers. "When will the ET get here?"

"'Bout thirty minutes, Detective," answers Danzinger. "They're sending Saxon."

"Best news I've heard all day. Gallagher's the best evidence tech we got." Frenchie belatedly glances around to make sure no one takes offense, but his unabashed baritone makes it too late for any kind of tact. "I mean, the other ETs are awesome, too."

French bends down and hands me an autographed picture. A gorgeous woman. Melanin-blessed skin, wide smile. Hair in bantu knots. A jade-green dress hugs her hourglass figure.

"That's Natalie Moore. Beauty influencer. Goes by @lezzismoore56 on her social media. Over twelve million followers on Instagram alone."

French opens TikTok on his phone. And there she is, Natalie, smiling ear to ear. "Get Ready with Me" stories, tutorials on proper skin care for dark complexions, advertisements on products to use, millions of views. *Tens* of millions.

"Anya loves her. She could barely put on foundation and blush, now the kiddo can do a mean smoky eye," gushes Frenchie.

Should I be impressed or disturbed that my fifty-something-year-old partner knows who Natalie Moore is and what she does?

I cock my left eyebrow so hard I nearly give myself a headache. "Can *you* do a mean smoky eye?"

Frenchie pushes up his glasses. "Pump the brakes, Red. Anya plays her videos all the time when I have her on my weekends."

I look over French's shoulder as he continues to scroll. Natalie is the new type of celebrity, the kind that doesn't need an agent to find fame, the kind who only needs a cell phone, decent lighting, perseverance, and some luck.

I crane my neck to look closer at his phone. "Is there anything trending under Natalie's handle?"

"I'll check." Frenchie scrolls through the feed.

I walk to the second bedroom. No men's clothes in the closet or drawers. Not much to go through. The bed is still made. Why two bedrooms if you're a couple? Maybe it was a last-minute booking and that's all the hotel had available or—

To my left, a shard of sunlight slices through the darkened room and rests on an orchid placed on the desk that faces the skyline. Next to the flower is a laptop. Saliva fills the back of my mouth. I almost vomit.

The icy breath of the air vents gently bends the stem of the orchid forward, as if beckoning. It must be my imagination. If I touch a bashful pink petal, it will disappear. Please, God. Let it disappear. I touch the orchid. It's real.

Nivea, Stacey, Annette, Olivia, and Mia.

I breathe in through my nose and hold it for three seconds. Maybe orchids are in all the hotel rooms.

I exhale long and slow. Maybe Natalie bought the orchid as a gift.

I inhale for three seconds. Maybe someone bought the orchid as a gift for Natalie.

I exhale. But why would she put it in another room?

Backing away, I bump into the door frame as I leave to find Teddy, who remains in the hallway near the elevator. I watch my stride. Not too slow nor too fast. I smile, or try to, with some grace. "What kinds of flowers are placed in hotel rooms?"

"Uh, housekeeping would know that."

"Mind asking?"

Teddy pulls his walkie from his belt. He walks a few feet away. A slight limp in his stride.

I return to the suite. Frenchie again emerges from Natalie's bedroom, still scrolling until he stops. He raises his hand as if he's in a classroom and waves me over. "Think I got something."

I avoid evidence markers, careful not to contaminate the scene. Standing next to French, I have a clear view into the second bedroom, the orchid, and the laptop.

French hands me his phone. On it, a semi-grainy minute-long video. I press Play. It's Natalie in the middle of a fancy restaurant arguing with another woman in a bold pink dress. The account that posted the video has a bunch of nonsequential letters and numbers. No picture. Three posts. The video has almost 134,928 likes and counting since last night.

The video's caption reads: *Out for a meal and I see @lezzismoore56 getting ready to fight. Dinner and a show! #thecathedral #fridaynightfights #letsgetready2rumble*

I can make out some of the back and forth between them.

Natalie: "*Get your hands off me or we're gonna have a problem. Don't let my makeup and nice clothes fool you. I'm still the same girl from the Wild 100s.*"

The other woman: "*And I'm still the same chick from Englewood.*"

Dayum! Neither came to play.

The other woman slaps Natalie. The video ends.

It now has 135,837 likes.

The chirp of a walkie needles my ear, and I glance up to see Teddy standing near the door.

I make my way to him. "You're quick. I'm impressed."

Teddy bashfully grins. "You know, I do what I do."

"So, does The Ivory put orchids in rooms?"

"I talked to Mecca—she's the head of housekeeping. Mecca said The Ivory has fresh lavender sent to rooms when they turn over. We don't use another kind of flower unless it's a special request."

"Was this a special request?"

"No," he answers.

I manage to choke out, "Thank you."

Returning to the living room, I find Frenchie rewatching the video. Natalie and the other woman. The slap.

"Looks like we got Lead #1," he says.

I stare at the orchid in the room across from us. Before I drag Frenchie into a situation that could get us hurt or disappeared or worse, before I again subject myself to humiliation, pain, and ridicule, I have to follow *my* leads on my own until I can trust where they take me.

Nivea, Stacey, Annette, Olivia, and Mia.

I inhale for three seconds, then slowly exhale.

"Let's not count anything out, Frenchie."

CHAPTER 7

Redding

June 14, 2025

If I wanted to take Emmett to The Cathedral, it'd be half a month's salary. But I'd put on my best dress—a one-shoulder fire-engine red fishtail bandage number. Emmett always looks hungry when I wear that—even after he eats. And he'd wear his harbor-blue suit, the one that's just the right amount of tight around his shoulders. And we'd eat and laugh and pretend like the mortgage is just a small inconvenience.

Frenchie peeps through glass so clean, it seems like he can step into the restaurant without needing to walk through the polished oak doors with heavy black curved antique handles to our left side. Above us, three small, evenly spaced cameras jut from the brick like goose bumps on flesh.

"Place doesn't look like much from the outside."

I ring the doorbell but feel no vibration through my index finger. "People pay for mystery and exclusivity, Frenchie."

He scoffs. "Fancy place like this, you'd think—"

The oak doors swing wide. French and I jump back in

enough time to not get winged by them. A short, stocky man with a flushed doughy face gives us the once-over. "Dinner service begins promptly at 6:00 p.m." He goes to shut the door, but French shoves his shoulder between it, forcing it back open. We flash our badges.

"We need to speak to your boss," says Frenchie.

"How do you know I'm not the boss?" he questions, suddenly holding himself up, barely meeting my 5'7".

"You answered the door," I say.

Doughy Face's skin color flushes something close to magenta. "He's behind you."

I turn to see a tan, wiry but muscled man with salt-and-pepper hair beckon to us in a black chef's coat from behind a door made of the sable brick that blended seamlessly into the storefront minutes ago. We walk over to him.

"Aidyn Ledger. *Chef* Aidyn Ledger," he says, ushering us into a darkened space with a freight elevator six feet away. Steel doors smoothly open without a squeak or groan. I'm greeted by refurbished polished metal floors with a small, cushioned bench four feet behind French and me, and a digital display on the right side, boasting tonight's specials.

"Most guests wanna feel like they're slightly slumming it before dropping the equivalent of someone's monthly salary on dinner," says Ledger.

A whole month. Still, might be worth it to see Emmett in that suit.

Ledger coolly exits the elevator as Frenchie and I follow. He's the only one who wears black. Servers are having a tasting of the evening's entrées. Others dart left to right in red uniforms, a swarm of fire ants ready to consume the evening, people's expectations, entitlements, and desires. There is a hum of energy and the expert *whoosh* of the stove's burners, whisks swiftly circling metal pots, the sharp chop of knives on cutting boards. Rosemary, lemon, saffron. Chocolate and butter; the slight tang of raw beef, chicken, and duck marry themselves to the steam. My mouth involuntarily waters.

Emmett tried to get a reservation at The Cathedral for our ten-year anniversary. He told me there was some sort of special list, which we never made. We spent that anniversary eating cheeseburgers and playing Monopoly with Hudson. It was perfect.

Ledger leads Frenchie and me past a wall of neatly framed awards and accolades. No pictures of celebrities or politicians or anyone famous. It's probably considered gauche. Ledger closes the door behind us as we enter his office. It's at least 16' x 13' with adjustable lighting crowning the ceiling and peacock-green walls. He makes himself comfortable in a rust-colored high-backed velvet chair.

To his left stands a gold display case full of awards and pictures of Ledger with celebrities, politicians, and all the others I expected to see in the hall. While the image of The Cathedral is to tastefully hide its connections, Ledger clearly wants the people in his direct sphere to know he's one of the best at what he does despite his bloodshot eyes and remnants of white residue that appear hastily swiped from his desk. Behind the chef, six black-and-white photos display cuts of meat and knives.

A chill shoots down my spine. "I'm sure you're busy and I wanna jump right into it. Was there an altercation at The Cathedral last night?"

"The fight between me and my sous chef? Me and my pastry chef? Or me and front of house? If we're not about to kill each other, we're not doing our jobs." Ledger extends his hand to French and me, offering the two seats on the other side of his desk. We both stand.

I snatch French's phone and thrust it in Ledger's face. The reel of Natalie and the other woman fighting already starting. "This fight. You remember *this* fight?"

Ledger watches the rest of the video and turns away for a moment, then his copper-colored eyes meet mine. The seconds ticking by are precious. They become the minutes and hours I can use to find Natalie and make sure she's safe. It might've been a public fight that got too heated and ended at Natalie's hotel room with them beating the crap outta one another. Or worse.

"I'm gonna need to teach you to look at the bright side of things, Red. Maybe it's my job. I bring it home with me, and I don't want to. Maybe it's 'cause your mom left us. Maybe it's me . . . maybe it's you. But, darling heart, there's good out there. I know it don't seem like it, but there is. Would I lie to you?"

The police psychologist I talked to before I was cleared to return theorized my pessimism was a defense mechanism against the disappointment I'd suffered in my life and career.

I mean, *duh*.

"You call that a fight? Last week, my chef de cuisine, the little guy who answered the door, pulled a knife on the sous chef who said his plate looked sloppy. They're roommates." Ledger laughs at his twisted recollection.

Okay, deflection it is, Chef.

I laugh with Ledger. I make it sound as genuine as possible. "You see a ton of crazy shit, right?" I rest my arms on his desk, close to the powdery residue. "And you probably like to take the edge off. Dude like you, in this place, stress gets to you. I feel that."

Ledger rapidly flexes his jaw. He opens his mouth to lie again.

I hold up my hand. "Do what you do, but I need to do what I do." I pause the reel on a frame clearly showing both women. "And what I do is find the people who hurt people. Natalie came here to have a nice meal, probably to post about it. But now she's missing after this lady hit her." I point to the mystery woman. "To find Natalie, I need to find this lady."

Ledger's eyes focus on the woman in the picture. There is no flicker of confusion on his face when he looks at the paused reel.

Natalie's not safe; I can feel it. Another body to supplant the ones snatched. A victim in a depraved search to eradicate a bottomless hole of loneliness.

Her orchid blooms near the window and I *know* there's a line of poetry somewhere nearby. I need time to look for it. Without French attached to my hip. To keep him from poking a hole in every theory, every instinct telling me that Natalie could be like the others. I have to prove it to myself, then prove it to him. Then I have a chance of finding Natalie, grasping at some chance of closure.

"I'd say we only need to peek at your reservation logs, but we don't need to do that, do we, Chef? You know her."

Ledger remains silent. He drums his fingers. Doughy Face bursts through the door. "Willa is on the phone asking about the menu for Governor Whitlock's birthday. Can you—"

"Fuuuck! I'll be there in a minute. You see I'm busy," bellows Ledger.

"Fine, deal with them. I'll deal with your girlfriend," Doughy Face mutters and slams the door.

French retrieves his phone from my hands. "We'll get out of your hair if we can get a reservation list."

"I know how this works," says Ledger, his voice is pitchy, his breathing uneven. "You need a warrant or something."

My urge to respond "*You know nothing, Jon Snow*" is so strong right now.

"Maybe we do. Or maybe we can visit tonight. In front of your guests. All cheap clothes and shiny badges," I say. "What's your pleasure, Chef?"

"You can't—"

"What's your pleasure, Chef?" I repeat my question, adding the grit to my voice I used when Hudson refused to go to bed as a toddler. Or when Emmett and I fight.

"If we don't find Ms. Moore safe and sound, could that make you ripe for an obstruction charge, accessory . . . eh, who's to say," says French who then eyes the white residue on his desk. "Possibly possession."

Ledger swallows hard, stealing a glance at the gold display case to his left. "Giovanni Mason. The other woman in the video is Giovanni Mason."

I grab my notepad. "Where can we find her?"

"Probably in the lobby. She basically lives here." He wipes the desk with his right sleeve.

"Frequent guest?" asks French.

"Giovanni's the chief concierge."

I look up and over at Frenchie who bolts from Ledger's office and scuttles down the hall in the direction of the freight elevator.

"Thank you, Chef," I say.

Ledger crosses his arms.

Emmett and I can forget about ever eating here considering the little chat I've just had, but I never want to step foot in this restaurant again.

I catch up to Frenchie and we hop in the elevator. The doors open and we are in the sleek black, white, and brass décor of The Ivory's lobby. The chatter. The guests. The smell of lavender. Not an orchid in sight. I scan faces. Young. Middle-aged. Old. Mostly white. I search for people who look like me. Check-in staff. Porters. Valets. Maybe a guest or two.

Giovanni isn't at the front desk. Did she call in sick? Is she missing, too?

No. She strolls through the lobby. A man with a cart full

of flower arrangements follows her. Giovanni is a woman on a mission, and she's clearly the woman from the video. Possibly the last person to see Natalie alive.

Maybe Suspect Number One is in front of me. Maybe I can find Natalie even if I can't find the others. There are a lot of maybes. But I'm certain of one thing. This chick has answers and I'm going to chip away at her until I discover what she's hiding.

CHAPTER 8

Giovanni

Two Hours Earlier
June 14, 2025

"Who are these from?" I arrange the expensive raspberry-red calla lilies on our cheap white plastic dining room table.

Natalie doesn't look at the flowers. "I don't know."

"Come on—"

"Let it go, Gio. I got a lot on my mind." Natalie holds up mail her parents would open if they weren't buried in a cemetery two hours away in Chicago.

I sigh in defeat. "We still gonna look at John Wick *2 tomorrow?"*

"Yeah . . . I . . . um, I'll make it up to you."

"Sure. Okay." I walk to my bedroom and close the door.

The pain in my head is excruciating. So is the birdsong outside the windows in my living room. Reaching for my phone, I knock over a wine bottle. Rosé spills onto the rent increase notice and my secondhand gold-and-white-patterned rug. Catching the neck of the bottle, I minimize some of the damage, but it's gonna stain if I don't wash it out immediately. I sit up, giving myself time to adjust.

My eight-hundred-square-foot Hyde Park apartment is blurry shapes and blended colors. The empty Flamin' Hot Doritos bag stuck to my elbow floats to the floor as I will myself to not vomit, to forget.

Forget the fight. Forget last night. Forget Natalie.

Cotton caresses my sore body. I'm amazed I was lucid and coordinated enough to put on pajamas. My dress is draped on my chair near the window. The dress is ripped, a hole near the bottom, the vibrant pink streaked with dirt and oil.

What the hell?

I ball up the wet paper declaring my rent increase of $500 per month, then gather the wine bottles in my arms and trudge to the kitchen. Stubbing my toe on the box next to the door, pulses of pain radiate through the back of my foot. I pour the last of the rosé down the sink and throw away the notice and the bottles. I find the white wine vinegar and mix it with dish soap, like Mecca taught me.

My scraped-up hands sting as I run them under warm water. They look like shadows, but I turn on the light. Irregular-shaped, violet-hued patches of skin above the wrist on my left arm and a larger one, the color of blueberries, brand the upper shoulder of my right arm.

Memories come in clips. Laughing. Eating. Fighting. Slapping Natalie. Drinking. Details elude me, as if someone scrubbed my memory as fiercely as I am scrubbing my rug. My stomach can't take any more jostling. I stop and lean against the couch. The box near the door isn't labeled. When did I get a delivery? Carefully, I stand and make my way over to open it.

My phone pings. A high-pitched mechanical tune assigned to one person. Willa. I abandon the box and almost break my neck to grab it. Hangover be damned. I ignore last night's two texts from Mecca and open Willa's.

Need you @ The Ivory. ASAP!!!!

If Willa knows about last night, I'll probably be fired. I can't afford that. Momma can't afford that. Maybe Willa needs me to cover a shift. Maybe someone has no-showed again.

I peruse some other texts from last night. Momma's good-night message with more emojis than words. Willa's constant string of demands. And . . . Natalie. Her last message:

in the lobby. i'm hungry. where u @? 😋🤔💋

I type. Erase. Type. Erase. Look over at the torn dress on my chair. I don't even have the memories to put together everything I'm sorry for, but I gotta say something.

My fingers fly over my screen with a speed Natalie would envy.

Pls call me.

Abandon all hope, ye who enter here.

That line dances across my mind when I swipe my badge and walk into the Back Entry of The Ivory, a place bereft of the lobby's handblown glass chandeliers, large windows pregnant with light, water sculptures, and lavender scents. If the suites, The Cathedral, and the lobby are like Heaven, then the Back Entry on its best days is Purgatory. The days when someone brings in leftover fish to heat up in the microwave of the 12' x 12' kitchen with two tables and six seats, the Back Entry becomes Hell.

An employee badge is the only way you can access this part of The Ivory. Every request and room service order is fulfilled within these walls. Each clean pillowcase, bottled water, lampshade, and light bulb can be found in the cramped quarters of storage rooms, laundry facilities, and service kitchens. This eternal religion of service, convocation of bodies in and out of hidden spaces, is the microcosm of The Ivory that makes it . . . well, *The Ivory*.

The leftover Back Entry space is dedicated to small side-by-side offices for the heads of departments not deemed as important as Willa and others. My office is here. I pass pale cinder block walls plastered with corporate goals, customer service slogans, and OSHA rules. I can barely keep weak tea on my stomach.

Whenever I focus on myself twelve hours ago, there's . . . nothing. When I walked out of the liquor store last night, there are no memories *after*. I woke up with a hangover, but I don't remember putting the wine to my lips. My new $400 dress tattered and stained. I have bruises and no memory of falling. I've been drunk before. But I've never blacked out. Ever.

What I can remember, I wish I could forget. Slapping Natalie. Her shock. My . . . satisfaction when I hit her. There was a moment of regret, then justification. She deserved it. I deserved wine. And in those anarchic moments, I remember leaving The Ivory. Clutching my bounty of liquor and Doritos. The bus stop. Then . . . then I . . .

Did I go back to The Ivory? Finish what I started with Natalie? Is that why Willa wants to see me?

What did I do? Where was I? Why can't I remember . . . ?

Bon Iver's "Beth/Rest" blasts through my headphones. Sweat rolls down my neck. I glance at my arms, then check my phone again.

I punch in the code to the electronic lock of my office. It

works. Good sign. I turn off my music and search Natalie's TikTok feed. There's a new post tagging her.

I flex my fingers as I tap the play button. It is . . . us. Our fight. I watch the replay of me and Nat. Our movements. Our words. It's the ugliest I've ever behaved. Well, second ugliest. The reel is gaining views by the second.

I read a few of the comments.

hatethagame_908: who wanna know who @lezzismoore56 fighting with? Chick fights sexy af

millienialfractionproblems: That other female need to answer 4 what she did. who wanna find her? ✋

machinegunna12_765: Englewood vs Wild 100s, my $ on Wild 100s

no_chill_chi: U crazy Englewood whup Wild 100s ass

magatruth0323583: thats what u get in the ghetto

Exactly what I expected in an online comment section—a digital brew of inane debates and internet trolls.

millienialfractionproblems: That other female need to answer 4 what she did. who wanna find her? ✋

Breathe in.

You have a booming headache.

Breathe out.

Someone recorded a devastating public argument with your former best friend.

Breathe in.

Where is Natalie?

Breathe out.

What happened after I left The Cathedral?

Breathe—

"Giovanni!"

A voice pulls me back to the surface.

Mecca stands in my doorway. The hall is empty-ish. Not too many listening ears.

"You need something?"

"Shouldn't you be at home?" asks Mecca.

I adjust the sleeves of my blouse, making sure my bruises don't show. "Willa called me in."

Mecca leans against my door frame. "Humph. Willa can slide down a razor blade to Hell, far as I'm concerned."

I flex my arms back to relieve the tightening in my shoulders. I go over again in my head what happened after I left the liquor store. I check Uber. No rides last night. Then I must've taken the bus home. The 6 Jackson Park Express runs at night. Did I rip the dress trying to catch the bus? The ride to my place is around half an hour. So, I must've made it home by 11:00 p.m. Then drank. And drank. And . . .

"You hear what I just said?"

"Yes," I lie, placing my phone in my pocket.

Mecca scans my face, like a doctor trying to diagnose a disease. "Listen, sweetie, you got more important things to worry about."

She hasn't called me *sweetie* in almost a year. Did she find a hundred-dollar bill on her way to work? Did Idris Elba propose to her? Probably not. More likely that Mecca heard about my fight. Which means she feels sorry for me. Which means I really messed up if I got a kind word from her.

"I hear you."

"Focus on yourself. Go home. Willa can find somebody else to do her work." Mecca steps forward to hug me but stops herself, enters her office, and closes the door.

"You turn small battles into wars, Gio."

Momma's words replay in my head as I step into the service elevator, and it rattles its way to the sixth floor. Operations. Willa has the second largest office at the west end of the hallway. The only office larger than hers belongs to the director of operations, and he rubber-stamps everything Willa does.

Willa picks up a remote and smashes a button, turning the clear glass opaque, and walks behind her desk. She barks into her phone, "I don't care. Lie. Cheat. Sell your kids. Make it go away by end of day."

She hangs up and coolly brushes a loosened chestnut curl from her oval-shaped face. "We have a Code Indigo on a High Floor, Gio. If guests ask why the police are here, say it was a party that got out of hand."

Whatever situation Willa is keeping hidden shouldn't matter to me, but I haven't been able to find answers for myself about last night. Not yet. So, knowing something about last night even when it has nothing to do with me provides a measure of calm I haven't felt since Natalie checked in on Thursday.

"The Code Indigo is for which room? What's going on?"

Willa takes in the scenery from her office, an uninterrupted view of modern and classic architecture with the Chicago Riverwalk beneath. "I said if guests ask why the cops are here, say it was a party that got out of hand." She lays her phone on her desk, then focuses her Arctic-blue stare on me. "Now, do you wanna tell me about what happened at The Cathedral last night?"

Nope!

"Small debate between old friends."

"From what I hear, it wasn't small. It was, however, loud. And physical. *And* the video of you two is trending on social media." Willa lights a cigarette.

I remain near the door. I don't want to smell like cigarettes when talking to guests.

She takes a drag and says, "You know I fought for you to replace me as chief concierge, right?" She exhales. A toxic plume wafts and disappears next to the no-smoking sign.

"This was a . . . hiccup. I always do my best to represent The Ivory's high standards. You know this."

"Do I, Gio?"

Willa calls me "Gio" like I'm her little pet. A pat on the head or a swat on my ass with a newspaper will keep me in line.

"Fight the battles worth fighting." Momma's words come to me quickly.

"You do." I take a deep breath, then cough. The tobacco from her cigarette traveled faster than I anticipated. "If anyone asks about what occurred yesterday, I'll say it was a party that got out of hand."

"Good girl." Willa hits the button again on her remote. The glass regains its clarity. "Sign off on those employee reviews, too. You know my login."

I flee from her office. Mecca was right. Willa can slide down a razor blade to Hell. I normally take her slights and insults without a thought to my pride, but now I want to pop Willa in the mouth, strip her of her arrogance like she tries to strip me of my dignity.

What did Natalie unlock in me? Or am I using her as an excuse to entertain a violence that was always there? A violence that I displayed last night. Just once with Natalie. Well, twice if I count five years ago, but like the last time Natalie started it. Yes, it sounds juvenile, but do I always have to be the bigger person? The doormat? The victim?

Shouldn't I fight back sometimes?

Edgar Kelly from E. Kelly's Flowers and Gifts blasts through The Ivory's doors, pushing seven different, gorgeous arrangements toward the front desk. The Ivory uses a few florists, but he's the best.

I raise my hand, walking toward the front desk. "I got you over here." Edgar peeks from behind the cart and nods, making his way to the fourth station.

"I'd normally take these around the back, but it's a crazy busy day and I'm the only one doing deliveries." He slides the invoice to me.

I turn my attention to my computer but, to my right, I catch a front desk clerk staring before quickly returning to typing. People know. Like Willa. Like Mecca.

My headache now resembles the whole horn section of Stevie Wonder's "Superstition." If I could remember how I got home, how I got those bruises . . .

A few feet beyond, a porter and a valet look at their phones and whisper. One of them looks in my direction, then quickly drops his head. I lift my hand, signaling him to the desk. "Take these arrangements to Events. The last two are special orders for Housekeeping. Are we clear?"

"Yes ma'am, Ms. Mason."

"Okay, because if you need some more work . . ."

The porter shakes his head and hurries off. The partner-in-crime valet scurries to the front entrance.

"Oof! I'd hate to be on your bad side, Giovanni," says Edgar, running his calloused hand through his mane of thick white hair.

"You're one of my favorites." I smile as fake and hard as I can and hand Edgar his confirmation of payment.

"I know." He nods, then jogs to his van.

If I can't remember last night, there's a way to reclaim my time and start my search for Natalie. I log out of my account and log in under Willa's NexusLuxury account. I check if Natalie used her keycard to enter her suite, if she ordered anything from room service.

Nothing.

A balding older white guy closer to sixty than fifty steps up, a light stain on the left side of his shirt. The woman next to him is older than me, maybe early forties, clad in an off-the-rack business suit. The collar of her yellow blouse is slightly askew. The detective badge clipped next to the gun in her holster is perfectly straight.

"Ms. Mason, I'm Detective Redding Stark. CPD. I wanna talk to you about Natalie Moore. Got a minute?"

I left the liquor store with two bottles of rosé and a large bag of Flamin' Hot Doritos. There was a bus stop in front of the liquor store. And . . . and then . . . I took the bus home . . . and probably made it home around 11:00 p.m.

Didn't I?

What happened to my dress? Why do I have bruises?

What the hell happened last night?

CHAPTER 9

Redding

June 14, 2025

Giovanni presses her lips together and takes my card. She offers one of her own, a slight tremor in her fingers, then she closes her eyes. When she opens them, I'm standing in front of a different person. Calm. Centered. Composed.

"As you can see, we're pretty shorthanded today," she says.

"Shouldn't take that much time. We need a rundown of when you and Natalie—"

Giovanni leans forward, her voice lowered. "Can we speak about this *after* the rush has died down?"

She looks beyond us to a small cluster of employees. They fail to maintain any casual grace to their nosiness. People need to learn how to be less obvious ear hustling, I swear!

"How long you need?" asks Frenchie.

"Half an hour." She swallows hard, plants a watery smile on her face, then studies Frenchie. "Have we met before?"

"Can't afford this place," says Frenchie.

Giovanni nods and flexes her hand in a "come hither" motion.

A small breeze creeps along my back. A young man, barely a few years older than Hudson, is on my right. His tall, skinny shadow elongated on the off-white floor tiles.

The young man ushers me and French to a large sitting area. I sink into the cerulean-colored fabric chair that gives me a clear view of Giovanni.

"My name is David. Allow me to get you both some refreshments."

"It's fine, we don't need—" Before I finish my sentence, David disappears.

"Like something out of a movie." French leans back, sinking into the chair across from mine. A circular marble and wood table, similar to the check-in desks, separates us.

"I guess."

David returns with an assortment of cookies and two drinks balanced on a brass tray. "These are The Ivory's handmade Italian shortbread cookies. And this is our strawberry and lime acqua frizzante." Paper-thin slices of strawberries and limes float in the tall cylindrical glasses.

Frenchie screws his face up and opens his mouth, but before he can ask, David says, "Acqua frizzante is Italian for 'sparkling water.'"

French takes a sip. "Niiice."

David smiles. "Don't hesitate to ask for anything."

He retreats near the entrance greeting guests, most of whom ignore him. He remains close enough to be of service, but far enough away not to crowd us.

Frenchie grabs a cookie from the brass tray. "So, what's her deal?"

"Giovanni?" I leave my drink untouched. Cookies uneaten. "She's said all of ten words to us—I can't tell yet."

"Yeah, but she did slap the hell outta someone. In public," he says, taking a bite.

"Most of us have been driven to wanna slap someone. Or punch. Or worse." I shake my head, glancing toward Giovanni, the lilt of her fake laugh hitting my ears.

"Of course, but she *actually* did it," he says. "You ever been that mad, Red?"

I shrug.

If I own my rage, I acknowledge it, and if I acknowledge it, I have to face it, face what caused it. And I'm already exhausted.

Crinkling paper draws my attention. Frenchie takes a few packs of Ivory-branded Italian shortbread cookies and puts them in his pocket. He keeps his head low. "Best we get at Area Three are stale donuts."

"Not true." I open my phone to see if Emmett has texted me. He hasn't. "Frenchie, call Anya."

"Call An—"

"She knows about this stuff. You just told me she was a big fan of Natalie's, right?"

Frenchie opens his phone. Anya's cherubic apple-shaped face appears on his screen.

"I was just gonna call you and tell you how much I love you and to bring me some Portillo's." Anya giggles.

"Hey, birthday girl, I'll grab you two Italian beefs, extra dipped, if you help me and Red." Frenchie angles his phone to show me. "It's about Natalie Moore, the beauty influencer."

"Red!" she screeches.

I blow her a kiss. "What's going on with Natalie? What's the drama?"

"We don't say that." Anya lightly rolls her eyes. "But Natalie is super big now. Blew up over the last few years. TikTok, Insta, you name it. And she has, like, brand deals with tons of companies. Now, she did videos and shorts with other influencers, and one of them was Phoenix. And they were, like, tight. Best of friends. They said they were starting a makeup line or something. Then, like, a few weeks ago, Phoenix was throwing shade and tagging Natalie in a bunch of, like, posts and reels about fake friends and memes about how you can't trust everybody."

"What'd Natalie do?" I ask.

"Natalie ignored the shade. Didn't really post much on her account until like, last night. It was, like, pictures of food. Then someone tagged her in a fight with another lady." Anya covers her mouth with her hand for a moment. "You see it?"

"We saw it, sweetheart," says French. "What else?"

"Phoenix said she's still doing a makeup line. I think she's supposed to be at bellezza2025, it's some kinda huge convention for beauty influencers."

"What's Phoenix's tag or alias or whatever you guys call it?" I ask. "You know her government name?"

Anya cocks her head to the side. "Her what?"

"Her birth name, sweetheart," says Frenchie.

Anya scrolls through her phone for a few seconds. "Oh, it's Deiserae Waters. Her handle's @fee-nixxx_fiyah." She spells out the tag for us, then eyes Frenchie. "Don't forget you promised—"

"Portillo's. I keep my promises, kiddo."

"You're the best! I'm gonna put you in a *really* nice old folks' home." Anya giggles again.

Frenchie laughs. "Alright, smartass."

Anya blows us a kiss and hangs up. The abiding grin on Frenchie's face reminds me of Dad.

"Girl, you think I went all the way over to Lem's Bar-B-Q to get you some hot links?"

"Yes, 'cause I'm your favorite daughter."

"You're my only daughter."

All focus and flaming red hair, Saxon Gallagher, ET extraordinaire, marches through the hotel lobby. Frenchie scoots to the end of the couch.

"Stay here. Eat your cookies and keep an eye on Giovanni."

He eases back in his chair. "Well, you're lead on this case so I'm gonna have to do what you say."

"Must be tough." I adjust my jacket to hide the slight bulge of my 9mm SIG Sauer P320.

Frenchie mumbles, "So damn tough." He grabs another cookie he doesn't need. His face resembles a chipmunk storing nuts for the winter.

In room 4329, Saxon puts her hair in a tight ponytail and retrieves her camera. She checks the settings and begins snapping pictures of the living room. The used crystal tumbler. The shattered vase. The scattered flowers. The mechanic *whir-click* is the only noise in the room. I take her immersion in her job as my sign to perform an investigation apart from the one everyone has before them.

I grab a new pair of gloves from my pocket and return to the second bedroom. The orchid still sits in the ample sunlight. I put the gloves on and lift the plant. There's nothing special about this flower or the terracotta clay pot holding it. The other orchids looked the same. But they weren't gifts, they were blooming harbingers of something wicked and ugly, from someone disturbed and calculating.

I open the laptop and turn it on. Password protected. Besides, I need a warrant and a request to Area Technology Centers before I'm allowed to touch it. But why does it matter if I try on my own instead of waiting for ATC? I already have unauthorized copies of case files at home for a case I shouldn't even be investigating.

Nivea, Stacey, Annette, Olivia, and Mia.

Do they care about me following the rules? No. They want to be found.

I fix my gloved fingers over the keyboard. What do I know about Natalie? Not nearly enough to figure out what her password could be. If I'm caught, I have no reasonable explanation for why I'm breaking protocol, other than I'm willing to sacrifice damn near everything to find Natalie.

I need a victory more than I need to be a detective. It's that simple.

I type in her handle @lezzismoore56. A notification pops up. Incorrect password. I have three more tries before I'm locked out. Laughter bursts through the space. I slam the laptop shut.

No one's in the doorway. Saxon remains in the living room. Head tilted as she returns the camera to its case and walks in a half-moon arc around the living room table. That laughter was a sign stopping me from destroying my life. My heart still thumps unevenly, but it's regaining its normal rhythm. Why does Saxon look confused? She backs up again, picks up her camera, and takes another picture.

I leave the bedroom. "What's up?"

"The glass fracture of the vase is . . . it's off. If someone is fighting, bumps the table, and the vase falls, the shards should be concentrated to one side of the table, with fewer and fewer pieces of glass toward the sectional. Same thing with the lavender." Saxon bends down. "But the lavender and glass shards are more evenly spread like someone held the vase over their head and purposefully shattered it."

"You sure?" I back up, repeating the same half-moon walk I saw Saxon do from the second bedroom.

"Of course not. Still gotta finish processing the scene. Send for labs. You know this."

The glass and flowers are near the sectional and the mounted television on the other side of the wall and near the minibar. "Damn good catch."

Saxon grins, the freckles across the bridge of her nose prominent. "Too bad Webb wasn't here. I'd have gotten a coffee out of it."

That's why Frenchie adores Saxon to the point of worship. Detectives follow clues, use our instincts to help us determine if what comes out of a victim or perp's mouth is a lie or the truth, but the nuances of angles and light and bullet trajectories, blood splatter, the mechanics of the crime—detectives wouldn't be nearly as effective or solve as many cases without people like Saxon. But the problem is the case load. Saxon's and mine.

I have forty-seven open cases. Saxon no doubt has more. Once upon a time, I loved starting a case, the adrenaline, the blood pumping so hard in my ears I could barely hear my siren as I rushed to the scene, but now I dread it. Telling another family I'm doing everything I can while staring at a six-inch-high stack of manilla folders.

Why the hell am I still doing this?

Saxon's pale hand waves in front of my face. "You okay?"

"F-fine. I'm fine." I smile as fake as Giovanni and point to the cell phone. "Can you get anything from that?"

"Probably some data if it's been stored to the cloud, but the phone's smashed to hell, and the SIM card is missing. I swear these true crime documentaries are a step-by-step guide on how to make our jobs harder."

That leaves the laptop. Maybe Natalie left something that will lead us to her. Maybe someone else left a clue. Have you ever wished for something to be and not be?

"Come with me a sec." I walk to the second bedroom. Saxon enters, but I remain in the doorway. "Could you, uh, talk to ATC? See if there's anything written on this computer within the last twelve hours. Might belong to one of the people staying here, Natalie Moore or Fleur Winstead."

"Any particular reason? Something specific you want them looking for?"

"Something that sounds poetic or a lyric. Could point me in a certain direction. I've had luck with stuff like that," I lie.

"It's always the little things that solve big cases. My dad used to say that."

"I'll put in a request for ATC to take a look once—"

"Yeah, yeah, we get a warrant." I pinch the bridge of my nose. "What about fingerprints? DNA from the blood? How long?"

"Not a fortune teller, Stark." Saxon pushes the orchid to the side and places the laptop in a black Faraday bag with a see-through pocket.

"Humor me."

Saxon's lips press together in an annoyed frown. "Fingerprints and DNA? Four months . . . give or take. The usual. Depends on how much the state lab has on its plate. It's gotten better, but analysis, *proper* analysis, takes time. You want it done quick, or you want it done right?"

"Knew what you were gonna say, but I was hoping for an optimistic timeline."

"And I'm hoping to go home this evening to the twins tucked in bed and a clean house," says Saxon. She zips the Faraday bag. "You sure this woman's a victim? She could've trashed the room."

"Can't rule anything out." I peek at the orchid before I leave.

French drinks another refill of sparkling fancy water. He's taken my seat to keep an eye on Giovanni who remains at the desk speaking to another guest.

"Learn anything interesting upstairs?" he asks.

"Actually, Saxon thinks *maybe* the scene was staged."

Frenchie puts his almost-empty drink down. "Staged?"

David reappears with another refill and a small cake. In thirty minutes, Frenchie has graduated to cakes. I wait until David leaves.

I whisper, "Saxon thinks the pattern of the glass looks like someone picked up the vase and threw it down instead of it getting knocked off a table while fighting."

"I'm gonna grab Saxon a coffee or something."

I chuckle. Saxon should consider becoming a detective. She's good at predicting people's patterns.

"But why stage a fight? Where did the blood come from?" I hold up my notepad. "Plus, Natalie wasn't alone and—"

French clears his throat. Giovanni stands in front of us.

"Detective Stark, Detective Webb, I'm ready."

CHAPTER 10

Redding

June 14, 2025

There's only the slick hum of the elevator as Frenchie and I ride with Giovanni. She stands in front of us wearing a black dress shirt, sleeves to her wrists. Peculiar fashion choice when today's temperature is almost ninety degrees.

"You cold?" I ask.

She nods as the robotic voice of a woman announces we've arrived on the fifty-sixth floor. Giovanni steps out and makes a right, taking out a set of keys. There's no sleek marble, expensive wood. Nothing ornate except the large bronze door, almost hidden underneath a set of black steel steps. Three panels, each with two diamond-shaped metal designs and a lock in the middle.

"Where we going?" asks Frenchie.

"Someplace private-ish," says Giovanni.

"The roof?" I ask.

"Yes, but there are two ways to get there. Elevator access. Or this way."

Giovanni reaches into her pocket and retrieves a single-toothed bronze key, which she inserts into the lock, jiggling it left to right. The beginnings of a grin decorate her lips. She's like a kid letting you into their secret fort. A 360-degree view of Chicago surrounds us as we step outside. Giovanni walks to the edge of the rooftop. Frenchie and I pick up our pace.

We gorge ourselves on the architectural buffet of brick and mortar, glass and steel enveloping us. The Wrigley Building to the east and Marina City to the west. The dark, dusty blue of Lake Michigan just beyond. It's magnificent, and I almost regain a sense of love for my city.

Giovanni turns around. "Natalie wants to press charges?"

"Don't know. She's missing. And it looks like you were the last person who saw her."

Frenchie chimes in. "And we have you on video assaulting her, so there's that."

Giovanni shoves her hands into her pockets, the slight jingle of keys hitting my ears. "Things got out of hand. Words were said . . . I . . . Nat knows my buttons and where to apply pressure, but I shouldn't have hit her."

"After your fight, you didn't call Natalie? Text her?" I step closer.

"I texted. She hasn't responded . . . yet." Giovanni takes a step back. "Besides, I was told there was a party in her room."

"A party *after* you and Natalie fought in The Cathedral?" I cross my arms. "And who told you there was a party?"

"Willa." Giovanni's face scrunches up as if she's smelled something rotten. "Nat never let much keep her from having fun."

"You go to her room?" asks Frenchie.

A slight haze coats Giovanni's cryptic brown eyes. "No. I left and went home."

People are great actors. Some are monsters hiding among us.

They can be teachers. They can be your favorite movie stars or singers. They can be your friends. Some monsters can take you away and no one can ever find you.

"And you didn't go to her room? Try and patch things up?" I ask.

"He just asked that question. I was home and in bed by 11:00 p.m.," says Giovanni.

"We didn't give you a timeline of events," says Frenchie.

"Doesn't matter 'cause I didn't see Natalie again after I left The Cathedral," says Giovanni, shedding her perfect grammar and diction like a snake does its skin.

I love it when Frenchie and I get into a rhythm. As much as I don't like being watched like some naughty toddler, Frenchie and I can play off each other when I get out of my own head.

Frenchie sniffles and grabs a napkin from his back pocket. "When someone gives me information I didn't ask for, it makes me . . . suspicious."

Giovanni shakes her head. "And when someone looks for reasons to poke holes in honest answers, it makes me . . . angry. Now, if you'll excuse me—" She pushes past Frenchie, just short of shoulder-checking him.

I step in front of Giovanni. "We're not done."

Giovanni breathes deep. "I answered your questions."

"We have more," I say.

Wind whips around me and Giovanni enveloping us like the breath of an open oven. Giovanni was calmer downstairs, composed. But with no guests watching, perhaps this is her true self. Smart-mouthed. Confrontational. Could I see her hurting Natalie Moore in this moment like last night?

Abso-fucking-lutely.

Dad said you get more flies with honey than with vinegar. Frenchie and I can't both play bad cop. I look past Giovanni to the skyline. "I know you're busy, but the quicker we find

Natalie, the sooner you'll never have to see my face again—" I glance over my shoulder "—or his."

Giovanni steps back, her shoulders slacken the slightest bit. "What else you need to know?"

"Can you tell us a little bit about Natalie? She married? Any family we can contact? Friends?" I ask.

Giovanni lightly scoffs. "I haven't talked to Nat in at least five years. But is she married? Didn't see a ring. She wouldn't even acknowledge the dude she checked in with was her boyfriend. And Nat's mom and dad died our senior year of college. Car accident."

"Fleur Winstead. The man she was with. Can you tell us about him?" I pull out my notepad, my brain syphoning the information into clues. "Natalie mention him over dinner?"

"I pressed. She didn't wanna answer." Giovanni gnaws on her bottom lip.

"That what caused the fight at The Cathedral? Asking her about Fleur?" Frenchie tugs at his ear.

"Probably. And old business from college," she answers.

Frenchie cocks his eyebrow in anticipation of more information. Giovanni remains quiet.

"What do you mean by 'old business'?" I take off my jacket.

"I'd rather not discuss it. And it doesn't matter 'cause Nat and I squashed it," she says, an edge creeping back into her tone.

"The way you slapped Natalie last night doesn't look like you squashed anything," says French.

Giovanni reaches back to futilely smooth the errant curls breaking free from her sculpted bun. A splotchy purplish bruise peeks from the left cuff of her blouse.

I grab her wrist. So much for trying to be gentle. "Where'd you get that?" I move the cuff up slightly before she snatches back her arm.

"Excuse you?" says Giovanni, as she pulls the blouse cuff

below her wrist. "Probably got hurt helping a guest with their luggage."

"You got those nice porters and valets. A fancy-pants concierge doesn't help with luggage," says Frenchie.

Giovanni snaps back: "A fancy-pants concierge does whatever they need to do. That's how they become a fancy-pants *chief* concierge, Officer."

"It's detective," he says.

Giovanni doesn't correct herself and crosses her arms.

If you're gonna lie, lie simple. Because the bigger the lie, the more details you gotta remember like when you got home, how you got those bruises, why you decided to reunite with someone you haven't spoken to in five years? I don't hate when people lie because it's wrong. I hate when people lie because it makes me think they believe I'm stupid.

I'm not stupid. And I hate it when people waste my time.

"Where'd you get that bruise, and the other ones that I assume are hiding under your blouse?"

"I didn't hurt Natalie," she says.

"Other than when you slapped her," says Frenchie.

"After dinner, I went home. Took the bus." Giovanni straightens her back, then utters, "I know you have other people to interview, like Fleur. So, I'll let you get on with it."

"Well, we have to find Fleur. He's missing, too."

"Sorry to hear that." Giovanni marches to the rooftop exit. She unlocks the bronze door and opens it. "Unless you'd like to spend the night up here instead of one of our premier suites, *Detectives*—" she eyeballs Frenchie "—I'd suggest you follow me downstairs to the lobby. Or —" she points to a camera hovering above the door "—you can take your chances and hope Security'll see you and come to your rescue."

I reluctantly trek to the door. So does Frenchie, but he retrieves a cookie from his pocket and bites it right in front of

Giovanni. "Afraid we're not leaving just yet. Still got to finish our business downstairs."

We ride the elevator in uncomfortable silence. All the lies, words left unspoken, mistrust, and secrets hover in the air as much of an odor as the flowered scents they pump through the vents. The doors open on the forty-third floor. I exit with Frenchie.

"Have a pleasant evening," says Giovanni as the doors close. She gifts us with the most courteous "Fuck you" smile she can muster. The kind where you tilt your head and grin while puckering your face like you smelled something rotten.

Cormac flirts with a girl in the corner of this Bronzeville café. She devours the attention. He devours the adoration. Until I interrupt it. And him.

"I'm Detective Stark with the Chicago Police Department. I would like to ask you a few questions about—"

He pushes the girl into me and sprints out of the door.

"Think she killed Natalie?" asks French.

I want to punch French in the mouth for already bending his mind in that direction. "I think Giovanni's lying. If she's smart, she'll tell us the truth before this turns back on her."

"Most times they're not that smart, Red."

"No, Frenchie. Most times, they're not."

CHAPTER 11

Redding

June 14, 2025

Willa Vanacore, The Ivory's general manager, greets me and Frenchie at the door wearing an expertly tailored coral-colored suit, two business cards in hand. "Detectives, thank you so much for all your hard work. At The Ivory, we're grateful for our first responders. They are the absolute backbone of our city."

How ironic the backbone of the city can't afford a stay in one of the rooms. But, yeah, go off with the fake appreciation.

Willa nestles herself behind a custom oak and glass table. Looking less like a corporate manager and more like a three-star general. "Please sit."

I begin my question before my ass hits the chair. "How were you notified about what happened in 4329?"

"Security called me around seven in the morning about the Code Indigo—"

"A code what?" interrupts Frenchie.

"Ah, it's a code for a serious disturbance in one of our VIP rooms," continues Willa.

"Anyway, I was on my drive in from Naperville. By the time I arrived, the police had the room taped off. It was simply a party that got out of hand."

"Is that what you were told by security?" I ask.

"Do you suspect it's something else?" asks Willa.

"A rowdy party with no liquor bottles and all the damage confined to one space . . . either it was a small party or a big fight." I tap my pen on the edge of Willa's desk. "Have you had any rowdy parties recently? Complaints about noise?"

Willa focuses on my pen. She grimaces for a moment then gains her composure. "At The Ivory, we do our best to accommodate all our guests. From intimate events to larger celebrations, we strive to create unforgettable experiences while maintaining the highest quality standards of safety, comfort, and elegance."

Did she memorize the hotel's website? Willa already knows there was no party that went down on the forty-third floor. Security would've given her as many details as they had when they called her or else they'd be fired.

"Uh, thanks for that . . . response, but you didn't answer my question," I say. "Have you had any rowdy parties recently? Any complaints about noise?"

"No," she says.

I play with her business card. "We had a chance to speak to Giovanni Mason."

"Oh, Gio. I hope she was helpful in answering any questions you've had thus far?"

"She was . . . helpful," I lie. "But she didn't seem to know much about what happened in that room."

I peek across the hall of her office. Perched in the left corner like a vampire bat is a small, angular black camera. "I'd love to speak to the security team. Footage from last night would be a big help."

Willa's formerly smooth forehead suddenly has so many lines I could write a book. "I'll check with our general counsel."

I lock eyes with Willa. "We can get a subpoena."

"I'm sure you can. However, it'll probably be a week or two before you hear from the state's attorney." She tilts her head and smiles. A frozen lake in Antarctica is warmer.

"Or we can go to a judge and have it much, *much* sooner," I counter.

Willa is unmoved and has likely been briefed on how to handle these situations. How to keep people happy while keeping the hotel's secrets. Toeing the line between host and enforcer. But I guess it pays well enough judging from her large office, manicured nails, and tailored clothes. She's ready to call my bluff.

"We're kinda in a rush," says Frenchie. "Anything you can do to speed up the process in getting that footage would be helpful."

"Understood. I'll shoot a text over to our legal team to see what we can do."

Willa doesn't reach for her phone, only folds her hands. A picture of her husband and children is turned outward. Not inwardly, as most people do for motivation. Doughy Face called her Aidyn's "girlfriend," not wife. Because Willa is someone else's wife. I wonder if Giovanni knows that about Willa. What does Willa know about Giovanni?

"Can you tell us more about Giovanni?"

"Well, Gio has been a model employee. Taught her everything I know."

French leans forward. "The one who can get you dinner reservations and tickets to a show or the one who slaps people at dinner? You know the woman she slapped is missing? So is the man staying with her. All that's left is the destroyed room from the 'party.'" Frenchie air quotes the word "*party*."

Willa swallows hard. Her phone buzzes. She looks down briefly and then at us. "I have a meeting in five minutes, and I've shared everything I know. I apologize if it isn't enough." She stands up and walks to her door. "But you have my card."

I slip between Willa and the door. "Giovanni said *you* told her there was a party in room 4329."

"At The Ivory, we always want to ensure our valued guests have the most pleasurable and safe experience on our luxurious property. We do all we can to make sure that happens," she says.

"So, did you tell Giovanni there was a party or did you tell her to say there was a party when there could be something more serious?"

"I do what's best for The Ivory and so does Giovanni. Now, if you'll kindly excuse me." Willa shuts the door with force, just shy of slamming it.

"Now, where's the hospitality?" asks Frenchie.

"We're not paying for it." I walk toward the elevator.

CHAPTER 12

Redding

June 14, 2025

Mecca's office has no windows facing the Chicago River. No fancy custom oak and glass table. The walls are cinder block painted pale yellow. She has three picture frames on her generic floor-model desk. They are all turned inward.

It's a cliché to say everything is spotless, but damn, I dare a speck of dust to settle here. Frenchie and I settle into a soft tan couch near the door.

"Can I get you anything?" asks Mecca.

"No ma'am." She automatically unearths a deference in me I typically reserve for church elders and family members, though she isn't much older than me.

"What about you?" She eyes Frenchie up and down, not in judgment, but anticipation.

Frenchie shakes his head, probably stuffed from the polish sausages, sparkling fruit water, and cookies. The man once had a six-pack and chiseled jawline. This job takes its toll. And it comes out in different ways. Some drink too much. Others blow up with anger, red-hot and raw. Or cry in dark rooms, biting on pillows so the sound is muffled. Some, like me, close themselves off to the world and pray their families understand the unreachable distance. Frenchie eats.

I begin, "Miss Mecca—"

"Just Mecca is fine," she says.

I hand her my card. "Mecca, I'm Detective Stark and this is Detective Webb. We're investigating what happened in 4329. We've spoken to a few people—"

"Humph, you started from the top down," she says.

"What makes you say that?" I slide my clipped badge from the left side of my utility belt closer to the middle. It doesn't mess as much with my scar tissue below my stomach when I do this.

"No one starts with back of the house first. We're not important until we are," says Mecca. There's no question in her voice when she says this, only the elemental knowledge of the place in which she works. "I take it you talked to Willa?"

"And Giovanni Mason," I add.

Mecca glances at a picture on the left for a few seconds but locks eyes with us.

I stand and walk to her desk. I reach down but look at Mecca first. "You mind?"

Mecca reaches across her desk and hands me the photo. One of her, Giovanni, and another woman, arms around each other. All smiles. All promise. On the lush green lawn of a college campus. Giovanni has a pretty smile when it's genuine.

"You've known Giovanni a long time," I say.

"All her life. Before that," says Mecca. "She and her momma, Diedre, worked with me in Housekeeping before Giovanni went off to college, got her degrees. She's the first Black chief concierge we've had at The Ivory. Hell, first Black concierge period."

I set the picture back down on her desk. "When's the last time you spoke with Giovanni?"

"Not sure. Today? Maybe yesterday afternoon? She needed a favor," says Mecca.

"What kind of favor?" asks Frenchie, putting his glasses in his pocket.

"Quick turnaround for a room, an R&R. There was a . . . disgruntled guest."

"I thought you said—"

"Giovanni worked housekeeping with me and her momma when she was a kid, then the front desk after she got back from college, moved up to a concierge, became chief concierge not too long ago."

There's a mix of pride, sorrow, and anger to Mecca's abbreviated retelling of Giovanni's career path. Remembering the good times and perpetual ache of missing the person and the bitterness that they left you without them.

"Didn't think concierges did that kinda stuff," I say.

"Most aren't Giovanni. She can handle a little bit of everything at The Ivory."

"The way Willa tells it, she's known Giovanni all her life, too. Got her where she is today," says Frenchie.

Mecca clenches her jaw, letting out a long slow breath.

"I take it you're not a big fan of Willa," says Frenchie, picking up on the same vibe.

"That girl hasn't given anything to Giovanni except heartburn and a guilt complex. Gio takes the #6 Wacker from her place in Hyde Park at the butt crack of dawn and doesn't leave until well after evening. She already has enough on her plate," says Mecca.

I stop writing. "Like what?"

She avoids my gaze for the first time since I've stepped into her office. "We all got things, Detective Stark. Home. Family. Our lives don't stop when we leave the back door of this place."

"I think you mean something specific, though," I press Mecca.

If whatever else Giovanni might be dealing with speaks to her mindset with Natalie, that's helpful. It can lead me to Natalie. Alive. Safe. Maybe even unaware of all the fuss her disappearance has caused. A happy ending. Well, severe property damage but a happy ending all the same.

"She sick?" asks Frenchie.

"No, she isn't," answers Mecca.

"Then who is?" I ask.

"It's nothing that concerns you," she says.

A pitchy chirp interrupts us; someone asks Mecca about protocol for how to deal with cleaning rooms on one of the High Floors. Mecca tells them to adjust the shifts for that floor. She then calls to the front desk asking them to alert her personally if someone on the forty-third floor or above complains about the longer turnaround times. I wait for her to finish.

"You have any personal interaction with the guests in 4329?"

"Guests don't pay housekeeping much mind unless their room goes uncleaned."

"So that'd be a no," says Frenchie.

"That'd be a no, Detective Webster," she says.

"It's Webb, ma'am."

"Okay," says Mecca, making no move to correct herself.

Frenchie clears his throat and throws me a desperate glance. He's not getting into it with Mecca. He's tapping out, leaving me to finish navigating all the unseen landmines when it comes to not only being Black, but a Black woman, in a large city that's as easy to welcome you as it is to discard you. Frenchie knows a wrong word or gesture could leave us with less information to gather, making a difficult job impossible. He's being wise, but he's being lazy. He's leaving it to another Black woman to clean up his mess.

America's go-to move.

"All these questions about Giovanni. I know y'all got other people to look at, right? Just because she had a fight with that other girl, it doesn't mean she did something to her," says Mecca.

Of course, she knows what's going on at the hotel. Information twists itself into gossip, stories that curve and dip and evolve, make people harder to track and the truth almost impossible to uncover.

"All we're doing is gathering information," I say.

Mecca scoffs. "Y'all are collecting suspects."

"I want to find Natalie and make sure she's okay. I believe Giovanni can help with that. There's no agenda." I stop short of holding up my right hand in pledge.

Mecca takes me in, determining if I'm lying or if I'm being honest. She says nothing, opens her laptop, and begins typing. Frenchie frees himself from the clutches of the tan couch and opens the door. Mecca has told us all she wants to reveal.

"Before you go, I double-checked my records. There weren't any special requests for orchids to be placed in a guest suite."

I look over my shoulder and whisper, "Thanks."

Damn!

Frenchie and I ride the elevator to the lobby. In silence. We walk. In silence. Frenchie looks straight ahead to the front entrance, his face an emotionless mask. I don't want to continue attempting to decipher it. I stride ahead of him until a woman blocks my path. Light citrus perfume. Square red-framed reading glasses. Book in her left hand. Victoria Andersen-Whitlock, the current governor's daughter-in-law. Her executive protection unit keeps watch. An officer from her EPU, clad in a navy-blue suit with a wide brow, flat green eyes, and buzz-cut blond hair, is less than five feet away.

"Excuse me, Detectives."

"How did you—" I begin to ask until I remember the adjusted position of my badge. "Umm . . . how can we help you, Mrs. Andersen-Whitlock?"

"Victoria's fine." She dismissively waves her hand as if physically shooing away formality. "What's going on?"

Frenchie slaps an amiable smile on his face. One of the two officers on her detail looks directly at me, ready to act at a moment's notice. The other officer keeps his eye on Julien, Governor Whitlock's son, talking on his cell phone with what seems to be a days-old black eye. He glances in our direction but returns to his conversation.

"Umm . . . is your husband okay?"

"It was an accident. He was bringing me dinner, slipped and hit his face on the door frame."

Julien hit his face on the door frame? If half of what I read online is true or see in those video clips of him cozied up with women who are not Victoria, then I wouldn't be surprised if she punched him.

Unofficially, I say good for her. Officially that's domestic assault and I'd have to arrest her.

"We're currently investigating an incident, but we can't divulge any details at this point," I answer.

Victoria nods. "Will everything be okay for the governor's birthday gala on Friday?"

"You should check with your head of Security, but I don't think it'll be a problem," Frenchie chimes in.

"Thanks. Well, I'm sure you both have plenty to do and event planning is not one of them." She laughs, the hollow sound amplified by the high-arched lobby ceiling.

Victoria returns to her seat. Julien hasn't looked in our direction. Frenchie's good-humored smile vanishes as he now walks ahead of me toward the automatic revolving doors. I make it to the car before he does.

I pull into traffic, heading south on North Wabash, then make a right on East Wacker Drive.

"Why did she mention orchids?" asks French.

"We gotta pull Natalie's phone records. See the tower where her phone pinged off last."

"Goddamn it, Redding! Why did the housekeeper talk about orchids?"

I finally utter, "You know why."

French puts both hands to his face. "You can't be this hardheaded. It's a flower. It's only a flower."

Nivea, Stacey, Annette, Olivia, and Mia.

Each woman could teach or entertain or mend what was broken in cloth or bone or alleviate the crushing pressure of the world with calm and cannabis. Everyone has something to offer this world. These women have something to offer him.

But what?

"The Ivory only puts lavender in their rooms. Natalie can be another one he's looking for. Maybe she's the one who can replace whatever, *whoever* he lost. Maybe all of them together re-create her."

"Her?" says Frenchie. "Someone could've bought the orchid for Natalie. It doesn't mean it's him."

I blink back tears. "So, you believe there's a connection."

The ebb and flow of skyscrapers slowly breaks away to smaller squat brick buildings and fast-food places. French hunkers himself in silence, his thin lips pressed in a grim line.

I repeat, "You believe there's a connection? Natalie, Mia, Olivia, Ni—"

"I think . . . you want redemption, but you can't save everybody, Red. There are people who leave their lives behind. Overdose and die, and no one finds the body. Sometimes awful, violent things happen. It's a reminder, a warning."

"A warning?"

"Go home, hug your people. Let this go, before . . ." He trails off.

"Before what?"

"We gotta make it okay before we lose everything."

My vision clears. The burning in my throat remains. "Not yet, Frenchie. Not yet."

CHAPTER 13

Giovanni

June 14, 2025

I knock on the door and Teddy opens it, his body almost fully blocking the entrance. He's the only one in the office. Security is located two levels under the Low Floors. This floor and this office aren't accessible to anyone but other security employees or higher-level management.

"Where's everyone?" I look around and sit in an empty chair next to Teddy. My heels slightly sink into the carpet.

"Patrol. We're down three today. And I had to get a new badge 'cause I lost mine last night," he says, his eyes focused on the twenty screens affixed to the beige walls in front of him. "Been a helluva day so far."

Teddy unclips his walkie from his belt. "I'm gonna need two at the front entrance. Group of four's gettin' a little rowdy. De-escalate if necessary."

Someone radios back confirmation. Teddy studies the screen. He winces as he bumps his toe against the too-short desk. "I only got the cushy job 'cause my bunions been actin' up."

"You got it 'cause you work hard and you're good at what you do."

"Thanks, doll."

"One time I tell you to not touch my white dress because your hands were dirty. I've been 'doll' ever since."

"What five-year-old says that?" Teddy holsters his walkie then scribbles something on a clipboard.

"One with good sense. Besides, I'm not all dainty like you make me out to be."

"Sheee-it!" Teddy stops and looks around the room. He let his mask slip. He clears his throat. "I know. I'm the one that taught you to fight. That left hook of yours alone is proof you ain't soft."

Teddy laughs as he returns his attention to the clipboard, then lays it down below the organized rows of car keys belonging to The Ivory's fleet.

I roll my chair closer to him. "Paperwork?"

"Gotta sign off on the driving logs with Transportation since we gotta keep the keys in here now. Like we don't got enough to do," he says. "Willa send you to check on me?"

"Not trying to step on toes, but she needs footage from the forty-third floor near ten at night, maybe a little after." My phone vibrates. A notification my student loans are due. "Ugh. Speak of the devil."

I pull out my cell and pretend to text. I use my peripheral vision to watch Teddy log in to NexusLuxurySecure. I might need access when he's not here. Teddy enters his first initial and last name and a code: 782 . . . 25 . . . what are the last digits? Ah, 681!

I type *78225681* as a text and send it to myself. Yes, I'm a horrible person for betraying Teddy's trust. I'll repent later. Free. In my apartment and not in a jail cell.

"Alright, here ya go." Teddy scoots back from the monitor,

allowing me a better view. The time stamp on the bottom right-hand corner displays 9:45 p.m. Natalie returns to her room from The Cathedral and closes the door. And . . . the screen goes black.

"What the . . ." Teddy pushes me out of the way. I almost topple out of the chair but catch myself.

His hands fly across the keyboard with the skilled ease of a jazz pianist. An empty hallway flashes on the screen with a 10:42 p.m. time stamp. Nearly an hour is gone. Teddy checks the lobby footage. All of it is still there, catching Fleur leaving The Ivory at 10:48 p.m. Teddy turns to me. "I'm gonna see if I can restore whatever's missing. Buy me some time with Willa."

"I got you." I put my hand on his left shoulder and squeeze.

What happened in that missing hour? It's erased like my memories of last night. It's so . . . unsettling.

Teddy's bulbous nose almost touches the bottom screen, his lips pressed into a grim line. He doesn't look in my direction as he says, "This little situation stays in this room, doll."

I twist the doorknob to leave. "Our little secret."

It's whimpers, then sobs behind her closed door. I don't knock 'cause screw manners when Natalie's grieving and exhausted. I don't say anything. Just sit on her bed and hold her. Nat can only be happy for so long until something as small as a look or a television commercial or a color drags her back to a reality where she has no family but me. And I realize as I clutch her shuddering body to mine, that I will never be enough, but I'm all she has. Natalie asks me to sing something, anything. I do. A song Momma taught me "Precious Lord."

David Embark's cocky grin greets me as I step out of the elevator into the lobby. We walk outside and stop at the pedestrian bridge on North Wabash Avenue. The murky green of the Chicago River laps along, occasionally disturbed by the afternoon rush of tour boats.

I pull at the blouse sticking to my skin. "What'd they talk about?"

"You," says David. "And the fight you got into at the restaurant."

"It wasn't a fight!" I soften my tone. "Yeah, things got heated but we didn't fight, okay?"

He raises his hands in mock surrender. "I ain't judging."

"Yeah, but others are and those detectives broadcasting it in the lobby doesn't help."

"Actually, they were at a respectable whisper, but you know, I got them 'rat ears.' That's what my granny called 'em." David chuckles. "And to be fair, I heard about what happened soon as I clocked in. You know this place is luxurious with everything, including gossip."

Forget guns or knives or poison. Words spoken without truth or thought of consequences are far more dangerous. The valets and porters and the front desk are already stealing glances, quickly walking by me as if if they linger too long in my presence, whatever damage to my reputation thus far might spread to them.

David follows the water's movement before he says, "They were talking to someone on the phone. Getting the rundown about your friend, Natalie. Turns out you weren't the only one who wanted to slap her."

"Keep on crackin' jokes and I swear I'll fire you."

"Okay, okay," he says, stifling his laughter. "Them cops said your girl had beef with some other chick named Phoenix. Her government name's Deiserae Waters. Her social media name is @fee-nixxx_fiyah. They were supposed to do some business or project together. Makeup, skin care, or something, but your girl dropped out."

"Business and friends don't mix."

"More like money and friends," he says.

Natalie hinted at this over our dinner before we argued, before I . . . hit her. She said she didn't want to work with Phoenix anymore, that you can't trust anyone, couldn't trust influencers.

But friendship is volatile. Chosen sisterhood can become destructive. Small complications become insurmountable problems. White lies become conspiracies. Adoration morphs into animosity. And love becomes your hands around a neck in the dirt.

I breathe through the abyss of space where memory should be. *I took the bus. That was the only way I could've gotten home. I took the bus, but I probably fell when I got off the bus and that's how my dress got torn. Right?*

David's voice drags me back to the surface.

"The female cop kept checking you out," he says, pulling an apple out of his long black pants. He shines it as best as he can on his vest.

"Uh, I . . . yeah, probably trying to get a read on me. I do it to guests all the time." I lean on the railing overlooking the churning water. "The older guy with Natalie, he come back?"

David clears his throat. "I ain't seen him. But if something comes up, I know who to call."

If Natalie's boyfriend disappeared, too, that only leaves Phoenix with possible answers about Natalie. She doesn't like Natalie. I get that. God, do I get that. And nothing bonds people like a shared dislike over someone else. Gossip spilling from ready lips, and among the gossip, clues to where Natalie might be.

But where is Phoenix? Her TikTok account might hold some clues. She has over a million and a half followers. I doubt messaging her will get me a quick result, if she doesn't outright ignore my message; I could be sitting in jail by the time she answers it. Besides, face-to-face discussions are the best way to avoid misunderstandings.

I play her latest video.

Thank you to all my Fiyah Flies who came out to see me at bellezza2025. Now, I know I been talking lately about loyalty and true friendship. More and more I realize you can't trust everybody 'cause someone's always gonna try and sabotage plans, tear you down. But there's always a way to get what you want, take what you deserve. Do what you gotta do, Fiyah Flies. That's my word for today.

David chomps on his apple and studies the river. "She was definitely talking about your friend."

"Natalie? Yeah, had to be."

My freedom depends on talking to Phoenix sooner rather than later. I rewatch the video. Take in the background. Phoenix stands in front of a large picture window where a squirrel scurries up a tree. Probably a first- or second-floor apartment. She ends her video while panning to the right.

Gotcha!

In her video, across the street, is Taqueria Cabral, one of the best hidden gems in Logan Square, and a place I frequently direct guests who are on the hunt for authentic Mexican cuisine.

Phoenix gave me her address without realizing it.

David tosses the remains of his apple in the garbage can in front of us. "Where you goin'?"

Passing him, I say over my shoulder, "Running an errand. I'll be back."

"Okay, Terminator," he teases.

That boy has no idea.

CHAPTER 14

Redding

June 14, 2025

Thousands of movies and television shows are dedicated to police: comedies, action flicks, dramas. But the one thing they never seem to get right is the amount of paperwork we fill out. Can you imagine how much John McClane had to do after all five *Die Hard* movies? I shudder to think about it.

I walk to the cramped kitchenette next to the bullpen. As soon as I open the refrigerator and grab a bottled water, the two detectives laughing moments earlier give me a quick nod and head toward their cubicles.

Groups of desks sit cordoned off by department at Area Three. Homicide is on the far right of the room. Frenchie, myself, and the rest of Violent Crimes are on the far left. Missing Persons are behind us. Arguments, negotiations, ringing phones, and the click of keyboards smother me in a blanket of noise. I imagine someone could once find a similar level of chaos at the Chicago Stock Exchange on La Salle Street, but at Area Three, we only trade in tragedy.

Settling back at my desk, I eat two bites of salad, then push it away and revisit my notes. All the details. The ransacked room. Glass patterns. Natalie. Giovanni. The Mystery Boyfriend. Motives. Secrets. It's a jigsaw puzzle with the funkiest pieces and I won't force them to fit where I want them. It's selfish and sloppy policework. Dad taught me better than that. Each person, each purpose, melds into a plausible story. I just need to know how to finesse each part to create the picture.

Deiserae is another piece to the puzzle, another person of interest, who'll either tell me the truth or lie or a bit of both. Even the truth, or the way we perceive the truth, can impede an investigation. Four witnesses can see the same thing but have four different stories. That's something I learned on my first day as a beat cop.

I can't trust myself and I can't trust my truth.

Turning on my computer, I log in to DataWarehouse. If Deiserae has ever been the victim of a crime, been arrested, or had any run-in with us, she should be in this system.

"I'm gonna see if Deiserae has any priors."

"Mmm-hmm." Frenchie slurps coffee from a mug that has an illustration of a pickle with the words *I'm kind of a big dill.*

"Eh, she got a couple tickets for speeding. Don't know if it's current, but the last known address is 2509 North Sawyer Ave., Unit 2." I grab a fresh GPR from my drawer. "I'm gonna go pay her a visit, but I'll have my report on your desk to sign by tonight."

Frenchie puts down his mug and rises from his desk.

I wave him back. "No. You being pissed at me right now is gonna throw me off my game. Just . . . let me handle it. Alone."

"I'm not . . . Red, your GPRs are cleaner than mine. I trust you."

"Yeah, you do. It's everyone else."

French gives me a sympathetic look but says nothing.

"Someone's gotta prepare the subpoena and email the state's attorney for The Ivory's video footage. Divide and conquer, isn't that what you taught me?" I ask.

"It's what your dad taught me." He shakes his head. "Okay, Red. You go. And I'm not mad at you, I'm . . . concerned."

I grab my jacket from my chair and adjust my holstered gun. "I know, Frenchie. I know."

Deiserae's last address is an unassuming greystone apartment in Logan Square nestled among generational family homes and hastily constructed new builds. An endless blend of traditions and trends. Taquerias and kombucha shops. Expensive grocery chains and corner stores.

The lawn could use a mow, but even the least architecturally decorative older buildings in this city have an ethereal craftsmanship and Deiserae's place is no different. The curtains on the second floor are drawn shut. I can't see anything. I open the wrought iron gate but catch movement out the corner of my eye.

Giovanni marches up the block, all attack, no plan.

I turn on my heel to intercept her. How did she know about this place? Did she follow me here?

"How'd you know about Phoenix?"

"I employ people who know how to listen."

David! He brought Frenchie and me those fruit waters and cookies. I wanna kick myself. I thought Frenchie and I were careful. Not enough apparently.

Giovanni folds her arms. "Natalie mentioned Phoenix first, but—"

"Natalie told you where Phoenix lived?"

"Everyone puts everything online. It's not hard to figure things out if you pay attention to what people show you," she says.

"Go home." I put my hand on my hip, revealing my badge.

"No."

Giovanni steps to my left. I go left. She goes right. I go right.

"I said go home, Gio."

"Don't call me Gio. And I left work for this so if I can't question Phoenix, then I'm gonna watch you do it. My freedom is on the line."

"So is my career!"

Giovanni hasn't moved and I haven't moved either. It's a battle of wills and egos. It's messy. I understand Giovanni's motivation, but my family and my career are hanging on by a thread. That's something I *know* she and I have in common.

"This isn't a buddy cop movie. This isn't how these things work. If you're here when I question anyone, a defense attorney can spin it as witness intimidation." I loosen my body, trying to release the aggression prickling underneath my skin.

Giovanni balls her left hand into a fist but backs away. "I won't go into the apartment with you, but I'm still coming in."

I walk back to the greystone. "I'll take what I can get. Just stay in the foyer."

"Fine."

I press the doorbell for Unit 2. Nothing. I press it again. No answer.

Giovanni reaches over me and presses the other four doorbells simultaneously. Someone buzzes us in thirty seconds later. "You'd still be standing outside if I wasn't here."

"Stay in the foyer."

I climb the stairs but glance over my shoulder for a moment. Giovanni remains at the landing, arms folded looking all kinds of pissed off.

The second-floor apartment's door is a sturdy hunk of oak that's at least a hundred years old. I knock. "Deiserae Waters. My name is Detective Stark. Can we talk?"

I wait and look down at Deiserae's welcome mat. It has the phonetic spelling of the word *audacity* along with a quip about people not calling before they come over.

The sliver of a shadow moves under the small gap at the bottom of the door.

I knock again. "Deiserae?"

Something heavy tumbles behind the door. Could be boxes. Could be a body. That's what it sounds like. A body. Or maybe that's what I want it to sound like. Maybe I want something bad to happen.

I press my ear to the door. I listen for a sound that shouldn't be inside of a peaceful apartment.

There's a curse. Then a scream, sharp and quick and muffled. I twist the ornate cast-iron doorknob. It's locked. I pound on the door. "Detective Stark. Chicago Police Department."

Drawing my gun, I turn around, and donkey kick below the doorknob with my right foot. I lean into the kick as hard as I can. The door splinters but doesn't break.

There are thumps and yelps. Deiserae's fighting. And so am I.

I imagine the door is the face of the man who took Nivea, Stacey, Annette, Olivia, and Mia. I kick again. Harder. The door gives. I rush in as Deiserae is on the floor crawling away from her assailant. A star tattoo on his left cheek. Lanky. Lithe. Lethal.

"Get your hands off—"

Another suspect stalks toward me. Big. Brawny. Bad. Identifying myself as a cop stopped nothing. These two don't care, which means they didn't come here to leave witnesses. As I aim, his muscled arm, the size of a regular person's thigh, strikes my shoulder. He moves faster than someone his size should. My gun falls and slides into a dim corner near an end table. Turning on my heel to retrieve my SIG Sauer, I'm lifted, my body trapped. His arms slide down and lock my elbows. Sweat from his body seeps into my shirt. At least he'll leave behind DNA. My chest tightens. I fight to breathe. To stay alive.

As Deiserae scratches at her attacker's face, he bangs her head onto the hardwood floor twice. Her body goes limp.

I should've taken Frenchie up on his offer. Giovanni was right. I need backup.

Now.

CHAPTER 15

Giovanni

Four Minutes Earlier
June 14, 2025

Tawny orange lights blind me. I grip the microphone. My fingers pulse as I hold it to my lips, but nothing comes out. The guitar and the sax and piano and the bass pull me close and seduce me, wait for me to open my voice. To sing. But I'm terrified. Why did I listen to Natalie? Why am I on this stage? Then I feel her breath hot on my ear. "You're not singing to them. You're singing to me, Gio. Show them what I see." She kisses me on my cheek. Leaves me. I look out. The band starts again. "Whatever I Am, You Made Me." I sing. I testify. Use memory and longing to tell a story. My story. Hands clap. People cheer. And I am who she wants me to be. Who I tell myself I am for her.

First Natalie, then Willa, now Redding. I'm forced to sing or serve or stand still. Well, I'm not forced. I allow it because it's worse to be seen as difficult than it is to sometimes comply. And living for others, doing for others first and not myself, is . . . exhausting. The word *No* is a whole sentence. So, no

I won't stand here while Redding gets answers that she could keep from me, that I need, for my search and my sanity.

I pass the foyer. I make it to the first step as Redding yells, "Detective Stark. Chicago Police Department!" She bangs on the door. I sprint up two flights but find no one when I reach Phoenix's floor. Large and small splinters of wood litter the hallway. The balls of my feet throb in my Christian Louboutin heels.

The kicked-in door hangs off the top hinge. The doorknob is loose. A semitruck of a dude bear-hugs Redding. He struggles to control her as she lifts her legs and drops down on her butt, trying to wriggle away from him. Her legs hit my left arm with such force, I tumble to the floor.

"What the—get the hell outta here," Redding orders. Her breath coming in short bursts.

"No."

A tall, wiry, and bug-eyed dude standing over Phoenix makes a beeline for me as she lies unconscious on the floor. Or worse. I wasn't planning on brawling, so I didn't come dressed for the occasion, but no one thinks about the outfit they'll wear when they kick someone's ass. Jeans or a business suit. It doesn't matter as long as you win your fight.

I kick off my heels. They slide toward the kitchen. I hoist myself up, using an old wood end table for leverage and reach for Redding's gun a couple feet away. My fingers graze the weapon, but Bug Eyes grabs my jacket collar, jerks me back and spins me around to meet his harshly angled face.

"Wrong place. Wrong time," he says.

"Get off me!" I put as much bass in my voice as possible.

He's amused at my command. He wants another person to hurt. But I'm not gonna make it easy. I cock my head back and propel my forehead toward his left eye socket. With everything I got. Bug Eyes falls back near Phoenix.

He clutches his face, hisses like a king cobra. "You wanna fight like a man, alright, I'ma treat you like one." Bug Eyes comes at me again, juking to his right, then smoothly countering left.

I dodge the right hook to my jaw, but I slip on the floor again. My head strikes the end table. My vision bursts with black spots that dance and shimmy. Bug Eyes straddles me. His spindly fingers encircle my throat and squeeze. I try to force air inside my body, but his grip tightens. My breaths are shorter. Is this what Natalie felt that night five years ago? I claw at his hands, his wrists. He smashes my head against the end table again.

A crystal-framed portrait clatters to the floor. It's closer than Redding's gun, but I see two frames. I reach for the one on the right. It doesn't exist. I reach for the one on the left. My fingers grasp something sharp and real and firm. I crack the frame across Bug Eye's crooked nose. He scurries back, trying to shake off my latest blow. Blood pours from his face.

Three months ago, The Ivory had a self-defense class. But the class didn't teach me to use everyday items like keys and picture frames as weapons.

Momma did.

I try to focus until I stop seeing two of everything. Including Redding, still in Semitruck's hold. She wriggles an arm out of his grasp and reaches back, digging her nails into his jaw. He howls and releases her. Scrambling to her feet, Redding whips around to face Semitruck. "Stop now and I promise you'll make it to holding in one piece."

Semitruck runs his hand down his jaw and examines the blood on his palm. He charges at Redding, and shoves her against the wall near the door. His fist raised, prepared to do damage.

"Hey, dumbass!" I barely recognize my own voice.

Even if you're in a life and death struggle, you'll react to someone insulting you. I don't care who you are. It's instinct. It's human.

Semitruck turns in my direction.

Redding stomps his left foot like it's the biggest, nastiest cockroach on earth. He bellows in agony and lumbers back a few feet. She kicks his left knee, then steps forward and comes down with her right elbow across his face.

"Fuuuck!" Semitruck screams.

I grab her gun and toss it to her. She catches it and points it at Semitruck. "Move, and I swear to Almighty God I'll make sure you can't use the right leg either."

Just like in the movies! Now, why couldn't someone have filmed that?!

Bug Eyes bolts toward the broken back door and down the fire escape. My head feels two sizes too big for my body. My throat is raw. I'm not relieved Bug Eyes is gone. I'm disappointed that I can't finish the job. I rush over to Phoenix, pressing my index and middle fingers against her neck. Her pulse strongly beats against my fingers.

Steady metal clicking hits my ears as Redding handcuffs Semitruck. The chains are a tight fit.

"Ma'am, ma'am, you're hurting my shoulder."

"We'll get another set to extend these." Redding reads Semitruck his rights. She then picks up her phone and dials a number. "This is Detective Redding Stark. Badge number 58122. Roll units to 2509 North Sawyer Avenue."

My heels are scattered near the tiny eat-in kitchen. I grab them and carefully tiptoe past the wood and glass and blood out of the door. I don't care if I've just fought Satan, I am not leaving my only pair of Louboutins.

I'd carry them and walk barefoot. Over fire. No problem.

The Ivory is chaos, but it's a bespoke chaos I'm used to navigating. It's civilized and sinister. This new chaos is brash and unapologetic. The sirens and onlookers. A man who would've just as easily killed us sits alive in the back of a patrol car. His sociopath partner still roams the streets.

I touch the back of my head, a small bump forming, but I'm not disoriented, not in enough pain to incur a medical bill that could bankrupt me. I'm aware enough to remember my name, the date, and what happened an hour ago. But the hours after I left The Cathedral still escape me.

"We should really check you out. Also take you to Dovemire Memorial," says an EMT, a wisp of a middle-aged lady with pixie-cut black hair.

I haven't visited Momma since yesterday. I swallow. It hurts. "I'm fine."

Semitruck is locked in a patrol car with a new black eye I hadn't seen him with earlier. Phoenix is alert and breathing. She's wheeled off in the ambulance next to mine, but she's not dead. I'll take that as a win. Redding talks with Detective Webb across the street as I make my way toward a bus stop. I barely have two hours left in my shift.

"Thanks for giving your statement. We're gonna get Phoenix, uh, Deiserae's tomorrow, soon as she's cleared by a doctor," says Redding as she jogs up from behind.

"What about the guy who attacked you. He say anything?"

"Only thing he said is 'lawyer.' We have patrols searching for the other suspect." Redding studies me. "You should've gone to the hospital."

"You're already at your job. I left mine to come here."

"You left your job to break the law and make it harder for me to do mine," says Redding.

I look down the street. The 56 Washington/Michigan inches closer to my stop. "You good?"

"Been hit harder than that. Been shot and shot at, too. Not that it's something I like reliving," she says.

"Didn't really answer my question."

"I answered it enough," says Redding, while massaging her right shoulder. "Just . . . stop playing detective. Let me do my job."

"Then do it right and I won't have to come rescue you next time." The bus squeaks to a halt, hisses, and settles in front of me. I step on, escaping one Hell to return to another.

CHAPTER 16

Giovanni

June 14, 2025

Clutching my phone in my hand, I stare at the screen, willing this machine to somehow return those lost moments, hours.

You piece of crap metal, glass, and microchips, tell me what happened last night!

I grip my phone tighter, suppressing my urge to smash it into pieces. I push it all down. The guilt. Almost being murdered less than three hours ago. My missing time. Momma's illness.

All of it.

I can't find Natalie if I dwell on all the circumstances of our reunion and its aftermath. So, I'll compartmentalize my trauma. It's simple. It's breathing.

It's survival.

Opening the drawer of my front desk station, I scavenge for aspirin to fight the headache gifted to me by Bug Eyes and find a bottle two months past its expiration date. I pop a couple, struggle to swallow them, then log in to NexusLuxury as Willa.

Our system isn't as good as camera footage, but it'll give me all the little tidbits security cameras can't—the information we collect on our VIPs. Likes, dislikes, favorite foods, restaurants, preferred vendors, known associates, triggers, quirks.

Everything.

This is a different kind of data mining. We obtain our knowledge the old-fashioned way. Observation. Listening to conversations, important and ordinary.

A good hotel fulfills a request. A luxury hotel anticipates your needs.

Under NexusLuxury's Guests tab, I click on Guests (Special). Winstead's account has a smiley face.

He has a reservation for a High Floor room. No special requests. Three-day stay in a double-room suite. Thursday to Sunday. Who wants two bedrooms when they're with their girlfriend? That could mean something or nothing. He enjoys a nice steak at Bavette's Bar & Boeuf. Prefers a late checkout. A couple of vendors. Winstead's job title was changed from Governor Whitlock's chief of staff to consultant a week ago. Nothing else stands out. By our standards, his profile is sparse, which means he's private. I barely got two words out of him on Thursday.

I Google *Fleur Winstead*. There are pictures with the governor. Smiling. Scowling. Whispering in ears of subordinates. Articles quoting him on Winstead's policies, Julien-related scandals, and his philanthropic endeavors. But the latest article in the *Chicago Tribune* is about his recent leave of absence.

> ". . . I remain Governor Whitlock's staunchest advocate and fiercest supporter, but I need time off to attend to personal matters. However, I expect to return soon refreshed, recharged, and ready to help reelect Governor Whitlock who remains an advocate for . . ."

One way to return "recharged and ready" could be to take a little getaway with your young girlfriend. I've met politicians, their staff, their families. I've never known them to take a break while ramping up for a reelection campaign. Was Winstead so stressed that he hurt Natalie? Is that what the missing footage would show?

Should I tell Redding about this tomorrow?

A pair of hands with mermaid-blue manicured nails sets a book down on top of my station. Victoria stares at me expectantly. "I ran into two detectives who said they're investigating an 'incident' here but didn't give me any details."

"A party got out of hand Friday night. Some property damage. That's all." I maintain eye contact and smile.

"A party?" She drums her nails on her book.

I cough. My throat clenches the slightest bit. "Yes."

As pleasant as Victoria is, and I say pleasant in comparison to her asshole of a husband, she's still entitled. Not getting answers to your questions when your father-in-law is the governor is clearly unacceptable. *Well, we can't always get what we want, Victoria.*

"And are you okay? I saw you at The Cathedral and—"

"Yes, fine. A simple misunderstanding."

"You sure? Your voice also sounds a little—"

"Allergies." I look past her. "Oh, I think you have a gift."

Edgar Kelly comes from behind, a bouquet of red roses cradled in his arms. Victoria shoos away her security detail and they return to their original position a few feet behind her.

"These lovely blooms are courtesy of your husband, Julien. He wanted me to deliver them personally. A note is attached." Edgar points to the tallest mound of roses, where a hand-written card in elegant cursive is perched. Edgar's handwriting, not Julien's. I've seen both of their signatures plenty of times to know the difference.

"Thank you," says Victoria flatly.

A nameless staff member takes the flowers, cradling them in her left arm, holding a constantly buzzing phone in her right hand.

"Did you enjoy *Macbeth*?" I ask.

"I don't like red roses. I like pink dahlias. And I don't like *Macbeth*. My favorite Shakespeare play is *Titus Andronicus*." Victoria sneers. "You wanna make someone suffer, kill what they love."

I'm not clutching my pearls at Victoria's words. I've heard worse from guests about their partners. Plus, an unsatisfied wife who gives her husband a black eye is the least of my worries.

"I—uh, you ladies have a wonderful evening," says Edgar. He scuttles off to his white van, hazards blinking, in the front driveway.

Victoria glances around the lobby. "Has someone named Zanthe asked for me?"

"Zanthe?" The thump in my head grows more intense. Hopefully the expired aspirin will kick in soon.

"Yes, Zanthe Yaeger-Gates?"

When I tell you wealthy people love these hyphenate names! They need that little piece of punctuation to make their high social standing official.

"I'm afraid not. Would you like me to page her?"

"Would you—" Victoria scans the lobby again. Her face relaxes and a smile decorates her lips, the first one I've seen since she arrived.

A tall, stunning woman dressed shabby chic saunters past the water feature. She pockets a silver lighter and warmly embraces Victoria. She smells lightly of cigarettes but mostly of rose perfume. Zanthe. I saw her at The Cathedral sitting with Victoria and Julien. Another witness to my fight with Natalie.

Victoria turns to me. “Giovanni, this is Zanthe. Zanthe, this is Giovanni, the chief concierge at The Ivory.”

I smile. “Nice to meet—”

“I owe you. I know your Hyde Park exhibit is on Tuesday,” interrupts Victoria. She swipes her book from my desk.

“Governor Whitlock’s daughter-in-law comes calling, I come running,” says Zanthe.

I close my mouth and swallow the other half of my greeting. Keeping my ears open and my face blank, I continue to search for any clues in Winstead’s file.

“I can’t believe the photographer canceled.” Victoria leans in close and whispers, “Honestly, I’m way more excited about seeing you than I am about this damn party.”

Zanthe laughs. “Like I said, here to help.”

“Julien can’t be bothered to lift a finger but has all the mouth to take the credit.” Victoria rubs her temples.

“That bad, huh?” Zanthe removes her woven sun hat, her dreads swing slightly along the mid of her svelte, muscled back.

“This is his what, third affair? I stopped caring long before we even got married.”

Zanthe looks Victoria up and down. “And what’s to stop you from having a little fun of your own?”

Victoria’s mouth opens and closes in surprise before she utters, “The thought has crossed my mind.”

“Has it now?” Zanthe smiles seductively. “Well, let’s talk more about that over dinner.”

Victoria nervously chuckles and turns to me. “Ah, Giovanni, would you mind giving Zanthe a tour of The Ivory tomorrow? I want her to see where the gala will be, figure out the best places to take pictures. All that good stuff.”

I’m visible again. I momentarily abandon Winstead’s file. “It’ll be my pleasure.”

"This place looks like it has more than a few ghost stories. Am I right, Gio?" asks Zanthe.

I have no desire to correct Zanthe when she calls me "Gio." Zanthe appears humble, not arrogant. She seems easygoing enough to balance Victoria's high-strung nature. She's . . . charismatic. Like Natalie was . . . *is*.

"I'll see you tomorrow at nine o' clock," says Zanthe.

"I look forward to it," I say.

I never blur the lines between guest and friend, but Zanthe could get me to make an exception.

Zanthe and Victoria leave, security detail in tow.

I return to my sideline investigative work. That brief encounter gave me the gift of almost forgetting my current circumstances.

Almost.

CHAPTER 17

Redding

June 14, 2025

Dad would work like this. Late nights. Little sleep. Even when his hands were swollen, or he had migraines or nosebleeds or couldn't catch his breath. Even when his kidneys failed him, then the rest of his body. He gave his life to be a detective. So, I can fight through fatigue. I've seen my father fight through worse.

I glance at Emmett loitering in the kitchen just before midnight, then close the browser window containing a fluff piece on Natalie. Pretty pictures. No important information.

The dull splash of coffee into a mug pulls me from my abyssic trance. Emmett stands to my right, grimacing at the sight of the files and papers fanned out before me like playing cards on a poker table.

Emmett sets the mug in front of me and sits in a chair two seats away.

"At least they're not taking up room in the bed."

"No. Just here." He points to his temple. "And here." He points to his heart.

I roll my eyes. "You're such a teacher."

He softly chuckles. "Can't turn it off. Like my wife."

I gesture to the files. "There's a woman who went missing from a hotel, The Ivory. Natalie Moore. When Frenchie and I got there, the room was a mess. Blood, shattered glass, and . . . an orchid. In one of the bedrooms." I don't look up. Not yet. I don't want to see judgment in his eyes. Or worse, disappointment.

"Probably a coincidence. Fancy hotels spend money on flowers. Could've been part of the decor," he says.

"The hotel's signature flower is lavender. Not orchids." I drink. A little sugar. No cream. That man always figures out the right amount of sugar to put in my coffee.

"The orchid could've been an exception, a gift from an admirer. Hell, she could be allergic to lavender," says Emmett.

"There was still lavender in the room," I counter.

. . . *the glass fracture of the vase seems off* . . .

. . . *the shards are more evenly spread* . . .

"There's something different about this case. Some of the evidence doesn't match what happened at the scene. It's possible it was staged."

"And maybe it wasn't, Red. You don't think you're reaching. Seeing what you wanna see?"

"What I see is a missing woman, one who looks like me." I focus on my coffee for a moment, then meet Emmett's eyes. "If it was Brianne with long blond hair and piercing blue eyes from Winnetka. If five white girls went missing back-to-back, there'd be a task force. A tip line, the FBI and James Bond's ass with Batman and three of the Avengers to save Brianne."

But not Nivea, Stacey, Annette, Olivia, or Mia. They have

none of that. They only have a missing person's report. Ms. Charlotte only has an unanswered text. And me, a detective assigned to every case except for the one that matters the most to this city. Even if other detectives don't see it. Even if Frenchie doesn't see it. Even if my own damn husband doesn't see it.

News vans are still perched like vultures across the street. At least the door knocking has stopped for a while. The back door opens and slams as Hudson runs upstairs to his room. I ease off the couch, not wanting to tear my stitches.

Emmett jogs after him. "Kids can be . . . unkind. But they're just mimicking their parents."

I take each stair carefully as I make it to his room. "Baby, open the door."

"Kids are singing 'Fuck tha Police' when I'm on the playground." The door remains closed, but Hudson says from the other side, "They keep saying you should be locked up for shooting that man coming home from work."

I lean against Emmett. "No one's figured out what happened. Who shot who. That takes time."

"How much?" asks Hudson.

My stomach violently cramps for a moment. "I—I don't know, son."

Emmett stares at the five thick files. Pieces of paper compiling the lives of vibrant women snatched away, not a trace left behind. Five families and countless others left in some weird purgatory of grief, fear, and hope. A quick look of loathing and rage overtakes his normally handsome face, but then he somehow quiets those emotions to something more compassionate, kind, again resembling the man I know. The man I think I still love and who I think still might love me.

"There were orchids in each of their homes. And a line of poetry," utters Emmett, pinching the bridge of his nose, exhausted that he's found himself rehashing the basics of this case with me. Again.

"A vanda orchid," I reply. "They were all taken—"

"Or disappeared," interrupts Emmett.

". . . at the beginning of the weekend," I continue. "It took a day or two before family and friends realized something was wrong. Except for Nivea. She was noticed right away 'cause she didn't pick up her daughter from Ms. Charlotte's house. Mia took the longest. Three weeks. She's originally from Seattle and moved around a lot. Didn't have many friends at Afya Wellness. Stacey wasn't noticed until she failed to show up to teach at Septima Clark. Annette missed singing at the opening of her fundraiser for Better Chicago Tomorrow. Olivia's partner at Englewood Design Alliance said she was absent at the last two weekly meetings before they realized something was wrong."

"But why them?"

"Why not? Different jobs. Single women. Some had found-families, some more traditional. There's nothing tying them together but the orchid, the poetry, and their skin."

"The orchids could be a coincidence," he says.

"And the poetry?"

"Who says it was poetry?" says Emmett. "Those lines could be song lyrics, the beginnings to a story, or something to do with the title of a photograph, a marketing campaign, or a painting. It could be nothing." Emmett puts his elbow on the table, resting his head in his hand. "My point is the connection is thin and what about this new case? Was there a line of poetry this time?"

"Haven't found that. *Yet.* I need to access Natalie's computer, but Digital Forensics has a backlog. Everybody's got a backlog. And I need to get a warrant." I crack my back, relieving some of the pressure of sitting too long. "Then there's the concierge at the hotel, Giovanni Mason. Granted, she's got something to hide, and she got in a fight with Natalie, but it's only been—" I glance at my phone "—yeah, a little over fifteen hours. Way too early to draw conclusions."

Emmett shifts to the chair closest to me and takes my hand. "You need some rest. Coffee isn't gonna keep you going."

"Thanks for going over the basics again."

He leans in and kisses my forehead, then rises from his chair. "You're welcome."

I can barely dance in this dress. It's heavy and white. And I hate lace. But Emmett twirls me around on the floor with ease. With Dad and Frenchie looking on from the side. Then Emmett gathers me in his arms. And we dance. And I swear to myself the only other person I'll love more than him is the one I've been carrying inside me for two months.

As he passes me, I grab his arm. I know why I do this. I need balance and love, even during the times neither he nor I deserve them.

We say nothing. No "I'm sorrys." No "I love yous." We go upstairs.

Together.

CHAPTER 18

Redding

June 15, 2025

"People are who they are, Red."

Dad sits on the couch and stares straight ahead at the television, then coughs. I examine the lumps in his arm from his dialysis treatments. Even looking at a movie drains his energy.

"Isn't this where you give me some kind of pep talk about how we're still supposed to see the good in everyone?"

"No. And don't waste your time trying to change anyone either." Dad grabs my hand and squeezes it. "'Cause I wouldn't want anyone trying to change you."

Frenchie hangs up his phone. "A guy matching the description of the perp yesterday was found a few blocks away on North Troy Street late last night," says French. "Says for now it looks self-inflicted, but they still gotta work the rest of the scene."

"You sure? White male. Skinny. Star tattoo on his left cheek," I say. "He killed himself? That doesn't make sense."

"Maybe he felt guilty for what he did," reasons French.

“Nah, he loved what he did. Loved hurting people. There’s more to it.”

“Well, I’m telling you what the detective on scene told me,” he says.

“This doesn’t make sense, Frenchie. You know it doesn’t.” A dull ache spreads through my stomach.

“Red, you look for anything that’ll support whatever theory you got in your head. Start putting together things that aren’t there.” Frenchie points toward Phoenix’s hospital room. “We got more than enough to deal with. It’s barely past eight in the morning. And I haven’t even eaten.”

I suck my teeth. “By all means let’s not keep you from stuffing your face after this.”

Deiserae inhabits her full Phoenix persona even as we enter her hospital room overflowing with unopened gifts and an array of bouquets. Five people are already inside the space that’s only supposed to have two visitors at a time.

“I want them to *see* my IV. Move to the left. Center me. And get me one of those boxes to open. They love when I open their shit on live. Makes them feel special,” she says.

A boy with bright blue hair and dark circles around his eyes holds Phoenix’s phone and counts down to one.

“Alright. my Fiyah Flies, as most of you know I won’t be at the second day of bellezza2025 because I was . . . attacked in my home. I got bumps, bruises, and a really bad concussion and I’m . . . shaken. Everything is so . . . raw, fresh. But I’m being released in a couple of hours, so the real healing begins when I return home.” A quivering breath escapes her mouth as she wipes away tears that she didn’t have a minute ago. “Being attacked like that is terrifying on a level I can’t describe. But if any of you have endured something like this, or worse, know you’re not alone. I want to thank you for all the thoughts and prayers . . . and these.” Phoenix opens the gift, a perfume set, cradling the box as if it's the most precious thing she's ever been given.

I stand in her eyeline, placing my hand on my hip, revealing my badge. Frenchie does the same. Phoenix notices us, glares for a moment, then returns her attention to her live feed.

"unicornbest3753, I can't wait to try this fragrance." She blows a kiss to the camera. "Be well and stay safe out there, Fiyah Flies. And don't forget to make sure you're following me on Insta, TikTok, and YouTube. Like, share, follow, or subscribe. We can all get through this . . . together. That's my word for today."

Frenchie and I snake in between the bodies surrounding Phoenix and stand at the foot of her bed. The boy with blue hair hands Phoenix a pill. She puts it in her mouth and swallows it down with water.

"Ugh. Damn pills," she says.

"Don't expect you to remember me, but I'm Detective Stark. I was . . . there at your apartment. This is Detective Webb. We'd like to ask you some questions about—"

"Hold on." Phoenix eyes her entourage. "Get out!" The vulnerability displayed on the camera gone from her high-cheeked, umber-hued face.

No one jumps and they file out. The alchemic mix of body sprays and perfumes stings my nostrils.

"I remember you. Barely," she says.

I don't offer Giovanni's name as the other person in Phoenix's apartment. The less she knows about Giovanni, the less of a chance those two possibly team up and cause me and Frenchie twice the headache.

"Well, I don't know . . . thanks. Can't say much more than that, I guess." Phoenix offers me the perfume set.

"Umm, no. Can't accept gifts. Besides that, helping you is my job."

"The perfume's cheap, anyway." Phoenix tosses the box to the side. "You catch who did it?"

"One suspect is in custody. The other one was found dead earlier this morning." I take a deep breath. "And we need to get your statement about what happened yesterday."

Phoenix holds up her arm with the IV attached. "Well, I can't be a suspect."

"No, a victim, at least for this." I grab my pen and notepad from my inside pocket. "Can I have your full name?"

"Deiserae Waters," she says.

She whispers her name like a curse, as if whatever glamour and fame she's acquired would be stripped. Deiserae will never again be enough.

"Want me to refer to you as Phoenix?"

She nods and pours another full cup of water from a plastic pitcher.

I search for the vulnerability she displayed for her followers, but it's still missing. Perhaps in front of a camera is the only place where Phoenix can find the truest, or most tolerant, version of herself.

"Can you tell us what happened? How those men entered your place?" I ask.

"They knocked." Phoenix scoffs. "I'm always getting packages. Sponsors' products on pre-release. Gifts from fans. Other influencers send me their shit, hoping I'll feature it on my channels."

"You didn't think twice about *two* men delivering a package?" asks Frenchie.

"I only saw one when I looked. The skinny one. The dead one." A faint smile spreads across Phoenix's mouth. "The big guy barged his way in."

"Seen them before?" I ask.

"Nope. Never." Phoenix reaches into a blue-and-white bag

and pulls out a set of makeup brushes. Unlike the perfume she offered me, she gently sets the brushes on her right. Her own little keep and discard pile. She looks at Frenchie for a moment, then me again. "Why were you at my place, anyway?"

"Wanted to ask you about Natalie Moore. You two speak recently? I heard she was supposed to be at bellezza2025 yesterday or today."

Phoenix rolls her eyes. "First of all, I'm the last person she'd talk to. Second, Natalie skips it every year."

"Thought she came to Chicago for this event," says Frenchie.

"Sponsors don't pay enough for her." Phoenix flips her black- and purple-highlighted hair to her left shoulder, grabs another gift and unwraps it.

Her humanity is stripped down to the two-minute reels she posts for her followers. It scares me that these are the people Anya might imitate, aspire to be like. What about Hudson? Who the hell is he watching on his phone? Vapid and harmful people are helping to shape our world. But then, is it so different from what happened before cell phones and clicks for clout? I'm fooling myself thinking my generation was better. We weren't. We just couldn't spread the damage as quickly.

I tap my pen on my notepad. "Well, we're hoping you can provide some insight into why Natalie was in Chicago."

"Don't know. Don't care. We good?"

"We're not good at all 'cause Natalie is missing."

"Sorry to hear that," says Phoenix. She takes a sip of water.

"Did you hear what Detective Stark just said?" asks Frenchie, finally coming out of hibernation. "Natalie is missing. You were assaulted. Maybe you were supposed to be next."

She raises her perfectly arched eyebrow and puts down her cup. "Black women under attack is a new headline for you, Detective? Really? We're always in danger. And for the most part none of y'all care enough to find the people who hurt us anyway. So, now you do care, and want me to set aside everything I'm working for, stop my life, to help you? One of the animals who hurt me is dead. The other one is in jail. I'll be alright, trust that."

"And what about Natalie?" I ask. "You care that she's missing?"

"I care that Natalie ditched me *before* she went missing. I trusted her with a dream. Those don't come often for me and my trust doesn't come easy, but I was gonna try. With Natalie, I was gonna try."

"Well, I get why you're annoyed," says Frenchie.

"I'm annoyed when my flight runs late. Natalie cost me $50,000. You expect me to be sad she's missing? Does that sound logical?" asks Phoenix.

Frenchie scratches his stubbly jaw. "Well, Deiserae, it sounds human to be sad. But what you're describing sounds like a motive."

Phoenix snorts dismissively and digs again amid the boxes and bags of presents from admirers and picks another gift.

"How'd Natalie screw you out of $50K?" I ask.

"I was gonna start a makeup line. Amour Noir Beauty. Been talking to Natalie about it for, like, a year," she says.

"Beauty. Tough business to get a foot in the door," says Frenchie.

"That's any business for us or are you willfully ignorant?" asks Phoenix.

"Just the normal level," quips French.

"I didn't want us to just be the next big thing. I wanted us to be *the* thing . . . icons. But being icons doesn't come cheap and it's not like they're throwing money at Black women to start companies run by us for us."

Phoenix unwraps another offering from one of her followers. "And Natalie was all for it a few weeks ago. Went to Chicago. Met with the grant people. Then she came back talking 'bout 'she doesn't wanna do it anymore.' Then ghosts."

I write as fast as possible, trying to keep her facts, or what Phoenix believes are facts, in order. But as I collect her side of the story, I have questions.

"What grant people?"

"The D.A.R.E. to Dream program," she says. "Stands for 'Diversity Application Resource and Engagement.' Memorized that name for nothing."

"How'd you hear about it?"

"I go a lotta places. Meet a lotta people. A lady told me about it," says Phoenix. "Said she knew me from my socials. Heard I wanted to start a makeup line and the D.A.R.E. program is built for people like us, women like us."

Frenchie sniffles. "Get a name?"

"I don't remember the people I meet ten minutes ago let alone someone I met a month or two ago," says Phoenix. "I think the governor's backing it or something. Probably the only way a Black Republican is getting a fraction of the minority vote in this city."

I don't keep up with politics like I should, but I know when any politician, no matter the party, does something positive for minorities, they shout it from the rooftops like they've erased centuries of oppression and should be next up for a Nobel Peace Prize. Why is this program barely marketed?

"Why was Natalie the spokesperson? She lives in LA now," I ask.

"Natalie's got more followers, but still repped Chicago in a lot of her posts. Plus, she was excited and . . ." Phoenix trails off and crosses her arms. "*He* probably got into her head. That's why she ghosted."

"Who got in Natalie's head?" asks French.

"Ronan. Her husband. He was really checking up on her. Especially these past two or three months. Maybe he was tired of sharing her. Maybe she didn't wanna do it anymore. Wanted to try that trad wife lifestyle instead. I don't know." She grabs her cup of water. Drops spill over the rim onto her fingers. She drinks and empties her cup.

"Ronan? Is he an older guy? Natalie was seen at a hotel with an older—" I ask.

"What? Ronan is, like, maybe one or two years older than Nat, but he's not old like him." Phoenix gestures to French.

"Am I the universe's punching bag?" French shakes his head. "What's this guy's last name? Ronan what?"

Phoenix shrugs.

There are people in some of Natalie's pictures, maybe the last images she captured still alive. Please God let her still be alive. I scroll through them. The newer posts aren't as crisp, careful, curated as the rest of her feed. Random. They were taken at The Cathedral. Some food. A picture of the bar. A picture of someone near the host stand. A group in a booth. No captions. I can't find a picture of anyone over thirty-five years old.

"That's him. That's Ronan," says Phoenix, pointing to a post on the third row. She again refills her cup to the brim with water.

There's a picture of him with Natalie. They look happy. He looks like . . . I toggle back up Natalie's feed. Ronan's a dead ringer for the man at the host stand.

Someone knocks on the door. A guy in a red-and-white track suit sporting a low fade and sunglasses pokes his head in. "Yo, we got two minutes 'fore we gotta start the next video. The hospital's gonna kick us outta here in, like, a few hours."

Phoenix puts her water down and waves her entourage back in without asking if we're finished. She grabs a small black bag and retrieves lipstick, then begins reapplying a bold fuchsia gloss perfectly complementing her skin. "Umm, no offense but even if you are cops, I got money to make, and you're not adding to it, sooo . . ."

I hand Phoenix my card. She stares at it.

"They might come back for you. Maybe not the same people, but you might wanna think about it."

Phoenix's mascaraed almond-shaped eyes grow wide. She takes my card and puts it on the table next to her bed.

We exit. Someone closes the door behind us.

It's an avalanche of people and facts and moving parts. A quicksand of information that's sucking me in inch by inch. I'm close to suffocating.

French wearily runs his hand down his face. "So, Natalie ditches a business plan and $50K. Was in town for a conference she wasn't attending. Gets into a public fight with a friend in a fancy-ass restaurant. Disappears. *And* she might have an older boyfriend and a husband stalking her? What the hell is going on?"

My feet slap the pavement down East 43rd Street. Cormac has stamina. He looks back at me. I take deep breaths and close the gap. I'll find Nivea. He knows where she is. Where the others are. I know it. Justice, any kind of justice, please let it be done. Cormac looks back again, then makes a right and cuts down an alley and runs faster. So do I.

"I don't know, Frenchie. Wish I did."

CHAPTER 19

Giovanni

June 15, 2025

I check my inbox. Nothing from the Art History Department chair or the Title IX coordinator. It's been three days. Nat goes to her professor's place when she thinks I'm asleep. I've followed her. Watched them kiss as he pulled her inside.

She knocks on my open door. "Hey, I feel bad I keep blowing you off. Lemme make it up to you."

I close my laptop. "It's fine. I'm not your only friend."

"You're not my friend, Gio. You're my sister. Blood means nothing." Natalie hugs me from behind. "You gonna keep making me kiss your ass 'til you forgive me or are we going to this party tonight?"

I smile. "Both."

Bale puts on a fake smile—one that doesn't reach his eyes—and approaches me in the lobby near the water feature. I'm an expert at fake smiles. I always make sure my eyes crinkle. I can lie with my whole face. That's not the best thing to brag about, I suppose, but I should embrace all of me. The good. The bad. And the messy.

But the messy part can't remember a twelve-hour block of time last Friday.

"Morning," says Bale. "Uh, you know where there's a pharmacy around here?"

"I hope you're feeling well." I keep my tone as light as possible. The last thing I need is for Bale to take offense. He seems the type to always find a bee in a bouquet of roses.

"Nothing like that. I . . . uh, anyway, the pharmacy?"

"Sure, there's one about a block east. If you're not feeling well, you can call the front desk, and we can have a doctor sent to your room."

"Not that serious. Thanks," says Bale as he makes his way to the front entrance and out of the door in a few seconds.

He was calm. His voice was low. He said "Thanks." Bale seems different than the entitled, angry man I met on Thursday. But a good moment means little when it comes to behavior. A sustained pattern, good or bad, normally tells me everything I need to know about a guest.

"Gio!" Zanthe calls my name, leaving her emphasis on the *o*, a funny little tick of a sound that makes me smile.

I extend my hand. "It's nice to see you again, Mrs. Yeager-Gates."

She takes my hand and does a faire la bise, kissing me on each cheek. "Stop it. It's Zanthe. I'm not like these stuffy little Karens in here."

Behind Zanthe stands a man, around six feet with a muscular build, high cheekbones, and beryl-colored eyes. A black wedding band on his ring finger. And Zanthe has a simple black band on her ring finger as well. No large diamonds or other jewels adorn it. She didn't have a wedding ring when we first met. I *always* pay attention to a person's ring finger.

Zanthe turns around, "This is Gideon. My husband. My better half and my little spy."

She laughs. He doesn't.

Gideon reaches out to shake my hand but says nothing.

It feels tense between them, but it almost seems like they're used to being at odds. Natalie and I would go through spells like this in our sisterhood. You're just as comfortable in the chaos as you are in the calm.

Zanthe loops her arm in mine. "Now that introductions are out of the way, tell me all about this place."

As I walk forward, I feel a hand tugging me backward. I release Zanthe to see Mecca, brow furrowed, examining me, her mouth parted as if she wants to ask something.

I turn to Zanthe. "Please excuse me for a brief moment."

Mecca and I walk toward the left bank of elevators, a few feet away is a small, dim alcove where the porters store their carts.

"Are you okay?"

Mecca widens her eyes and steps closer in the already cramped space. "Are you?"

I whisper, "I couldn't get you to say 'Boo' to me two days ago. Now you're texting, stopping by my office."

"I'm concerned," she says.

I left the liquor store and went home and went to bed. I tripped over that box near the door. That's how I tore my dress and got my bruises. That has to be it, but where did the dirt on the dress come from? Nah, I tripped and fell when I got off the bus. Right?

"I'm good. This whole thing with Natalie is a . . . small bump in the road."

"Giovan—"

"I can't keep guests waiting." I release Mecca's hand and stride back to Zanthe.

Confidence in my walk. Smile on my face. Anguish in my heart. "Apologies."

Zanthe again loops her arm in mine. "Ready to give us all the dirt on The Ivory?"

"Can't say there'll be much dirt, but I'll tell the truth," I say.

"The truth is as dirty as you can get." Zanthe giggles at her joke.

Gideon remains behind us. I keep track of his reflection in the mirrored glass as I lead them to the left and down the hall. Clearing my throat, I begin my speech, the one I've recited hundreds of times before about The Ivory, its history, the big and little things that give a place its hauntings.

"The Ivory was constructed in 1914 by the architecture firm Wallace & Fox. A wealthy oil baron named R.I. Willowbrook fancied himself more of a hotelier than oilman, and he set about to build one of the grandest luxury hotels ever known in Chicago and around the world. Willowbrook named it The Ivory Hotel as he believed the color ivory exuded purity and sophistication."

I stop in front of a collection of brass-framed pictures on an onyx-painted wall. Less than ten feet away sits the small greenhouse near the rear of the hotel, which leads to the outside pool used in the summertime.

I point to the picture at the top, an unsmiling man with a shock of brown hair on his head, a pug nose, thin lips, and thick mustache. "This is R.I. Willowbrook. And, after the stock market crash of 1929, he leapt off the roof of The Ivory to his death."

Zanthe gasps, a catch of breath reminiscent of the one you take before a roller coaster takes its first dip. "How much did it cost to build The Ivory?"

"Figures go up to approximately one to one and a half million dollars. If my math is right, it's almost $50 million today."

Gideon sneers. "A lot of money to spend on a dream."

"Some would say not enough," counters Zanthe. "Whatever it takes to achieve a vision. Money, time, anger, blood. Willowbrook probably felt like it was worth it. I would."

"Well, his vision might not have totally matched yours," I say.

If this were another guest, I'd keep these next facts to myself. Most guests don't want to hear the unpleasant stories underpinning the expensive marble, brass fixtures, and thirty-foot water feature, but Zanthe seems to crave these types of details. You don't get the pretty without the ugly. Judging from Gideon, Zanthe doesn't mind a little ugly.

I lower my voice so the other guests walking past won't hear what I say unless they eavesdrop. "Willowbrook was a notorious racist. Believed in eugenics. It's rumored another reason he named this place The Ivory is because he felt white, in all things, was the superior color. The hotel didn't even get its first Black porter until well into 1971."

"Now I don't feel so bad he jumped," says Zanthe.

Gideon remains stone-faced. I didn't expect the revelation to move him. He hasn't been stripped or denied an opportunity because of his looks or race, as a matter of fact, he could've been given more than his fair share of chances because of white skin, blond hair, and blue eyes. R.I. Willowbrook would've completely welcomed him at The Ivory while Zanthe and I wouldn't have even been able to get jobs as maids.

Over a century later, I'm chief concierge. Even as tenuous as my position is right now, I truly hope that Willowbrook is rolling in his goddamn grave.

I point three rows below Willowbrook's picture. "And here we have a young Governor Whitlock and other pictures of the Whitlock family. They've been coming to The Ivory for thirty, forty years, at least."

"There's Julien," says Zanthe, referring to a picture to my left.

Julien Whitlock, no more than seven years old, stands among a group of young men. The governor is centered in the last row. The thirty-year-old picture is still amazingly crisp. I can make out Julien's mischievous glare, the governor's haughty grin along with all the other men decorating their faces with obliging smiles.

"You've known Julien for a long time?" I ask.

"I'm closer to Victoria," she says, looking off toward the greenhouse near the back of the hall.

Gideon checks his watch, an oddity in this cell-phone-obsessed climate, but given the detail and craftsmanship, it's expensive and worth showing off. It's also a passive-aggressive way to reinforce he'd rather be anywhere but here at The Ivory with me and Zanthe.

"Why don't I show you to the Elizabeth Grace ballroom, named after Willowbrook's mother and the place where we're holding the governor's birthday gala."

I lead Zanthe and Gideon west, in the opposite direction of the History Wall, to the hallway, just shy of the elevator bank leading to the High Floors.

"Tell me about yourself, Gio," says Zanthe.

This seems more an order, a need for her to make herself at ease around me. And though I like Zanthe, I'm not ready to share my life with her or my current circumstances.

"Nothing special. Born and raised on the South Side. Englewood. My mom is . . . well, she used to work at The Ivory. She'd bring me along all the time. I fell in love with this place. Hard not to. And I've been working on and off here since I was about sixteen. Promoted to chief concierge a few months ago. Yourself?"

"Raised by my mom. My grandma took over when I was eight. Didn't really talk to my dad until a few years ago."

I catch Gideon rolling his eyes in the reflection of the crystal-clear glass doors leading to the ballroom.

"This room is breathtaking," says Zanthe walking toward windows spanning right to left on the east wall. "It gets a lot more light than I thought."

Zanthe whips out her camera and snaps some shots from a few different angles. Frowns or smiles at what she's captured. She then makes her way toward the west end of the ballroom. Taking pictures. Frowning. Smiling. Zanthe then stands in front of the stage.

Wash. Rinse. Repeat.

Though her movements are repetitive, the passion with which she performs her job is fascinating. I wonder if this is how guests see me. For better or worse right now I know how my coworkers do.

Zanthe returns from her temporary creative adventure as Gideon steps beside me.

He keeps a few feet between us. "You know it is admirable that you've . . . pulled yourself up by your bootstraps for lack of a better term."

My face tightens into a frown as I turn to him. "Thank you." The inflection in my voice positions this as a question.

"I only meant that you should be proud of what you've accomplished," he says.

"Yes, I am proud. *Very.*" I walk toward the front of the ballroom to the stage, putting some distance between me and Gideon. My footsteps are muffled by the red-and-gold-patterned carpeting.

He moves closer. "Good. I don't want you getting all sensitive on me when I'm only giving a compliment." He smugly grins, his eyes are the color of blue toilet bowl water.

Zanthe steps between us. "Gio, do you like art? Photography? Of course you do. You're cultured obviously more than some of us." She cuts a look at Gideon. "I'm having an exhibition on Tuesday. I'd love for you to come. L'Atelier Rouge. Hyde Park."

"I'm familiar with the gallery," I say. "I've directed a few guests there if they wanted to explore a place . . . off the beaten path."

And by "off the beaten path" I mean places with people

who don't quite match the heavily white world in which some guests have cloistered themselves. One guest said to me, unashamed and out loud, that she wanted me to suggest the kinds of places where she'd see her child's teacher, nanny, or the landscaper. In that order.

"So, you'll come?" asks Zanthe.

I look past Zanthe and meet Gideon's glare. "I hear it's getting quite the buzz. Managed to snag some exclusive up-and-coming artists."

Zanthe loops her arm in mine again and we leave the ballroom and return to the lobby. "You're deflecting, Gio. I'm too smart for flattery and you're too smart to think it'll work."

Victoria will be there, and wherever she'll be, Julien will surely be lurking. Mixing business with something resembling a burgeoning friendship with Zanthe might not be a good idea. Plus, I am not vibing with Gideon. After-Work Giovanni would call him an asshole in seven different languages.

Zanthe peeks over her shoulder at Gideon a few steps behind us. She leans in and whispers, "I have him under my thumb. No need to fear Gideon."

"I'm not worried about *my* safety."

Zanthe giggles. She's fun. She's engaging. She's beautiful. Like Natalie. And I care less about the long-term and relish in the refreshing embrace of something decadent and new. Which means Zanthe could be dangerous if I don't keep my guard up. But not everybody is Natalie. Not everything will end in ruin.

Bodies restlessly churn around me and Zanthe like unsteady waves beating against the shore. Gideon has passed us and is now perched at the exit.

An exclusive exhibition. Making nice with someone who's friends with the governor's daughter-in-law. Unintentional social climbing isn't a skill I'd put on my résumé, but it's nice to know I can do it when the opportunity presents itself.

“What time?”

“Six o’clock, but no one arrives to these things on time. I won’t. You shouldn’t.” Zanthe unhooks her arm from mine. “I’ll put your name on the guest list. You’ll be one of three people I’ll be happy to see there. Myself included.”

She kisses me on each cheek again and heads toward the exit to Gideon.

I touch the bump on the back of my head. It’s lessened but it’s still there. And despite feeling something that is not panic, anxiety, or terror for a few moments, these beastly thoughts return, clawing at the back of my head. Though what still gnaws at me almost as much as my missing time, is what does Redding know that I don’t? She’s visiting Phoenix today at the hospital. What has Phoenix told her? Has she held anything back from Redding that she’d tell me?

Can I trust Redding?

I power walk past the valets and porters, then hail a taxi. It’s about a five-minute drive to Dovemire Memorial. Just a little chat with Phoenix. Redding won’t know.

What harm could it *really* do?

CHAPTER 20

Redding

June 15, 2025

I open a new browser and Google the D.A.R.E. program. Their social media pages are . . . sparse. The same few pictures of Julien Whitlock with grant recipients. No captions. No tags. The D.A.R.E. website is nondescript. Stock images and a link to the application. I click on "Meet the Board," and a smiling picture of the governor's son assaults my eyes. Below is a quote:

> "An emergent issue in our community is the lack of social programs serving underrepresented groups as well as resources given to Black entrepreneurs longing for a chance to prove their worth in a world failing to acknowledge the role reinvestment plays in revitalizing neighborhoods . . ."

I scrunch my nose at this line. Not because it isn't true. It absolutely is, but because he's using this problem to exploit others and gain votes for his father. Hartwell Whitlock eked out a win three years ago and that was only because the Democratic candidate passed away and his replacement couldn't garner enough support a month before the election.

Frenchie's phone pings and a deep frown creases his face. "Aww, dammit." The first few words he's spoken since we returned a little over an hour ago.

"What?"

He shoves his cell into my hands. "She didn't give a damn about Natalie missing, now she's posting about it?"

Phoenix says in a trembling, melodramatic voice, "*I'm not gonna say we didn't have our differences, but I still loved Natalie. Family fights, but it's still family. The police just told me my sister is missing. First, I'm attacked. Now this?*"

Phoenix continues, "*Approximately 2,300 people are reported missing every day in the US. There's no information on how many are Black women. The media, this city, this country, don't care when we're hurt, when we're killed, when we're disappeared, so let's make them care.*"

Phoenix keeps the camera framed on her perfectly shaded cheekbones and waterproof mascara. "*If you know anything about my attack or Natalie's disappearance, please drop a comment below with #BringNatalieMooreHome. And don't forget to like, share, and subscribe to this channel. Let's hunt those bastards like they're hunting us.*"

It's not surprising that she'd capitalize on Natalie's circumstances to her advantage. It's bold, smart, and heartless. Her outcry for justice is bombastic and reckless. But it's the world we now live in or perhaps it was the world we always lived in.

Frenchie scrolls below the video and we read some of the comments.

teebaby23432: u know police not looking 4 @lezzismoore56

fandombike1111: 🙏 🙏 🙏

fxckdawrld0824: clout chasing

blssdnhighlymelanted: been saying this for years but they aint trying to listen

The thud of the closing security door draws Frenchie's and my attention to Commander Justin Markham. Wearing a bespoke tan linen jacket and pants, Markham waves us over instead of yelling over the din of voices surrounding and suffocating us.

"Oh God, what does Suits want?" asks Frenchie. He peeks over at his desk to a picture of Anya taped to the wall and makes the sign of the cross.

Frenchie isn't the only one who calls Commander Markham "Suits" behind his back. Markham is a social climber and an asshole, and he doesn't wear nice clothes because it helps his confidence or because he's especially into fashion. He does it because at any given time, he expects to be at a press conference. For me and Frenchie, Area Three is our safe space. To Markham, it's a stepping-stone.

We follow Markham to his corner office, a glass box to our right, visible over six rows of cubicles. He shuts his door and lowers the beige blinds on the windows as soon as we enter his domain. Markham works, congratulates, and berates in public. If we're having a private chat, it's about to go down.

Markham focuses on Frenchie. "Tell me what happened at The Ivory Hotel yesterday morning."

Whoever contacted Markham has wealth and power—attributes that he respects, worships, and covets. That's the only reason Frenchie and I are in this room.

Frenchie adjusts his glasses, then says, "A woman named Natalie Moore and her . . . companion, an older male, went missing between late last Friday or early Saturday. They were last seen at The Ivory Hotel and Resort. Security was patrolling the floor around 6:00 a.m. yesterday, and observed blood seeping from under the door. Upon entry, the room was heavily damaged and there was also blood throughout the living room. Scene's being processed by ETs, well, Saxon. The hotel isn't being super cooperative about giving us video footage so I'm working on a subpoena. Gonna be sending that to the State's Attorney's Office soon as we leave." Frenchie keeps his head down and scratches his ear.

Markham flexes his squared jawline but says nothing.

Frenchie continues, "There's a person of interest. Giovanni Mason, chief concierge at the hotel. Giovanni was seen fighting with Natalie hours before Natalie disappeared. There's also a video of Giovanni slapping Natalie *and* we saw some bruising on her arm."

"Why the hell isn't she here?" asks Markham.

I'm tired of this two-way conversation. "Because she isn't the only person who had a reason to hurt Natalie. There's also Deiserae Waters. She goes by Phoenix on her socials. She's pissed off that Natalie dropped out of a business arrangement. Says it cost her over $50K. I uploaded the report to R-Case a few minutes ago."

Markham opens his mouth but hesitates for a few seconds before he finally looks at me and speaks. "Did Deiserae, or Phoenix or whatever, slap Natalie?"

"No," I answer.

"Did you or Webb notice any bruising on *her* body after the victim's disappearance?"

"No sir. But—"

"And Phoenix or whatever her name is, does she have 24/7 access to the hotel?" counters Markham.

I unclench my left hand relieving a slight throb. "No, sir."

"Uh . . . Detective Stark *and* I questioned Deiserae at

Dovemire Memorial. She was attacked yesterday," says Frenchie, to redirect Markham's attention to him. "Stark got there in time to help. Apprehended one of the assailants. The other one was found dead this morning."

He leaves Giovanni's name out of it for now. Good boy, Frenchie.

"This Phoenix girl give you anything useful?"

"Phoenix posted a video about the case from her hospital room," says Frenchie, preferring to deliver the bad news, keeping me safe from Markham's additional wrath.

"Goddamn it!" Markham pounds his ham-sized fist on top of his desk.

"It's not all bad, sir. We still have other people to talk to, including Natalie's husband, a guy named Ronan," says Frenchie.

"The man she checked in with? Didn't you say he was missing, too?" asks Markham.

"Different guy," I say. "Natalie checked in with a man named F.T. Winstead."

"The governor's former chief of staff?" says Markham, a sudden, light tremble in his resonant voice.

"Eh, there also might be a link between Natalie and a grant program run by Governor Whitlock's office," I add.

"That angle's off the table." Markham wags his finger. "I want this closed sooner. Not later. And no mention of Governor Whitlock in the files. Now that's point-blank and period."

I'd love to investigate, find Natalie alive, and say this was all one big misunderstanding. But I watch Disney movies. I don't live in them. And if Natalie is number six, I can't let this go.

No matter what it costs.

"We wanna do this right, Commander. We can't control the people who are involved. And with respect, it takes the time it takes."

Markham puts a finger to his ear, pushing it forward. "Excuse me?" He stalks from behind his desk and stands close, I can taste his cologne on my tongue. Cardamom and vanilla. "If we don't act, gather suspects and evidence, we have no way to get in front of this thing. And I'm not gonna let this case be the next social justice cause that gives the public yet another excuse to shit on the police or have the superintendent, the mayor, or governor up my ass," Markham says. "Mason's got the assault, the bruising, and access to the victim." He counts each point on his fingers. "Anything else?"

I straighten my jacket. "All due respect, Commander, but the way to not make this a 'social justice cause' is to do the work even if it's hard, even if it takes us outside of what we want the narrative to be."

"You should've looked in a damn mirror and said those words to yourself last year before you cost this district a fucking fortune," says Markham. He looks down and lowers his voice to a sinister whisper. "Maybe you're hard of hearing, Stark, or you forgot how things work here. You've been . . . gone a minute. So, I'ma be nice and repeat myself. Focus on Giovanni Mason. Close this case. And leave Whitlock's name out of it. Simple."

"I hear you, *sir*." I smooth the edges of my hair.

"Now, I called in a favor to the state lab. You and Webb should have some news on the DNA from The Ivory, a day or two at the latest." He stands up and straightens his suit jacket. "But, Stark, if you cross me, if I even *think* you're working an angle I don't like, I'll make you radioactive. You won't be able to get a job in Avant, Illinois. You know that's where I started out. I'll make your life hell and enjoy it. Every. Single. Minute. We clear?"

"Absolutely."

Markham walks to the door, his fist enveloping the brass knob. He smoothly opens it. "Thank you."

I leave the office with French, swallowing the pride, anger, sorrow, and regret back down to the dank pit of my stomach.

Markham said, "if we don't gather suspects *then* evidence." He has his own narrative to craft. This is how investigations lose cases and cost lives. This is how trust is lost in communities. Just because some facts point to Giovanni doesn't mean she's guilty. Giovanni has secrets. That's obvious, but so does Natalie. There are parts of ourselves and our past we hide. And if they're discovered, we never know what we're truly capable of doing or who we're truly capable of being.

I retreat to a dim corner and dial a number. It rings. A robotic voice asks me to leave a message.

"Hello, Charlotte. It's . . . Red, uh, Detective Stark. I don't have any new information on Nivea. Wish to God I did, but there's another young lady missing. I'm not sure if it's related but seeing as how you've got your ear to the ground, I was hoping, praying, really, you could answer a few questions for me. I don't know if you're up to talking about this, but . . . I need your help. Got no right to ask for it but . . . Anyway, thanks."

That was a rambling mess. Seeking absolution via voicemail.

Frenchie emerges from his cubicle. "Just emailed the subpoena. I'm gonna grab Anya's birthday gift while we wait to hear from the state's attorney about that subpoena for The Ivory's video footage. Cover for me with Suits." He turns to face me. "You alright there, Red?"

I smile and lie. "Never better."

CHAPTER 21

Giovanni

June 15, 2025

Momma's room is empty, but it's a few minutes past noon. I must have just missed her, and the chemo sessions last around three hours. I want to see her face, put my head on her lap, not be strong for a few precious moments. But I didn't come to see Momma.

I came to see Phoenix.

Getting in to see her, that's the problem. I don't know her room number, and I know I'm not on a list of friends and family who can visit, but when there's a will there's a way, and my will is damn near made of vibranium. I leave the Hartwell and Julianna Whitlock Oncology wing of Dovemire Memorial Hospital and make my way to the emergency room.

Behind the counter, a nurse picks up the phone—overworked, annoyed, unappreciated. I remove my work badge before I approach her.

I slap on a smile. "Excuse me, do you know if Detectives Stark and Webb are still taking Deiserae Waters's statement?"

"Hold on." The nurse hits the mute button on her phone. "They left I think, but you need to question her, too?"

"Crossing my I's and dotting my T's."

The nurse points near the exit to a group of people with bags of gifts, bouquets, and balloons. "Her friends are waiting for her. She was just discharged, but I think she's still in the room."

"Number?"

"Oh, room 729."

I nod and walk away.

I didn't impersonate a detective. I just didn't correct the nurse's assumption that I am one. Fine line to walk, but I'll ask for forgiveness later. Whatever Phoenix tells me could help bring these last nightmarish forty-eight hours to a close.

As I step out of the elevator, Bale rushes inside. He had to go to the pharmacy earlier, did whatever he have take a turn for the worse?

"Umm, uh, Mr. Bale, are you okay?"

Bale says nothing as the doors shut in my face. I guess his earlier politeness was a blip in his otherwise jerky personality.

I walk down the hall to Phoenix's room. Her door is closed. Perhaps she's still getting dressed, gathering the last of her items. I knock and wait for an answer. I listen for a television or the shuffling of feet. The muffled close of a closet or bathroom door. Nothing.

I knock again. I could've missed Phoenix leaving but why close the door? This isn't a hotel room.

"Phoenix? Deiserae?"

Nothing.

I open the door and enter the hospital room . . . where I find Deiserae on the bed asleep. Asleep when her friends are waiting downstairs? Asleep with her eyes . . . open?

I inch toward the bed and place my index and middle finger

and press gently on her neck. Her skin is warm, but there's no pulse. Orange pills are scattered on the nightstand.

A doctor orders me to step away while she and a nurse assess Deiserae and begin compressions. They shout orders. They inject her. They shock her. They begin compressions again. Until they look at each other and . . . stop.

What the . . . they stopped!

An hour ago, I was a social climber entertaining the idea of friendship. Now my only lead to Natalie's disappearance is dead, and I'm the one who found her.

Momma plays the lottery. Loves it. Thinks she's gonna hit the Mega Millions one day. She calls me her good luck charm. She is dead-ass wrong.

I'm a walking, talking, breathing herald of bad luck.

Deiserae Waters is proof of that.

I'm screwed.

CHAPTER 22

Redding

June 15, 2025

Dad would call these "deep valley" moments. When you're so rooted in a situation, your ability to find your way out is lonely and rough. Standing in the room where I spoke to Phoenix *alive* hours ago at Dovemire Memorial is the deepest of deep valley moments. Two connected victims; different crime scenes. Well, one confirmed crime scene and one potential crime scene, a suspicious death . . .

And Giovanni is the only link.

Late afternoon sunlight seeps through the clouds, some bloated, threatening rainfall. Chicago weather never knows what the hell it's doing. And it appears neither does my partner. I try his cell phone. Again. French picks up after the second ring.

"It's rush hour traffic, Red. I'm doing my best. Even with lights and sirens it's a nightmare."

"I know you were getting something for Anya, but just . . . hurry."

He ends the call, and I examine the scene, half expecting Phoenix to sit up and say this is all part of some morbid hoax to gain more followers. But her body lies on the bed. They've removed the tubes and wires. Closed her eyes. Her shoes are still on her feet.

Next to the bed sit my card, scattered sherbert-colored pills and a full cup of water.

Ugh. Damn pills. Phoenix shuddered when she had to take one hours ago and downed at least three cups of water when she talked to me and Frenchie.

I step out of the room and make a call. "Hey, Doc."

There's a slight clang of metal behind Dr. Shayla Ross as she navigates her duties, our requests and brutal demands, overworked and abundantly traumatized, just like the rest of us.

"You good?" I ask.

"Fine. I'm . . . multitasking. I have a vic's family coming to ID a body in an hour." She clears her throat. "Assuming you're calling about the body at Dovemire."

"How did—"

"You're my second call. Attending physician beat you to it. But I wanna hear the scene in your words. See if there's any discrepancies."

"Well, our victim was found at the scene unconscious. Medical staff attempted to resuscitate but were unsuccessful. Near the body we have some pills." I pull out a blue latex glove from my inside pocket, walk to the nightstand, pick up a pill, and study it. "Don't think it's prescription, but there's no insignia or calling card that would let me know where they originated."

"Might be a homicide or it might not be," she says. "It may just be someone who didn't think something so tiny could kill them. Between heroin and fentanyl alone . . . well, you know the statistics, but unless there are signs of a struggle or a letter . . ." Dr. Ross lets her unfinished sentence speak for her. "I'll know more once I examine the body. Run tests. Toxicology, tissue . . . I refuse to make a determination until then."

"How long before we hear something?"

"For the autopsy? Depending on how quick I get the body, the complexity of the case . . . few hours to a few days, but the report could take three weeks. More. Your case isn't the first one on my plate. Nor the last." Dr. Ross wearily sighs.

"Understood. Thanks." I end the call.

Two patrolmen leave as I approach Giovanni near Phoenix's room.

"Detective Stark." Giovanni smooths her jacket and stands up straight. Her heels give her two inches over me.

"What were you doing in Phoenix's room?"

Giovanni takes a deep breath, then says, "I wanted to talk to her about Natalie. If she knew why she was attacked yesterday." She leans against the wall again and closes her eyes, but it doesn't prevent a tear from escaping. "I just wanna find out what happened to Natalie."

"Do you? Because I know, like I know French's cholesterol is bad, that you're hiding things. And if you don't tell me, I can't help you. Or Natalie."

Giovanni is a person of interest, but I need video footage or her fingerprints on a pill bottle to make something stick. And I won't get fingerprints or DNA from the state lab for at least four months. And that's the hopeful estimate from Saxon.

Markham wants me to focus on this girl and common sense says that someone at the center of a disappearance and a possible homicide has got to be guilty of something. What are the odds Giovanni's luck is *that* bad?

Cormac's stride is wobbly, as he slows down and reaches inside his jacket. I stop and reach for my gun. I don't know if he has one, but I have seconds, less than seconds, to react. I don't want to kill him. I won't find out where he took Nivea. If I kill him, she'll never see her daughter or her mom. Bullets sound like peals of thunder. My ears ring and I feel warm. I feel . . . blood. My blood. But it can't be my blood. I'm not supposed to die before I . . . before . . .

I step closer. "Listen, how about we talk someplace private. Without prying eyes."

Giovanni studies Phoenix's room for a moment, then says, "Tootchie's Restaurant in Hyde Park. Near the corner of 56th and Stony Island. Green brick storefront. Red awning. You can't miss it."

"8:00 p.m., tomorrow?"

"Alright." Giovanni pushes herself off the wall and heads to the elevator.

Even if everything your eyes tell you leads you to one conclusion, there's always another possibility. Most things that happen in this world appear improbable, but they're not impossible. I've learned to take a step back and examine all the possibilities, revisit my notes. Ask the same questions over and over and over.

Because when I think I know everything, that's when I come to the inevitable conclusion that I haven't even scratched the surface.

CHAPTER 23

Giovanni

June 15, 2025

I swipe my badge again arriving on the fifth floor. Teddy is still the only one in the office. His brown face reflecting an eerie blue-gray glow from the mini-screens, stacked in four rows, five screens wide. Teddy's left foot is elevated on a swivel chair as he writes something on the clipboard.

"You here, doll? Figured you'd probably head home for the day. Seeing as how—"

"You heard about what happened at Dovemire?" I interrupt.

"One of the valets also works part-time as a janitor there. You know how it is. Anyway, he saw you, so now . . ."

"Yeah, all The Ivory knows." I roll my neck. "Just one problem on a list of many. Regardless, figured it's best to finish my shift. At least try and focus on something else."

Teddy reaches past me and clips his badge onto his belt. "Don't wanna lose this one."

I'd give anything for my worst problem to be a missing work ID. I want to forget what happened two hours ago, but that's an idiotic wish, so I want answers. Why is Phoenix dead? Where is Natalie? How do I play a part in all of this?

"Need a favor," I say.

Teddy scoots his chair closer to the monitors. "Still working on that corrupted footage. Probably gonna have to troubleshoot with IT. That's gonna take five years off my life."

"Pull up the footage again, Teddy. Friday, the 13th. Any time after 9:30 p.m. on the forty-third floor."

He types, then places his hands on a dial to his left and time speeds forward, minutes tick by in seconds, and at 9:45 p.m., Natalie returns to her room, the screen goes dark. Natalie's boyfriend, Fleur, leaves the lobby at 10:48 p.m. Outside cameras catch him strolling on North Wabash Avenue toward the Chicago Riverwalk.

Where the hell is he going?

Phoenix was the best and only lead I had. Now she's dead. But I have this footage and if Willa won't give it to Detective Stark and her smug cookie-eating partner, then I'll give it to them. Create doubt. There's someone who possibly wanted to hurt Natalie and they killed Phoenix, too. I just know it wasn't me. I may have lost hours, but I didn't lose my soul. I didn't hurt Natalie. I didn't kill Phoenix. And that brief run-in with Bale at the hospital is some kind of proof. *Right?* That counts for something.

Doesn't it?

Doesn't it?

"Teddy, if I asked you to . . . share that footage with me, could you accommodate that request?"

He opens the right drawer and grabs two USB drives, inserting each one into a small rectangular slot underneath the monitors and above his keyboard. There are five slots in total.

Teddy removes both drives and hands them to me over his shoulder.

I place them in my pocket. "I got these from no one. And I wasn't here, as I'm sure my badge login credentials will testify."

Teddy retrieves some food from his book bag. "I'm just here eatin' my chips."

Before I turn around and leave, I see my picture on the monitor and swipe logins from the fifth floor highlighted in red, then nothing but a black screen.

My dude.

Willa's office windows are opaque again. I can make out her shape and others. The door swings open a few minutes later, the director of operations exits, a scowl on his round face. The tailored collar of his shirt catches the sweat from his thick neck. He brushes past me, lumbering back to his office. The PR director also emerges, a low exhale escaping his mouth as if trying to dispel whatever venom was transmitted in that meeting.

"What the hell happened, Gio? Where were you?" Willa flops into her chair, clutching her phone. "The gala was almost canceled. A trashed hotel room and the governor's former chief of staff was one of the guests? Cops and detectives in and out of here."

Willa doesn't care about Natalie. She doesn't really care about Fleur Winstead. Only his title, political connections, his money.

"How'd you know about Fleur?"

"You didn't think I'd check the credit card to make sure we could bill for repairs? I taught you everything you know," she says.

"Did you?"

"What'd you tell that cop?" She opens her top drawer and pulls out her lighter and a cigarette.

I place my hand in my pocket, running my thumb over the USB drives. "Detective Stark?"

She rolls her eyes. "Were you talking to any other cops yesterday?"

"The same thing I'll tell you. That the . . . misunderstanding I had at The Cathedral was unfortunate and I don't know anything about Natalie's boyfriend." I swallow the lump in my throat.

"Her story is gaining traction over socials. PR is starting to get a few calls for comment. ABC, NBC, CBS. All local stations. No national ones, thank God." Willa shakes her head. "You just couldn't keep your hands to yourself. Should've left you in housekeeping with the rest of them."

A burst of sunlight is blunted by the opaque tint. My jaw throbs. I've lost count of how many times Willa has belittled me, tried to put me in my place because of her assumed authority, mentioned she's the reason I have my position. Disregards my bachelor's degree. My MBA. The fact I'll do things like stay six hours past my shift to help Ms. Niyanzawa find her pet turtle, Aaron Burr, when he escaped from his habitat. Willa will never acknowledge the literal goddamned blood, sweat, and tears I've given to The Ivory. That Momma, Mecca, Ms. Evon, and others have given to The Ivory.

A guest hands Momma $100 for a tip and whispers something in her ear. She coyly smiles until he walks away. Her smile morphs into a scowl etched in sorrow and disgust until she catches me watching her. Momma smiles again and shoves the $100 in her back pocket. I sit in the lobby and eat a sandwich Mecca took from the kitchen.

"Y'know, we all have choices." I close the gap between me and Willa. "For example, I choose not to tell people that you and Aidyn have been using empty rooms to carry on your morning get-togethers." I stand in front of her desk and look down at her. "But I can choose to stop being quiet."

Willa bolts from her chair before she's sure of what to do with her body. "After all I've done for—"

I wag my finger in front of her face. "I've done this for myself. *By* myself. I do your job, too. And while you're busy patting yourself on the back for pretending to not see color and the Board is busy being terrified of it, I'm still here. And I'm still going to do my job. Just stay out of my way while I'm doing it."

Willa looks down at the picture of her husband and her rosy-cheeked kids. Her shoulders drop. I take that small sign as my victory and turn around to leave.

"How did you know?" asks Willa.

"You'd text me to take messages. Aidyn would leave The Cathedral. A few minutes later, you'd follow. You didn't hide it because your title is your protection. It's your power. But it's all you are. And the sad thing is that it's enough for you. I thought it'd be enough for me, too, but I just realized . . . I'm better than you. I always have been."

Willa puts the cigarette to her lips but can't get the lighter to work. I can hear it clicking as I walk to the door, every step, loosening the ropes that strangled my voice, bound my will, tangled and turned me into an unrecognizable mass of flesh and breath.

"One more thing. I'm Giovanni to you. Not Gio. That name is reserved for people who mean something to me. You're not one of them."

I keep my back to Willa and close the door behind me.

CHAPTER 24

Giovanni

June 16, 2025

My head beats harder than snare drums played by Questlove. More staring eyes and stolen glances. Ducking into my office, I grab the digital thermometer from my desk's top middle drawer and press it against my forehead. It reads 98.2°F. I'm normal. Well, my temperature is normal. Disappearances. Death. Four hours of sleep. Unbuttered toast. And weak tea. My soul is subsisting on fumes.

A notification with Natalie's name slides across my screen. Let it be a text, a missed call, anything letting me know she's okay.

No. A TikTok from Phoenix is waiting. Posted fifteen minutes ago. She's not uploading from The Great Beyond. Must be a scheduled post.

Phoenix is positioned in front of the camera. She draws her perfectly arched eyebrows together as she straightens her back in her hospital bed. She's stitched the video of Nat and I fighting. "*Still no news reports on Natalie. Police have made no state-*

ments. We're talking about a popular influencer and we're the only ones who care about her disappearance?"

She continues, "*Before Natalie disappeared, she had a fight with this unknown woman. Who is she? Are the police questioning her? I will not be quiet. Be overlooked. Be disappeared. One Black woman going missing is one too many. Join my fight. Raise your voice! Together we can bring Natalie Moore home. Be sure to share, like, and follow . . .*"

I shouldn't have eaten anything today. I shove my phone in my pocket and leave my office for the lobby, I peek in Mecca's office. She's not there, but Ms. Evon lingers near the service elevator as it descends, turtle slow, to the Back Entry.

"Good morning." I press the up button even though it's already lit.

Ms. Evon slightly jumps. "Oh hey, how're you?"

"A little worn out. This week is gonna be busy with the Whitlock gala."

Ms. Evon chews on her bottom lip like a well-done steak. "Mmm-hmm."

This stilted exchange of small talk from Ms. Evon is foreign. She is bubbly and expressive, not stiff and tight-lipped. She gives great hugs and makes even better German chocolate cake. The reluctant echoing groan of the elevator is the only noise exchanged for the next minute.

She keeps her hands folded in front of her. "You know what, I'm gonna go ahead and just take the stairs. Do my knees some good."

"Shouldn't be too much longer."

"It's fine," she says, trekking to the stairwell around the corner.

Two porters and a valet walk past me toward the break room, talking among themselves, laughing.

I turn around to greet them. "Morning, fellas."

"Hey," says one.

The others drop their heads toward the ground. They pick up their pace, breezing past me. It's official, I'm persona non grata.

"Morning, Gio," David says from behind.

"You're the first person who hasn't tried to bolt at the sight of me."

"I'ma say 'hi' to you regardless," he says. "I'm a rebel like that."

I almost hug him, but I keep my distance and hope my smile communicates all the gratitude I feel for his small act of kindness. Being shut out, on the outside looking in, is devastating. The Ivory is my home, despite the pettiness, arguments, and chaos.

No one's home is perfect.

The elevator doors finally open. We both step inside. I press the L button for *Lobby*. As the elevator rises, David pushes the emergency stop button. He jumps right in.

"Listen, a lot of people are . . . uneasy with you here, right now. The fight in The Cathedral, finding that chick dead in her hospital room, telling Willa to sit on your middle finger and spin—"

"I didn't say that exactly and how did you—"

"You taught me how to ear hustle. She was talking to old dude, Aidyn, about what you said." David smiles ear to ear. "Wish I could've been there, but Willa is making it known dealing with you could mean a lack of benefits, maybe even getting fired. It's not that people 'round here don't love you it's—"

"They love a roof over their heads and eating more. I get it." I massage my wrist. "Thanks for the heads-up."

David presses the emergency button again and the elevator resumes its climb. The only way to regain any sense of power and any sense of peace again is to find Natalie. And to do that,

I need to track down the one person not even Redding seems focused on.

I press the emergency stop button. "Need a favor."

David braces his left arm on the wall at the sudden jolt. "Worth my time?"

"I'll make it worth your time." I lick my suddenly dry lips. "I need you to low-key make inquiries into F.T. Winstead—that was the man who paid for Natalie's room. I think he's her boyfriend. And it's not as easy as looking up his VIP file in NexusLuxury."

David plays with his ear. "You wouldn't be asking me if it was."

"There's got to be *someone* who knows Winstead or helped him with something. I find them, Natalie can't be far behind."

"I got you."

The thumping in my head has lessened. I press the emergency stop button again and we both arrive in the lobby a minute later. David walks left. I head in the opposite direction to Zanthe floating through the lobby in an off-shoulder peach sundress. Gideon isn't with her. Thank God. She bounds toward me as if I'm the most important person in her world; as if she's happy to simply be near me.

"Excited about Friday? The exclusive photographer of Governor Whitlock's birthday gala."

Zanthe places her hand under the trickling flow of the water feature. "Of course I was gonna do it. Family is cheap labor."

Family? Victoria never mentioned she and Zanthe were related. They don't look alike. Both women are beautiful but their heights, body shape, and mannerisms don't resemble one another. But what do I know? When Natalie and I were in college, people always assumed we were sisters. We weren't, but at the apex of our closeness, I wished we were, prayed that somehow my absent father was a rolling stone. Five months before we graduated college, four months before the fight that ended our friendship, Natalie and I took one of those AncestryDNA tests. We weren't sisters. And I cried. Not a few tears. I sobbed. It felt like someone died.

"Girl, we don't need blood to tell us we're sisters. We have our history and our love. That's all we need, right?"

"You should see your face, Gio." Zanthe laughs—it's a musical and reckless sound.

"Apologies. I was . . . caught off guard."

"Come on. Who do you think is funding my little exhibit?" She leans closer. "I'm used to being the dirty little secret. Governor Whitlock loves the appearance of the happy nuclear family, but not the work needed to have one." She removes her hand from the waterfall and presses it on her neck. "Politicians and their wives don't want the affair baby front and center at a birthday party, but the affair baby can take the pictures. Art is irony. And attention. I adore both," she says.

"Regardless, your secrets are safe with me."

Zanthe smirks but says nothing.

The unspoken part of my job is managing all the well-hidden disfunction behind The Ivory's glossy exterior. I excel at that, performing as an obedient and replaceable cog in this well-oiled and glittering hospitality machine. There's no need to keep Zanthe's paternity hidden. It's surely one of those open secrets that everyone in the governor's inner circle and outer circle know but have the political and survival instinct to not mention in wider spheres.

"You still coming to the exhibition tomorrow?" she asks.

I'd be out. At night. Alone. Alone like Phoenix. That wouldn't happen, right? Someone trying to hurt me? Kill me?

Gideon saunters through the lobby. A valet asks if he needs help, but Gideon shakes his head without acknowledging them.

"Your poker face is zero for zero today," jokes Zanthe. "Yes,

Gideon will be there, too. I know my husband comes off as well . . . abrasive. But he's harmless."

Zanthe blows Gideon a kiss. "I swear that man has the emotional depth of a puddle."

Gideon maneuvers through the throng of guests. He smiles, but it's an alien movement of his mouth, like his brain can't quite get his lips to comply with a joyful human emotion.

"Look, I know some fun people. Plus, Victoria will be there, and Julien can keep Gideon busy with what they do," she says.

"And what's that?" I ask.

"Being co-presidents of the Assholes Club. Underqualified and overconfident are the main requirements."

I cover my mouth, but my hand fails to cover the arch of my cheeks. Zanthe can still elicit a warmth and fleeting sense of peace. She's gorgeous, effortless, and funny.

When it comes to friendships, I clearly have a type.

"See you tomorrow, Gio."

Zanthe makes her way to Gideon. He gives me a tight nod and they both head toward the Elizabeth Grace ballroom. Willa stands near the edge of the lobby waiting for them. She spots me then quickly looks away.

My phone alarm buzzes. Meeting with R. @ Tootchie's, 8:00 p.m.

I silence the reminder and replay Phoenix's TikTok.

These few moments of horrible judgment captured on a camera will burn my life down. Everything I have built, the sacrificed dignity, the lost time, is it worth finding Natalie? Memory is short on social media. The hottest story on Monday can fade into obscurity by Friday. Online outrage can quiet itself again into whispers and then silence.

But can I live with myself if I do nothing?

CHAPTER 25

Giovanni

June 16, 2025

I lean slightly to the left and look over my shoulder. Water pours down the picture windows of Tootchie's with a consistency and passion normally reserved for April or May. A group of three UIC students huddled under an umbrella cut off Detective Stark as she enters and walks toward me near the rear of the restaurant next to the kitchen.

"You good?" she asks.

I put down my phone. "No, Detective Stark."

"You can call me Redding or Red," she says. "You prefer Giovanni or Gio?"

"You can stick with Giovanni. Friends call me Gio."

"This is the spot I would've chosen," says Redding. She pulls out the chair facing me, the somber scrape reverberates across the almost-empty restaurant.

"Watched enough cop action movies and TV shows to know that."

"Then you should know not to sit with your back to the door," she says.

I've also seen enough cops in real life, in my community, in my city to not trust them. It doesn't matter if we share the same race or even the same gender. Our agendas are different. Our lives are different. The way we view Chicago is different. Though I suppose if all you witness is the worst humanity has to offer, then maybe it becomes harder and harder to see people as human. Maybe it becomes harder to see yourself as human.

Redding flips through the menu.

"Try the fried catfish with the garlic mashed potatoes and mac 'n' cheese. The yeast rolls alone make it worth the trip." My mouth involuntarily waters.

Melodic baritone and tenor voices flow through the speakers, cadenced singing and rhyming about a preacher that went hunting. It's a bouncy tune, but the sound isn't as crisp or polished. It's classic, older, but Redding mouths the rapid-fire lyrics with little difficulty.

"'The Preacher and the Bear.' A group called The Jubalaires sing this," she says. "My dad loved those guys."

I set my utensils on my left side instead of my right. "How old *are* you?"

"Old enough to remember when restaurants had smoking and nonsmoking sections," she quips, a small smile flickers across her lips. "Grow up in Hyde Park?"

"Englewood with a single mom. But you know that already."

"I do. And Natalie is from the Wild 100s."

Her question was a test to see if I'd lie about something small. If I'm willing to lie about something innocuous, then I'm capable of lying about far greater things. Redding's deciding if she can trust me and I'm deciding if I can trust her. But it takes more than a dinner and a chat to build trust. Trust, like love, is fragile and it only takes a moment to be destroyed.

"Englewood. Tough area," she says.

"What you know about it?" I lean back in my chair.

Redding stops reading the menu. "I grew up near 117th and Princeton Avenue. Just me and my dad."

"The Wild 100s. Like Natalie."

Redding nods. "It's a small world, even in Chicago."

Englewood and the Wild 100s are two places constantly in the news and mostly never for good reasons. Great things happen in these neighborhoods, and great people have always lived there. But disenfranchisement, food deserts, crime, and poverty metastasize, through every home and family, block by block. And every politician promises to fix these issues but never does a damn thing about it, causing the chasm between what is and what could be to grow wider, consuming all the hope and potential these communities possess.

But what do I know? I've only lived in Chicago my whole life.

The table leg hollowly knocks on the floor as Redding leans forward. "What happened? Before Phoenix? With Natalie."

"Nothing. Things we thought we got past, but we didn't."

"Obviously not," retorts Redding. She takes a sip of water. "Why did you and Natalie end the friendship?"

Partygoers gather around us. Cheap liquor in red cups jostling to get the best view.

"It wasn't your business!" she says, knocking the drink out of my hand.

"He's using you," I say.

Nat pushes me. "I can't love anyone else but you, that it?"

"You stupid bitch. You're pretty. He's old. He's using—"

Natalie slaps me. I slap her.

We're on the ground. There's dirt and sweat and blood and tears. My hands are around her neck, and I squeeze. For every time I comforted her, put her needs and wants first, sacrificed my peace to her chaos, I squeeze. My fingers press into the hollow of her throat. Natalie claws at me. All I wanted was for you to love me? Why couldn't you love me? Why couldn't you see me?

"I didn't end it." I shift in my seat; the wet fabric of my pants temporarily lifts from my skin.

"Natalie, then?"

"Let's stick to the present. We had a fight. Yes, it was dramatic. Yes, it was filmed. But it stopped there. After I left The Cathedral, I went home, went to bed. And . . . if Natalie hadn't disappeared or left or whatever, we'd have patched this up by now. You and me—" I gesture between Redding and myself "—would've never met."

I cup the USB drive under my palm and slide it to Redding. She covers it with her hand, taking up the relay, and places the drive in her inside jacket pocket.

"What's this?" she asks.

"Footage. Might help you figure out what happened to Natalie."

I'm not telling her that I have a copy for myself. Just because Redding is my best option to help me find Natalie and clear this cloud of suspicion around me doesn't mean I'll give her everything.

A server comes to our table, pouring ice water into our cups. We politely wait until he walks away.

"There's gotta be enough on there to prove I'm not the one you're looking for," I say.

"Where'd you get the bruises on your arms, huh?"

She screams my name. It's dark until I see the lights coming at me. It's quiet until I hear the screech of a car. And I fall.

I don't know where I got them. If I knew, I could trace my steps. Find Natalie. And return to my life as mayo-mild and toxic as it was. If I lie and Redding finds out, she won't trust me and whatever she knows she won't share with me. If I tell the truth about not remembering, she has more reason to suspect me and more reasons to get a warrant and search my apartment and tear my life apart. There are no good options.

"Like I told you on the roof, I probably hurt myself helping a guest with their luggage."

"Sounded like a lie then, too," she says.

What is driving her? I know it's her job, but something about the way Redding is approaching this case seems like it's personal. Why is she here without her partner?

"Why do you care so much about Natalie?" I ask.

Redding writes something on her notepad, then on a white sheet of paper. "It's my job."

"Why did you become a cop? Was your daddy a detective? Was your family poor? Who abandoned you?"

Redding slows the pace of her breakneck writing and then stops.

Ah, she can dish out the questions, but she can't take them.

I continue, "Takes one workaholic to spot another. You wear the same style of shirt but different colors. Same with your pants. You don't wanna think about what you put on your body. Your hair, the same slicked-down ponytail. No makeup. Thank God our melanin does the heavy lifting. So, what is it? Natalie is your chance to make something right? Your chance to un–fuck up your past?"

"Women like Natalie, women like us, most times no one cares when we leave and don't come back. They don't look for them. Not like I do."

"Women like us?" I ask.

Redding cocks her eyebrow. And I can tell; it's not that she's afraid to say Black and Brown women go missing and aren't looked for with the urgency of white women. It's that she's tired of saying it.

"Who's *them*?"

Redding lays down her pen. Her questioning brown eyes darken. "Giovanni, I'm gonna need you to stop that cold read shit you do."

"Natalie's disappearance, her case, it's gaining traction on social media. Or so I hear."

"Yeah, there's pressure to find a suspect. Quick. And you're making it kinda easy," she says.

"You sound like the old bald guy, Fred."

"His name's French," she says.

"I know." I refold the slightly askew cloth napkins on the pumpkin-orange table.

"What do you have against him? Us?" asks Redding.

Cops. Public pressure. Media attention. It's a recipe for disaster. It's enough to haul my ass in with only circumstantial evidence. Why do you need facts when you've got fear and a blind need for justice?

"It's not like cops inspire a great deal of confidence in this city, or anywhere else."

Do I subconsciously choose to start fights in restaurants? Is it some weird fetish?

The server returns to our table and takes note of our resting bitch faces. "Umm, I'll give you ladies another moment to look over our specials." He vanishes like my dad when my mom told him she was pregnant.

I carefully place the fork and spoon back onto the newly folded napkin. "Anyway, if you're saying Natalie's in trouble from someone specific—"

"Like you?" she counters.

I hold the knife a beat longer before placing it back on the napkin with its counterparts.

"I didn't kill Phoenix." My bottom lip throbs from biting it.

Redding says nothing in response.

"I didn't hurt Natalie. Well, not any more than she hurt me, or we hurt each other, but that's in the past and—"

"You wanna share that past?" she asks.

I remain silent and think about ordering some peach cobbler. Momma loves Tootchie's peach cobbler.

Redding grabs her pen and scratches something else down in her notepad. "I'm not the neighborhood gossip. I need to know what I can about you. The more I know, the better my chance at finding Natalie."

"That's fair." I toy with the tip of the dull knife.

"Besides footage of Natalie, what else is on the drive?" she asks.

"Fleur Winstead, her boyfriend. The person who you should be looking for."

"What can you tell me about him?"

"Fleur Winstead is a VIP. Used his credit card to book a room on the High Floor with Natalie."

"High Floor?"

"Yes. There are three tiers of guests. Three tiers of floors. Three tiers of service. The Low Floors are from 7 to 20—usually reserved for first-time guests and families; the Mid Floors, those are floors 21 to 37—reserved for more loyal guests, rich guests, or those who like to pretend they're rich, or lucrative business accounts that allow their higher-ups to stay for conferences. Then we have the High Floors; those are the top-level suites, floors 38 to 52—for the wealthy, VIPs, hotel board members, politicians, and celebrities."

I finally drink some water. I forget how exhausting it can be to explain the nuance, the spoken and unspoken rules of The Ivory.

"Fleur is Governor Whitlock's former chief of staff. He left The Ivory a little after a quarter to eleven, 10:48 p.m. to be precise. Apparently, he's on a leave of absence. I had a . . . connection provide the video."

"And who's your connection?" asks Redding.

"I'm not your only suspect," I say.

"At this point, you're a person of interest." Redding digs in her pocket, pulls out her phone, scrolls through, and hands it to me. It's Natalie's feed, pictures from the night of our argument. "You seen this guy? Goes by the name Ronan. He's Natalie's husband."

My mouth goes sour. "Didn't realize he was Natalie's . . . I saw him at Dovemire before I found Phoenix."

Redding sits up in her chair. "Are you sure?"

"I know his face. Had to look at it the past couple of days. H-he's a guest at The Ivory. His name is Ronan Bale."

If Natalie's married, that means she's having an affair with Fleur. I get it. Ronan's an asshole, least he was the few times I've dealt with him. He could've driven Nat into the arms of someone she believed could truly love her. I was that person for her once. But did he kill Phoenix? Could've been the jealous type. Didn't like the people Natalie associated with, didn't like the attention, didn't like her popularity eclipsing his. He wouldn't be the first man to want a woman to shrink herself for his sake. He wouldn't be the first to get violent about it either.

Far from it.

I scan the other pictures on Natalie's feed. The pictures Natalie was taking at The Cathedral were for her own safety. She wasn't documenting our meal, not really; she was documenting her stalker, Ronan—the potential killer of Deiserae Waters.

Natalie was calling out for me the whole time without saying a word. It was in front of my face. I glossed over details because I thought I knew Natalie, using her past to inform her present. But I knew nothing about her. I haven't for a long time.

"I mean, we still need the ME to determine an official cause of death, but I'm gonna need you to make a statement."

The rain stops. I put $20 under the saltshaker for food I'm not going to eat. Shouldn't leave the server with nothing for his wasted time.

"I wanna head back to The Ivory first. See what more I can dig up on Ronan. Plus, I'll see if I can find out more about Fleur. We keep files on our VIPs. Fleur's doesn't have much, but I know staff have probably interacted with him."

"I should take you." Redding scoots back, taking another look at the entrance.

"No. I'll call if I find something."

"Giovanni—"

"Didn't you say this isn't a buddy cop movie?" I stand up. "I said I'll call if I find something."

Wind whips through Stony Island Avenue, and behind me, a flash of headlights briefly enlarges my shadow on the rain-saturated sidewalk. I quicken my pace. Not fast enough to appear afraid but not slow enough to appear unaware. The northbound 6 Jackson Park Express bus stop is a few blocks away.

Keep breathing. Keep walking. The car keeps driving. And gaining. The bass thump of music grows louder. Louder. Someone soulfully belting a chorus about getting ready; about time winding down.

Faster, Giovanni. Walk faster.

There is laughter ahead of me, raucous and reckless. A group of six students. *UIC* etched on the backs of two fire-engine red T-shirts. The car slows. Headlights feature the stiff, quickened movements of my shadow. The car swerves and screeches in front of me. A sleek black sedan. All four doors swinging open.

I search for an empty beer bottle to break. A jagged tree branch to swing. I jab my hands in my pockets feeling for my house keys, then tighten my fingers around them.

The men in the car jump out and run . . . away from me to the group ahead. They dap up and hug and laugh.

And this is what happens when you listen to paranoia, Giovanni. You feel stupid, small. Yes, you're dealing with secrets, but not a conspiracy. I step into the street for a minute to bypass the group overtaking the sidewalk. *Not everyone is out to get you.*

Peach-tinged street light filters through a cluster of overgrown trees, remnants of rain drip from leaves. The bus stop is barely two blocks away. Cars and trucks zoom up and down Stony Island. Lights turn red then yellow then green. And I'm safe. I'll make it back to The Ivory and figure out what the hell happened to Natalie. Who Fleur Winstead really is and how Ronan Bale connects with—

Arms grab me and pull me backward into the trees as the heels of my shoes drag against the mud and grass. Someone clasps their hand over my mouth before I can close it. My tongue grazes the rough palm, a bitter taste of cologne assaults my tastebuds.

A voice whispers, "Don't scream."

Is this what happened to Natalie? Is this my end? Why didn't I take Redding up on the damn ride? Will Mecca take care of Momma for me?

My body jostles against the man forcing me into the small grove. I can feel his heart rapidly thumping against his muscled chest. I look down. He's wearing hiking boots. In Chicago? What kind of kidnapper is this?

His neck keeps twisting from left to right. No one else has popped out to assist so it's just me and him. One-on-one. "Look, just do what I say and we're good. Okay? Okay?"

I say, "Yes," but it's muffled by his hand.

In The Ivory's self-defense class, the instructor said if someone tries to abduct you, stay calm and comply with their demands, then look for an opportunity to escape.

No, I'm not complying with demands. No, I'm not waiting to escape. Maybe that's what Natalie did and that's why no one can find her.

This jackass isn't breathing right. His bursts of air match his bursts of energy. His grip loosens slightly on my left arm. I reach into my pocket and grip my house keys, interlacing a finger between each key. I wriggle my arm out of my pocket, wrench it free, and jab behind me.

I catch part of his cheek and I hope his eye. He howls, staggering back. Now I'm free to run. To escape. Headlights pierce the canopy of leaves. And there he is. His face. It's Bale.

I drop my keys, turn around, and sock him with my right hand. A sharp pain shoots down my arm. I didn't lock my wrist like I should've, but I don't think I broke anything. Sprained, probably.

Bale crumples to the ground and I kick him. His ribs. His chest. His dick. He blocked his dick. With every violent move of my body, I only ask one question:

"Where is she?"

He says nothing so I don't stop. Everything these past days with Natalie; these past few months with Momma. All the times I wanted to smack Willa. All the times I wanted to tell a guest to go to hell. All the times someone overlooked me or underestimated me or left me.

This prick is getting all of it.

It's satisfying to let go. It's a pure act of justice. Some would call it vengeance. But whatever the label, it's immensely pleasurable.

Until I see the gun pointed at me.

CHAPTER 26

Redding

Ten Minutes Earlier
June 16, 2025

You coming home?

My unmarked Ford Explorer idles on Stony Island Avenue across the street from Tootchie's. I don't answer Emmett's text because I don't know the answer. I turn on the air conditioner and roll down the window, allowing the hot breeze to dissipate. That girl could be playing me like an instrument of ten strings, but I've been a detective long enough to know when someone is trying to play me and when someone wants the truth just as much as I do. My instincts aren't perfect but they're damn good.

I think.

Giovanni should've let me drive her back to work. Offering a ride was a way to keep her safe. Getting some more information on the way would've been a bonus. The more the layers are peeled back on this case, the more I discover another lie, another suspect, another secret. And Giovanni is the nexus holding all of it together.

I start driving. The northbound 6 Jackson Park Express is Giovanni's best route back to The Ivory. I know Chicago Transit Authority routes like I know my name. Pops always told me, "*You can't be a good cop in Chicago if you can't get around Chicago.*"

I accelerate past the thirty-five-mph speed limit. The northbound 6 Jackson Park is at the stop; the bus driver lowers the vehicle, allowing people to enter. Then the door closes. I don't see Giovanni among the passengers, but she could've already gotten on by the time I pulled up. It's not a good look if I rush on that bus to make sure she's there, right?

I'm doing too much. Giovanni is on the bus. Hopefully, she'll call soon with information. Everything can't be a disaster waiting to happen. The psychologist told me that once in a session. Focus and be thankful for the rare moments when things are quiet, when life is peaceful.

I turn the car around and practice my apology to Emmett and Hudson for another late night. Hell, forget practicing, if I hustle, I can make it to Original Rainbow Cone in Beverly and grab some pistachio ice cream for Emmett and salted Mackinac fudge for Hudson. No need for "I'm sorry" when I have ice cream and—

Movement from my periphery looks like someone is in mid-kick with someone else on the ground. Things blur as you drive, so it's probably not what I think. Still, I slow down, make a U-turn, and head eastbound on Stony Island. I stop.

Dammit. Well, no ice cream tonight. It's a fight. Well, not much of a fight. This chick beating this poor guy like he stole something. She might kill him. He pleads for her to stop. She doesn't. I reach for the dispatch radio and call it in, then flick on the sirens in the middle of the toggle system between the driver's and passenger's seats. Bolting out of the car, I firmly grip my weapon.

"Detective Stark, CPD! Let me see your hands! Let me see those hands!"

My voice is primal, fierce. My heart threatens to burst from my chest. I keep my gun pointed at the woman's back until she stops. She takes in deep gulps of air. Shoulders sagging, she turns around. "He grabbed me. I defended myself."

Giovanni. I should've taken her to the hotel. I pull her away.

"I only wanted to talk," screeches the man, still a hunched ball of flesh on the ground.

She pushes past me and grabs a set of keys near his body. "So, you grab me from behind and pull me into some trees?"

"Go over there by that streetlight," I order, holstering my weapon.

"It's Ronan!" Giovanni puts her keys back in her pocket. She stops at the light six feet away, then bends over to catch her breath. "The asshole wants to shut me up 'cause he thinks I know something about Natalie."

I stare at Ronan Bale cowering on the wet grass. Hello, Suspect Number One. Giovanni is now a distant second.

I offer my hand. Bale takes it and stands slowly. His face is somewhat unscathed except for a soon-to-be-black left eye and some cuts on his cheek. He grabs his stomach and sharply exhales.

"Need an ambulance?"

Bale shakes his head, then says, "She's crazy. I only wanted to get her attention. I didn't want anyone at that hotel to see us talk."

"You grab her off the street 'to talk' and she's crazy?"

It's the gaslighting for me. How can this situation be anything other than Bale's fault? He's a guest at the hotel where Giovanni works. He's had plenty of opportunities to speak with her but chooses to follow her, then snatch her off the streets to question her? Was a coffee at Starbucks out of the question?

His real problem is that Bale expected Giovanni to be easy. He expected her to cry and quake and acquiesce.

But she didn't. She kicked his ass. And now I'm going to arrest him.

I pull my handcuffs from my duty belt. "Turn around. Place your hands behind your back, Mr. Bale."

"Wait—I—"

"You have the right to remain silent . . ."

The blaring roar of sirens, at first faint, now drown out the ambient noise of crickets and cicadas. Units marked and unmarked surround the block. Officers and detectives stalk toward the scene, weapons drawn, then holstered when they witness me placing Bale under arrest. Detective Baltimore Elliott strolls up, his lean build hidden by an oversized navy-blue raincoat.

"They don't have enough criminals in your neck of the woods? You gotta come all the way to Hyde Park?"

"Plenty, but I happened to be in the neighborhood."

"Mmm-hmm," says Baltimore.

I walk Bale to my SUV. "Mind if I take lead on this?"

"My district. My perp, Stark."

I flag down a patrol officer who takes temporary custody of Bale. Baltimore and I trek half a block away. Misty rain falls again. Baltimore retrieves a Chicago Bears pocket umbrella and opens it. Not to shield us from the drizzle but from the watching eyes and listening ears.

"You taking him to Area One, right?" he asks.

"Of course, it's where the crime went down, but he ties in to my investigation."

"The investigation where you just happened to be in *my* neighborhood?" he asks.

"I got eyes on me, B."

"Commander Suits giving you the blues?"

I chuckle at him using Markham's secret nickname. "Yep."

"Always something with you. Like your old man. I love it. I hate it but I love it." He studies me with his sable-soaked gaze. "My case load is atrocious. Long as I'm in the room while you question, I'm good. But I'm assuming you want me to take the perp back seeing as how we can't have him ride with the vic, now can we?"

"No, we can't, B."

Baltimore closes his umbrella, puts it back in his pocket, and heads toward Bale.

I can't say I expected to have another set of eyes on the case, but it's nice to have a pair I can trust. Baltimore was one of the last people to train under Dad. I trust Baltimore with my life. Like Frenchie.

"Make sure I get my cuffs back," I shout over the din of sirens.

Baltimore gives me a thumbs-up as he escorts Bale to a patrol car.

I wave Giovanni over to the Explorer. "Bale's gonna be okay. Bumps, cuts, and bruises. Nothing too bad, Mike Tyson."

Giovanni tiredly snickers. "Teddy from Security taught me a few things when I was a kid."

"My dad taught me. It was a way to process my feelings after my mom left. All that anger—" I stop talking. Why the hell am I telling her this? I didn't tell Emmett about my mom until we were dating for six months.

"It's fine. I won't say anything. Natalie says I have one of those faces that makes people tell me everything." Giovanni massages her hands. "Well, most people."

A small crowd of onlookers gathers at the scene. It's best that I meet Baltimore at Area One sooner rather than later. Giovanni is no longer my main suspect, but she still doesn't trust me. I don't think she trusts herself. I unlock the car doors. Giovanni climbs inside as my phone vibrates in my pocket. I already know who it is before I type in my code.

E: Late night?

R: yes

E: Looking at a movie with H. Got pizza. Pequod's.

R: my fav

E: Yes

R: thought u and H were eating healthy? blackmail?

E: Yes

E: Come home

I steal a glance at Giovanni in the car. Her head is back. Her eyes are closed. Trying to gain some rest, some balance, some . . . peace.

I gather the courage and answer Emmett.

R: can't. love u & H

CHAPTER 27

Redding

June 16, 2025

Giovanni keeps her eyes closed as I drive. Her breathing is steady, but she's not asleep. Her body is too tense and unless she's a master of power naps, she won't have time, cause Area One is less than six minutes away. I check my phone again at the stoplight. Nothing back from Emmett. Which makes sense but still stings.

"Why did Ronan think you knew about Natalie if you two hadn't talked in five years?"

Giovanni opens her eyes, annoyed. "I don't know. Maybe he thought I knew about Natalie's affair." She scrolls through her phone for a moment, then tosses it on the dashboard.

We exit the car and trot down a curved pathway. The brown-framed mirrored doorways do little to warm the utilitarian feel of the entrance, flanked on one side by a larger wing of the building branded with pairs of long, skinny rectangular windows. Giovanni bridges the six-foot gap between our bodies. Sometimes, as Hudson tells me, I forget how to "human." I don't tell him this is my coping mechanism, but it doesn't make my son less right.

Through the tiled hall, mismatched plastic chairs sit against the walls. I find the one closest to the bullpen with the other detectives.

"Stay here. I'll be in ERI for a bit, but—"

"ERI?" interrupts Giovanni.

Remember how to "human," Red.

"Sorry, Electronic Recorded Interrogation. That's where they have Bale. Detective Elliott or I will show you a photo lineup and if you identify Bale, we'll be pressing charges."

"Then I can go home?"

"Yeah, I won't be far. You feel anything is off, flag someone down and they'll come get me, okay?"

"Okay." Giovanni sits.

Baltimore rounds a corner and I follow him to his cubicle, his walls covered with pictures of family, quotes from Bruce Lee and Malcolm X, and a calendar from 2022. As he fills out a GPR by hand, I eye his laptop in the corner.

I point to it. "May I?"

"Go for it," says Baltimore. "Password's taped under the desk."

"Chicago's finest," I mutter to myself, powering on the laptop. I enter the password and plug in the USB Giovanni gave me and open two .mov files. I watch a thirty-second clip of Natalie returning to her room from The Cathedral and closing the door. I click on the second file, a twenty-second clip of Fleur Winstead leaving the lobby at 10:48 p.m., then heading south on North Wabash Avenue toward the Chicago Riverwalk. That's it. He disappears.

"What's this?" asks Baltimore.

"Connected to my case. In addition to assaulting Giovanni Mason on the street, this dude could also be responsible for the disappearance of his wife *and* her new boyfriend, the governor's former chief of staff. They could've just trashed the room and left, but that's looking less likely by the second."

Baltimore scratches his stubbly jaw. "You got people vanishing at a five-star hotel? Damn, who else knows about this?"

"Frenchie, Suits, and now you."

Baltimore bends down and scans the footage at least three times on his laptop. "Well, let's go see what playboy has to say."

I follow Baltimore to the second room on my left, a white cinder block matchbook of a space with two wooden doors and two cameras angled in the corners near the drop ceiling. Baltimore sits in a chair a couple of feet behind me. I sit in the one across from Bale and Mirandize him.

Reaching over the square Formica table, the same color as the walls, I unlock my cuffs on his wrists and return them to my duty belt. "Want some water? Snack from the vending machine?"

"No."

"You prefer I use your first name, Ronan? Or your last?"

He takes in his surroundings, glancing at the cameras in each corner of the room.

"Man of few words, cool. Let's get down to it then. Why'd you attack Giovanni Mason?"

He scoffs, crossing his arms. Then winces in pain. Bale is exercising the silent part of his Miranda rights, but some people want to tell their story. I just gotta find his trigger. What can he tell me without telling me? Certain body language is easy to read. Closed postures tell me nothing other than this person doesn't trust me and is on the defensive. I'm tired and hungry and haunted. I could try that cold read crap Giovanni does and see if that works.

Bale wears khakis, a pink shirt, and hiking boots. Horrible kidnap attire. He didn't fight back when Giovanni beat him, only blocked her blows. Whether it's because he doesn't fight women or he can't fight at all remains to be seen. He's careful not to touch anything. His nose is scrunched up in disgust. The room doesn't smell like a bouquet of lavender at The Ivory, that's for sure. He's a novice to crime. At best.

"First time in an ERI?" I ask.

"A what?" Bale massages the skin around his wrists.

"Electronic Recorded Interrogation. First time?"

"That obvious?"

I nod. How does Bale fit into the puzzle? Why attack Giovanni instead of talk to her when he first arrived at The Ivory? Does he know Natalie was with another man? Did he leave the orchid in her room?

"Listen, I know you didn't wanna hurt Giovanni. Right?" asks Baltimore.

Bale bounces his knee, the vibration slightly shaking the table. "It wasn't like that. She just started hitting me."

"She said you came up from behind, slapped a hand over her mouth, and pulled her into some trees." I look up at the camera.

He does, too.

"I only wanted to ask Giovanni about Natalie. I made a bad call."

Baltimore leans back in his chair. "Criminal assault and attempted kidnapping are more than bad calls."

"Jesus Christ! I wasn't gonna . . . Natalie didn't like to talk about Giovanni, and if she didn't trust her, I didn't either. Plus, there's something about this city for Natalie. She's been to Amsterdam, London, Thailand, but never made the four-hour flight back home to Chicago 'til now?"

I lean forward. "What happened with those two?"

"No clue," he says, touching the new scars on his right

cheek. "But whatever happened, it must've been some nasty business."

"Yeah, lotta that going around," says Baltimore.

"You say you didn't mean to hurt Giovanni. What about Deiserae Waters?" I steeple my hands and wait for his reaction to her name.

"Who?" His smooth baritone goes up an octave to a trembling tenor.

"Deiserae Waters, also known as Phoenix to her followers. She was found dead right after you left the seventh floor of Dovemire Memorial?"

Bale looks down and gnaws on the inside of his cheek.

I tap on the table twice to redirect Bale's attention to me. "You know Phoenix told me you were jealous of Natalie, mad about the grant program, of the business she was starting?"

"That's what she told you?" Bale curls his fingers into fists.

"Yep. Maybe that's why you went to visit her at Dovemire," says Baltimore. "Set her straight."

I play a scenario for Bale. "You knocked on her door, asked her about Natalie. Figured you could charm her into answers. She wasn't cooperating. You got mad. Love makes us . . . unpredictable."

"Better if you tell us what you know, my man. 'Cause once the ME comes back with the report in a few weeks, the time to say something in your favor runs out," says Baltimore as he scoots closer behind me.

"I saw someone leaving her room. White, muscular, but I had him by a couple of inches. He was on the phone. Sounded like a three-pack-a-day smoker. Phoenix was in the bed. You could tell she was dead. Didn't step foot in that room. I just closed the door and left." Bale readjusts himself in his chair, sitting up straight, grimacing as he does. "And I *never* told Natalie to ditch the grant program." He grins, grudging but wistful. "Natalie did what she wanted. Period."

"The D.A.R.E. grant?" I ask.

Bale nods. "She was stressed out about it the past couple weeks, but I still supported her."

"You stalked her." I drum my fingers on the table.

"You can't stalk your wife," counters Bale.

"Uh, yeah you can, if she wants to get away from you, and she clearly wanted to do that," says Baltimore.

"Listen, I know you were at The Ivory to see Natalie. You even went to The Cathedral when she was at dinner. The hostess turned you away, right? You see Natalie with her new boyfriend?"

Bale rubs the back of his neck. "She was with Giovanni, not the old man."

"Ah, so you knew she had a new boyfriend. Older cat. Rich. Powerful. Who wouldn't go for that?" I taunt.

Anger could be Bale's trigger. Anger can make you explode, make you unleash everything in words or violence. Or both.

Bale covers his face but mumbles three words.

"Say it again," I order.

Bale's hands drop from his face. "Natalie was pregnant. Almost three months. We hadn't told anyone yet, but we were happy. Least I thought we were happy." He turns his face from me toward the left wall. "I got home, like three days ago, and Nat was gone. No text. No call. Her location's turned off. And she *always* told me where she's going—what she's doing."

I take a beat or two before asking my next question, measuring when Bale needs me to nudge him. "What did you do?"

"I have her passwords. I logged in to her accounts. Saw she bought a one-way ticket to Chicago, made a reservation at that hotel. Booked the first seat I could find leaving LAX and followed her. I knew she was talking to someone else, but Natalie wasn't like that. She was loyal to me. I'm loyal to her."

"Was she really? I mean, who's to say the baby's even yours," says Baltimore.

Bale's head shoots up. His nostrils flare as he stares daggers at Baltimore. "I know what's mine. She was mine . . . and so was our baby."

"You keep referring to Natalie in the past tense a lot," says Baltimore.

"Because we're talking about past events," Bale shoots back. "Don't make this something that it's not." He studies the camera in the right corner.

Is this a performance? A piece of acting a jury could watch and determine this poor man loved Natalie Moore and would never do anything to harm her. I could have it all wrong. Could be Natalie isn't connected to Nivea, Stacey, Annette, Olivia, and Mia. The only piece tying them together is that they are missing. The orchid in the second hotel bedroom could be a dark coincidence.

Baltimore scratches his jaw. "Natalie does what she wants. Cool. But you said you knew she wasn't cheating. How'd you know?"

"Checked her phone when she wasn't looking. Not proud of it. She was texting someone named Fleur W. I Googled Fleur W. and Chicago. Wasn't hard to figure out who she was talking to. I wasn't worried."

"Wait, what happened to 'she was loyal to me and I'm loyal to her'?" asks Baltimore.

"That's how I knew she was loyal," says Bale. "The texts were businesslike, professional. Thought he was someone from the grant program. That's all they talked about." Bale sighs, dropping his face into his hands. "That's all she thought about after she came back from that first meeting in Chicago. She was jumpy, touchy. She was talking on the phone a lot. Texting a lot. Then, I come home, and she's gone. I didn't know what to think. Natalie's my family. My only family. I'm her only family. What was I supposed to do?"

"Go to the police with your concerns. We're not a last resort," says Baltimore.

"And you still didn't tell us *why* you were following Giovanni," I add.

Bale lifts his head and focuses on me. "After Dovemire, seeing Phoenix, I, uh, was shaken. Wanted to make things right with Natalie. Went to a drug store, got a cheap pair of sunglasses. Bought Natalie a pair on our first date. She wore them the whole time. So, whenever I screw up, I buy her sunglasses." He cracks his knuckles and continues, "I overheard some valets talking about what happened on the forty-third floor. They mentioned Natalie's name. I slipped one a $50 and they used their badge and got me up there. There was yellow crime scene tape on the door. I panicked. A couple hours later, saw Giovanni back in the lobby, and . . . I—I decided to follow her, ask her about Natalie. I was desperate. I wanted my family back. That's all."

I've gotten answers from Bale. I've gotten answers from Giovanni.

And I still don't know what to believe.

CHAPTER 28

Redding

June 16, 2025

"I'm gonna tell you something no one ever told me, Red. Sometimes, it's okay to forget. The evil we see, the evil that keeps you up at night, is gonna kill you if you don't say something to somebody. It don't make you weak. Talking keeps you smart. Keeps you sane."

Dad squeezes my hand so hard my fingers pulse. "You hear me, Red?"

"Mmm-hmm." I ease him back into his bed. "Now get some rest, Pops. Keep up your strength."

"Keep up yours, Red. Keep up yours."

I flex my hands to stop the tremors. I splash lukewarm water on my face. I even try praying. Anything to gain clarity in the minutes just after midnight.

Nivea, Stacey, Annette, Olivia, and Mia.

Giovanni clears her throat. "Who are they?"

"Who's who?"

Giovanni peeks at each of the four stalls in the women's

bathroom. Turning her nose up in disgust until she finds a toilet that meets her exacting standards. "Nivea, Stacey, Annette, Olivia, and Mia. You kept repeating those names."

"It's . . . they're . . . nothing. It's nothing." I wash my hands for the second time.

"If you say so," she says, her still-scratchy, skeptical tone echoing through the compact space.

Dad said to talk to somebody. But should it be Giovanni? She's hiding things. How can I trust someone who is still at the very least a person of interest in her friend's disappearance? But who else do I have? I need someone who isn't another detective or a therapist or a husband. All who've held suspicion on the cases of these women or my sanity or both. I need someone from whom I'm free of judgment because they are also too screwed up to pass it. And maybe if I share my secrets with her, she'll do me the same kindness.

I flex my hands again. They're still shaking.

Giovanni exits the stall. She keeps her head down as she washes her hands, then heads toward the door.

"December 22, 2023, a woman named Nivea Dugrave went missing. She was an ER nurse. She vanished on her way home."

Giovanni turns around.

"Her mom, Charlotte, called the police a little after midnight. They told her to go to Missing Persons. Missing Persons told her they'd open an investigation. They did but didn't find much. Said Nivea was probably stressed. Needed some time away. Would call when she was ready. Charlotte was having none of that though. She was arguing with Teagues, one of the detectives. I overheard and asked Charlotte a few questions. I traced the route back home. Found Nivea's house keys, some pepper spray, and a smashed phone. And that began the longest eighteen months of my life."

"The other women you named . . . they're like Nivea," says Giovanni.

"I think so. Mia worked at a dispensary. It got robbed and she was supposed to be on shift that night. I got the case. Went looking for her. Couldn't find her. Landlord let me into her apartment. A flower and some lines of poetry were sitting on her desk. Stacey missed a week of school. Annette missed a gig to sing at a fundraiser. Olivia failed to deliver a custom wedding dress to her cousin. All of them women. All of them Black. All of them single. All of them missing. Each woman had a vanda orchid in their home or delivered to their work."

"So just a flower? Maybe—"

"There's also a line of poetry left at the scene. On an open journal or a laptop or something else. In Nivea's case, on a Post-it taped to the back of her smashed phone." My hands still shake, but it's lessened.

"What'd the poetry say?" asks Giovanni.

I recite each line from memory like I would Hudson's birthday or my badge number.

> Nivea Dugrave—My mother's daughter. My child's keeper. The whole world's weight as I wait. Freedom.
>
> Stacey—Open minds in tortured bloom. Marked memories and bled potential from open wounds.
>
> Annette—Elevated in onyx. Shaped in amber. I am created to be golden for you.
>
> Olivia—I make You and unmake You. I make Me and unmake Me.
>
> Mia—In long lines and lost connections, I have been here. Hidden by your dark excess.

"Just you and this theory and no one else searching for them?" she asks.

"You got it."

"You're torturing yourself over . . . over something you can't control and everyone else abandoned. Just because the world treats Black women like we should bear everything on our shoulders, like we're supposed to be superheroes, doesn't mean we always need to move under that burden."

Giovanni and I could've been friends if we met in a normal way. Bumped into one another at a store or in the community garden four blocks from my house. It's not our skin that binds us, but the common tethers of our tragedies and our willingness, healthy or not, to push them down and keep moving forward. I'm not talking to her about the case only to gain information but to gain her trust.

And keep it.

My inability to keep an emotional distance will screw up this case and my life even more than it already has, if that's even possible.

Giovanni hugs herself and glances at me, tears threaten to spill down her cheeks. "You believe Natalie is one of them, don't you?"

I bite my lip before I answer. "Found the same orchid when Natalie was reported missing in the second bedroom of the hotel room she shared with Fleur."

"Why her?"

"I've always thought this . . . person was searching for someone they lost in the women he's snatching now. What happens after . . . I . . . we've never found a body." My last sentence I know is no comfort, but that's all I can give to Giovanni.

"What was Natalie's line?"

"Don't know. It might've been on her laptop, but I need a warrant before I can get onto it. And I need you to be honest with me about *everything* that happened the night you two got into it."

"I *am* being honest."

"Did you know Natalie was pregnant?"

Giovanni's mouth hangs open, but she quickly closes it. "Our—" she clears her throat again "—conversation never got that far."

"And after a fight like that, you didn't call anyone, go talk to anyone? You just went home and went to bed? Mecca? Your moth—"

"I. Went. Home." Her anger is simmering, but there's still a politeness to it, as if showing me her full rage would be bad manners.

Giovanni was for a moment my priest as I poured out the sins of my failures and this is how I repay her absolution? It doesn't matter. I have a job to do. I have people to find.

Giovanni is still a person of interest. I'm still a cop.

"Where were you when Natalie disappeared? When did you go back to The Ivory? I . . . just tell me the truth. We can get ahead of whatever you're hiding."

Giovanni mumbles something under her breath.

"I didn't hear you."

"I said, 'screw you,' Redding." She wipes the single tear that flows down her left cheek.

I rub the back of my neck. "Listen—"

"I'm done listening to you or anyone else," says Giovanni. She steps closer. "In the past two days, I've been yelled at, found a dead body, and been assaulted. *Twice!* I told you what I know, what I remember. I was home by 11:00 p.m., after Natalie and I fought. I don't know where Natalie is. I didn't hurt Natalie. After this, the only time you or your janky-ass partner are gonna talk to me is through a damn lawyer."

I grab her arm. "Exercise your right to remain silent

while I drive you home. Make sure no one else tries to kidnap you."

"breathe again" plays on the radio as Joy Oladokun softly and soulfully croons about the complications of finding peace and humanity in a world hell-bent on destroying both. The night-slicked canal of West 51st Street welcomes us along its road. Giovanni sits staring ahead.

Joy's now singing "Sunday" and I'm mumbling a version of the chorus while a black Mercedes SUV stays two cars behind us in the next lane. After the past couple of days anything seems like a threat. I'm seeing opportunities for danger where there are likely none. Turning the radio down, I turn left on South Champlain Avenue to prove to myself that this car is not following us.

One. Two. Three. Four. Five.

Giovanni sits up and looks behind her. "What is it?"

I check the rearview mirror again. The Mercedes also turns left on South Champlain, remaining two car lengths behind me. Angling the truck, I veer into the left two lanes cutting off two cars, then make a sharp left turn onto East 50th Street, then a right onto South St. Lawrence Avenue. The blare of rageful horns rings throughout the Explorer. A hellish fire spreads throughout my stomach. My heart sputters along on an uneven beat.

"You gonna call somebody?" asks Giovanni as she grips her seat belt.

"Let me worry about whoever's back there first."

One. Two. Three.

The Mercedes appears behind us. They're not even trying to camouflage themselves now. I push the gas and veer to my right putting three to four car lengths' space between us, then swerve into an alley sharing its space with brick three-flats, greystone apartments, and newly constructed condo buildings. I make a three-point turn, switch off the headlights, and creep to the edge of the street. Pedestrians walk with little notice or care of me and Giovanni inside the car.

My gun only holds seventeen rounds per clip. I have two clips in my belt. I'm not scared. I'm terrified. What if I hadn't noticed these people and they snatched Giovanni at home? What if I'd led them to my house? To Hudson. To Emmett.

Anyone who tells you they're not terrified in a situation like this is lying to you and themselves. But I have a plan. I just need that SUV to be a decent tail.

Come on. Where are you?

One. Two. Three. Four. Five. Six. Seven.

The Mercedes speeds past with a dent in the front passenger's side door. A Toyota is behind it. I follow the Toyota and keep my headlights off.

Illegal yes. Necessary. Also, yes.

"What the hell are you doing?" asks Giovanni, sliding down in her seat.

"No one's *ever* followed me before. I'm CPD. If you wanna hurt me, you must have a death wish." I glance at Giovanni. "And if someone's willing to intimidate me, or worse, what do you think they'll do to you?"

"Okay, so just pull them over," says Giovanni.

"I don't have reasonable suspicion yet, but they're gonna give it to me."

The Toyota makes a left and it's just us stalking our stalkers, but I . . .

The Mercedes screeches to a stop. I come inches from hitting the bumper. Giovanni braces herself on the dashboard. A couple crossing the street stops mid-stride and glares at the Mercedes for a few seconds before continuing their journey. An arm reaches out of the window and adjusts the driver's side mirror, placing my car into their view, and speeds off, making a left down South St. Lawrence Avenue.

"Now I have reasonable suspicion. You can't go over thirty miles per hour on a residential street."

After flicking the switch in the middle panel, the sirens blare; I reach for the radio. "Dispatch, Detective Stark. Badge number 58122. I need marked units. Got a suspect fleeing. Just made a left on South St. Lawrence Avenue, heading toward East 48th Street and South Forrestville Avenue."

Less than three minutes later, the wail of other sirens echoes behind the Explorer. Two units in back. One in front, edging behind the Mercedes flying down the street toward Martin Luther King Drive. But making it to MLK, even at this ungodly hour, means more cars, more people, more chances for things to go wrong.

The officer behind the Mercedes inches up, aligning the cruiser to the rear of the Mercedes. He then strikes the truck, causing it to spin . . . and spin . . . toward me and Giovanni.

This wasn't a good idea. This is Cormac all over again.

I want what I want. I do what I do.

And someone else *always* pays the price.

As I slam on the brake, my arm shoots out to brace Giovanni's body as if she was Hudson. I prepare for the impact, for pain, and feel . . . nothing.

I smell burning rubber. I hear shouting from my fellow officers. I feel sweat trickling down my neck and the rise and fall of Giovanni's chest against my arm. I taste blood. I bit my tongue.

Giovanni and I see the Mercedes facing us, less than two feet away.

With Teddy behind the wheel.

CHAPTER 29

Giovanni

June 16, 2025

Two cops remain close to Teddy but are engrossed in conversation a few feet away. I stroll past with the false confidence of someone who is supposed to be among them.

Teddy rests his head against the partially rolled-down window. "I was just trying to keep tabs on the cop. I wasn't trying to hurt her. Or you."

"You know what this means?" I take off my jacket. The breeze does nothing for the warmth radiating from my skin. "Why, Teddy? We've known each other since . . ."

Teddy hunches over. "I gotta spell it out for you? I can't live on what they pay me at The Ivory. They give you crumbs acting like it's a whole loaf."

"I love Denzel, but he took down the whole cartel to save Dakota Fanning? Nope. Couldn't do it."

"Before you go judging people thinking you wouldn't do something, try to think about if you didn't have anywhere to turn to, no one else to lean on," says Momma. "No me. No Mecca. No one at The Ivory.

You just might burn the whole world down knowing you, my Aries baby."

I laugh, then eat popcorn. "Maybe."

"Don't talk with your mouth full, Gio."

The need to survive can turn men into monsters. Sometimes you do terrible things to stay alive. I smashed a crystal picture frame over a man's head in Phoenix's apartment. Kicked and punched Bale until he howled and begged for mercy. But it was me or them, so for a moment, I became a monster.

I bend down. "You felt like you didn't have a choice, Teddy."

His voice is thick with emotion. "It's not a feeling, doll. I didn't have a choice."

"We have a choi—"

Teddy scoffs and looks off. "I was working at the hotel, bouncing in the Loop, and gig driving. Three damn jobs and I'm still barely makin' it. Now—"

"Why didn't you come to me? Talk to someone?"

"It's The Ivory. You can't trust no one. And I'm not the only one who does special errands."

"You're not the only one in Security?" I ask.

"Security. Housekeeping. Porters. Valets. The right price can get you anyone. The right price you'll do what you need to and convince yourself the money's good enough and the risk is small enough."

An officer approaches me. "Ms. Mason, Detective Stark asked that I escort you to the station. Would you follow me, please?"

I turn away from Teddy and leave him to his fate.

The Ivory's corruption is never in the open for guests to see, but some know it's there and some revel in it. I willingly looked away or played the game for a hundred here or there with Julien Whitlock and others like him. I'm no better than Teddy.

The only difference between us is that I didn't get caught.

CHAPTER 30

Redding

June 16, 2025

I flex my shoulders again, praying for that relieving and satisfying *crack*. Nothing comes and I'm still left with the dull ache below my neck, tapering off at my mid-back from the chase.

Markham taps a sausage-like digit on my desk. "Come with me, now!" The picture of Emmett, me, and a seven-year-old Hudson in front of DuSable Museum almost topples over but I catch it.

"We should have another," says Emmett, wistfully gazing at Hudson as he zooms up and down the museum stairs.

"Uh, who's 'we'? Doesn't seem like you'd be doing any of the heavy lifting there, buddy."

Emmett laughs. "True, true. But you can't tell me Hud won't make the world better one day."

"Yeah, and I gotta do everything I can to make sure he gets there."

"Heavy burden to carry, Red."

Hudson runs back down the stairs and into me at full speed, giggling.

I lock eyes with Emmett. "I'll bear it. Happily."

As I shut the door to Suits's office, he pulls down the shades around the glass box. Markham's face twists into a rageful mass of dark eyes and bared teeth. Frenchie is there, too, but he won't look at me.

Whatever this is, it's gonna suck.

Suits anchors his bulky arms on his desk and leans forward. "News of Phoenix's death has broken. And she's left us one last gift. A final video about Natalie's disappearance."

I pull out my phone and search her TikTok handle. Tributes from her Fiyah Flies and fellow influencers pour in. People are stitching and reposting her video on Natalie's disappearance. She's a digital folk hero, spreading her social media message of outrage and apathy around our disappearances, our assaults, our invisibility.

Still no news reports on Natalie. Police have made no statements . . .

One Black woman going missing is one too many . . .

Join my fight. Raise your voice!

People are liking and they are sharing and reposting. Nothing brings people together on social media like tragedy and gossip. *#BringNatalieMooreHome* is trending. . I scroll through a few comments.

teebaby23432: 🙏 🙏 🙏

parasights5432: she posts abt blk women, then dies a day later? i'm waitin for the netflix doc

evermoors_rbg: nothing new under the sun. we're the only ones who care when we disappear. smh

akademikmindz_367: people always wanna make it about race.

persiankat_hydepark: my cousin works @ Dovemire where she was. He said @fee-nixxx_fiyah od'd 😭 😭 😭

I speak before Suits can. "We're investigating all possibilities, speaking to acquaintances. Making progress with this case. I mean whoever sent Theodore Upchurch to follow us—"

"All we have to show for it is a dead influencer that's still posting videos accusing us of sitting on our ass. It's already at 500K+ and growing by the minute." Markham grimaces. "This is open and shut. Giovanni works at the goddamn hotel where the victim was last seen! Your report said Giovanni had fresh bruises on her arms. Then she's caught in a hospital room with a dead body? She's the link! She could've been screwing the husband. Wanted Natalie out of the way."

"But she was attacked by Natalie's husband not even two hours ago," I counter.

"Yeah, probably because he wanted to keep her quiet about their affair."

I flex my shoulders again. No relief. "I just uploaded my GPR to R-Case. Bale said he'd never met Giovanni until a few days ago."

"Like men who have affairs tell the truth," he says, locking eyes with me.

Frenchie clears his throat. "Listen, Red—"

"Shut up, Webb," barks Markham. "So, why the hell isn't Giovanni Mason in ERI? Why is she sitting at your desk like some goddamn VIP?"

"Giovanni's the key to figuring out why Natalie's missing."

Markham turns his laptop around. "Or she's the reason Natalie is missing and Phoenix is dead."

I watch a two-minute video of a disheveled, stumbling, crying Giovanni in her pink dress on North Michigan Avenue, less than a mile from The Ivory.

The time stamp is June 14, 2025, 1:01 a.m.

"I told you what I know, what I remember. I was home by 11:00 p.m., after Natalie and I fought. I don't know where Natalie is. I didn't hurt Natalie."

I slam the laptop shut. "Where'd you get this?"

Frenchie finally speaks. "Parking garage, a few hours ago."

Sonofabitch! He wasn't getting a birthday present for Anya. I want to feel betrayed, but it's not like I didn't lie to Frenchie about what I was doing.

Natalie isn't like the others. For Natalie, the orchid was just an orchid. Some weird coincidence. A gift from an admirer perhaps. There was no line of prose because there was nothing to find. I muddied the waters, lost valuable time obsessing over something that had nothing to do with my case.

I open Markham's door. Giovanni is sitting at my desk, talking on the phone.

"After this, the only time you or your janky-ass partner are gonna talk to me is through a damn lawyer."

You're gonna need that lawyer sooner than you think, Giovanni.

CHAPTER 31

Giovanni

June 16, 2025

Redding is right. Solving crimes is nothing like it is in the movies. Lineups aren't dramatic and they don't happen in a room with one-way glass. The detective showed me six pictures, each on an 8" x 10" sheet of paper. Vending machines are the only source of nutrition in the building, but they also sell ibuprofen. I swallow a couple and wash them down with room-temperature bottled water. There's little to keep my mind spiraling when one of my coworkers is connected to the disappearance of my friend. It doesn't help that my last discussion with Redding almost ended with me squaring up for the fourth time in less than forty-eight hours.

Redding seems less aggravating in this picture on her desk. As a matter of fact, she has a nice smile, an adorable son, and a decent-looking husband. All the makings of a normal life, but something isn't connecting for me. Redding doesn't seem driven and content. She's driven and grieving. Her actions and attitude don't match the woman in this photo.

She wants to know my story, but what is hers? What are the parts of Redding's past that she doesn't want me to know?

Mecca rings my phone. I was expecting Willa. I walked out in the middle of my shift.

"Thank God! I've called, texted. Where are you? David hadn't seen you. I—I thought you did something or something happened."

I run my fingers across my collarbone. The welt from the seat belt is more tender than an hour ago. It's slightly bigger. "Who's covering for me?"

"Don't know. Don't care. I told Willa you got sick." There is an uncharacteristic waver in Mecca's voice. The rawness in her tone surprises me.

"I'm fine. I had . . ." I take a deep breath. "I went to the hospital to see this girl who knew Natalie. When I got there, she was . . . she was dead, and—"

"Yeah, all The Ivory knows. Are you okay? What did you—"

"Let me finish." I wait a beat to gather my words and figure out what half-truths to tell. "I had some . . . difficulties getting home, but I'm with Detective Stark."

I won't tell Mecca my difficulties getting home include Teddy. I'm still struggling with that and it's not my place to reveal this information. It'll probably mess with Redding's investigation or count as witness tampering or whatever.

Mecca doesn't interrupt, but the tension in her silence has me even more on edge.

"Look, don't tell Momma what happened. I'm fine, at the police station on 17th and State Street. They're gonna take—"

Redding swings open the door to an office to my right a few cubicles away in my direction. Is she ready for Round Two? Am I?

"I'm gonna call you back."

"Gio, wait, what's—"

I end the call. I'll apologize for the disrespect later. I stand before Redding makes it to her desk.

"Come with me," she orders through clenched teeth.

I trail Redding down a hall to our left and step into a bleak room with cameras in the corners, painted in white and smelling of musty bodies and old food. She closes the door and sits down on the side of the table with her back to the wall, facing the door.

"We need to be in here to take my statement?" My phone buzzes again. It's Mecca.

"Where were you Friday, June 13th at 11:00 p.m.?"

"Are you for real, right now?" I back up to the door and twist the handle. It's locked. "I told you the next time you asked me this, you can talk to my lawyer."

Redding extends her hand to the empty chair across from her. "Good, then you can explain to them why you lied to me."

"I didn't—"

Redding bristles. "Five minutes ago, I saw a video of you stumbling along North Michigan Avenue, two hours *after* you told me you were home."

Detectives lie to people they suspect of crimes. It's well documented. Clearance rates are more important than justice. Natalie's case is starting to garner local attention. Who's to say it wouldn't go national. The more attention on Redding and the CPD, the more pressure to close this case. The greater the need to find a suspect, any suspect. Redding is lying. I wasn't on Michigan Avenue.

I twist the handle again. It's not giving way, but my legs are shaking. I sit across from Redding. "A video?"

Redding nods. She reaches over and cups my left arm gently raising the sleeve of my blouse. She does the same with my right arm. "Where did you get these?"

"Fighting with you."

"These bruises are older, starting to get a little yellow on the borders. You didn't get these with me in the apartment fighting, Gio."

Heat rushes to my face. "Don't call me that."

"What happened that night after you left The Cathedral?"

"I went home."

There's a bitter and brisk cloak over three-day-old memories. Yet I remember the names of guests' pets, what they did on holiday, that Julien got Victoria an emerald necklace for their third anniversary last year. I remember Momma sang "Precious Lord" by Thomas A. Dorsey whenever I was upset. I can hear her voice.

"This isn't the first fight you and Natalie had, right? Old wounds reopen. Things happen."

"No. I . . . I wouldn't hurt Natalie."

"Can you show me something, *anything*, that can tell me where you went? Receipts? A friend? Locations on your phone?"

I close my eyes. Memories, thin as wax paper. The Cathedral. The river. Food on plates. Natalie laughing. Me laughing. Us shouting. Me slapping. Then . . . *come on* . . . then . . .

"Why were you on Michigan Avenue? What happened that night, Gio?"

"Don't call me that!" I screech back in my seat. "Stop trying to act like my friend. You're not! I'm done. I wanna leave."

"We can figure it out. If you hurt Natalie, we can figure it out. Tell me. Just tell—"

"I don't know! I remember leaving The Cathedral and it's just . . ."

Natalie and Momma and Redding. Questions and expectations. My failures and our masks. How we wear them. How we can never say what we want, be who we want. The weight of this, the guilt of it. I stuffed my pain into places where I thought the detritus would remain until it came spilling forth, until I lost myself.

Until I lost time.

And I don't know how to get myself back, get my time back.

The door opens, French silently beckons Redding out of the room, there's a mechanical click of the lock as it closes. I'm trapped. I'm a suspect. I'm going to jail. And I can't remember what I did to get there. I lay my head down on top of my arms, like when I took a nap in kindergarten.

When I was a child. When I was safe. When I was free.

I remain like this for a few minutes or a few hours. Until a hand is on my shoulder. I flinch and open my eyes.

It's Redding. The door is open behind her.

It's time. I wait for Redding to pull the handcuffs from her belt.

"I'll be in touch about Ronan Bale, possible charges. Okay?" She walks to the door. "You can go."

"After . . . after all that? I can go?" I wipe my eyes.

Redding bites her bottom lip hard, as if trying to trap words behind her mouth. Maybe the words "I'm sorry." Slumped posture. Uneven breath.

I have questions, but I'm not asking her. I pass Redding, try not to run. I never again want to see the inside of a police precinct, station, whatever you call it.

Four detectives discuss the best place to grab a meal that's still open. I follow them and stay quiet, tepidly smile at them and keep my head down. They enter a security door at the end of the hall then go down a flight of stairs through another security door. They don't pay attention to me. I'm back to being invisible.

And it never felt so damn good.

The first floor is enveloped in ordered chaos. The unhoused searching for a place to stay cool. An older woman demanding a police report for a traffic accident in which she claims the man next to her is at fault. He claims the opposite. Frustrated parents, crying babies, and . . .

Mecca and David.

CHAPTER 32

Giovanni

June 16, 2025

I don't cry in Mecca's arms, but I hug her. I'm probably smothering her, but I don't care. I have my people. The ones I know mean me well. The ones who love me.

"You hung up so quick. I left The Ivory. Told David to drive me here."

"It's supposed to take twelve minutes, according to the GPS. Got us here in eight." A cocky grin adorns David's face.

I burst out of the front door, breathe in the fresh air. Well, the gasoline fumes, newly poured asphalt, and grilled onions from the twenty-four-hour diner down the street.

I'll take it.

David opens the car door for Mecca, then me. I playfully punch his arm and hug him before I get into the back seat of the 2025 black Mercedes-Benz GLS 580, one from The Ivory's fleet. Newer than the one Teddy used to stalk me and Redding. The vents blow cool air. I sit on soft leather seats. Revel in the privacy of tinted windows. I pretend I have no problems as I dial the number for Momma's room.

"Take me to Dovemire. I wanna see Mom before I head home."

"Take us to Giovanni's place." The order tumbles from Mecca's lips.

The phone rings. "I know visiting hours are over, but I can get one of the nurses to let me see her."

"We need to talk, Gio." Mecca rubs her temples and whispers, "Do what I said, David."

David drives toward the expressway and merges onto I-55 North. Mecca can have this one thing. I hang up. Whatever she said to Stark got me out of that dingy white room and back to my apartment with a tattered pink dress, the empty wine bottles, and unpacked boxes.

The outlines of homes and small businesses rise from the indigo-dyed horizon as David inches up on Harper Avenue. Old and new, dirty and clean, cars line the street with a foot or so between spaces. The U-shaped apartment building warmly embraces the block, with tuck-pointed tan brick. Hyde Park is not a neighborhood where life or parking come easy. But it has moments of peace, and pockets of prosperity thanks to the University of Chicago thriving at what so many businesses and institutions fail to do—financially and socially invest in an area where Black and Brown people live.

I exit the car. So does Mecca.

"I can make it in by myself. I'm done with playing detective."

"Told you we needed to talk," she says.

I enter the foyer of the building and turn around, holding the heavy maple door. "And it can't wait until tomorrow?"

Mecca brushes past me.

Odors of uncorked wine and garbage welcome us as I close

the door. My tattered pink dress remains neatly draped and displayed over the seat next to my front window.

"Instead of riding with David you're left with either babysitting me or taking an Uber."

Mecca slogs to my couch. "Sit the hell down. I'm not asking."

It's the tone that unearths an emotion close to fear. She sounds like Momma did before she'd snatch me by my collar. And though I'm almost thirty years old, her voice gives me pause.

I turn around and sit on the opposite end of the couch. "You couldn't stand me on Thursday, but these past couple of days, you're texting, talking, visiting, ordering me around."

Mecca puts her face in her hands for a few seconds, then looks at me. Tears spill down her sunken cheeks. "I can't . . . I won't watch you keep doing this to yourself."

"Do wha—"

"I thought you were putting on a brave face on Saturday. Thought you talked about Diedre in the present tense because you didn't want anyone to know what happened. I know people, especially you, value privacy. But you kept doing it. And in the car when you asked David to take you to Dovemire. Gio, baby, something's wrong. I don't know how to help except tell the truth. Plain as I can, and pray to God it takes, that you accept she's gone . . . Diedre . . . your momma . . . died."

I don't realize Mecca's holding my hands until I snatch them away, almost hitting her face. "No. She's sick. Really sick. Momma's not dead. I'd know. The hospital would've called me."

"I called you. I texted. Diedre's vitals were going down. They were working on her. Second time I called, you picked up. Said you just got back from dinner, I think." She wipes fresh tears from her face.

Whatever sick game Mecca is playing, I don't have time for it. I've been through too much, seen too much, done too much. Yes, I lost time, but I'd remember Momma dying. As loving and smothering and wise and short-sighted and hilarious and judgmental and fierce as she was.

Is!

I'd know if she took her last breath. I am from her. I am of her. I wouldn't put her in an abyss, lose her in cheap wine and self-pity and tears.

She deserves more than that.

She taught me to be more than that.

We deserve more time.

There's screaming . . . no, wailing.

Am I wailing? I am out of my body.

Mecca's hands on my arms keep me still.

Someone bangs on the door. Mecca shouts, "We're fine. Little accident. That's all. We'll quiet down."

The banging stops. As long as there's no more noise. As long as there's no blood. There'll be no police. And I don't want to see any more like Redding.

Today. Tomorrow. Ever!

She continues her story, my story, of what happened after Momma . . . left me. After she . . . died.

"She waited for you, for us," whispers Mecca. "After you left. I followed. You were in a daze and walked against the light. Into traffic. A car clipped you and you fell. Car kept going. I took you home. Got you outta that dress." She gestures toward the chair. "You were already drinking before I called you. I let you finish the last half bottle of rosé. I almost snatched it from you so I could finish it, but I didn't. Just stayed with you 'til I had to go to work."

I've stopped struggling. Mecca lets me go. She picks up the box near the door and places it in front of me. I reach for it, then draw my hand back as if I touched fire. I try again, managing to lift the flaps. A pair of blue jeans, a size too big, that used to fit snugly on her hips. A black hoody with a sun wearing sunglasses and the words *No Sweat*. Her Bible, her favorite verses highlighted in different colors. Three pairs of pajamas. A pair of white house shoes.

And an envelope that slipped to the bottom of the box. I open it.

My Gio . . .

I refold the paper, stuffing it back into the envelope.

You trust a hospital with a person and sometimes you leave with a cardboard box or a plastic bag of belongings. And you don't have the person you loved.

Only their things.

And that is everyone's story. Despite the fight between wealthy versus poor, one race versus another, Liberal versus Conservative.

Death equates us. Loss binds us. Regret tortures us.

All of us.

Redding released me because Mecca provided an irrefutable alibi for Natalie's disappearance.

I can't be Natalie's killer or stalker if I watched my mom die at the time.

I wanted to prove my innocence. I wanted to guarantee my freedom. I wanted my life to return to normal.

I got two of the three.

CHAPTER 33

Redding

June 16, 2025

"Have you ever heard of something like that?" Frenchie keeps pace with me as we trek down the hall back to ERI.

"Uh, yeah. Dissociative amnesia. A police psychologist talked to me about it before I came back. She told me it can be a natural response to trauma."

Frenchie stops in front of the room where we're holding Teddy. "You've had a helluva day, Red. It's your second interrogation in what . . . two, three hours? First with Baltimore, now with me. This Giovanni mess. You can take a minute if you need to."

My hand grips the cold silver doorknob, but I don't twist it. I stare at Teddy through the slender rectangular window. I need more than a minute. I need at least a year to process the past two days. I need a decade to process the last year and a half. But this job doesn't give me time to heal. It doesn't give me time to apologize. It gives me questions and deadlines, paperwork and protocols, suspects and victims, who sometimes are one and the same.

There are four ERI rooms at Area Three. I walk into the second one. Teddy sits up as Frenchie and I enter the 11' x 11' space, smaller than the rooms at Area One. Frenchie remains behind Teddy, and sits in a worn black ergonomic chair.

I Mirandize Teddy again.

"Hey, I gotta call my aunt, see if she can keep my daughter."

I sit in front of Teddy. "Answer my questions and we'll see what we can do about you making that call. Sound good?"

"Well, how long 'fore I get arraigned?" asks Teddy.

"Day or two," I answer.

Frenchie plays with his ear. "Attempting to flee the police *and* trying to intimidate a detective? These actions tend to also . . . stretch things out."

Teddy moves with surprising agility as he whips his body around to Frenchie, then back to me. "I wasn't trying to intimidate you. Just spook you a little bit."

I smirk. "That's the same thing, Teddy."

"I didn't even know I was following you!" Teddy's voice rises two octaves. "They just gave me a description of your car and the license plate. I was just trying to keep tabs. I wasn't trying to hurt Gio. Or you."

"That doesn't make it any better, friend-o," says French, rocking back and forth in the black chair like some unbothered retiree on their front porch. "And who is 'they'?"

"Don't know. I got a text. Go to the Second District on 51st and Wentworth Avenue. Follow this car. Deliver the flower when no one was home."

I lean forward. "What kind of flower? Deliver it to who?"

"Don't know," he says. "I was supposed to get those instructions after I checked in, but then the chase happened."

"Was it an orchid? A vanda orchid?" I ask.

Teddy puts his face in his hands. "Told you I don't know."

Validation, no matter how small, can be absolution or damnation. In my case, it's both. After Cormac, after my scars, and the leave of absence, the isolation, the fights. Being followed means I'm getting closer to him. Revealing who he is. And he's scared. But I'm still no closer to finding out who has taken these women. I can't even confirm if the flower Teddy was supposed to deliver was an orchid or who it's meant for—me or Giovanni.

"Still got the text?" I ask.

He looks up. "Nah, I delete 'em. Always."

I fall back in my chair. "You're smart, Teddy. There's got to be something about the texts, or the people you worked with. Something you remember."

"You're right. I'm smart. Smart enough to know the type of people who want things like this done don't like loose ends. I'm smart enough to stay dumb about things."

I take in the four cameras affixed to the corners of the room. These places vary in size and slightly in layout, but there are always cameras in corners, capturing every truth, every lie, every confession or request for a lawyer. Some suspects rely on revisionist history. Try to take charge of the narrative to elicit sympathy or worse doubt if the recording lands in front of a jury or judge. Paint me as an overly aggressive cop. Paint me fighting for my life as a misunderstanding. Teddy is a good but misguided citizen. Wrong place. Wrong time.

"Why'd you run," I ask.

Teddy responds, "It was self-defense. Kinda. You were chasing me."

"Did you not hear the sirens?"

Teddy has two options. Help me or don't. I have two options, be strategic or a smartass. Dad told me plenty of times,

"You can either be right or be happy, and you sho' nuff love to have the blues don't you, Red?"

I can be right, or I can solve this case. Find Natalie. Figure out who's behind her disappearance and maybe heat up five other cold cases.

I rap my knuckles on the desk to recapture his attention. "This situation is out of your hands, but if you help us, it'll probably make you look better 'cause you can't look much worse than you do now, right?"

French pushes his glasses up on his nose. "The court bus to 26th & California should be here in about an hour to pick you up."

"Whatever, man. Whatever." Teddy weakly throws up his beefy hands in surrender. "Ask your questions, I guess."

Frenchie leans forward. "You're sure you can't identify anyone?"

"Whenever I took one of these jobs, most times it was alone. I had to check in at certain times for my next instructions. And if I had to partner with someone, we didn't exchange names. We didn't talk much. My rent's a week late. I'm behind on daycare. And it was an easy $1,500." Teddy hangs his head. "I'm an idiot 'cause there's no such thing as 'an easy $1,500.'"

I walk to the door with Frenchie close behind. "I'll see what I can do about you calling your aunt."

"Yeah, thanks." His voice cracks.

Teddy broke the law. That doesn't mean he's lost his humanity. It doesn't mean I've lost mine. I can still feel bad about where Teddy's actions have led him.

And I can still do my job.

Charlotte's name pops up on my text notifications. I lay the phone back on my desk for a moment, staring at it. Charlotte's text could be a string of rightfully deserved curse words or a simple message saying she doesn't know anything. But I can't remain frozen, afraid of either outcome. Even if I can't bring Nivea home, maybe Charlotte can help provide the one thing her family still seeks—closure.

I pick up the phone again and read the text.

Charlotte: Got your vm. Setting up for the rally tomorrow morning. Come through when you can.

It's almost three in the morning. Too late to visit Giovanni, but I'll stop by after Charlotte. I need to make sure she's okay. Just because Teddy and the guy who assaulted us in the apartment are locked up, just because one of their accomplices is dead, doesn't mean I'm safe. Doesn't mean Giovanni's safe. Far from it, according to Teddy. But I'm closer to finding Natalie, maybe that means I'm closer to finding the others. Or I'm selling myself a dream. I just hope I'm tired enough tonight to have one.

CHAPTER 34

Redding

June 17, 2025

"When you can't find your way to the end, start at the beginning."

Too many facts. Too many suspects. Too many motivations. So, I'll go back to where everything began. An obvious and simple piece of wisdom from Dad, but one I overlook more than I care to admit. He was probably frustrated repeating himself like I am when I tell Hudson to pick up his socks off the floor for the umpteenth time.

I smile briefly thinking of Hudson and Dad as I turn right onto East 68th Street. My phone rings. Saxon's name pops up as I turn off the car across the street from Hasan Park.

"What's up?"

"Not too sure what you did or who you know, but I got results back from The Ivory. Blood and fingerprints in the room match Fleur Winstead." Saxon shushes her kids in the background, then resumes, "That wasn't difficult to track. You know most gubernatorial staff have their prints and everything else on file. Fleur is type A+, which was the majority of the blood collected at the scene. But . . . therc was no match for the other blood type at the scene. Prints either. We do know it's a female with O+ blood. I can't say Natalie is a match nor can I exclude her because we don't have her DNA on file. She's not on CODIS, was never a government employee, no military background. I checked DataWarehouse, too. Not so much as a parking ticket. But I have a call out to a colleague working in the sheriff's department's forensics unit in LA County."

"Anything else?"

"Put that down or I swear to Christ . . ." Saxon returns to the phone. "Uh, yeah. I'm damn near certain that scene was staged. It looks too clean. The items were all broken in a certain place. Whatever 'supposed' fight that occurred didn't migrate toward the bar or the rooms. So, it was either a fight that was interrupted or staged. My professional opinion, I'm going with staged."

"That it?"

"For now, yes," she says.

"Thanks."

"You got it," says Saxon. "Stop hitting your brother!"

I end the call and let Saxon deal with a burgeoning crime scene of her own.

Charlotte Dugrave moves like most Black women do when setting up an event. With urgency and purpose. A compact, manicured green space, Hasan Park sits nestled between the cross streets of South Oglesby Avenue and East 69th Street in the South Shore neighborhood. Charlotte unpacks a well-loved cardboard box on the trunk of her red 2015 Kia Sportage. She hands a stack of flyers to a volunteer and cranes her neck every few minutes toward the play area. Her granddaughter, Ava, swings back and forth, pumping her legs, going higher and higher.

Making my way to Charlotte, my legs feel as if I'm walking through tar. Will she cry when she sees me? Will I cry if she starts crying? I finish scanning the street for suspicious cars as Charlotte lifts her head again toward the play area and notices me. Barely two feet separate us.

"Hi, Ms. Charl—"

Charlotte hugs me. It's warm and full and loving. I return her embrace, holding her as tight as she holds me. Tears spring to my eyes, but I blink them back before she lets go.

"It's good to see you, Redding. How're you doing?"

"Fine," I lie. "Can we . . . uh, go somewhere and talk?"

She tilts her head, searching and finding the true answer to her question on my face, but she decides not to press. She points to an empty part of the park, near a daycare center separated by a wrought iron fence.

"Granny! Granny!" Ava runs up to us and stands between me and Charlotte. "Where you going?"

Ava is taller now. Bright eyes. Hair French braided into an intricate zigzag pattern down the sides of her head leading to one interwoven braid down her back. She's Nivea's twin.

"'Where *are* you going?' You know your momma doesn't like you using poor grammar," corrects Charlotte.

Ava grabs Charlotte's hand. "Where *are* you going, Granny?"

"With Detective Stark. You remember her, right?"

"No, ma'am."

Charlotte kept Ava confined to her room during the early days of Nivea's disappearance. "I want to keep a child a child," she told me. I didn't expect Ava to remember me. I'm relieved she doesn't.

"I'm gonna be right over there, baby. You can see me, and I can see you, okay?"

"You promise?" Ava squeezes Charlotte's hand.

Charlotte bends down and kisses Ava's hair. "Yes, baby. I

promise." She turns to her other daughter, Isis, and says, "Don't let Ava outta your sight."

There's a tortured urgency in her edict and with it surfaces a riptide of regret and guilt that nearly pulls me under. Isis takes Ava's hand and leads her back to the playground, then watches like a Secret Service agent. I want to sprint back to my car, but I stay.

I have no choice.

We stop under an oak tree. A warm gust of wind shakes the leaves above us and blows Charlotte's freshly pressed silver bob away from her heart-shaped face. "Another girl's missing, like Nivea."

"Yeah, Natalie Moore. I wanna run down a theory. It could lead to me finding her. It could lead to nothing, but I'm gonna try." I pull out my notepad.

I take a moment to gather my thoughts, weigh my words to find the ones that might do the least amount of damage. "Natalie applied for a D.A.R.E. grant and—"

"Humph!" Charlotte crosses her arms. "You mean the 'dirty D.A.R.E. grant.'"

Her tone is bitter, her stance rigid. I've seen Charlotte on the worst days of her life, but this is as close to scorn as I've ever seen from her.

"Why do you call it that?"

"*This* grant program runs a little different." Charlotte glances at Ava playing on the swings.

"How so?"

She returns her attention to me. "If I was younger and my ass was a bit tighter, I guarantee you I'd have gotten that grant money."

"So, there wasn't a . . . diverse application pool."

"Nivea was supposed to go. But she . . . anyway, when I was in that office waiting for my interview, everyone who applied besides me was at least thirty years younger and fifty pounds lighter. I know about others who've been denied the money. Men, women who aren't the kind of pretty they're looking for, older folk like me," she says, pushing her hair out of her face. "Don't need money like that. It always comes with conditions, and I'm sure a few of them girls wish they never took it. But no one cares about this."

"I'll talk to some people. See if I can figure out where the money went."

"Baby, you can look up who's awarded grants online. It's a law. Type the name of the grant and it lists the organizations that got the money." Charlotte snickers. "Close your mouth, Red. It's hanging open."

"I—I didn't expect it to be so simple."

"I'm sure in your line of work things rarely ever are." She peeks over at Ava again. Still swinging. Still there. Isis hasn't moved an inch.

"You know the name of it? The website?"

"Sorry, sweetheart. Got too many things roaming around up here."

I finish my notes just as a small group of people enter Hasan Park, wearing white and black T-shirts with Nivea's face printed in the middle, smiling, enigmatic, hopeful. Frozen in time when she was safe and never had an idea anything like this would ever happen to her or her family. Beneath Nivea's face is the date, *December 22, 2023*—the date she went missing.

"People care about you. About Nivea."

"I know there are people who care, but none of them anchor a news show or write for a paper. Not that I didn't call or email or walk to the stations and beg and plead. But I don't have anything scandalous or salacious enough to offer. Just my pain. Not that I'll stop trying."

"I'm sorry."

Charlotte sniffles. "You don't apologize. You didn't visit this evil on Nivea, on me, on my family. But I know you'll find the man who did."

I flex my fists open and closed to distract from the rising heat in my bones, blooming in my chest. "You're goddamn right."

"And when you do find him, Redding. Make. Him. Pay."

CHAPTER 35

Giovanni

June 17, 2025

The last time I called in sick to work was four years ago. I had a 102° fever and still felt guilty. I was brainwashed by my bosses and their bosses, by this city, by this country into believing there was still more of me to give, to sacrifice. But today, I have nothing else.

Feeling the back of my head, there's only a small raised patch of flesh. I stare at the textured ceiling, imagining patterns and shapes that aren't there: hands, faces, lips. I go beyond the patterns and shapes to imagine a life I no longer have. With Momma. Maybe with Natalie. Perhaps I did something different in my life on the textured ceiling. I worked at the Field Museum. I got married. Or divorced. But no kids in my imaginary worlds. I'd never make a good mom.

In the cracks of my unlived lives, untethered memories claw through. Sharp scenes. Sounds and sights and smells. My screams. Mecca's arms supporting my weight but also holding me back as the doctors and nurses worked and worked until they stopped, until Momma's body, jolted and pressed and pounded, was still, until there was an eerie quietness in room 1411 that reeked of antiseptics and medicine and the perfume I wore to dinner with Natalie.

Real life shreds my imaginary life until the truth is all that I can see behind the tears that fall from my eyes and create tiny wet spots on my pillow. I can't touch or hug Momma anymore. I trudge to the living room and sit cross-legged in front of a curated memorial of her belongings stored in a cardboard box.

I grab the envelope first. If I can't hear her voice, I can read her words. It's all I have left.

> My Gio,
>
> We know what's happened if you found this letter. And to be clear, I'm not happy I had to leave, but I'm at peace because I know you have people left on this earth who love you. Most important, you have you.
>
> If I made your world too small, make it bigger. Remember to keep working for what you want because no one owes you anything. Watch your temper. You're an Aries. I know how you get when pushed too far.
>
> Please listen to other people. Even when the truth isn't something you want to hear. Learn to forgive others. Learn how to forgive yourself. Live your life and love yourself enough to admit when you need help. If this disease has taught me anything, it's that.
>
> Gio . . .

Her letter ends at the beginning of a sentence—she had so much more to say but wasn't given the time to say it. I search for something to punch that won't cost me a security deposit.

I turn on my phone. Phoenix's last TikTok video has over a million and a half views. So many comments, but I don't want to read any more about Natalie. I don't want to know if internet sleuths have discovered who I am. I close out of the app and delete it from my phone. My stomach grumbles. I enter a clean living room. The wine bottles are gone and the garbage is empty. A delicate citrus fragrance floats in the air as Mecca lies on my couch asleep, the last of her energy expended on cleaning up after me. Doing her job after she's left work. I can't be her job. I can't be her burden. I'm gonna stop playing detective. I turn off my phone.

The dress is still draped on the chair. Folding it in three parts, I stare out of the window. Branches sway and bend under the morning breeze. People walk up and down the block. A familiar SUV parks across the street from my building and Redding climbs out.

Normally, it takes five minutes to reach the courtyard.

I grab a jacket, my wallet, and keys, still making it outside in three minutes.

Redding holds her hands up before I start down the brick-paved walkway.

"I wanted to say I'm sorry for your loss, first off. And—" she begins.

"Leave."

"I wanted to make sure you were okay. I owe you that," says Redding. Her tone calm. Her words practiced.

I thrust my hands in my pockets. I don't trust what I'd do with them if they're free. "I'm very far from okay. You have your status report."

"We need to talk," says Redding.

I remember the last time we talked. In that tiny room. Waiting for me to break and confess to something I didn't do.

I turn on my heel without a word.

Redding steps in front of me, but she keeps her hands to herself and only utters, "Please."

I clutch the fabric lining of my pocket. "Now you care about me?"

"I always cared, but I have a job to do," says Redding. "You were keeping secrets. I need to find Natalie."

"Goodbye, Detective."

"The orchid Teddy was carrying, he didn't know who it was for." Redding glances over her shoulder, then back to me. "Someone paid him to follow us, to terrorize us. Who do you think's following you?"

She isn't acting. Her fear is real. Mecca is still upstairs. If there is someone who wants to hurt me or worse, if they were the ones who disappeared or killed Natalie, then what chance do I have? What will they do to the people I love? I don't have many of them left. I crane my neck scanning the windows; all of them only reflect cold sunlight in my direction. If someone was watching us right now, I wouldn't know. Neither would Redding.

Would they try and kill me alone? Absolutely.

Would they kill me if I'm with a cop? Probably not.

I push past Redding, shoulder checking her. "I'm pretty sure if someone is watching us, it's best we don't give them a show. Maybe talk somewhere else."

Redding jogs in front of me, shielding me with her body so I stay a step behind. "My thoughts exactly, but you weren't too keen on letting me in the front door."

"You blame me?"

Redding doesn't answer and gets into the black Ford Explorer.

I open the passenger's side door and put on my seat belt. "I know a place."

CHAPTER 36

Giovanni

June 17, 2025

"Good spot," compliments Redding.

"Last place anyone would look." I flick on the lights to my office. "We need to be in and outta here quick. I called in sick. That doesn't leave a lot of us on the floor." My phone buzzes. It's Mecca.

I text: I'm fine. Explain later.

"That Willa?" asks Redding.

"No. She knows to stay outta my way."

"Do I wanna know?"

"She's having an affair. She knows that I know, and she doesn't want anyone else to know."

"So, blackmail?"

"Yeah, and I'm not really worried about morality at this point. Kinda had my hands full the past couple of days," I answer, the bitterness in my voice untamed.

Redding swallows hard and chokes out, "Yeah."

I almost say "I'm sorry" to Redding. Almost. But why should I apologize for her discomfort?

Redding fidgets with her blouse. "Got some results about the room Natalie and Fleur shared. Most of the blood was Fleur's. Other blood found in the room is possibly a match for Natalie, but the ET can't—"

"ET?"

"Sorry. Evidence tech, Saxon, she can't say for sure the blood's Natalie's. Can't say for sure it's not."

It's taking everything to not lie down and crawl into a ball and cry.

It's not the pain of falling. It's the blood gushing from my knee. The callous roll of my bicycle wheels causing me to wail.

Momma kneels in front of me. "If crying would help, I would lay down and cry with you, but since it won't, I need you to get up and try again. Okay, Gio?"

Redding sits on my couch. "Natalie ever mention the D.A.R.E. grant program or any dealings with Julien Whitlock?"

I dab a tear from my eye. "Nothing about Julien. She just told me about a bad business deal with Phoenix. Didn't give me the details but said ending it was for the best."

"Something's screwed up with the D.A.R.E. program. Ronan said when Natalie came back from Chicago after the grant interview she was anxious, then left their home and met Fleur." Redding lays her head back. "You learn anything new about Fleur?"

I open my laptop, logging in to NexusLuxury. "Not really. Got someone looking into it for me."

"Who?"

"Doesn't matter as long as you get what you need."

"Legally. As long as I get what I need *legally*, Giovanni."

I didn't give David a set protocol when I commissioned him to find whatever he could on Fleur Winstead. And after helping Mecca to rescue me *from* Redding and still working at The Ivory, he hasn't exactly had the time to do what I asked.

I navigate NexusLuxury's program and click on Guests (Special). I scan Fleur's file. Nothing new. Nothing I don't know. Nothing Redding doesn't already know. An alert pops up. Room 4329 has been released by the police.

"Wanna go upstairs to Nat and Fleur's room and see if there's anything you missed?"

Redding drums her fingers on her thigh. "Most of the evidence is being processed as we speak so we can't say if there's anything I missed."

"Can't say if you didn't either."

"Show me the way." Redding wearily lifts herself from my couch.

I swipe my master key and enter the foyer. I step over the dried crimson puddle in room 4329.

Old blood, wilted lavender, and a lingering metallic scent mixes into a witch's brew of foulness. The handmade cream-colored shag carpet has precise squares surgically removed. The sectional has slashes across its back. Momma wouldn't have flinched if she was here. She'd know how to get rid of the odors and the stains. The Ivory offered Momma a single night's stay in celebration of her twentieth-year anniversary.

Twenty years of service gets you one night in a suite on the Low Floor on the second Wednesday in January. I resist the urge to break another vase or add another slash to the sectional.

"If you need to stay in the hall, that's fine." Redding studies me with concern.

"Ford & Mumford are gonna charge a fortune for this room."

"Ford & Mum—"

"Biohazard services firm we use for these . . . situations," I say. "Am I wrong for being worried about that and Natalie?"

"Now who's the bigger workaholic?" asks Redding.

"You by a country mile."

Redding heads to the second bedroom on her right. She digs into her pants pockets, then an inside jacket pocket, retrieving a pair of latex gloves.

"Still here," she says, relief and disappointment in her voice.

"Is that—"

She picks up an orchid on the nightstand. "Could be."

I step closer and reach for the flower. "Then we need it."

Redding blocks me. "If we take this, the evidentiary chain is tainted. The orchid is going to Saxon. We can use it to find Natalie, prosecute whoever is responsible for . . . hurting her."

Redding might be holding on to hope that we'll find Nat alive. I'm holding on to that same hope, but I need to prepare myself for the likelihood that Natalie is dead, so I don't lose myself in grief again so deeply I may never be able to find a way back to something resembling peace.

Redding takes out her phone, snapping pictures of the orchid and the bottom of the terracotta pot.

I turn on my heel. "I'll meet you in the lobby in ten minutes."

I don't wait for Redding's answer as I leave the room.

CHAPTER 37

Giovanni

June 17, 2025

I wait for the elevator to close before I swipe my badge and enter the empty security office. It's oddly quiet without the sounds of Teddy snacking. The screens flicker. Guests. Employees. The pool. The lobby. The Ivory at my fingertips. Answers I may have overlooked.

Whoever's taken Teddy's place was smart enough to log out. I'm smart enough to have stolen Teddy's passcode. Maybe smart isn't the word. Devious. Subtle. Evil. Those words are more apt.

I enter Teddy's first initial and last name, then type 78225681 on NexusLuxurySecure.

I delete the record of my entry, then glance at the security screen a row up and two screens over. I navigate again to June 13, 2025, after 10:30 p.m. Same thing. Fleur leaving the hotel at 10:48 p.m., then walking south on North Wabash Avenue toward the Chicago Riverwalk. Natalie arriving on the forty-third floor at 9:45 p.m., going to her room, and closing the door. The footage blacks out in the same spot. At least I know I did nothing to Natalie during that missing time.

I was too busy having a breakdown on Michigan Avenue.

A clipboard lies on the desk to my right. I close out of my search and stand, my knee bumping the desk and knocking the clipboard to the ground, a dozen pages cover the floor.

Damn it!

I gather the security logs, arranging them by date, almost two weeks' worth. Most of the papers are initialed by Teddy and logged into NexusLuxurySecure. At least that's what I remember Teddy saying when The Ivory had the annual hotel "Bootcamp" where we learned about all the other departments. Willa headed up the concierge department with the presentation I wrote for her.

I flip through the pages until I find the entries for June 13th. Were any cars taken near or just after midnight? I study the signatures. Teddy's signatures are quick slashes for a "T" and an overly curved "U" with the rest of his last name meticulously written, except for June 13th at 10:30 p.m. Those signatures are different for Teddy. They mimic the *T*, but the *U* is too slender. It almost resembles a *V*. The rest of his name is haphazardly scrawled. Those are the last signatures for the evening.

Who signed Teddy's name?

A beep draws my attention to the rapidly opening door. A man, lean with sallow skin and an unsmiling face, enters clad in the same uniform Teddy once wore.

I rise. "Knocked these over. Sorry."

"I didn't leave the door open," he says, his sunken eyes narrow. He closes the door and stalks to the security console.

"You did."

I'm not surprised at how easy the lie comes. I lie to guests all the time. I lie to myself the most.

I place the papers back on the table. "I was waiting to ask

about a security measure, but I just missed a call from Willa, so, if you'll excuse me." I swerve away from the guy. My back to the door, I blindly reach for the handle.

His jaw clenches. "I completely logged out before I left. Whose login is this?" he asks.

"A guest lost her handbag. No one was here. She's quite upset, so I was searching for it."

"You didn't answer my question."

"And you weren't here doing your job, so here I am." I infuse my next words with as much authority and entitlement as I can. "*I'm* the chief concierge of this hotel. I don't answer to you."

"Now, listen—"

"No. I don't think I will. Now, if you'll excuse me, I got a meeting and you're making me late. Don't want Willa or Detective Stark to come looking for me." I put as much emphasis on *detective* as I can. Hoping Willa's name and Redding's title will deter this guy from asking more questions.

This man could have nothing to do with the twisty alliances and shady conspiracies enshrining The Ivory, but I don't know that. I don't know him.

I thought I knew Teddy.

I escape the security office. The guy doesn't follow me to the lobby where Redding waits near the History Wall.

She stares at the pictures, not looking in my direction. "Successful errand?"

"Maybe." I stand next to her, sweating. "You want the long version or the TLDR of The Ivory's history?"

"TLDR, please."

I point to the portrait of R.I. Willowbrook. "Racist bastard founds hotel in 1914. Spent a million and a half dollars in the 1920s on the vanity project. Killed himself." I point to the rows below. "Here are all the white people who've run the hotel." I point to the last three rows. "Here are more white people and a young Governor Whitlock, who's about the Blackest thing on this wall. Now the hotel a white man had built hires minorities but barely pays us a living wage. The end."

A vent blows cool air above me. I move two steps to my left to cool my burning skin. "I noticed something was off with the transportation logs. Signatures for Teddy don't match for June 13th, the night Natalie went missing, but the log is for 10:30 p.m. Maybe someone took a car out for a joy ride?"

"You really believe that?" asks Redding.

"No."

The *whir-click* of a camera pulls me out of my thoughts. Zanthe stands six feet away from Redding and me.

"Sorry, couldn't resist," she says, lowering her camera.

"Next time, ask permission. I don't like having my picture taken," says Redding, pushing her body past mine.

"Apologies . . ." says Zanthe.

"This is Detective Redding Stark," I introduce. "Detective Stark, this is Zanthe Yaeger-Gates."

"Oh," says Zanthe. "I can delete the picture. Though, it'd be an absolute shame. It's an enchanting candid."

"It's cool, just think to ask people before you do something," says Redding.

Beyond Zanthe, the mouth of the lobby opens greedily consuming those making their way from the pool back to their hotel rooms. Victoria stands near the water feature with Julien.

Zanthe nods, fiddles with her camera, then turns her attention to me. "You still coming tonight, Gio?"

"A lot has . . . well, it's been a rough few days." I rub the back of my neck. I like Zanthe but I can't trauma dump about a missing friend, a dead mother, and an uneasy alliance with a CPD detective.

"How 'bout this, I'll put both your names on the guest list. Both of you should come. Have a little fun."

Zanthe leaves us, strolling toward Victoria and Julien. Their protective detail is posted near the front desk. Willa walks up a minute later, glaring at me before speaking to Victoria, her face then morphing into something pleasant and serene.

Redding turns her attention back to the History Wall. "What's she talking about?"

"Her photo exhibition in Hyde Park at her gallery. L'Atelier Rouge."

"Will Victoria be there?"

I nod.

Redding sizes up their security. "Proximity to the governor's child is better than nothing. That exhibition is the way in."

"Which child?"

Redding turns her head in my direction. "Excuse me?"

"Zanthe is Governor Whitlock's kid, too," I whisper. "She and Julien are half siblings." My skin prickles revealing this bit of gossip.

Zanthe wasn't shy about revealing her paternity to me. Still, it's probably not something she shares with everyone. But Redding isn't everyone and keeping information from her at this point won't hurt anyone but Natalie.

"It's a viper's nest. I should go to this exhibition thing alone," says Redding. "I'll report back on what I find."

"Either you're gonna let me help you, or I'll find out what happened to Natalie by myself." I lean against the wall. "We're connected for better or worse, like a marriage. And like a marriage we need each other but sometimes wanna fight each other."

A reluctant grin crosses Redding's face. "True."

"So tonight, we're gonna put aside our differences and figure out at the gallery what Victoria and everyone else is hiding." I stop shy of the lobby and glance at the History Wall full of captured faces and lives and secrets frozen in a moment. "For Natalie."

"For Natalie," repeats Redding.

CHAPTER 38

Giovanni

June 17, 2025

Encased in cedar with gigantic sable-paneled glass windows from top to bottom, L'Atelier Rouge dominates the other boutiques, restaurants, and shops alongside it on East 53rd Street. The looming three-story art gallery beckons me, emitting a sultry electric glow. The cell phone in my pocket bumps against my thigh as I make my way to Redding. She waits by a slender man with an aloof attitude and chestnut-colored hair. He checks his clipboard for our names and waves us past the waiting crowd.

We stand in two separate lines as a male and female state police officer wand each guest. I lift my arms and allow a skinny piece of plastic and metal to roam over my body. I should be with Mecca making arrangements for Momma's services. I don't think I told Mecca that Momma wanted to be cremated, not buried. She didn't want a repast either.

I try and keep myself together, but tears leak from my eyes because emotions are rebellious little shits that don't give a damn about my surroundings. I pretend to sneeze so people will think I'm suffering from allergies and not grief.

Redding passes the security check. We enter through a set of massive doors that lead into a cavernous room teeming with at least two hundred guests, servers, and tepid laughter. Dozens of photographs in black metal frames are equally spaced apart on exposed brick walls.

I gracefully snake my way through the crowd taking a drink from a polished silver tray, careful not to step on the hem of my flared one-shoulder rose-gold dress. Redding clocks the others around her. The deep V of her tailored black suit shows off her ample chest and round hips in a way her off-the-rack clothes never could. More than one head turns around. She only frowns, an injustice to the exquisite sheen on her neon red lips.

I whisper in her ear. "Take the stick outta your ass and act like you do when someone confesses their crimes to you. Makes you feel powerful, right? Hold on to that feeling. Imagine everyone here is a criminal and strut accordingly."

Redding glances at Julien and Victoria. "Everyone here probably *is* a criminal."

I smile. "I said be confident, not judgmental."

Zanthe and I lock eyes across the room. I raise my glass as she glides toward us with Gideon in tow.

I scan the photographs near me. Some are black and white. Others are in color. The one Redding and I stand in front of is a crisp capture of a summer day. Sunbursts from the edge of the frame illuminate a mom spraying her children with a garden hose in the front yard of an apartment. The boy with green and yellow swim trunks chases the girl with French-braided hair and barrettes. Everyone's mouths are open in expressions of joy and delight. The moment is candid and curated. It is pure and I feel right there with them.

"It's called *A Summer Wednesday* That one's mine," says Zanthe, planting a light kiss on each of my cheeks. "Thanks for coming. It means a lot." She extends her hand to Redding. "I'm sure you had a hand in convincing Gio to leave her little perch at The Ivory."

Redding takes her hand. "Something like that."

Zanthe's toned figure is snugly nestled into a long maxi cocktail dress. Her hair is styled in an inverted mohawk updo; she's added violet highlights to the tips.

"These are stunning pictures. Reminds me of my mom." My throat clenches and burns.

"Zanthe's got quite the following from her little hobbies," says Gideon. He downs his champagne and quickly flags down a server.

"Art is a calling, not a hobby. I can take a picture and tell a story about race or poverty or injustice. Just because it doesn't affect you, doesn't mean you can't learn a little empathy," says Zanthe.

"But at least your picture is one of the few that shows happy Black people. Most of this 'art' only wants to divide us, promote the narrative that you're all somehow still oppressed." He flicks his boney index finger at the rest of the pictures on the wall. "Like this one is from another BLM protest. The one next to it has a man standing outside of a liquor store with a sign asking for a handout. It's just depressing."

Heads turn our way, Gideon's voice temporarily drowning out the soulful crooning of Boyz II Men over the speakers. He has the luxury to tote his ignorance around like designer luggage. Like Momma, and so many before her, said, "You can't change what you don't acknowledge." Maybe I should help Gideon finally acknowledge his ignorance.

"So, you presume to tell Black people how we should express our lived experience in this country? You don't find that arrogant?"

Gideon takes a healthy gulp from his glass. "No one wants wokeness shoved in their face 24/7."

"Ah, *wokeness*, the word people use when they don't want to acknowledge how they benefit from a system built on the oppression of others." I peek at Redding who remains stone-faced at my words.

"If you keep telling yourself you're a victim, then that's all you'll ever be." Gideon puts the flute to his lips and realizes it's empty. "Look at me with your nose turned up all you want. I have the right to express my feelings."

"Like your wife. Your *Black* wife." I cock my head and smile, a poisonous action of my mouth that I pray carries home my disdain of Gideon's attitude.

Redding grabs my wrist and squeezes amid the gentle crush of bodies. "Well, social justice can come in all forms including this grant program I've heard about . . . D.A.R.E. to Dream?"

"Someone mention my baby?" Julien slinks up behind Zanthe and puts his arm around Gideon who then moves a few feet away. "What? I could hear you on the other side of the hall." He sniffs. "You know I came up with the idea."

"Really?" asks Redding.

"I mean, I had help, but the concept was all mine." He scratches his temple, the brash purples and nauseating greens fading from around his eye.

Gideon mutters something under his breath. No one likes being stripped from the narrative. It's funny how he can appreciate that when he's been done harm, but outside of his existence, others don't matter.

Redding turns to Gideon. "You feel the grant program is helping the community?"

"Yes," he says.

"I heard you're helping a lot of Black-women-owned businesses get their foot in the door," she says.

"Suppose so." Gideon holds up his empty glass. "If you'll excuse me. Need something a bit . . . stronger." He turns on his heel and disappears into the crowd.

Redding flexes her jaw and cuts her brown-black eyes to me. I had to have the last word and that shut Gideon down.

Humph, such an Aries.

I down my champagne, place it on a roaming silver tray.

Julien continues bragging. "We don't want people in the community to think just 'cause we migrated to a different political party that we don't care about the place that birthed us."

"Weren't you born in Naperville?" taunts Zanthe.

"I still rep for my city," says Julien.

"Which is Naperville," says Zanthe.

I stifle a laugh and touch Julien's arm. "I mean, the suburbs are still part of the Chicagoland area."

He smiles down at me. "Exactly."

I'd feel safer with Freddy Krueger right now, but I return his smile through my disgust and his arrogance. I didn't stuff myself into Spanx, this dress, and three-inch heels for nothing.

"Let me tell you how I finally got Victoria to go out with me. So, I rent a helicopter, like the movie *Pretty Woman.* Hand to God . . ."

Edward took Vivian on a private jet, not a helicopter, idiot.

Victoria remains on the opposite side of the gallery, just before a small entrance leading to a hallway blocked by her security detail.

"Excuse us," says Zanthe as she slides her arm in mine.

I turn to Redding who nods and stays with Julien.

Zanthe guides me toward the entrance to a small nook on the right side of the double doors. The space is barely wide enough for three people. She props open a window and pulls out a cigarette from a pocket hidden in the folds of her dress.

"It's illegal to smoke in here." I don't know if it's hanging out with Redding or my natural need for order inside a room that has me point out the obvious.

"What're they gonna do, throw me out of my own place?" quips Zanthe. She ignites her square with a silver lighter, a Black power fist colored in red, black, and green engraved on the front.

I step under a vent near the window. The mix of the air conditioning and balmy June winds is oddly satisfying. "Just wanted to talk about the D.A.R.E. program. I'm starting an internship program at The Ivory. Maybe there won't have to be another century that passes before a concierge or general manager who looks like us."

"Gio, they'll rip you apart like fresh bread." She takes a satisfying drag.

Zanthe stares at a picture of bodies jammed together on a bus. Sitting. Standing. Sleeping. Faces annoyed or resigned or peaceful. People trapped together for a time in their desolate worlds. Alone.

"First time I made some real money for one of my pictures was about seven years ago. I bought a gravesite and a headstone for my mom." Zanthe touches the bottom of the frame. "They never found a body. Just her belongings scattered along Dearborn Street Bridge. I kept her lighter." Zanthe massages her left temple, perfectly balancing her cigarette between her fingers. "It's been . . . twenty-five years. You can declare someone dead after seven."

I observe the profile of Zanthe's face as she continues to look at the photograph. "What was her name?"

"Iris. Her name was Iris," she says reverently.

"I'm sorry." I count backward. Every tale of loss is a trigger. I don't know how much strength I have left to listen to someone else recount how they're grieving a part of themselves that they can never recover.

"You're good." Zanthe steals a glance at Gideon near the bar. "I'm creating something beautiful out of the ugly despite the critics."

I wonder where Zanthe buries her rage. Her dead mom. The politician father refusing to publicly recognize her as his daughter. A golden child brother. A resentful husband.

"If Gideon is so bad, why'd you marry him?"

Zanthe puffs on her cigarette one more time before extinguishing it with her index finger and thumb. "Dad tends to arrange these things. He did it for Julien. Did the same for me. Kids still want to believe in Santa Claus or the Easter Bunny. We still want to believe in love."

"Yeah, Prince Charming and all that."

"Not romantic love, Gio. A father's love. I wanted to believe in that once. Don't anymore, but there are benefits." She gestures around the massive hall where we're surrounded by her accomplishments paid for by Governor Whitlock's money.

"Wish I could say that'd be enough for me, but . . ." I shrug.

"I may share this place with Julien, but I do my work. And no one bothers me." Zanthe closes the door and turns to me. "And I can always count on Dad to manage his own self-interests, so if I or Julien find ourselves in some . . . difficulty, we have a way to avoid consequences. I don't take the governor up on it as much 'cause I'm smart, but that's Julien's go-to. That's why you need to stay away, Gio. I don't wanna see you get hurt."

Zanthe has long since abandoned hope of attaining Governor Whitlock's love. Julien holds on to this dream like Momma did of one day hitting the Mega Millions.

"I know how men like Julien work. Flattery and flirting get you everywhere."

"See, my mom was like you. Thought she knew everything there was to know about everybody. Thought she could talk or fight her way out of any situation. And she couldn't," says Zanthe.

Iris was alone in a city with millions of eyes, yet no one watched. It was easy for someone to snatch her, leaving remnants and destruction in their wake. Zanthe is right, I can wind up like her mother. But I have someone in my corner. I scan the crowd for Redding. She remains close to Julien.

Sadly, Iris didn't have a Redding.

I do.

"I burned my bridge with Gideon. So, I'll take my chances with Julien," I say, studying Zanthe over my glass as I finish the last of my champagne. "It'll be fine."

I leave Zanthe in the claustrophobic space near the gallery's entrance as I hear her say, "No, it won't."

CHAPTER 39

Redding

June 17, 2025

Dad pulls me away from Shawn, who holds his bloody nose in front of our apartment on 117th and Princeton. He wouldn't stop running his mouth. About my mom. The fact I don't have one. So, Shawn got what he got in front of his friends and most of the block watching.

I stand in the small living room waiting for Dad to take his belt off, but he doesn't.

"If you're gonna fight, Red. It can't be about you. Think beyond that. Fight beyond that. Understand?"

I nod fiercely, thankful for no whipping.

Dad grins. "That right cross got his ass, didn't it?"

Giovanni strolls with Julien out of the gallery as I press my way toward them. There are too many people crammed in here. She's betting on that; on more alone time with Julien because she knows I won't let her do what she wants.

Working your own agenda can get you into trouble, but here I am again. Without authorization. Without backup with someone who doesn't listen to a damn word I say. No doubt Frenchie would laugh at this irony.

As Giovanni and Julien disappear around the corner, an officer from Victoria's protection detail whispers something in her ear. Something important. Victoria's artificial smile slips for a second and she excuses herself from her conversation.

What did the officer say? Do I leave Giovanni with Julien? Pursue this lead?

Investigations work better if you chase all the angles. Gather as much information as you can, parse out the nonsense and deliver whatever measure of justice you can.

I abandon my path to Giovanni and move toward Victoria who's planted in front of a picture of a woman singing on a stage with tawny light enveloping her.

I ease up keeping a casual distance. "Beautiful picture."

"It is, Detective Stark. Your partner here?" Victoria glances over her shoulder for Frenchie.

"You remember me?"

"Keeping up with names and faces is part of the job. *I* appreciate details," she says.

Victoria's crafted polite and bubbly persona from The Ivory where we first met has vanished, replaced by someone who is exhausted of the curated demeanor, of masks. The covenant of political life and the stripping of humanity to gain power is a burden that I wouldn't dare shoulder.

"Saw that officer say something. You seemed upset."

Victoria tilts her head. "So, you came for gossip?"

"No. Woman to woman, I wanted to make sure you're okay."

"But you know I'm not. You're not dumb and you're not a narcissist. Most of the people here are one or both," she says.

"Including Julien?"

Her phone buzzes. Victoria reads a message. The frown

returns. She looks at the hallway where Julien left with Giovanni but makes no move toward it.

It's 8:45 p.m. Giovanni left with Julien five minutes ago. She can't get into that much trouble in five minutes, right? I'll give Giovanni another five minutes. Then I'm going after her. But I need to make headway with Victoria. If Giovanni can't get anything out of Julien, then Victoria is our strongest chance, probably the last one, to find a lead on Natalie.

I'm leaving here with something!

"Your husband ignores you. You remain the dutiful wife. You clean his messes. Stand by him even when he hurts you . . . or others." I stare at the picture of the woman singing, beyond it, to my reflection. "Family. It's love, duty, tons of regrets."

Victoria returns her phone to her purse. "Detective, I think you're a little confused about family."

"Not as confused as you might think. Your family's powerful."

"Jesus! This isn't *Game of Thrones*," says Victoria.

"No, it's Illinois politics. Way worse." I step closer. "You wouldn't still be talking to me if you didn't have something you wanted me to know but didn't want Julien to hear. So, what is it? Another affair? Something about the D.A.R.E. program? You don't wanna keep living like—"

"I'm not!" Victoria puts her hand to her mouth for a moment and takes a calming breath. "I'm not."

Victoria walks to the hallway where Giovanni and Julien entered but makes a left and enters a small office adorned in ebony and gold paint with wooden bookshelves flanking each side and a 42" television mounted in the middle. Below the television sits a round oak table and six comfortable-looking leather chairs. Victoria's detail remains outside.

"I'm leaving him." Victoria sits. "If you'd have told me five years ago when we met . . . I—well, yeah. I've had enough. Enough tears. Enough prayers. Enough chances. Enough apathy."

"Were you done when you gave him that black eye?"

"Julien has an extraordinary talent for pushing people too far." Victoria smirks. "Besides, I told you he was bringing me some food, slipped, and hit his face on the door frame. It doesn't even matter. After the gala, I'm done. With him. With his whole family. They spread like a disease."

"Why now?"

"There's no reason as to why one moment over another is the one that pushes you to make a decision that'll change your life, but I can tell you when it happened. Last Friday at 5:01 p.m., before dinner at The Cathedral. Julien was sexting some influencer he met through his little grant program. That's how he meets most of these girls."

I steady my breathing. Struggling to keep the questions straight in my head. "Who was Julien texting?"

"Fifi . . . Philomena? Does it matter?" asks Victoria.

"Yeah, it really does," I say.

"Ferris, Fiona, Flora . . ." Victoria lists the names as if they're groceries instead of potential mistresses.

"Phoenix?"

"Yes! Phoenix!" says Victoria. "Who names their child Phoenix?"

I flex my neck, side to side. "A child names themselves Phoenix."

"My husband has a type," Victoria bitterly quips.

"What do you know about the grant program Julien heads?" I ask.

"Julien and Gideon are both on the board and Julien uses it to find new conquests. That's it," she says. "I stay far away. Plausible deniability." She stands up and heads toward the door. "This will stay between us. For another week at least. After that, I don't much care how you crucify that bastard or his father."

Victoria paints Julien and the governor to be the villains of the story, but villains have a support network. People who turn a ready blind eye and blurt out a feeble excuse for harmful behaviors with devastating consequences. Yes, Victoria could be seen as a victim, but she could also be just as bad as the rest of the people she's denigrating. She tells herself the story she has to tell to survive.

Like Giovanni.

Dammit!

I look at my phone. Five minutes to nine.

It's been ten minutes.

I leave Victoria, rushing down the hall, searching for Giovanni. I tell myself she's okay as I scan each room until I find her. With Julien.

She slaps him and Julien's face twists with fury.

I swing open the door.

Time to use my right cross.

CHAPTER 40

Giovanni

Ten Minutes Earlier
June 17, 2025

Julien migrates to the opposite end of the gallery. I take out my phone, open my camera app, and press Record. As I approach, he turns from his conversation, taking me in without shame. I let him. I'll shower when I get home.

I force a smile that reaches my eyes. "So good to see you outside of The Ivory, Julien."

"Ah, Gio, you know I don't mind mixing a little business with pleasure."

"Speaking of business *and* pleasure, I was hoping to speak with you about the D.A.R.E. grant program. I'm interested in applying, but . . ." I peer into his muddied brown-green orbs. "I would like my application . . . expedited. That possible?"

I peek over his shoulder. Redding presses toward us, but the sudden influx of bodies slows her down. I caress Julien's forearm and squeeze. "Is there somewhere more private?"

Julien offers his hand, and I take it as he escorts me out of the main gallery past Victoria who continues speaking with an older woman. We stroll down a short hallway with an officer from his detail trailing us.

"Go to the main hall. I have business," he orders.

The red-haired officer blocks Julien's path. "But, sir, I—"

"Leave or I'll make sure the only thing you protect for the next six months is a goddamn porta potty." Julien doesn't shout, but the gleeful malevolence in his voice is disturbing.

"See, you've frightened poor Gio. She's shaking."

"I'll wait in the main hall, Mr. Whitlock," he says.

"Good boy," says Julien, straightening the jacket of his pea-green two-piece suit.

The quiet hatred in the officer's face is an expression I recognize well. It's the same one I've had with Willa countless times before. Julien's lucky he didn't act on what he's feeling. Willa's lucky, too. Though part of me is morbidly curious what would happen if I or that guy acted on our impulses.

To our left is the north wing entrance named the Iris Walker Memorial Hall.

"Who's Iris Walker?" I ask, playing dumb.

"Uh, some lady Zanthe knew." Julien unlocks the small glass-fronted exhibition space. "Now, let's talk about all your dreams and how I can help you make them come true."

Are these the same clichéd, tired lines Julien fed Natalie? Did he take her here?

I let go of his hand. "You're too good to me."

"If we have enough time, I can show you a few secret rooms." He smiles and licks his lips.

I gravitate to a painting. A child sits on the top stair of his front porch, pouting face, deep in thought. "If I hypothetically had a community program that needed funding, how likely would it be that I'd get approval?"

"Oh, Gio, for you, let's say it'd be a sure bet." Julien closes the distance between us. "Paperwork isn't even necessary. I do you a service and you . . . do me a service." His index finger discreetly trails my shoulder.

I hope it's quiet enough for my phone to pick up every self-serving, philandering, creepy word coming out of his mouth.

On the wall to my left is a painting of three women. They sit in a circle. Another woman is off to the side barely in frame. Julien slinks behind me, his cologne is a suffocating mixture of cedarwood and vanilla. I search for cameras. There are two on opposite ends of the room, but do they pick up sound? Is anyone watching us?

Julien embraces me from behind, but I push away from him and step to my right, creating distance. "You're getting awful familiar considering you were messing with that influencer Phoenix before she died."

Julien blinks in surprise, his mouth quickly opens, ready with a lie.

"People always talk around The Ivory. I keep my ears open." I grin.

"I mean, I'm sorry she's gone, but we already got what we needed from each other and ended it, like adults," he says.

Julien is on my phone admitting to misusing grant funds, adultery, and being a callous dickhead, though you can only possibly go to jail for one of the three offenses. That might get him to admit what he did to Natalie.

"What about Natalie Moore? She's a big-time influencer and I'm just . . . me."

"Natalie, pshh . . . she was a stuck-up bitch. Gio, darling, you're special. *So special.*"

Natalie could've experienced a version of this conversation a few weeks ago. The way Julien called her a bitch with such casual vitriol makes me wonder what he's capable of.

"Come on, you almost got into a fight with her at The Cathedral. Natalie knows how to push buttons."

"Mmm-hmm." My phone slaps against my thigh as I step back from him.

The entrance is ten feet away, but it might as well be a hundred feet. My back hits a wall that tapers off into a small nook with no light and no way for a camera to see what's happening behind it. Julien plants his palms on the wall, trapping me.

"Do you know how long I've waited for this?" he asks, his hot breath close to my face, reeking of shrimp and champagne.

"Victoria's gonna wonder where you are."

"No, she won't," says Julien.

I turn my head to avoid his kiss. "Stop."

"Ah, you wanna fight a little? That gets you going?" He chuckles.

"I made a mistake." I brace my weight on my back foot, push him away.

Julien stumbles toward the painting of the little boy on the top stair. I take those precious seconds and rush to the door, making it almost halfway until he grabs my arm and yanks me back.

"Y'all girls always wanna play with men. You flirt. You giggle. Now you wanna run off? Nah, I'm getting what I came for."

"Like Natalie? You get what you wanted from her?" I jerk my arm from his grasp and slap him, adding a little color to his fading black eye. My left hand stings; thin vibrations course down my arm as I back away. Just like Natalie, but this time, slapping someone feels good.

It feels *really* good.

Julien holds his left cheek for a few seconds, then his glare hardens. He holds his body like a weapon. Fists and hands ready to punch, pummel, and strangle. But I'm not getting ready to lose this fight. There's a sculpture to my right. It looks light enough for me to grab.

It's about to go down.

Julien charges at me. I move toward the sculpture, but a fist that's not mine glides past my face and connects with his left jaw. Julien crumples to the ground. I look up and see Redding pulling her fist back.

Muffled voices shout from behind. A group of guests gather in the previously closed-off north wing. Victoria among them, watching Julien writhing on the floor. She suppresses a smile, then quickly regains a flat expression.

Someone helps Julien up as he shrieks, "I'll beat you like I shoulda beat the old man!"

Cell phone cameras flash. People record, bodies robotically turn left to right, allowing them to create a piece of art, a social media narrative of their own.

"This place is bigger than I thought," says Redding.

I don't look in her direction. "Thanks."

Redding adjusts her jacket, making sure she's not giving spectators another show. "You okay?"

"Yeah. You good?"

Three additional officers surround me and Redding. There's no talking or fighting our way out of this.

Massaging her right hand, she says, "No, not really."

CHAPTER 41

Redding

June 17, 2025

I rotate my shoulders a few times to work out the stiffness. Giovanni massages her wrists where the handcuffs have left indentations. Across the street, Frenchie speaks to someone in a black suit and buzz-cut snow-white hair who looks over at us, then whispers to an officer who wordlessly marches over, returning my purse and Giovanni's phone.

Giovanni quickly scrolls through it, her face scrunched in anxiety, then softening in relief. "It's still there." She mouths a silent prayer.

"What?" I text Emmett, then Hudson, that I'll be home late. Again.

"I recorded me and Julien." She hits the play button; the video only shows black, but Julien's and Giovanni's voices are clear.

"Paperwork isn't even necessary. I do you a service and you . . . do me a service."

"Ah, Natalie, pshh . . . she was a stuck-up bitch. Gio, darling, you're special. So special."

"Do you know how long I've waited for this?"

"Ah, you wanna fight a little? That gets you going?"

I shudder at the last words. There's grunting, straining, a Morse-code-like thumping of Giovanni's phone against her body.

"Go home." I scan the street and find Frenchie still talking to Black Suit. "As soon as I got something, I'll tell you."

"I'll beat you like I shoulda beat the old man . . . who was the old man?" asks Giovanni.

"You hear what I said?"

"Yeah. I'm not leaving." She leans against an unoccupied car. "Who was Julien talking about? Governor Whitlock? Julien probably got smart one too many times and got popped in the face by his dad. Like you did to him an hour ago." She laughs.

I shake my head and chuckle, in spite of myself. "My money's on Fleur Winstead. If your girlfriend got hit on, even if you're an older man, you'd probably try to get a lick in. Maybe that's why he went on a leave of absence."

"We gotta find Fleur to ask him. And what kind of money you talking?"

I extend my hand. "One dollar."

Giovanni shakes it in agreement. "One dollar."

I slip off my jacket and check for a response from Emmett. Nothing. This time of the night he's probably asleep and snoring. Loudly and aggressively. Hudson begins typing, the dreaded three dots hovering, then nothing, three dots, then nothing. It doesn't take this long to type "good night" or even "gn" as these youngsters seem to only reply with acronyms and emojis.

Frenchie walks up, closes his red-rimmed eyes, and takes a deep breath. "You see that guy across the street in the black suit? That's Carl, head of the protection detail. And if Carl and I hadn't grown up together in Canaryville, they'd have hauled you off to jail, regardless of that badge." He looks at Giovanni. "And they'd have put you under the jail, Ms. Fancy Pants Concierge."

"It's chief concierge. And thanks for the recap of your white blue-collar upbringing, and the privileges it brings, but you do realize Julien assaulted me an hour ago, right?" says Giovanni. "And I've got a recording—"

Frenchie holds up his hand. "Here's a quick law class, free of charge. Illinois is a two-party state. You need permission from the person you're recording, and I know damn well Julien Whitlock didn't consent to being recorded, so what you have is useless."

"It wouldn't be on my socials," Giovanni fires back.

"The Whitlocks would sue you so hard your great-great-grandkids would be in debt," says Frenchie.

Giovanni raises her eyebrows as if it's a personal challenge to see how much IDGAF energy she can rain down on the people she believes are responsible for her situation. I get it, but we gotta be methodical about our approach.

"You do this, then whatever good will Frenchie used to get us released will be squandered." I step in front of Giovanni, so she focuses on me. "We'll find a way to link Julien to Natalie. The right way. We need to dot all our I's and cross our T's if we're gonna accuse the governor's son of kidnapping and . . . worse."

I don't say the word *murder.* Worse could mean Natalie's hurt badly, not that her body is rotting in a place where we may never find her. For now, Natalie is simply somewhere. She can't find us and we can't find her. Because in this generalized and naive pattern of thought, I can give Giovanni hope.

I can give myself hope.

The tint in Frenchie's face has faded to a light crimson. I can count the number of times on one hand that I've seen Frenchie angry, and two of them involved Giovanni.

Frenchie mumbles something under his breath, then turns to me. "Suits knows you punched Julien. Couldn't stop that. He wants to see you, Red. And I've never seen him this pissed."

I glance at my phone again. Nothing from Hudson. "I'll head over to Area soon."

"I'll meet you over there," Frenchie says, plodding to his car.

Giovanni and I trek two blocks away to my car in our cute outfits and sore feet after making a mess of an investigation.

I unlock the doors. "Frenchie isn't trying to be an asshole. He's just protective."

"Why does he think you need protection?"

"What happened between you and Natalie?" I ask, pulling off into traffic.

Giovanni's lips press together. She fidgets with the dashboard vent. This is a silence holding every unforgivable action, every putrid word, every moment Giovanni became someone she never wants to remember again. I feel at home in this silence, but I know the destruction it will wreak on her life if she doesn't let go of it. If I don't let go of it.

"There was this guy, Cormac, and he was . . . stalking Nivea, one of . . . the others. He asked her out. She said no. Three weeks later, Nivea went missing. And I knew I needed more, but I thought everything lined up perfectly. A prior misdemeanor charge for assault. Red-pill-type posts on his socials crying about what women owed him 'cause he was a 'nice guy.' He loved to write poetry. I kept calling. He kept ignoring my calls. So, I showed up at a place he frequented. And he ran. I shouldn't have chased him, but I was tired of dead ends and crying families and . . . failure." I turn off the air and roll down the windows. "Every foot I ran, every block I passed it felt like . . . I was getting closer to finishing something. Finding Nivea. Finding the others. Anyway, Cormac got tired of running and turned around. He had a gun. I drew mine. I fired.

He fired. I got his left leg and arm. He got my shoulder and stomach, but . . ."

I gather the fragments of that moment into a fractured bit of memory. The beat of seconds and sticky air of a June evening suspend me in silence.

"But . . ." Giovanni presses.

"A man coming home from a late shift. Investigation determined it was Cormac's bullet. Not mine."

"Did he . . ."

"He made it, thank God. Settled with the city a few months ago." A bitter laugh escapes my mouth. "I got desk duty for thirty days, but I took a few months off work 'til the story died down."

"Cormac?"

"Lawyer worked their magic and got him five years downstate. Claimed Cormac was scared for his life and didn't hear me identify myself as a cop." My hand tightens on the steering wheel. "As far as Nivea, there was CCTV footage of him filling up at a gas station on the North Side when she went missing."

Giovanni studies my profile. I study the street. The puzzle pieces fit. Cormac was a bad man. But he didn't snatch Nivea. I focused on him, saw no one else, and missed any signs that could've led me to the one behind all of this.

The precinct comes on like a bad flu—suddenly and all at once. I walk through the doors with Giovanni half a step behind. She sits at my desk as I enter Markham's office. Frenchie is already there.

"I shoulda never let you come back," growls Markham.

"Julien Whitlock was assaulting Giovanni. That's the only reason I hit him," I say.

"We don't know what went on between those two," says Markham.

"We know *exactly* what went on between them." I don't

measure my tone, my voice likely carrying outside of the office. "Giovanni recorded the whole thing! Look, I know that the recording isn't admissible, but I can testify that I saw Julien assault her."

"Did you see the start of the fight, Stark?" asks Markham.

I cross my arms. "No."

"Julien said Giovanni slapped him first," says Markham.

"He's lying," I say.

"Is he? 'Cause last time I checked Ms. Mason hauled off and slapped Natalie Moore first. Who's to say this isn't a repeat?" He shakes his head. "I know what y'all say about me. Calling me 'Suits' behind my back. I'm a 'kiss ass.' Whatever. I don't give a good shit because I do my job. I follow the leads. I follow the rules. Everything was leading to Giovanni. Fine, maybe, *maybe* I was wrong about that, but you still refuse to follow orders. And all of us pay for it. Not just you. *All of us.*"

I glance over at Frenchie who intensely studies his brown wingtips.

"So instead of a commendation for stopping a crime, I'm getting a damn lecture?"

"No, you're getting suspended. Effective immediately," says Markham as he walks to his door and opens it. "Now, if you'll excuse me, I have to call the governor's office and kiss some more ass, make sure they don't take back that firearm enforcement grant. If I lose that money because of tonight, Stark, forget Avant, Illinois, you'll be lucky to get a job as a security guard after this."

The eyes of every detective and officer follow Frenchie and me as we leave for our desks. I measure my steps carefully so my heels don't tear the hem of my black suit.

There's a process to getting suspended. It's not like the movies. Again, there's paperwork. I have to drive to CPD Headquarters on 35th and Michigan Avenue and fill out a Suspension

Notification form (CPD-44.102). That piece of paper states I'm no longer acting under the jurisdiction of the Chicago Police Department.

Frenchie stops me just before we reach my desk. "We'll get a union rep on this, Red. It'll be okay."

Frenchie can do whatever he wants.

I have a choice and my choice is to keep going.

Damn the consequences.

CHAPTER 42

Giovanni

June 17, 2025

French and I stare each other down like in an old spaghetti Western. I know this dude. I just can't place his face.

I put in ear buds and compile a damning clip of Julien bragging about the grant program, his power, his immorality. My thumb hovers over the share button. How many views would that get?

The feeble squeak of the door draws my attention as Redding walks toward us, with her gun still holstered on her hip.

"They let you keep that?" I say pointing to her waist.

"I fill out a form and turn in my badge. I keep my duty weapon. I paid for it, after all."

French puts his hand on Redding's shoulder. "I'm gonna go home and crash, but we'll figure something out." He heads off to his car.

I wait until he's far from us and ask the questions haunting me for the past few hours.

“Is that it? Is French gonna look for Natalie? Are they giving the case to—”

“I’m still looking for her. Wanted to give Frenchie some plausible deniability because we’re truly on our own,” says Redding.

Redding grabs her phone and scrolls through pictures she took in Natalie’s suite. She lands on one of the orchid, the bottom of its pot. I try to make out the sticker, but Redding flips to another picture.

I snatch the phone from her hand and return to the picture Redding glossed over. Zooming in on the bottom of the terracotta pot, I read the name on the sticker: E. Kelly’s Flowers and Gifts.

I return Redding’s phone. “I know our first stop in the morning.”

CHAPTER 43

Redding

June 17, 2025

I take residential streets all the way home. I park on East 51st Street, three blocks east. Just in case. Every car rumbling past, every tinted window, every shift of streetlight shadows, shortens my breath and roils my stomach. I keep my hands free and ready to fire my weapon at any moment. Telling Emmett and Hudson about my suspension isn't as high on my list of priorities as making sure we all survive whatever hellish conspiracy I've unearthed.

Emmett's car sits in front of the house. The upstairs lights are on as always. I walk to the end of the block and up the alley to the back gate of our wooden fence. I grip the black metal door handle and twist as I feel something wet and sticky on my fingers. I ease my hand back, staring in disbelief at the blood coating my palm. I draw my gun and Maglite. The bone-white glow illuminates the drops of crimson dotting a ghastly path toward the back door. Tears sting my eyes, but I blink them back. I take slow deep breaths.

What have I brought to my home?

The trail continues through the unlocked back door, small streaks of blood like macabre modern art run down the kitchen countertop and bottom cabinet closest to the refrigerator. I brace myself to find Emmett or Hudson in the living room. But there are no bodies. There's no sound. No television. No music. Only the creak of my footsteps on the floor and the sobs trapped in my throat.

Who lies in wait? Am I the last person on their list? How will I die? Whoever I'm chasing has power, which means they can make people disappear then craft a narrative to their liking: a troubled detective who could no longer handle the pressure, who was suspended from her job, went home, and killed her family. Then herself.

Case closed.

Other detectives will whisper they always knew something was wrong with Redding Stark. She could never let things go. Kept chasing after things that weren't there.

It was only a matter of time before she snapped.

The Maglite catches a slippery shadow, tall, a raised arm . . .

"Drop it! Drop it now!" I see nothing but the person who is trying to kill me, who probably killed Hudson and Emmett.

Liquid splashes on the ground. Two bags full of bandages, cleaning supplies, and a busted bottle of hydrogen peroxide, leaking on the floor toward my shoes.

Hudson, my son, my baby, eyes deep amber orbs full of fear. His hands are raised, touching the top of the door frame. Emmett is behind him, his face contorted in anger and horror and . . . hate. I quickly holster my weapon.

I gather Hudson into my arms. "Baby, I didn't know. I didn't know. I'm so sorry. I'm so sorry. I thought you were someone else. I—I thought . . ."

My son pushes me away, and runs upstairs to his room, slamming the door.

I've proven to Hudson that the things that he's seen on the news, or experienced in some subtle or profound way, are true. He's perceived as a threat first and a child second. He'll be given no chance to tell his story. My fear, my stress, this case, the indoctrination of justice by any means, caused me to make the worst decision of my life. I am the enemy they speak of in my community.

Emmett bends down and starts shoving the groceries back into the plastic bags. "We went for a late-night run. He fell and scraped up his arms. We went to the store to get some things for him and stuff to clean the blood up."

I grab paper towels to mop up the hydrogen peroxide. "I'm sorry. It . . . I came home to an unlocked house. Blood everywhere . . . this case . . . what was I supposed to think?"

"You had a gun pointed in our faces!"

"Someone is out there." I stop cleaning. "Someone followed me the other night. I thought maybe they sent someone else to the house . . . I . . . this case—"

"Enough with the case, Redding! Just . . ." Emmett drags his fingers down his face. "Do you know what I thought when I got the call you'd been shot? I thought . . . good. I was happy. You realize how messed up that is?"

"Em—"

"I'm tired of sharing you with dead people—"

I interrupt, "You don't know if—"

"They're dead or they don't want to be found and the only person who can't accept it is you!"

I won't deny Emmett the righteous part of his anger, but there are too many clues. The deeper I go, the more I find. Whether he believes in me or not, I won't stop what I'm doing. And in that, I'll lose everything.

Emmett places the ruined groceries on the breakfast bar. "I think we need to go somewhere for a while."

"I can't—"

He holds his hand up. "Me and Hudson. We need to get away . . . from you."

I swallow the acid-laced lump in my throat. "Where?"

"My brother's."

"Gainesville?" I blink tears back.

"Well, Georgia's nice in June. Hud'll get to see his uncle and his cousins," says Emmett.

I'm pretending we're talking about a trip we already planned because the reality of my family disintegrating in front of my eyes is untenable. Another unhealthy coping mechanism, but humanity has still managed to plod along living in denial and compartmentalizing their emotions. And it's not like I've been taught to do anything different. Dad, my community, my profession, it encourages me to bury what I'm feeling and never exhume the pain. So, I push through. Find peace in a hell of my own creation.

Emmett makes it to the landing before Hudson, two large suitcases downstairs clutched in his hands. Hudson follows his father with newly bandaged arms and a bag that weighs almost as much as him slung across his lean frame. He flinches as I hug him. His arms remain at his sides.

"I love you, son. And . . . I'm so, so sorry."

"I know." His body relaxes in my arms the tiniest bit before he wriggles away.

We both watch Hudson as he walks to the car and gets in the front passenger's seat.

Emmett turns to me. "I love you, Redding. Still. But I love Hudson more." He props himself against the door frame and looks at his feet. "I knew I had to share parts of you with this job, with this city. I signed up for that, but we don't even have *some* of you anymore. We have none of you."

"You have every part of me that fights for you, for Hudson. That has to make sure I can carve out a piece of the world for us that is safe. And the only way I know how to do that is doing this job." I stand in front of Emmett and caress his face.

He leans into my hand and covers it with his for a few seconds before he pulls away.

I ask the question that's been anchored on my tongue since they started packing. "When are you coming back?"

"I . . . Redding . . ."

I back away. "Be safe," I choke out.

He nods and closes the back door, still streaked with blood. I wait until the taillights no longer bathe me in a scarlet glow, then allow myself to slide down the wall and sob.

Hudson and Emmett.

Nivea, Stacey, Annette, Olivia, Mia, and Natalie.

Dad.

Everything and everyone. Every crisis. Every failure.

Blood. Death. Regrets.

Frenchie told me to make things okay before I lost everything.

I didn't listen.

Why didn't I listen?

CHAPTER 44

Giovanni

June 18, 2025

Edgar Kelly's West Loop storefront is an unassuming cardinal-colored brick building, nestled in the middle of a mom-and-pop deli and a four-star restaurant. The clash of familiar and trendy is the iconic badge of the West Loop.

Edgar peeks from behind his green door. "You don't make in-person requests, Giovanni, so to what do I owe the pleasure?"

"Could be my birthday or I might have a craving for some gourmet toffee."

"Your birthday is April 7th, and you prefer caramel to toffee." Edgar studies me with a mix of affection and suspicion.

The narrow hallway expands into a large greenhouse. We pass rows of carefully pruned and watered plants and flowers. The whites of Redding's eyes are pink, but they were like this before we arrived.

I touch the stem of a yellow rose. "You remember selling an orchid on Thursday or Friday?"

Edgar steps behind a green plant with floppy dog-ear type leaves. "I sell so many things. It's difficult to remember."

"But you can remember Giovanni's birthday and that she prefers caramel to toffee?" says Redding. Badge or not, there's an authority to her voice, a practiced cadence to her questions, ready to jump on any inconsistency or lie Edgar might attempt to utter.

"Things come and go," says Edgar. He bends down and tries to lift the pot, but it slips from his grip.

I step over and lift the pot with him, setting it on the table. "We're not talking about HIPAA or attorney-client privilege."

"No, but we're talking about people who respect privacy. And the people who pay well for it could make my life hell if I open my mouth."

Edgar speaks about the Whitlocks like the characters in *Harry Potter* speak about Voldemort. Or maybe it's not just the Whitlocks but all the people like them, keeping those below oppressed, beholden to their power without a way around or through it.

I cover Edgar's hand with mine. "What you say to us, stays between us."

Edgar huffs and prunes leaves. "That godforsaken bell didn't stop ringing. My video feed pops on and there in black and white I see him. Says he needs to purchase an orchid and it's past ten at night!"

"If it's such an inconvenience, why not ignore him and go back to bed?" asks Redding.

Edgar holds his thumb and index finger in front of us about two inches apart. "For that amount of money, I got my old ass out of bed and gave that boy the orchid. This location doesn't pay for itself, dear."

"Boy?" I ask. Wasn't it an older man who bought the orchid? Julien? F.T. Winstead?

"Your little protégé, Damo—Danie—David. David came by. Figured it was for some VIP, you know how those people have outrageous demands. Remember that Ms. Niyanzawa mess? Who names their turtle Aaron Burr?" Edgar shakes his head. "So, ladies, we done here?"

I can't find my voice, and back into Redding as I turn around.

"Thanks," says Redding.

"Security. Housekeeping. Porters. Valets. The right price can get you anyone. The right price you'll do what you need to and convince yourself the money's good enough and the risk is small enough."

First Teddy, now David. Was I the only one who never took advantage of these arrangements? Have Mecca or Momma ever performed a side job? College wasn't cheap, but Momma somehow was always able to help me with rent or groceries. Was that simply Mom magic? Or was it something else?

I breathe in air unburdened with the heavy scent of roses and gardenias and lavender. "We're going to David's house next."

"Is he gonna be home?" asks Redding.

"Let's hope so. I wrote the damn schedule."

I bang on David's back door a third time. Ruthless. Incessant. The way Redding banged on Phoenix's door. Redding studies the yard and desolate alleyway where she parked her car. A dark blue Subaru Forester. I had her pegged as a Dodge Challenger type.

"You good?" I look up at the second and third floors. For-rent signs are propped against the empty windows.

"Why?"

"Your eyes look a little pink is all."

Redding crosses her arms. "Allergies. Probably the flowers at Edgar's."

Movement beyond the beige curtains blocks my view of the inside of David's place. "They were like that before we—"

"Giovanni," she begins with an acidic bark, "I said I'm fine."

I bang on David's door a fourth time. Someone pulls back the curtain ever so slightly. With the sluggish click of a lock, a shirtless David slips his lanky frame through the opening.

He takes in me and Redding. "You bringing cops to my house?"

I step inside without invitation. "The sooner we talk, the sooner we're gone."

David leads us through his first-floor apartment to the living room with a three-paneled picture window, a red couch, a black plastic table with two chairs, and mismatched lamps on the dark wood floors. Monastic existence at its finest except for the framed autographed poster of Rihanna on the wall above the couch.

"I need you to tell me where you were Friday night," I say, leaning against the wall closest to the window.

David ruffles through a laundry bag near the table. "Working at The Ivory."

"All night? 'Cause someone said they saw you at the flower shop. Edgar's," says Redding, inching closer to him.

"People can say anything," counters David, as he finally settles on a white Captain America T-shirt and puts it on.

"We didn't pull your name out of thin air," says Redding.

"Like you can't pull a badge out of thin air," he counters.

Redding clenches her jaw. "I could've forgotten it this morning."

"I don't know you, but I know cops. You'd forget to breathe sooner than you'd forget your badge," he says.

"You do that cold read mess, too?" she asks.

David looks at me. "Giovanni taught me everything I know even when she didn't know she was doing it."

A mixture of pride and regret wells up inside me. I took David under my wing like Mecca took me under hers, then

Willa. The difference between me and them is that I didn't try and mold David into what I wanted him to be. I encouraged him to find a way to do the job and not lose himself in it. I let him choose his own path.

I walk to David, gently grabbing his pointy chin, forcing him to meet my eyes. "Forget she's here—" I wave in Redding's direction "—she can't do anything, right? I only wanna find Natalie. You say I taught you everything you know, so I know I taught you some version of right from wrong."

David flops in a chair near the table, the cheap furniture groaning under his weight. "Winstead paid me two months' rent to do a couple favors. So, I dropped by Edgar's to get that flower."

I kneel beside him. "Tell me everything. Bit by bit."

"It was, like, 10:00 p.m. He sent me out to buy the flower. He was in a rush y'know, but . . . focused."

I pull up a chair next to David and sit down. "You told me you didn't see him—"

"I hadn't seen him, not those past few hours at least," says David.

"A lie of omission," interjects Redding. "What was the other favor?"

David scrunches his face up. "What?"

"You said you did Fleur 'a couple favors,' right? What was the other favor?" she asks.

"I . . . uh, drove him to a house."

"What house?" asks Redding as she walks toward the windows.

"Twenty-five miles northeast in Black Oak, Illinois. A mansion. Brown brick. At the west end of the city on Delbrook Lane."

"*You* signed Teddy's initials that night. I knew that driver's log was off." The chair wobbles under my weight as I lean forward. "But you don't have access to the security—"

"Lifted Teddy's work badge," he says. "They had him doing so much. Wasn't hard," says David. "Told Winstead to leave through the front but walk a couple blocks to Lower Wacker Drive. Scooped him up there."

"Was Natalie with him?" asks Redding.

"No," he says.

My earlier feeling of pride is now twisting into a pulsing dread. "And the missing footage?"

David nods. "There was an eviction notice on my door. Had to do something." He waits for a beat or seven. "Am I fired?"

I put my hand on his shoulder and squeeze it. "Yes."

"That's fair. But I was just trying to survive."

"I know. I still love you, dude."

David stands, arms out. I reach for him, but I'm being pulled away and down. My head knocks against the floor. Redding covers me with her body as a rapid succession of cracks shred my ears.

Bits of drywall and shards of glass litter the floor. The noise doesn't stop. Bullets don't sound like firecrackers. They're louder. There is a deathly purity to the sound.

I don't scream. I think of Momma. Her smiling face. Her arms open and ready to embrace me as I was ready to embrace David. He's lying feet away; crimson now blooming from his body. He shouldn't die alone. I'll make sure he won't.

I'll see you soon, Momma.

CHAPTER 45

Redding

Three Minutes Earlier
June 18, 2025

A black truck with tinted windows passes by the apartment for the second time. I'm living on two hours of sleep and a single text from Emmett half an hour ago simply saying: We made it. I'm exhausted and sad, probably seeing the evil in everything.

Giovanni is damn good at getting people to trust her, reveal their secrets. She already fired the kid, but he'll be okay. I'm gonna need him to talk to Frenchie, get him formally questioned. It doesn't matter who gives you the information. Who's responsible for getting it. It only matters that you get it. I repeat Dad's mantra in my head.

The black truck returns and pulls into the driveway. No license plates. Three men, dressed in black, exit. They scan the street twice. The one next to the passenger's side door closest to the building spots me.

Six feet separate me from Giovanni. Nine from me and David. The Three pull masks down onto their faces. I don't need to be clairvoyant to know what's gonna happen next. They raise their guns . . .

I sprint and tackle Giovanni to the ground, covering her with my body as David is torn apart. His arms and legs performing a horrific dance of panic and agony before he collapses on the floor beside us. Giovanni wriggles beneath me. Her hand reaching out for David as another volley of gunfire erupts from outside. Shattered glass from the framed poster flies across the living room cutting my cheek. Giovanni frees herself from me and pulls David toward the kitchen. His body limp, head lolling from side to side.

"He's gone!" I drag her away from him. Her hands are stained with blood, but it's not her blood and that's all I care about.

We can't afford generosity or mercy. It is them or us.

It's quiet now. They're reloading. We head toward the kitchen until I catch a shadow slithering toward the back door where David let us in. Giovanni and I turn around and leave through the living room, running into the hall as the door of the apartment's front entrance rattles in its frame eight feet away. The unforgiving bang of the foyer echoes behind us. I stay on Giovanni's six. If anyone comes through the front, I'll get hit first. At the end of the hall, I yank open a door labeled Storage, then lock it, leading us downstairs. Giovanni tears away from me as boots stomp above us near David's apartment. I left his door open.

Damn it! Too many rookie mistakes. My SIG Sauer has all seventeen rounds. I gotta make them count. Keep us alive. Hudson's last memory of his mom will *not* be me pointing a gun in his face.

A smaller room to our left is separated by an archway leading to four cheaply assembled metal cages holding furniture, knickknacks, and clothing. A tool bench sits next to the last cage on the right.

I yank on each door and listen for The Three. "It's okay to be scared. I'm scared."

"I'm not scared," says Giovanni, walking to the tool bench, lifting a weighty, rusted pipe wrench.

"You're lying. Again. You can be angry *and* terrified."

"Fair, but you saw how I handled myself at Phoenix's. Now you wanna superhero yourself outta this alone?" she asks.

"You're not helping me." I try another door that mercifully opens. Footsteps draw closer. Gunfire hits the lock near the stairs.

I shove Giovanni into the musty-smelling closet. "Stay here. Be quiet."

"I can—"

"Surviving is the bravest thing you can do right now. If I don't make it back. Talk to Frenchie. Only him." I rip away the pipe wrench from her hands. "I'm gonna need this."

Giovanni grabs my hand and squeezes, then searches the floor and grabs a jagged piece of glass. I shut the door and position myself at the archway. I grip the pipe wrench instead of my gun. I need to drive the fight upstairs. One wrong ricochet could cost Giovanni her life. Rubber-soled boots on a damp concrete floor make a muted slap. I hear the click of a magazine being loaded into a gun. I'm weirdly grateful these assholes started shooting on the lawn. My ears would be useless if the fight started inside. One of The Three steps past the threshold before he's able to clear his corners. I raise the pipe wrench and bring it down like a lumberjack chopping firewood. He wails, the gun falling from his hands. He drops to his knees and I swing the pipe wrench, connecting with his back like Jackie Robinson hitting a home run.

The satisfying crunch of bones yields the same rush as last Saturday night with Emmett. This is self-defense. It's okay to feel good about this, right? I rip the mask from his face. Blood drips from his lips. Tan skin. Buzz-cut black hair. Earpiece. I snatch it and put it in, inserting it in my left ear.

"Dagget, target's down. You find the bitch peeking through the window?"

I drop the pipe wrench and keep my gun holstered. I grab Dagget's piece, a Heckler & Koch MP5A2, and strip him of his remaining five magazines. I leave Dagget's bulletproof vest on his widely muscled body. It won't provide me with much protection.

"Dagget? Sweep the third floor. Cops are 'bout five or six minutes out. Come in," orders a raspy voice.

Creeping upstairs, I nudge open the destroyed door, clearing my corners, and inch down the hall back to David's apartment. Crossing the threshold, the second of The Three stands over David, his body near the kitchen where Giovanni dragged him. A streaked trail of blood stains the floor. I struggle to keep down whatever's left in my stomach. I can shoot him in the back, can't I? He murdered David. He tried to kill me and Giovanni.

All's fair.

"Dagget's not answering," says Raspy Voice as he emerges from the kitchen. "I'm not waiting for 'im. Go get—" He locks eyes with me and the gun to his crony's back. He draws his weapon.

I fire mine. You miss a hundred percent of the shots you don't take. I miss five of the seven, but two hit the sonofabitch standing over David's body. One in the left shoulder. One in the right leg. My hands shake. Muffled siren blare invades my now-ringing ears. So much for taking the fight outside.

Raspy Voice tries to hook Sonofabitch's wounded left arm around his shoulders. Sonofabitch howls in pain.

Good.

Sweeping left to right, I shoot again, praying I hit something.

Nothing lands. Raspy Voice returns fire as I pull back. Shrapnel from the door frame slices my right leg. Spiky, lava-tipped agony radiates from my thigh to my calf. I still have five magazines left. Gripping the Heckler & Koch like a life preserver in a raging sea, I again wait for the shooting to cease. It does, or at least I hope it does, as I enter David's apartment. Sonofabitch, still curled on the ground, pushes Raspy Voice away from him. He sprints to the back door, where Giovanni and I entered twenty minutes ago.

Sonofabitch raises his gun, and I shoot first, one of my bullets clipping him in the neck. Sonofabitch's eyes grow wide in terror as his piece clatters to the floor. He clutches and presses down on his pale, torn flesh as hard as he can. His horrified ice-blue stare begins to dim. His grip loosens. His breathing slows.

I have no interest in watching a man's last moments. I also have no interest in helping him either. Bracing myself on the wall, I hobble down the hall and back downstairs to Giovanni. She's out of the closet, placing the pipe wrench back on the tool bench.

"I knew you'd be okay." She steals a glance at Dagget motionless on the floor. "Better they don't know what exactly took him down."

"Tampering with evidence?" I say, almost out of breath, adrenaline rapidly fading.

"You mean saving your ass." Giovanni offers her hand and hooks my arm around her neck, the same way Raspy Voice tried to do for Sonofabitch.

We exit the small room, Giovanni leads me to the left instead, a basement door opens into the backyard. My car is twenty feet away. "How'd you find—"

"Lived in an apartment like this with my mom. Figured it had the same kind of footprint."

We scan left to right, making sure no one witnesses us running for our lives from a crime scene. Less than forty-eight hours ago, I'd have instructed her to wait for the sirens. Talk to the detectives. Tell her side of the story. But what is there to tell?

I'm investigating a case as a suspended cop and I killed someone? Yes, in self-defense, but I broke a lotta laws in the process. Now's not the time for a debate about right and wrong, how laws meant to protect people sometimes prevent justice.

Giovanni digs in my pocket and takes out my car keys. I enter the passenger's side as blood now leaks from my leg onto the leather seats and the once clean floormat. She puts her hands on the steering wheel, ten-and-two, and drives out of the alley, in the opposite direction of the patrol units gathering in front of the building.

"What now?" she asks.

"David gave us a starting point." I study people walking down the street, strangers to my pain, but intensely familiar with their own. "You know how to get to Black Oak, Illinois?"

CHAPTER 46

Giovanni

June 18, 2025

I wash David's and Redding's blood from my hands using lukewarm bottled water from the back of the Subaru. Cars rush past as I try to get myself together on the shoulder of the Edens Expressway.

Redding hobbles over with her phone and mine in her hand and hurls them at the concrete barriers. "Hurry up," she orders, returning to the car.

I flinch at the volume of her voice. She finishes wrapping gauze around her right upper thigh and swings her legs back into the passenger's side of the car. The bleeding has stopped.

Easing back onto the expressway, I drive but keep replaying how long I was on the floor as pierced flesh, shredded drywall, and shattered glass swirled around me. About two minutes. It took five seconds to know David was dead, but I still haven't accepted it.

"Sorry for rushing, but we couldn't stay on the shoulder too long. Trooper pulls up on us, it's over." Redding tosses her first aid kit to the back seat.

She grabs a flip phone from the glove box, dials a number, and puts it on speaker.

A weary voice answers. "Detective Webb."

"Frenchie—" begins Redding.

"All I wanna hear is that you're at home reading a book," says French. Someone barks orders in the background.

"For your sake, I'm at home reading a book," she says. "Where are you?"

"No need to yell, Red. Bad connection?"

"Yeah, yeah." Redding pulls at her ear and lowers her volume. "Heard there was a shooting near 77th and Ashland Avenue. One of Giovanni's employees might be a victim."

"There was and he is. David Embark, the server with the cookies. Thought this might have something to do with Natalie's case since he worked at The Ivory. Homicide's saying it's gang related."

I check the rearview before swerving into the left lane. "David wasn't in a gang."

"Giovanni is reading with you, huh?"

"Yep, we got our own little book club." Redding shoots me an exhausted but furious look.

I can't let that cop talk about someone he didn't know. They'll entomb his apartment in yellow and black tape and rush to a conclusion about David that isn't justified or true because of his neighborhood and skin color. He was a good person who made bad choices like everyone else. But he was ambitious and funny and, when he got out of his own way, wise beyond his years.

"Look, Frenchie, I'm going to assume you found a couple other men there. Caucasian. Early thirties. That sound like a gang hit to you?" asks Redding.

"Dammit, Red. How did . . ." Frenchie says nothing for a few seconds. "There was one deceased Caucasian male found at the scene with David. Do I think it's a gang hit? No, but nothing is what it's supposed to be in this case. That probably includes your friend."

I change lanes and accelerate. The outline of skyscrapers once clear and commanding now appear faint and ghostly.

"Look, I'm gonna get back to reading with Giovanni."

"It's not my scene, but I'll keep my ears open. Keep . . . reading." French hangs up.

"This was set up to look like a gang hit. Reckless by approaching the front and shooting at the windows, but they were expecting David to be home alone. The guy downstairs, Dagget. His hair was buzz-cut. Those dudes were military trained. And close." Redding rubs her wounded thigh. "What South Side Chi Town gangster is taken out by a trio of white hit men?"

Bravado slides off me like wet paint on a canvas. I don't have an answer to Redding's question, even if it was rhetorical. I read the road and highway signs, mouthing them, giving my brain something to focus on other than flying bullets, dead bodies, and dank storage closets.

We cruise by hastily constructed homes in clashing architectural styles nestled in gated subdivisions and separated by sprawling acres of yet undeveloped land with portraits and promises of more McMansions to come. Many of The Ivory's guests hail from Black Oak, Illinois, and other suburbs like it.

I head toward the west end of Black Oak until Delbrook Lane comes upon me suddenly. The street sign is almost hidden by a tree branch. I turn left into an overgrown driveway that stops at a twenty-foot-high ornate black wrought iron gate.

The large brown brick house David described is behind the gate at least ten yards away.

Redding grimaces as she exits the car. "Guess we gotta hoof it and find a way around."

"How's your leg?"

"I can put pressure on it. It's just sore. My ears are still screwed up from earlier. Movies never talk about how gunfire makes you damn near deaf for hours."

"Yeah, don't ask me. My references include *Point Break*, *Face/Off*, and *Bad Boys*."

Redding chuckles. "Those are good movies though."

"A 1990s Keanu Reeves, yeah. I'm always down."

Redding stops and looks behind us for a moment, then observes our path going forward. She signals it's okay to continue. "You ever gonna tell me what happened between you and Natalie?"

I brace myself on a tree. "That won't help us."

"Let me determine that," says Redding. "It'll at least take my mind off this case and stuff I got going on at home."

"With more trauma?"

"I'd like to reflect on someone else's for a bit," she says.

We've fought each other. We've fought others. She's saved my life. I've been through more with her in the past few days than anyone. I owe it to Redding to tell her the whole story. And though I don't see how this will help her find Natalie any quicker, it will help me to share my pain instead of letting it rot me from the inside out.

I take a deep breath.

"Nat was dating her art history professor. I saw his texts to her. She started becoming secretive about where she was going. We stopped hanging out as much. Stopped hanging out at all, really. She was getting flowers and gifts delivered to our apartment. And I know how this looks. I wasn't jealous. I was . . . worried she was gonna get herself into a situation she wouldn't be able to get herself out of. Her parents had died, like, only nine months ago at that point. And I could see the train wreck coming."

Redding says nothing. Only the crunch of her boots over dirt and twigs lets me know she's here. I allow the lilac and coral bands of the evening sky to guide me through the small forest toward the rear of this estate.

"If you had the ability to stop something bad from happening to someone you love, you'd do it, right? Anyways, I followed Nat around, took pics of her and the professor. Went to the Title IX coordinator and the department chair. Thought it'd be anonymous."

The apparitional shape of a house appears ahead. We're close to getting answers or ending up where we started. I finish my confession to Redding, my temporary priest. I'm not even Catholic.

"We were at a party. Natalie came up and slapped me. I slapped her back. And then we stopped slapping and started hitting and punching and scratching. I said some venomous stuff. Her too. Mostly . . . I remember being on top of her and my hands were around her neck."

A scurrying field mouse darts from our path. In that moment, I got how people can kill someone they love. All the big and small things I let slide before with Natalie came together and I just squeezed.

"Took three or four people to break us up. By that time Nat was crying. Said that the professor loved her. I didn't understand why she couldn't see he was using her, weaponizing her loss. He left Nat a couple weeks later when she found out she was pregnant. Said he was going to Ibiza to study contemporary art.

"Nat wanted to re-create the family she lost. A first-year psychology student could see that. She thought it was love. She wanted so badly for it to be love. And it wasn't. I was right. And I still lost her." I stop and stare skyward. "After he left, she called me, and I drove her to . . . Well, I drove her. We graduated a week later. Didn't speak after that."

"Until last Thursday," adds Redding.

"Yeah." I continue walking.

Why keep secrets from me? Secrets, keeping them, is what I do. Fixing things. Arranging things. I learned how to do it for Natalie. She was The Ivory before The Ivory. Why couldn't I make her happy enough to stay with me?

"Don't move another muscle," growls a voice to our left. The clear click of a gun putting the period on the end of his order. Shadows slowly give way to the familiar outline. Beneath the wrinkled clothes and unshaven face, he remains just as aloof and curt as the day he stepped foot in The Ivory.

Fleur Winstead holds his weapon pointed directly at us.

Redding slowly pulls her hand up to her right side.

"Ah, ah, don't do that. I'll kill her. Then, I'll kill you and leave your bodies for the critters."

I slowly raise my hands. It's hard to catch my breath.

Fleur motions with his gun for us to walk ahead of him. As he steps backward to let us pass, he trips, tumbling onto his side. I dive for the gun held at my chest moments ago. Fleur scrambles on top. His weight pressing me into the ground. I push up on my right hand and jab my left elbow backward, the slight vibration in my bone and Fleur's pained grunt confirming I connected.

I can hear Redding shuffling to reach us both. I grab at grass and dirt and wet and squishy things I don't want to think about. I just want that gun. Is this what he made Natalie feel? Did she beg him to spare her? I still feel the stickiness of David's blood on my hands. It makes it a little hard to close my fingers as I clasp the gun, swing around, and point it at Fleur.

Both of us out of breath, but now only one of us scared.

"Get up." I don't recognize my own voice. Frenzied. Rage-filled. I check the safety. It's off. Fleur doesn't move, staying huddled beside Redding.

I grab him by his collar. "I said get up. Get the hell up!"

Redding eyes me. "Giovanni . . ."

"I'm not gonna kill him." I don't believe my words. I don't know if Redding believes me either, but she doesn't move to take the gun away.

I motion with the gun the same way Fleur did minutes ago. "Take us to wherever you . . . left Natalie."

He stands and dusts off his already dirty clothes, but he doesn't walk. I press the barrel to the middle of his chest. "Take. Us. Now!"

He plods in front of us. Sure of his steps but reluctant in every movement. Did Natalie suffer? Where did he bury her? What did she think about before . . . Before?

In a paltry clearing sits a one-story guest house. Unlit. Uncared for. Broken panes of glass on the front and sides. A worn cedar roof. Peeling paint. And . . . a smell—pungent, tangy, rancid. Death. Fleur walks to the cabin and unlocks the door.

My finger hooks around the trigger. No one would hear it. Redding is just as deep as I am in this—would she tell anyone what happened? One less monster in the world . . .

I lift the gun to his back. I see Fleur's end. I see my justice. I see . . .

Natalie.

CHAPTER 47

Giovanni

June 18, 2025

In the past few days, I've been prepared to kill and die more than once. I've unearthed parts of myself I didn't know, or believe, existed. All of it for Natalie who stands before me—alive, exhausted, still beautiful. I lower the gun as Fleur steps in the cabin. Redding now stands at my side. Her mouth open, head tilted. Like me. Folie à deux. We're sharing the same delusion.

Aren't we?

Natalie emerges from the cabin and touches my hand, the one not gripping the gun, and leads me inside. Her skin is warm. Her grasp is firm, but there are cuts on her left arm. She smells of soap and citrus. Redding follows us. The stench of death still slaps me in the face as we enter the cabin.

Natalie blocks the smell with her free hand. "A coyote killed a deer just past the trees. Happened the first night I got here. Thought it was some kind of omen."

"How *did* you get here? You didn't come with Fleur," says Redding.

"Told her to take a cab. Gave her cash," says Fleur. He sits down at a table near the barely functioning kitchen. "Paid the boy. He told me he'd take care of the cameras."

"The driver dropped me off a few blocks from the house. Fleur made me memorize how to get the rest of the way," says Natalie.

Redding closes the door behind us. I'm still holding Natalie's hand.

Why the hell am I still holding Natalie's hand? Why haven't I yelled at her? Slapped her in anger? Cried in relief? Why am I . . . numb?

There was an optional seminar held at The Ivory about a year ago. It was called *Inspiring Women to Advocate for Themselves.* The speaker talked about how it's okay to voice your disappointment and anger when you've been wronged by another person. She didn't mention how to voice anger and disappointment if someone faked a disappearance that led you to become a suspect in a police investigation. She also didn't mention what to do when you confront that person and have a gun.

And the safety's off.

"I'm so sorry, Gio," says Natalie, her breath shaky.

I snatch my hand away from hers. "You vanished and *everyone* started looking at me. Your followers, your rivals, my coworkers. I don't even know if I have a job anymore and . . . my mom . . ." I search for the words about Momma. They won't come and I can't share that with Natalie or Fleur. I point to Redding. "She and her partner thought I hurt you . . . and worse."

"Being a bit dramatic, aren't we, dear?" Fleur flexes his trembling left hand as he pulls a small gray case toward him. He takes out six prescription pill bottles. "And had you kept your temper in check at dinner, you wouldn't have served yourself up on a silver platter as a suspect."

"Excuse me?"

Redding grabs my arm before I close the distance between Fleur and me.

"Nothing about this is dramatic. You wouldn't be hiding if it was. And you're right to hide 'cause whoever is chasing you is chasing us now." I turn to Natalie. "And they got to Phoenix. She's dead."

"Wh-what?"

"There hasn't been an official cause, but it looks suspicious, at least to me," says Redding.

Natalie stares at her feet as if they're the most interesting objects on earth. "I didn't mean for anything like this to happen. I know it's a cliché, but that doesn't make it less true."

"Your husband's worried about you," says Redding, turning to Natalie.

"Bale grabbed me off the street to get answers," I add, finally switching on the safety and tucking the gun into my back. "I kicked his ass, too."

Natalie's eyes stretch, puffy, red, and devoid of mascara. "He did what?"

"Last I checked, he's awaiting an arraignment," says Redding.

I step closer to Natalie and stumble over an uneven floorboard. She reaches out to steady me. I let her. "You left him for Denzel Washington–lite. What's he supposed to do?"

"I didn't—"

"He's worried about you . . . and the baby," interrupts Redding.

Natalie sits beside Fleur. They look at one another debating if they can tell us the truth. Figuring out if we'll believe them. Because whatever it is that drove them to fake a disappearance and hide out in a broken-down guest house will stretch the belief of the closest confidant or kin, never mind an estranged friend and a suspended cop.

Natalie adjusts her off-the-shoulder mint-green shirt. "Phoenix came to me with an idea of starting our own makeup line, Amour Noir Beauty. I mean, the market is saturated, but not for Black makeup products. I thought that with my following and sponsorships, it'd be easy, well, easier." Natalie swipes her hand across her neck. "Securing capital for a business is hard enough. Securing capital for a Black woman–led business is damn near impossible. Now it's easier to openly declare war against anything that doesn't directly center whiteness.

"We were . . . desperate. Truly. And I didn't want to give up. You know, once I get my mind set on something . . ." Natalie raises her head, searching my face for understanding. I don't know what she finds in my face, but she returns her gaze back to the termite-eaten floorboards. "Anyway, Phoenix heard about the D.A.R.E. grant program. I didn't wanna get involved in anything close to the governor, but Phoenix said it was our last option. She said it was best I go to the interview by myself. So I did, like, two weeks ago. Met Julien Whitlock. At first, he seemed nice, a little flirty, but nothing I couldn't handle. Least I thought so. He wanted to do the interview at a gallery in Hyde Park. Fancy French name," she says.

"L'Atelier Rouge." Redding and I utter the name at the same time.

"He took me to the north wing to show me some art. I kept a distance but everywhere I went, he was there. Trying to kiss my neck, touch my body. '*We got plenty of money. Name a price.*' Like I was fine being bought and sold."

I try to quiet my breaths. But I'm back there. Julien's loud cologne. Rough hands. His weight pressing against me. A scream trapped in my throat. I swallow it, bury it. I'm not there anymore.

Natalie continues, "I told him I had to use the bathroom. I

tried to make it sound flirtatious. Didn't want him to get mad. You know how we do."

Fleur tilts his head. People with power never recognize the powerless. He doesn't understand "how women do" to keep safe if we don't want to engage with a man who's pushing himself on us. Fleur can't fathom the anxiety we feel. Or the danger we put ourselves in.

Saying no can kill us.

"I left the north wing, made a right, looking for an exit that wasn't locked. I heard footsteps. Julien's voice." Natalie wrings her hands. "Tried a couple of doorknobs until I saw a cleaning lady leave an office to get something. Ran inside and hid in the closet. Smelled like flowers and old blood."

"Do you remember anything else about the office, the closet?" asks Redding, massaging her leg.

Natalie wipes away tears. "Umm . . . I leaned against the back of the closet to rest, but it didn't feel . . . solid. There was a false panel or wall or whatever. When I moved it, there was an opening to another room and a small staircase on the left. I thought the staircase was another way out of the building. But it led to a concrete room that had . . . pictures. Of me." She begins to rock back and forth. "Leg chains bolted to the wall." Natalie clasps her hand over her mouth, muffling her sobs.

"How'd you escape?" I ask.

"Went back the way I came. One of the custodians let me out. She wasn't surprised. I wasn't the only woman she'd had to sneak out of the gallery." Natalie wipes her face with both hands. Her rocking slows. "After that, I backed out of the deal. Phoenix was . . . pissed is an understatement. Enraged is a better description." Fresh tears spring from Natalie's eyes.

"I get not telling Phoenix about what you saw, but why not tell your husband?" asks Redding.

"What was I supposed to tell Ronan?" she counters. "What I saw was evil. It was death. I knew that. But . . . I didn't want people I knew or people I loved to be touched by it."

I pivot to Fleur. "Why did you help? Some guys wouldn't think of doing this for their wives, let alone a girlfriend."

"Fathers always help their children," he answers.

CHAPTER 48

Redding

June 18, 2025

"You said what now?" I take a step closer to Fleur, keeping my weight on my left leg.

This case is a riptide. It will pull you under with every twisty current of secrets and you may never resurface. I take them in, noticing that Natalie and Fleur have the same lips and eye shape, but there isn't a striking resemblance. Dad and I looked alike. Most people called me his twin. I never knew if they were just being nice or if they didn't know who else to compare me to since Mom left us.

Giovanni waves her hand as if she can swat away Fleur's words. "Nat's dad is dead. Killed in a car crash with her mom."

"My stepfather died," whispers Natalie. "Fleur is my bio dad."

"You never mentioned—" she says, sitting down.

"There was never a need to. Fleur left me and Mom when I was a baby. When he tried to get in contact a couple years ago, I ignored him until this mess with Julien," says Natalie. "He's the governor's chief of staff so . . ."

Natalie leaves us to fill in the blanks of her motivation. She didn't use Fleur to get into the D.A.R.E. program, she used him to free herself from Julien's grasp. She'd never asked for anything from him before. She was owed.

Fleur takes the regiment of pills sprawled out before him on the table, then flexes his left hand a few times but the tremors still course through him. He places his hand on his lap under the table. "Well, I'm currently on a leave of absence."

Giovanni leans forward in her chair. "And why is that?"

"They found out you were sick?" I say pointing to his now hidden hand.

"Hartwell couldn't care less about illness as long as I continue to show myself useful." Fleur stands and carefully walks over to an old white refrigerator, its hum drowning out the cicadas. He grabs a bottled water. "Actually, after Natalie relayed recent events, I had a . . . chat with Julien." He tries to open the bottle.

I gently take the water from him, twist the cap, and hand it back. "This chat involve words and maybe a left hook?" I ask.

Fleur meets my eyes, a sly grin gracing his face. "Yes, it did. Hence, my leave of absence."

Giovanni rummages around in her pocket and hands me a crumpled dollar bill. I was right in who hit whom, but technically, neither of us were correct in what prompted Fleur to punch Julien.

I still take the dollar and shove it into my front pocket. "With all your connections, you couldn't find a better way?"

"My connections don't compare to Hartwell's," says Fleur.

"And I had a plan," interrupts Natalie. "But God must've been laughing his ass off when I made it. I . . . *we* were gonna show people who Julien really was, in a way the public couldn't ignore, and it would've ensured the governor couldn't save him." She bounces her knee, the floor creaks under the action. "After dinner with Gio, I was gonna 'bump into' Julien and ask him upstairs. Make it seem like I wanted to apologize for what happened at the gallery and get him to talk about it. I had everything set up to record him. I even took pictures of Julien to keep Fleur updated."

"I have a few trusted contacts in the press. The recording was going to them," adds Fleur.

"Then Julien would be ruined. Disgraced. Hopefully in jail once they found his hidden room at the gallery." Natalie shudders. "Out of our lives. Everyone would be safe."

My leg throbs. I search for a place to sit that won't require me needing a tetanus shot. "You should work for Disney. They're great with fairy tales, too."

Natalie glares at me. "I did what I thought was best. But Gio and I fought, and Julien saw me."

"So, at The Cathedral, you weren't just taking pretty pictures of your food or Bale?" asks Giovanni.

"Didn't even know my husband was there, crazy as it seems. I was only focused on doing what I needed to do."

"Which wasn't catching up with me." Giovanni crosses her arms as if shielding herself from the realization she's just spoken out loud.

Natalie rises from her chair and walks to Giovanni keeping a foot or two between them. "You weren't a prop. You were . . . *are* my friend."

Giovanni doesn't make a move to hug or hit Natalie. "What happened after you went upstairs? I deserve to know everything. Every damn thing."

"There was a knock on the door. Thought it was Fleur." Natalie hugs herself. "There was . . . an arm and a can of mace or pepper spray. I couldn't see. Someone put their hand over my mouth. I tasted leather. We crashed into a table." She gestures to the abstract pattern of cuts on her left arm. "But Fleur came back. Scared the guy off."

"Julien?" I ask.

"Don't know. He was covered head to toe. Black everything. Gloves. One of those balaclavas covering the face. Blew past me. Couldn't chase him," says Fleur.

"What about Phoenix?" I ask.

"What about her?" He takes a sip of water.

"She was making a lot of noise on social media about Natalie, their failed business partnership."

"I was trying to save Phoenix. She is . . . she *was* a pain in the ass, but I didn't wanna see her hurt," says Natalie. "All that and I still couldn't save her."

I lean on the table to take some weight off my leg. "Your story—"

"It's the truth," whispers Natalie.

The flip phone in my pocket gently smacks against my right thigh as it throbs. "Well, your . . . account of what happened is compelling, but there are holes. From how you tell it, we should've only found a broken table, but the room was trashed and—"

"To play up the scene for dramatic effect. I knocked over some furniture, smashed the vase and . . ." Fleur raises the sleeve of his shirt, though the bandage is tightly wrapped around his forearm, small pools of blood seep through. "Cut myself trying to fight off the bastard who attacked Natalie, but it takes months to get back DNA results, and I'd probably be dead by then anyway." He shrugs matter-of-factly.

"My boss put a rush on the DNA. Didn't take our forensics team long to figure out it was you . . . so if we know, then bet your ass Governor Whitlock probably knows now, too," I say. No fear behind my voice. That'll come later. Not now.

"Why'd your long-lost dad buy an orchid?" asks Giovanni.

Fleur leans forward in his chair. "Why do you think? It'll tie Julien to those other disappearances."

I move toward Fleur. "What disappearances?"

He raises his eyebrow. "You know what I'm talking about. How do you think I know about the orchids? Unless I was there." He rolls down his sleeve. "And considering my diagnosis two years ago, I can guarantee I was not."

"How'd you know *I* was investigating? I didn't make a lot of noise."

"You made enough," says Fleur. "Hartwell had me prepare a file."

"On me? My family?"

He nods.

This is the point I'd have told a lawyer that I blacked out. I didn't remember what happened next. And I'd be lying. The numbness is retreating and in its place erupts a blinding, reckless rage.

I grab Fleur by his collar. I jerk him back and forth. I don't care he's sick and I don't care if I'm making it worse. All the questions and late nights and anxiety, the fights with Emmett, missed opportunities with Hudson, the self-hatred are boiled down into one question I can't help but repeat.

"Why?"

Natalie and Giovanni pry my hands off Fleur. I wrench myself from their grasp and walk to the grime-caked window allowing a paltry shard of moonlight to brighten the floorboards below.

"If you know who's responsible, why're you saying something now? If you could've stopped this years ago, why didn't you?" I study the meadow outside. My voice begins to crack. "There are some secrets we don't get to keep."

"Is this the part where I'm supposed to feel guilt for my

decisions, Detective? The world is as deep and dark as you think it is. Even darker. And that is where real power resides. There is no guilt. There is no love. There is only action, success, and power."

"You didn't leave a line of poetry behind. Least I haven't found it yet. If you wanted to imitate Julien, why not leave that behind, too?"

He shrugs. "Didn't know about that detail, Detective. I use what I know. It's gotten me this far."

I turn around and face Fleur. "All that maneuvering and you didn't think about usurping the governor? Using his secrets to put you on top? That either makes you stupid or a coward. Which one?"

Fleur flexes his jaw, then smiles. Wolves baring their teeth look more welcoming. "Playing bad cop, Detective? What a feeble approach. But to answer your trite question, I'd only heard snippets of conversations. About Julien. About other things. Snippets and suspicions aren't tangible proof. You wanna know about tangible proof." Fleur brings out his phone, types on it, and shows me an account with over $14 million and another account with $12 million. "My bank accounts in the Cayman Islands and Belize, that's tangible. What I did for Natalie isn't about love. It's about legacy."

Natalie flinches at Fleur's last statement. She may try to remain aloof in their arrangement, but she wants what every daughter wants at many points in their lives—a dad who loves and accepts them. She has neither.

She has Fleur.

The faintest glimmer of empathy crosses Giovanni's face, but she makes no move to comfort Natalie.

Fleur continues, "I don't truly know if Julien's responsible for the disappearances. If he is, then he'll finally pay for what he did. If it isn't him, he'll still pay for the other awful things he's done. Karma. She comes for us all." Fleur finishes the last of his water, then takes his pill bottles and shoves them into the gray case.

"But if it isn't Julien—" says Giovanni.

"It's Julien," says Natalie. "I know what I saw."

"Natalie's alive. Maybe the others are, too." My fingers are wet. Blood from my injury.

Nivea, Stacey, Annette, Olivia, and Mia.

"Doubt it," says Fleur.

"Nobody asked you," I shoot back.

I grab an abandoned chair by the hallway, drag it to the head of the table, and sit. "Listen, the only way to take Julien down is publicly. Not a secret recording. Everybody's gotta see it, like the gala on Friday. Problem is Julien doesn't trust any of us. We've all burned our bridges with him."

Natalie raises her hand as if I'm holding a class. "As far as Julien knows I'm sorry for everything. I could reach out. Ask if we can still meet."

Giovanni folds her arms. "Yes, and he might promptly try to kill you. Again."

"All the more reason to use me as bait," counters Natalie. "Maybe he won't be able to help himself if he thinks we're alone." She touches her stomach. "I can't hide forever with Fleur. I need a way out. We all do."

It's quiet in the cabin. Chittering and howling are the only communication outside. The low wattage bulb flickers then holds steady, creating stretched shadows on the stained shiplap walls. Tenuous threads of trust and shared hatred are the only bonds connecting us, and the more I focus on my dislike of Fleur, the greater my anger, and the chance for us to put away a predator decreases. I have to grit my teeth and work with this man. But we can't formulate any plans without a safe place and some time to rest.

I push away from the table and stand. "I got somewhere else we could stay."

"I'm assuming it's safe," says Fleur.

I don't look at him. "It'd be the last place I'd search."

Giovanni grabs the keys from my pocket without permission. "Where to?"

June 19, 2025

I knock again just as the porch lights switch on. I shield myself from the sudden onslaught of light like a vampire during sunrise. Luckily, no one is roaming this block of Hyde Park near three in the morning. Locks are disengaged. The door opens . . .

"Need a favor." I don't recognize the sheepishness in my tone.

Baltimore looks past me, taking in Giovanni, Natalie, and Fleur. "Nah, Red. You need a damn miracle."

CHAPTER 49

Redding

June 19, 2025

Baltimore trudges up the stairs and puts five manilla folders in my hand along with my set of house keys. I catch my notepad as it falls out of the first folder.

"Thanks." I nod and yawn, clutching the folders to me as we enter B's home.

A car rumbles down South Harper Avenue. Baltimore and I both watch until it disappears from the block. My car is in his garage, but paranoia is warranted. I can't "put nothing past nobody," as Dad would say. The Whitlocks are powerful. I am not. But I'm smart when I get out of my own way.

"Before you ask, I wasn't followed."

"Either way, it'll all be done one way or another tomorrow." I clutch the burner phone in my pocket. Should I call Emmett?

No. If I tell him where I am and what has happened, I can guarantee that he'll stay in Georgia with Hudson.

Baltimore engages every lock, then tugs and twists on the doorknob to make sure we're secure. In the living room, I place the files on the table across from a sleeping Fleur, hunkered down on an expensive-looking cobalt-blue couch. Giovanni and Natalie sleep upstairs directly above.

Baltimore plods to the partially open kitchen and pours himself some coffee. He sets a mug in front of me. "I went through the back door, like you asked, but . . . what the hell happened at your house, Red?"

"An accident." I offer nothing else.

"If you say so."

"I do." I reach for the sugar.

"Hudson and Emmett, safe?" he asks.

"Mmm-hmm." My stomach cramps sharply. "You angry?"

"Do I like putting my ass and my pension on the line? Hell no, but I figured something like this might happen." He grabs coffee creamer from the refrigerator. "You don't listen to anybody. You're gonna do what you need to do. Like your old man."

I say nothing but wear Baltimore's last words like a suit of armor. If I have to be like anyone right now, I'd rather be like my father. Then I can push myself to do what's needed—and live with the outcome no matter what.

I sip my coffee. Too sweet. Emmett would've made it just right. I blink away tears as a rustle of paper interrupts the silence of the early morning. I set down the mug and round the half wall separating the kitchen from the living room to catch Fleur rifling through the files.

My files.

"You were asleep." I snatch the folders from him.

"Was I now?" A smug grin crosses his lips. "I don't remember Hartwell mentioning these names: Nivea, Stacey, Annette, Olivia . . . Mia."

Fleur sits up in a fresh set of clothes, newly showered, smelling of narcissism and cocoa butter. I open each folder, making sure they're still in order. The last folder holds a picture of Olivia's smiling face, full cheeks with dimples on each side beaming at me from behind a sewing machine. Besides their skin color, the orchid, and the poetry, what concrete evidence links them? What can I prove? How can I tie these lives to Julien, and, if necessary, their deaths?

I pluck pictures of Nivea, Stacey, Annette, Olivia, and Mia from the files and lay them on the table in front of Fleur. "Did you ever see Julien with *any* of these women?"

His sharkish eyes scan the photos in seconds. He shakes his head. "Don't remember their faces."

"The D.A.R.E. program, what do you know about it?"

"Not much. Kept my distance from it *and* Julien long before this situation with Natalie. Hartwell started the whole thing to give his son something to do besides get in trouble. He was always trying to make that boy something he wasn't."

"A politician?"

Fleur scoffs. "No. *Him*. Hartwell wanted Julien to be a better version of him. But Julien couldn't even be a better version of Julien."

Is Fleur really judging someone for their shortcomings?

He taps his fingers against his jawline. "If those girls were D.A.R.E. recipients, they should've been invited to the party. Hartwell wanted this year's grant winners at his big bash. Show them off, garner goodwill with Black voters." He theatrically gestures his hand in the air. "Hartwell doesn't care about the inner city or the burbs. They're props. He's using them for re-election to garner whatever portion of the Black vote he can get. Prove that he still knows where he comes from."

Nivea participated in the D.A.R.E. program but she disappeared before the face-to-face interview. Charlotte told me she went in her place and wasn't awarded the grant. I reach back in my mind to remember what else Charlotte told me. I flip through my green notepad. My observations, thoughts, and an underlined phrase: grant website.

"Baby, you can look up who's awarded grants online. It's a law. Type the name of the grant and it lists the organizations that got the money."

Charlotte's words, barbwire sharp, tear through my memory. I shove Fleur over as I flop on the couch and pull out my phone, Googling "Illinois grant recipients." Natalie applied for the D.A.R.E. grant. Charlotte said Nivea applied but disappeared before her interview. Results populate with websites tracking grant awards and their recipients. I scroll through the results. Fleur's finger shoots in front of me.

"That one. The DCEO website—"

"The . . . what?" I angle my phone away from him.

"The Illinois Department of Commerce and Economic Opportunity. They're responsible for grants, which probably includes the D.A.R.E. program. Lonnie, the director, makes sure his department keeps track of everything. Has a stick so far up his ass I think he might be part oak tree." He laughs at his own joke.

I almost thank him, but he doesn't deserve gratitude. All the trouble and confusion and heartache he's caused, this is his reasonable service. I scroll to the bottom of the page, click on the "Award Grants" link, and type "D.A.R.E. to Dream" in the search bar.

No Results.

I type "Diversity Application Resource and Engagement."

Nothing.

I turn to Fleur. "Maybe Lonnie is trying to cover the governor's tracks, too. Can't find anything on D.A.R.E."

Fleur sucks his teeth. "Try the organization applying for the money."

I grab Olivia's file and scan information I've read hundreds of times. She oversaw the Englewood Design Alliance in South Shore. Mia worked at Afya Wellness in Bronzeville. Stacey taught at Septima Clark Elementary School in Auburn Gresham.

I search again and filter using the year 2024. Englewood Design Alliance, Afya Wellness, and Septima Clark Elementary School. Here we go. Each of them recipients of a D.A.R.E. grant. The amounts vary between $1,500 to $10,000.

Is that what their lives were worth?

Fleur smiles wide. "There's your link. That's how Julien got to them. You've gotta love the illusion of transparency. You're told who received the money but none of what they had to do to get it."

I repeat Charlotte's words. "The dirty D.A.R.E. grant."

"That's an apt name."

I take my files and leave Fleur, walking into the den Baltimore transformed into a makeshift bedroom. The possible trail of destruction left by the D.A.R.E. program isn't limited to Nivea, Stacey, Annette, Olivia, and Mia. Or Natalie.

Peripheral links—the skinny punk in the apartment and Phoenix—are eliminated even on the slight chance they can be weaponized against him. Because finding the one he lost, through the missing, is the goal.

It is all that matters to him.

I grab my burner.

"Cook County Medical Examiner's Office. Dr. Shayla Ross speaking."

"Hey."

She yawns. "Shouldn't be talking to you, Stark."

"Haven't hung up though." I sit on the bed, steadying myself on the unusually soft sofa bed. "I only need to know about Deiserae Waters. Just the basics."

Silence.

"Hello?" I tighten my hold on the phone.

"Cause of death is an overdose. Fentanyl. But . . ." A muted clicking of Dr. Ross's keyboard fills the silence.

"But?" I clutch and twist the bed sheet with my free hand.

"I noticed petechial hemorrhaging in the eyes, which is consistent with some overdoses, but . . . there was a hairline nasal fracture."

"Phoenix made her money off her looks. She'd have complained about pain in her nose. Doctors probably would've noticed that," I say.

"Doctors don't catch everything," says Ross.

I let go of the bed sheet. "Someone could've held her, made her swallow something against her will. Put a hand over the nose and mouth. A little too much force could cause a fracture, right, Doc?"

"That's a plausible theory, I guess," she says.

Bale said he saw a muscular white guy leaving Phoenix's room before he found her dead. A guy who sounded like a three-pack-a-day smoker. Raspy Voice from David's apartment fits that description. He sneaks into Phoenix's room, holds her down, puts the pill in her mouth, then puts his hand over her nose and mouth to make her swallow. Used too much force, broke her nose.

"Anything else?"

"This is all you get from me, Stark. You want something else, you better seek Jesus. Not me."

"Understood. Thank—"

Dr. Ross ends the call.

"—you," I finish.

The sheets are soft and smell of detergent. I lie down and wrap myself like a burrito and sink into the bed, closing my eyes. All I see are Emmett and Hudson. My throat begins to burn. My eyes begin to sting. So, I open them. A desk sits across from the unused slate fireplace. Pens, paper, and envelopes neatly arranged on top. I unwrap myself from the sheets and get up.

I write.

To Emmett.

To Hudson.

I lay out my love and my apologies. My hopes. Our memories. My goodbyes. My tears stain the paper, creating small ripples on the surface. They'll dry by the time Emmett and Hudson read their letters. If they read them.

If I die.

I'll probably die. And I can never say everything, but I can say something, let them know that though I gave my all to be a detective, I loved them more. I wanted to make our city, our world, safer. For us.

Baltimore is heating up food when I reenter the kitchen.

"Thought you were going to bed," he says. "More coffee?"

I glance at the cerulean base of the horizon inching up to claim the muted stars. I place both letters in front of him. "If anything happens—"

He sets down the coffeepot. "Red—"

"If anything happens," I begin again, "give these to Emmett and Hudson. I know I've asked a lot of you, but this is the last thing."

Baltimore hugs me, slightly wrinkling the envelopes between our bodies.

"It's gonna be okay. One way or another," I mumble.

He lets go. "I know."

Baltimore takes the letters, his face somber. "Red, can you promise me you'll do everything you can to make it out? Alive. You don't have to become a martyr."

"I promise. I wanna at least live to see Markham eat his own words."

"That's definitely something to live for," says Baltimore.

CHAPTER 50

Giovanni

June 19, 2025

"I can hear you thinking," says Natalie, her body turned toward the wall.

I'm angry with Natalie, jealous of her, and happy for her. All at once.

"You think about our time together?" I ask.

"A lot more now, yeah." Natalie hasn't turned to face me. "I think about that slap mostly."

I wince at the memory. Bitterly regretting my lack of self-control. "I'm sorry about that night . . . truly."

"Compared to what I've done, and what you've gone through because of it, we're even. More than even."

I take a beat to gather my thoughts. "The night of our fight . . . my mom died, but I pushed it down, forgot it, denied it the days after you went missing. I buried my trauma to find you."

Natalie turns to me. "Oh my God." She grabs my hand and squeezes it. Tears dance at the edges of her eyes.

Late night confessions are ones where you can free yourself, in the peace of darkness, when your words are no longer anchored by what you fear to say in the sunlight.

"Somewhere deep down you loved me. And you do, or did, but not the way I loved you." My hand cramps but I don't let go of Natalie.

"Gio, I love you. I do." Natalie sniffles. "But the way you love is . . . suffocating. You can be . . . I don't always feel joy at love. Sometimes I feel burdened by it."

I pull my hand away. "You think love is an obligation, but it's an imperfect act." I interlace my fingers and rest my hands on my heart.

Natalie sits up, drawing her knees to her chest. "You . . . you wanted *me* to see you. What you'd do for me even at the sacrifice of yourself. Like at the talent show. Or the dinner at The Cathedral."

"Something like that." My voice cracks. "You didn't ask me to love you as deeply as I did. But you used my love. And I used you to feel like . . . like I mattered."

"I see you, Gio. I do." Natalie lies back down. "That's why I'm putting myself in front of Julien. To protect you. Me. All of us."

"I don't need protection, Nat. Our . . . bond, our sisterhood, it can be powerful, but it can be destructive. We're like the elements, you and me."

Soft and steady air blows through the vertical vent on the right wall. I pull hanging covers over my rapidly chilling body. I've said what I needed. I'm lighter. My body is cradled in the bed I share with her. A tree branch taps on the bedroom window. And I hum the first and only song I sang on stage.

"Whatever I Am, You Made Me."

But I am remaking me. Stripping myself of what I wanted to be for others. I am what I am for myself.

And I'll learn to make that good enough.

CHAPTER 51

Giovanni

June 20, 2025

We keep Natalie in front of us as we walk down the alleyway toward The Ivory. Redding and I aren't letting her out of our sight.

I'm not relieved to find her. I'm still confused, mad, happy, and scared. Really scared. I should've said no when Natalie invited me to dinner a week ago. But regret solves nothing. Redding looks down at her burner phone and frowns.

"What?"

"Frenchie just texted. Bale's getting arraigned today. And you were right. David had no known gang affiliations." She runs her hand down her face. "Markham's putting a rush on the DNA for David's apartment. My blood, our fingerprints, it's all there. We gotta pin this on Julien, get all roads to lead to him, or we're done. Charges, jail, who knows."

I pat the sweat from my forehead as I walk up three stairs and swipe my card to access the Back Entry. A beep pierces the alleyway. A red light flashes. "What the hell?" I swipe my badge a second time. The door to the Back Entry remains locked.

Trucks full of linens and flowers and food are parked at the freight entrance seven feet away. Servers and hotel employees rush back and forth for Governor Whitlock's gala. They tightly smile, lips ready to only speak a few phrases: "How may I be of assistance?" "Yes ma'am," "Yes, sir."

I return the tight smiles. Heat rushes to my cheeks.

"You good?" asks Redding at the bottom of the stairs. She clocks the movement behind us.

I swipe my badge again. Beep. Red light. "We're gonna have to find another way in."

"Let's go through the front," suggests Natalie behind me. She smooths the back of her sculpted updo. The edges of her hair twisted back revealing a simple elegant pair of small hoop earrings.

"Nah, security," says Redding from the bottom step, massaging her right leg. "And after I knocked Julien on his ass, I'm sure his detail will remember me and Giovanni."

"This plan depends on Natalie getting into the gala, getting a public confession from Julien, then all of us leaving. Alive."

"We gotta get in first, Gio," says Natalie.

I think of David cleaning an apple on his vest. I rub my badge on my pants. Swallow the lump in my throat and swipe again.

Red light. Beep. Dammit!

A rush of cool air embraces me on the small landing. Ms. Evon steps back and tilts her head, her body keeping the back door propped open. She hugs me. "I'm so sorry to hear about Diedre."

"Well, y'know, figured Momma wouldn't want me avoiding my responsibilities." I release Ms. Evon and hold the door. "Besides, being here will take my mind off things."

It's some version of the truth. I need a little honesty to make my lies believable.

Ms. Evon makes her way down the stairs past Natalie and Redding. She takes them in but only utters a politely weary hello, then trudges toward State Street. We stay to our left in the Back Entry's winding tributary of bodies and duty. Mecca peeks out and waves us inside her office. On her couch are two suits, the spare from my office and one from my apartment. Redding will have to be okay with some extra room. I grab the suit on the left and begin dressing. None of us so much as blush at the shedding of clothes and temporal bare skin. Modesty is the least of anyone's concern.

"My badge didn't work." I button my blouse then grab my keys from Mecca's desk.

Mecca opens her middle desk drawer, pulls out a work badge, and slams the drawer shut. "Willa's been telling everyone you're taking a temporary leave of absence. Checked NexusLuxury. Your name's already grayed out."

"Temporary." I scoff. "Wonder who she's making do her paperwork."

But revenge on Willa isn't the priority. It's getting Natalie past security and into the presence of Julien while Redding and I remain as backup.

Natalie looks up from her phone. "Fleur's set. He'll wait for one of us to call by midnight. If he doesn't hear anything, he'll call Detective Stark's partner."

"Hopefully, Frenchie won't be comatose from Pequod's Pizza or Al's Italian Beef," jokes Redding, slipping into a pair of low-slung black heels. She puts on her holster, slides her gun inside, and adjusts her jacket.

We half-heartedly laugh, grasping at anything to alleviate the anxiety, tension, and fear weighing down the air. I could lose my freedom. I could die. But worse than that is doing nothing and letting another Black woman disappear at Julien's hands.

Mecca hands the work badge to Redding. "This should get you most places you need to go. Make sure I get it back."

"Yes ma'am," says Redding.

Natalie tugs at the waist of her recently delivered azure-colored strapless ruffle ball gown. "I should've gone up a size."

"You look fine." I walk to the door and open it.

Mecca clutches me to her for a minute before letting go.

I look to Nat and Redding. "Let's go."

We conceal ourselves in the numbing movement of bodies. They follow as I lead them to the left hallway past the break room and the odor of perch. To the left of the break room is a rusting door that reads Maintenance. That's the fourth key on my chain. I open the door. It's musty and damp. The buzzy bulbs barely illuminate the path ahead. Redding passes me, texting on her phone. Perhaps something to her husband and son.

Natalie clenches my shoulder to keep her balance. To my right, we pass the back stair entrance that leads to every floor of the hotel. Our heels click on the concrete. I remember Momma rushing me along this corridor on the nights when she couldn't afford a babysitter. I thought of it as an adventure, and she was my guide.

Now I'm the guide and I wish to God I was going anywhere else.

To my right is a familiar door. That's the fifth key. I twist and open. Bold electric glow almost blinds me as I step into the carpeted hall. The Elizabeth Grace ballroom is less than ten feet away.

It only took six minutes. Not bad.

I turn to Natalie. "That was a lot easier than I—"

"Ladies, I'm gonna need to see invitations or we're gonna have a serious problem," says a voice from behind.

I spoke way too soon.

CHAPTER 52

Giovanni

June 20, 2025

Will I go to Hell if I ask God to help me lie?

Natalie steps back, but Redding stares through me. Maybe she's thinking of a way out, but I'm not telepathic and I don't have an answer for the hulking brown-haired security guard in front of us.

"There you are," says Victoria as she glides up the hall. "These are my guests."

"But ma'am, I caught them sneaking in through this entrance," he says, gesturing to the door.

"Which means they were lost." Victoria crosses her arms.

"Mrs. Whitlock—"

"Mind your business," orders Victoria.

Skin the shade of cardinal feathers, the officer says nothing and retreats to the main ballroom entrance. Victoria swings around in her strapless turquoise gown. "You have something on the bastard?"

"Yes," says Redding. "Thanks for answering my text so quickly."

"It's fine. I'm practically glued to this," she says, holding up her phone.

I elbow Redding. "That's why you weren't worried."

She cracks a small grin. "Figured we might need a backup plan."

Without preamble, Victoria turns on her heel with all of us behind her. She waves away the security with hand wands as we enter the ballroom. Redding's gun remains undetected.

Concentric circles of politicians and partygoers cocoon Governor Whitlock. Mrs. Whitlock and the mayor fake laugh at jokes. A digital slideshow of Governor Whitlock, from birth to present, plays in a loop on the twenty-four-foot-wide projection screen.

Gideon sulks and orders a drink from the bar. The click of a camera and bursts of light to my right announce Zanthe's presence. She gracefully navigates her way through the crowd taking candid shots, invisible to those around her.

Julien stands in front of the windows that span right to left on the east wall. Natalie saunters toward him. He takes the bait, meeting her near the front entrance. Julien's security detail remains a few steps behind on his left.

Redding moves to follow Natalie, but I pull her back and unhook the third key from my chain. "You're gonna need this. You remember how to get to the rooftop?"

"Yeah." She puts the key inside her jacket and winds her way through the crowd, staying inconspicuously behind Natalie.

Now I must do my part.

I retrace my path back to the entrance and reenter the dank hallway, rushing to the back stairwell, now on my left. I book it upstairs to the fifth floor, but I stop, out of breath, on the third floor and reconsider my options. Or lack of them.

My badge doesn't work. Willa revoked my login access. And I have no friends left in the security office to help me. Redding and Natalie need me to figure this out. Now.

But I'm out of options.

I'm out of moves.

I'm out of time.

Unless . . .

CHAPTER 53

Redding

Five Minutes Earlier
June 20, 2025

Voices grow louder in my direction. Probably security making rounds to ensure they weren't followed. I pocket the badge Mecca gave me and insert the key, jiggling it right to left and twist. It doesn't budge.

Isn't that what Giovanni did?

I remove the key from the lock and try again. Right to left. Twist.

The door doesn't budge.

One of the voices is talking about baseball. They're arguing about last month's Crosstown Classic—White Sox versus Cubs.

Right to left.

Twist.

The definition of insanity is doing the same thing over and over expecting a different result.

I insert the key, jiggle *left to right*. Twist. The door opens. I slip through and hope the shadows hide the small hint of evening coming through the crack in the door. I wait until the rivaling baseball buddies pass before I close it with a creaky thud.

The elevator access to the roof is ten feet away on the opposite side. Natalie and Julien are in the middle. I remove my shoes and inch closer to a small storage shed casting generous shadows. Natalie walks toward me and the cameras attached to the storage shed. Julien follows her.

"Why didn't you stop by last Friday?" she asks.

"Victoria," he scoffs. "She's always been so needy, y'know? Couldn't get away until the next day. Then I saw police and . . ."

"You weren't worried about me?"

Julien theatrically takes a breath. "Baby, of course I was. I just couldn't think straight. I tried calling you . . ."

Liar. I wonder if Natalie is thinking the same thing. Her face reveals no loathing nor longing.

She takes a step closer. "You should've been worried. I was attacked. I swear someone tried to kill me."

Julien sweeps Natalie into his arms, and she lets him hold her for a few moments.

She steps back. "Do you know who tried to hurt me?"

"I'd never hurt you. Trust that. Trust me. I'm falling for you. You're not like anyone else I've ever met. It's beyond your beauty, baby. It's not just words. I wanna help you."

Liar!

Julien delivers all the lines less experienced girls would fall for. The words tripping over themselves to shower you with adoration and the elusive possibility of love and stability with the kind of man the world tells them that they need.

"That's why I came to you about the D.A.R.E. program, for help. But I don't know about that now," says Natalie.

"Why, baby?" Julien unbuttons his jacket.

Natalie bites her lip. "I heard things. Some of the women applying for your program going missing. At least five of them."

"Got any names?"

"Nivea, Stacey, Annette, Olivia, and Mia."

Julien's eyes don't even twitch. "I'll ask Gideon. It's his job to keep track of applicants."

Evil takes a practiced, prolific, and nurtured callousness, an unchecked decay of the heart and soul. I hoped to read something in Julien's face when he heard their names, but I'm not surprised I didn't.

"You think Gideon has anything to do with the disappearances?"

Julien brushes a strand of hair away from Natalie's face. "It's a big city. People come. People go."

"I don't believe you, Julien. I really don't."

Natalie turns away, but Julien grabs her arm, forcing her to meet his face.

"Whoa, whoa, whoa. Don't turn your back on me. I told you I wanna help," he says. "Listen, Nat, I'm a genie. I make wishes come true. I can still make your dream come true."

I emerge from the shadows, dropping my right shoe and gripping the other, heel facing outward. Natalie catches my outline over Julien's shoulder and mouths the word *No*.

Julien leans forward, his face hovering over Natalie's. She wrenches herself from his grasp. "I told you I'm married. I want to keep this professional. I didn't change my mind about that last time we met at the gallery or now."

"So, my words don't mean anything?"

"They're the same words I'm sure you've said to Victoria and Phoenix and God knows how many other women. I'm just one who's telling you 'No.' Respect that."

Julien takes a step closer. "You can't get something for nothing. You're not innocent. You know what you're doing. You can't look like you do. Wear what you wear. Then turn around and tell me I can't have it. It doesn't work that way, Natalie.

And this New Age feminism fantasy about women can do what they want and be who they want without a consequence, that's not the world we live in."

"Well, it's the world I'm living in," says Natalie. "The world I'm fighting for."

Julien looks around at what he believes is the empty rooftop except him and Natalie. He takes a cleansing breath. "Fine. Have it your way, Nat."

As Julien lunges toward Natalie, the elevator access opens a few feet away. His executive protection unit bursts from the doors and grabs him. "It's live! It's live!" one of them shouts.

Julien has no time to register what they're saying before they shove him into the elevator, leaving Natalie and me alone.

I put on the heel I was ready to blind Julien with and open the bronze door with Natalie close behind. We ride downstairs to the first floor and press our way toward the ballroom through throngs of people. Some leaving, others rushing in the same direction.

Julien's voice booms: "*You can't get something for nothing. You're not innocent. You know what you're doing. You can't look like you do. Wear what you wear. Then turn around and tell me I can't have it. It doesn't work that way, Natalie. And this New Age feminism fantasy about women can do what they want and be who they want without a consequence, that's not the world we live in.*"

Four people gather near the multimedia setup at the front near the stage. Giovanni stands next to Zanthe at the bar.

Reporters swarm Governor Whitlock, microphones out, ravenous with questions. The governor's executive protection unit pushes their way through with punctuated shouts of "no comment" from the governor.

Natalie and I smile.

CHAPTER 54

Giovanni

Fifteen Minutes Earlier
June 20, 2025

I didn't need to leave the ballroom. I was so busy being clever, I forgot to be smart. My login credentials no longer work, but Willa's do. I run back downstairs to the first floor, pretending I'm not out of breath when I reach the landing and open the hallway door. But he blocks my path.

Gideon.

When God closes a door, He opens a window. And beneath that window are barbed wire and lava.

Gideon swaggers slightly, side to side. "Running to stick your nose in someone else's business?"

I try and push past Gideon, but his body doesn't give. "You gonna move?" No time for manners. No "sirs" or "please."

There's a meager slur to his words. He's tipsy but not drunk. Gideon can step through the door, land a punch, and connect. Is it that farfetched to assume this is the next move? He's condescending and rude. Zanthe called him and Julien *co-presidents of the Assholes Club*. Is Gideon also a partner? Not to Zanthe but to Julien. He could partake in Julien's crimes. What if *his* face is the last face they saw?

What if *his* face is the last face I see?

He steps forward and I tip back. Almost losing my balance but bracing myself on the cold cinder block wall.

"You don't belong here." Gideon reaches out and grabs me.

When Bale snatched me into a small grove of trees, he thought force was the way to quiet me, make me obedient. Orders. Compliance. Silence.

Fear.

Gripping the edge of the steel door, I use every inch, every pound of my body and slam it on him, catching his elbow. Gideon howls in agony and slides to the ground as I open the door, sprint down the hallway, and enter the ballroom. I weave in and out of the crowd until I reach the unguarded multimedia control deck near the bar. Opening the laptop near the projector, I navigate to the NexusLuxury landing page and enter Willa's login information like I've done a million times before—to handle her schedule, department budgets, or annual reviews. I did Willa's work. Cleaned up her messes. Hid her secrets. And Willa never changed her login because she was too arrogant to believe I'd cross her.

Grabbing an HDMI cable from the drawer below, I plug it into the laptop, then toggle to Security, search for the rooftop camera next to the storage shed, click on the icon, and press the live button. Natalie's voice blares from the speakers.

Natalie: "*You think Gideon has anything to do with the disappearances?*"

Julien: "*It's a big city. People come. People go.*"

Guests slowly stop their chatter and pay attention to the screen. News cameras turn their lenses toward the front of the ballroom. One by one, then two by two, then a dozen by a dozen, guests raise their phones like lighters at a concert, capturing the release of secrets and decaying morality.

People love messy. And Julien confessing to adultery and mismanagement of a charity's funds is damn messy. People will post and TikTok and chat and gossip and speculate. My heart grows bigger than the Grinch because after every tear, every insult, all the fighting and suspicion, I might know real peace tonight.

If a criminal court won't convict Julien, the court of public opinion will eviscerate him.

When Momma was alive, she would tell me not to rejoice when bad things happen, that karma deals in thought as much as it deals in action. But in this case, I think she would be fine rejoicing in this because of what it means for me. For Natalie. For Redding. If she was here, Momma would probably give me a hug. I want that hug almost as much as I want to watch Julien's world burn.

Almost.

CHAPTER 55

Giovanni

June 20, 2025

Redding and Natalie are linked arm in arm to withstand the barrage of bodies crashing their way. I wave my arms to get their attention, pressing toward them. A hand grabs my shoulder.

Zanthe.

"I couldn't have asked for a better early birthday gift," she shouts as if we're at a live concert.

"It's your birthday?"

"Tomorrow." She grins, then links her arm with mine as we press our way to Redding and Natalie.

Should I tell her about Gideon? Would she care?

Nah.

Outside of the Elizabeth Grace ballroom, I lead them to the Back Entry. I turn to Natalie. "Stay with Mecca. We'll come back for you, but we gotta go to the gallery."

"My gallery?" asks Zanthe. "Why?"

"I found a room when I met Julien there," says Natalie. "It was in a hidden part, kind of a basement. There were chains. Pictures." She places a hand protectively over her belly. Instinct.

"He was using L'Atelier Rouge as cover." I squeeze on Zanthe's shoulder.

"Are you sure?" she asks. "Could be someone else."

"Could be Gideon," I suggest.

"He doesn't have the balls to do something like that," says Zanthe, her voice the closest to contempt I've heard since I met her.

"If I was a creep whose secrets just got broadcast to most of Chicago's elite and the news, I'm cleaning up *any* evidence," adds Redding. "Let's go now. Debate later."

Natalie enters Mecca's office. Zanthe and I leave with Redding who speeds toward Hyde Park. Beating Julien to L'Atelier Rouge before he destroys any evidence, or just beating Julien, is my goal. I can't speak for Redding or Zanthe though I suspect they'd allow me a lick or ten before they call the police to arrest him. At least Gideon is one less thing (and I do mean *thing*) to worry about. I'm sure I broke his arm.

L'Atelier Rouge is empty, encamped in murky pale light, but my knowledge of what lies beneath its floors now informs how I perceive every inch of this place.

"I don't see his car yet, but I'll keep watch." Zanthe emerges from the back and hands me a key. "This should open Julien's office."

Redding enters first and flicks on the lights. I follow her into the neat space. Behind his desk is a closet with a couple of suits. Redding and I press against the back, but nothing shifts or bends.

"His phone keeps going to voicemail," says Zanthe, walking into the office.

I grab Redding's burner from her pocket. "Whatever Julien's hidden, he accesses it from somewhere else." I head toward the north wing, and call Natalie.

"When you left the north wing, how many offices did you pass?"

There is silence a few seconds before she answers, "It was two."

I make a left at the north wing and pass two offices. Julien's office is the third and only option according to the directions. "Nat, his office doesn't have the closet you described. Maybe he just replaced it. It's been a few weeks."

"There's gotta be *something*," she says. "This can't be it."

"I retraced the steps from the north wing. I made a left—"

"Gio, I said, 'I left the north wing and made a right.'"

I rub my temples and walk to the end of the hallway. I make a *right* and pass two offices but . . .

"Gio . . . Gio, you still there?"

The goose bumps dotting my arms have nothing to do with the air vent directly above. It's the name. The name on the door.

Zanthe Yaeger-Gates.

CHAPTER 56

Redding

June 20, 2025

What am I missing?

I have the place. I have a witness. But I don't have the evidence. I can't link Julien to Nivea, Stacey, Annette, Olivia, and Mia. At this point, I can barely link him to Natalie. And one good piece of misinformation, an internet troll, or a $1,500-an-hour lawyer can turn it into a he said–she said story.

My right leg throbs again. Each thump matches the beat in my temples. I turn to Zanthe who lingers behind me. "I'm gonna look in some other places. Maybe Natalie got her directions mixed up."

"Details don't come easy when you're terrified," she says.

"When you can't find your way to the end, start at the beginning."

I walk to the front gallery of L'Atelier Rouge, searching for any subtle indents in the walls. On the right side of the locked ebony-encased doors is a larger alcove. Small sconces illuminate a group of images. All of them shot by Zanthe. Three rows of five pictures each. I press against the wall. It's solid.

I remember the picture of the mom spraying her children with a garden hose. *A Summer Wednesday.* They moved it with the rest of Zanthe's collection. Below that photo is another one. A mother holding her child's hand as they walk down the street. *Child's Keeper.*

The phrase used on the sticky note after Nivea's disappearance . . .

It's a coincidence. *Child's Keeper* is a common phrase. Writers, photographers, painters have probably all used that phrase at some point.

But . . . the picture next to it . . . a room of students, hands raised; the teacher, open-mouthed eager to answer questions. It's called *Tortured Bloom.* On the left side, an image with bolts of fabric lying at the feet of a woman confidently holding a pair of scissors in her left hand. *Made & Unmade.* The next picture in the collection, a winding line of people waiting outside of a cannabis dispensary. *Long Lines and Lost Connections.* Six inches away near a corner, hunkered on the wall, a woman sings on a stage, a tawny light enveloping her. *Golden for You.*

> Nivea—My mother's daughter. My child's keeper. The whole world's weight as I wait. Freedom.
>
> Stacey—Open minds in tortured bloom. Marked memories and bled potential from open wounds.
>
> Annette—Elevated in onyx. Shaped in amber. I am created to be golden for you.
>
> Olivia—I make You and unmake You. I make Me and unmake Me.
>
> Mia—In long lines and lost connections, I have been here. Hidden by your dark excess.

When you can't find your way to the end, start at the beginning.

The answers are here. My torture, hate, and anguish perfectly framed in photographs of strangers with art posing as evidence. I touch my SIG Sauer with as much reverence and comfort as someone would touch their rosary beads.

I have the place. I have a witness. But I had the wrong person. Julien is a predator, but not the type I suspected. It was someone who was never in my periphery. Or Giovanni's. And that's what made Zanthe so proficient at her game. Unless Fleur jumped the gun and called Frenchie, Giovanni and I are trapped with Zanthe.

But where's Giovanni?

CHAPTER 57

Giovanni

June 20, 2025

Natalie's voice is far away. It begs me to answer. It tells me that she's scared.

There'll be time to feel betrayed later. There'll be a time for regret later. There'll be a time to mourn later.

I need to act. Now.

"I'm here. Sorry, Nat. It's, uh . . . the office you entered wasn't Julien's. Just . . . stay on the line with me, okay?"

"Okay." Natalie murmurs to Mecca that I'm fine.

Natalie said there was another opening on the other side of the office. The only room directly sharing a wall with Zanthe's office is the utility supply closet. It's unlocked. A shelf stocked with bleach, air fresheners, gloves, and garbage bags partially blocks the wall connected to Zanthe's office. I kick off my shoes, anchoring my feet, and push the shelf three feet to the right, praying nothing falls. I press my fingers on the back wall. It bends. I push harder; the left edge of a panel finally puckers. The panel isn't heavy and slides away. Behind the wall to my right is a stairway. I brace myself on the wall as I descend the stairs. My eyes water and my nostrils burn from a chemical meant to smell like flowers. An unsettling hum from the lights turns my attention to the wall.

And the pictures.

One of me and Redding standing near the History Wall last Tuesday. One of me talking to Gideon in the ballroom. One of me helping a guest. Zanthe took those photos. This can't be who she is. Maybe Julien is framing her. Maybe Gideon. I didn't notice anything wrong with Zanthe. I saw me in her. So, if she's a monster, then what am I?

"Nat, I found the room. And . . . it's not Julien's office. It's Zanthe's, his sister." My mouth is sour.

"Oh my God," she whispers.

I take pictures. Of the walls, the chains. Two white bookshelves against the back laden with records, neatly folded clothes, reprints of pictures. Her mother. Grandmother. None of her. A gold-plated memory box. A doll. And a framed jigsaw puzzle of the Sears Tower. A shrine of memories with no idea of what they mean to Zanthe. If they provide her comfort or sorrow or a measure of both.

I switch to video and film the room along with the shelves on the opposite wall full of lenses and unmarked containers with unknown fluid. I touch nothing as I leave. Redding would be proud.

Upstairs, I don't exit through the utility supply closet. I turn left into Zanthe's office. It's the only way to convince myself this isn't a bad dream. Natalie's faint breathing on my phone is the only sound. I put my cell in my back pocket and press against the false panel. On the desk, a sepia-toned photo of an older woman with flawless mahogany skin, adoring eyes, and a cigarette tucked behind her ear. A girl cradles the woman's face in her small hands. Iris Walker, Zanthe's mom who disappeared twenty-five years ago. There's no time to study the picture, pick apart Zanthe's villain origin story.

Redding is alone. With her. I cover my hand with the bottom of my blouse and open the door.

I'm free.

I'm not.

Zanthe steps toward me. "What are you doing, Gio?"

CHAPTER 58

Giovanni

June 20, 2025

"This place is so big. Guess I made a wrong turn." I smile. I make sure it reaches my eyes.

"And the wrong turn involved coming *out* of my office?" Zanthe mirrors my smile. It reaches her eyes, too. Her smile is now a strange and vulgar thing.

"Thought I heard something. Figured maybe it was Julien." I shut the door. There's no blood on her clothes or hands, so Redding's probably okay. I try to move around Zanthe.

She blocks me. "I keep my door locked. And I gave you a key to Julien's office. Not mine." Zanthe looks down. "Where are your shoes?"

That meme of Sweet Brown pops in my head.

I didn't grab no shoes or nothin', Jesus. I ran for my life.

"My feet are killing me. Kicked 'em back off in the north wing. Was on my way to grab 'em." I step to my left.

Zanthe matches my move again. "Your grammar and diction

take a little dive when you lie. Not many people notice that about you, but I do. I notice everything, Gio."

"Please call me Giovanni."

Zanthe grabs my arm and squeezes. "We're not friends anymore, Gio? Is it because you and Natalie reconciled?"

I jerk my arm away. There are only flat walls and hardwood floors. Nothing sharp I can use to cut or stab. At least the utility closet had plenty of options. The heel of my foot touches the door as I step back with my right leg. I bend my knees and tuck my chin like Teddy taught me.

"Giovanni!" Redding calls me with equal measures of alarm and relief. "I, uh, got a call from Area. French needs me to fix some paperwork. I gotta drop you off." She waves me over to the end of the hall.

No need to fight my way out if I got a cop with a gun who can shoot her way out. Suspended or not, Redding is still a detective, a CPD detective.

I take Zanthe's momentary distraction and force my way past her. I close the space between me and Redding ready to spill everything I've seen and documented since we split up, but her face is pinched and she's sweating though the gallery is cool.

She swallows hard. "I know."

Redding didn't see what I saw in that horrible room, but she came to the same conclusion. Zanthe is the villain. We say nothing and walk to the back exit. Two locked glass doors and beyond them an empty parking lot. Zanthe walks toward us like a bohemian chic Michael Myers. Steady gait. Confident. Relentless.

Ready for the kill.

CHAPTER 59

Redding

June 20, 2025

I pull again on the handle of the back door as if it'll magically open this time. I have a surge of adrenaline so intense I might vomit. Fight or flight is no joke.

"Let's ease our way out the front or side," suggests Giovanni. She glances over her shoulder.

"Front's locked. Side exit, too. Tried those first."

"You were gonna leave me to throw hands with a psychopath? You know I got trust issues." The ghost of a grin then bends her lips.

"You know I'd go down before I let that happen."

Giovanni's face softens and I might've hugged her if we were far away from Zanthe and Julien and the insidious threat of the Whitlock family.

Zanthe finally stops a few feet away. She studies us, waiting for the game to begin. Who has the best moves? Who will live?

Who will die?

"Umm, the entrances are locked and, like I said, we gotta

go." I keep my tone even and put my hand on my hip casually revealing my gun.

"Thought you were still looking for evidence." Her voice is teasing, there's a singsongy cadence to her words.

I straighten my back and clear my throat. "Still best that I check in with my sergeant."

"Do suspended cops keep in touch with their sergeants?" says Zanthe, walking closer to Giovanni.

"Suspended?" I try to laugh. The sound tinny and unfamiliar. I step to my left, covering Gio with as much of my body as I can.

Markham. The ink is barely dry on that form. I wonder how much his soul was worth. But I'm sure it was easy for him to sell what he doesn't have.

Zanthe's right arm dips into her black sequined jacket.

"Whoa. Whoa." I step forward and pull my gun as Zanthe pulls hers, but her arm is angled just to the left of me.

"I wouldn't try that," she says.

Giovanni isn't behind me anymore. She's a few inches shy of pulling a fire alarm. I try to protect her. She tries to protect us.

"Give it," Zanthe orders.

I place it in her free hand. She tucks it in the holster under her jacket, her aim never wavering from Giovanni. I seriously regret I didn't grab the Heckler & Koch before I left Baltimore, before I told him what to do with the letters to Emmett and Hudson if I didn't return.

Giovanni glances at the cameras.

Zanthe clocks her movement. "Oh, sweetie, I already thought of that." She pulls out a memory card with her free hand.

Now I know what she was doing when she was "looking out" for Julien.

"You know I can't let you leave. My story is my own," she says.

"And what is it?" I ask.

Zanthe scoffs. "Is this my Bond villain moment?"

The only way to stall whatever unique piece of Hell she has planned for us is to get her talking. Yes, this is her Bond villain moment. We all want to be heard. And I've got more than a hunch being heard is a rarity for Zanthe. That's why she does what she does.

That's why she's become what she's become.

"Doesn't it gnaw at you? Whatever you've done and the reasons you've done it are overshadowed by Julien. Everyone is looking at him. Not you."

"It's true," says Giovanni.

It's the "not you" that burns Zanthe. All her preparation, planning, the money, the shadows. All that sacrifice for her bombastic, philandering, idiotic half-brother to gain the spotlight?

Zanthe keeps the gun focused on Giovanni. "Why don't you take us to The Dark Room, Gio? You know the way. And if you think about trying something, Redding, I'll kill Gio, kill you, and make it look like you did it. Am I clear?"

"With you the lone survivor. Bet you'll sell a lotta pictures then," taunts Giovanni.

Even with a gun to her face, she has no chill.

None.

Giovanni eases from behind me and treks down the hall. I tread behind with Zanthe's Glock 19 pressed into my back.

"Art is my church and it's my weapon," begins Zanthe. "I use it to scream about our injustices, about women like Iris. Missing. Black. Nothing changes. Files with our faces gather dust. Then there's another case, and another. Right, Detective?" She nudges my back with the gun.

I remain silent. I'm angry at being held by gunpoint, but I'm livid that she's right. This is the weirdest version of Stockholm syndrome. We walk into a utility supply closet toward a tall shelf stacked with supplies and a loosened plywood panel. I pass through a macabre version of Narnia.

She continues, "No one looked for Iris. And I grew up with Granny who beat me for every mistake, big or small. In her mind, she was keeping me safe. If I was disciplined to perfection, I wouldn't go out one night, meet friends, and never come home. Hartwell Whitlock never came for me. 'Cause he sure as hell wasn't gonna raise his bastard Black daughter in the suburbs with his white wife and newborn son."

There's a set of stairs to the right. Our heels gently clicking against the concrete. Giovanni's bare feet make no noise.

Zanthe plants herself in front of us. "Art always gives you what you need. Not what you want," says Zanthe. "My initial subject, that influencer girl Phoenix, caught my eye. That's who I approached. But she brought along Natalie. Then you both fought at The Cathedral. It was all there for the press to devour. And . . . nothing. Well, some social media noise, but no news articles. No national story. Not even a local one. I gave them everything to look at us and nothing happened." She laughs, bitter as grapefruit. "*I* didn't even know where Natalie was, and I put this thing in motion. She's a survivor."

All these answers, like a ghastly bounty, lie at my feet. But there's more I want to know. Is it wrong of me?

"How'd you find them? Nivea, Stacey, Annette, Olivia, and Mia?" I ask.

"Julien used the D.A.R.E. program to find pretty women. I used it to find my . . . subjects."

"Victims," interrupts Giovanni.

"There are tons of neighborhood programs we run. I'd casually mention the D.A.R.E. program. No matter how good a person someone believes they are, no one says no to free money." Zanthe ruefully shakes her head. "The rest wasn't terribly difficult. I got random people, some from Gio's little hotel, to deliver the orchids."

Zanthe turns away from Giovanni to me. "And you were the only one to pay attention. Bravo, Redding. No one else cared but you."

"And Governor Whitlock?" I ask. "Did he know about you?"

"Why do you think Gideon and I are married? Love? Gideon's my father's own little informant. He needs money, and my father can't be governor if I'm . . . well, me." She laughs. "My father has eyes everywhere."

"Markham?" I ask.

Zanthe smirks. That's the only answer I need.

"Though the little war parties my father sends to tie up loose ends aren't my idea. Too messy. Phoenix was such a waste." Zanthe lays her free hand against her chest. "And I'm sorry about David."

Giovanni's eyes widen and just as quickly narrow into sharp vengeful slits.

"What happened to Iris, so many before and after her, shouldn't've. But why?" Beads of sweat trickle down my forehead. "To replace the mom you lost? None of these women could take her place. Counseled you. Cared for you. Loved you. They were frightened and would've told you anything to return to their *real* families. You haven't honored your mother's memory. You've destroyed it, just to become what you hated."

"And what have you become, Detective? What have you done?" Zanthe asks. "Looked at dusty files? Cried over the women you couldn't find? This country's apathy when we go missing is damn near criminal, but you're inside of the justice system perpetuating our trauma and grief. And you *still* can't do anything to stop it. That makes you worthless. At least I'm trying. I'm doing horrible things, but I'm trying to fix it."

"When does it stop?" whispers Giovanni.

"When we don't bury empty caskets," says Zanthe.

I search for a pipe, a shard of glass. Something to shatter a bone. Cut through flesh. But this place is cleaner than the state lab.

Zanthe points the gun at Giovanni's head and racks the slide. "I won't stretch this out. I owe you more than that. It's nice to know you'll be the ones to keep my secret."

CHAPTER 60

Giovanni

June 20, 2025

"You don't belong here."

Gideon tried to warn me about Zanthe at The Ivory and I broke his arm for it. Well, he was an asshole who drunkenly attacked me, so all's fair.

"Gio, take that soda bottle on your left. Pour it around the back of the room and around you and Redding. It better not touch me," says Zanthe. Her last instruction is low and menacing. "If it does, I won't give you the merciful way out by shooting you. I'll put you both in those leg irons and let you burn."

I open the old green soda bottle. My eyes water. I baptize the perimeter of the back wall and shelves, scan for exits. Nothing. I empty the last of the chemical around Redding and me.

I'm not some badass that's not afraid to die.

I'm terrified I haven't left anything of value behind. And years of stellar service at a five-star hotel doesn't grant me automatic entry into Heaven. But at least Nat isn't here. She'll be safe. So will her baby. So will that sonofabitch Fleur. My last regret is Redding. She has a family.

Watch your temper. You're an Aries. I know how you get when pushed too far.

Zanthe pretended to be my friend to watch me suffer. She killed Phoenix. She killed David. She's gonna kill me, burn me alive. But if I can distract her, maybe Redding can take her down.

Zanthe keeps her aim on me while she fishes a lighter out of her pocket. The same one from her exhibition, silver with the Black power fist engraved on the front. Her mom's. The flame wavers, then steadies. Redding's body tenses against me. She's going to make a move. And I don't stare at the gun pointed at my head. I stare at Zanthe's waist. I crouch and I tackle her. I hear a gunshot, but I feel nothing.

Did she shoot Redding?

Slamming into Zanthe, I land funky on my left wrist. Her gun slides near the left corner and the lighter clatters out of her hand across the floor like a bad game of spin the bottle, connecting with the chemically saturated bookshelves.

Jesus!

I can't win the lottery, but I can get a lighter to make a one in a million shot and connect to a flammable wall?

Zanthe scrambles to her feet as I struggle to mine and catch Redding's movement toward the flames that barrel higher, quickly consuming the shelves and treasures along the back wall. Zanthe throws a right cross, rattling my left cheek. She goes for another hit. I barely bring my arm up in time to block her with my left. Her blow adds more damage to my pulsing wrist.

Zanthe knows how to fight. Not the windmill, flailing arm moves that women get stereotyped for. Her aim's precise. Her power comes from her legs and hips. She doesn't try and pull my hair. She goes for my face, for my body.

Someone taught her and taught her right.

But someone taught me, too.

Sirens faintly echo above. My eyes water. Zanthe coughs, trying a sloppy right hook as acrid smoke fills the room. It connects with my left shoulder, dull steady pain telegraphs down my elbow. I can barely protect my left side. I can barely see. If by some miracle my wrist isn't broken, it will be if I hit her.

Zanthe senses my weakness. She wouldn't be a good predator if she didn't. She tries a left jab. I bend my knees, missing her strike. I slide right and counter with a right hook, grazing her chin. She stumbles back but recovers and eases forward. She jabs with her right this time, then follows it up with a left cross. I take it on the jaw. Blood fills my mouth. I spit on the floor.

It's getting harder to breathe. Redding's arm covers her mouth as she searches for anything to quell the rising blaze, now separating her from us. I'm done playing games with Zanthe. Her lies cost me. My peace. My freedom. David. Momma. I've lost so much. I thought I was gonna die tonight, but I won't.

I can't.

"Live your life . . ."

Teddy always told me if you're in a tough spot and want your enemy to go down fast, "*Stop going for the face. Kidney shot. It'll take 'em out. Every damn time.*"

My right hook lands near her lower back, near her spine, and below her ribs. Zanthe cries out and crumples. She kicks at my right knee, and I lose my balance dodging her. My head hits the floor.

Yep, that's a concussion.

The sirens are no longer far away, the ruthless roar is on top of us, but head injuries tend to have you believing things are happening when they aren't. A rippling blanket of flame creeps forward that will consume us and the oxygen in this horrific place. But let it consume Zanthe first, God.

Please!

As I rise, I stay low to the ground and make out the blurry outline of Zanthe standing up, reaching for her holster to retrieve the gun she took from Redding. I stumble and rush forward, grabbing at whatever resembles her arm and the gun. I twist it until the heel of her hand points north.

She drops her weapon, shrieking, falling back against the wall near a steel post. Her weight pulls me with her. She claws at my throat. Frenzied, desperate, rageful.

I grip both sides of her head and ram it against the post.

Once.

Her eyes shift from sharp to dazed. I slam her head again. Zanthe's body slumps down, but she's still breathing. I wait until she hits the floor. My left arm pulses in an odd rhythm with an unexpected burst of searing pain every few seconds. I don't care. I bend down and grab Zanthe's head with both hands, ready to slam it against the post a third time before I'm stopped. By Redding. There's white residue at the bottom of her pants and feet. She holds an empty box of baking soda. She made a small path to reach me.

I still hold Zanthe's head in my hands. I focus on Redding and ask the question that she's asking herself, but is too afraid to utter: "Are you sure?"

Redding looks back to the ever-hungry fire. "Yeah."

Her reasons for stopping me from killing Zanthe have nothing to do with mercy or forgiveness or preventing eternal damnation. If I kill Zanthe, Redding's chances of finding any of the women Zanthe abducted and murdered vanish.

I remember their names.

Nivea, Stacey, Annette, Olivia, and Mia.

Redding tosses the empty box and takes Zanthe's left arm. I grab Zanthe's right. We climb the stairs, dragging Zanthe along. I'm helping to save someone who's destroyed so many lives in her wake. But we should thank Zanthe. The previously locked doors are automatically open because she tried to torch the gallery.

Fire trucks, police cars, and ambulances greet us in front of L'Atelier Rouge as smoke billows from the back. My right arm tingles from Zanthe's dead weight. My left arm is a weird mixture of thumping and throbbing. I'm tempted to let Zanthe fall headfirst into the fire hydrant three feet in front of us, but now I'd have witnesses.

"Are we gonna be okay?" I ask.

Redding looks at me, her face somber but oddly serene. "No clue, but I can live with that."

CHAPTER 61

Giovanni

Two Hours Later
June 21, 2025

Natalie never hung up.

She called 911 and merged my call with the dispatcher. Zanthe confessed to emergency responders, law enforcement, and anyone with a halfway decent police scanner. One-way recordings might not be admissible in an Illinois court, but 911 calls are.

"I'm not just a pretty face, Gio," says Natalie.

"I never thought you were a pretty face, Nat." I instantly regret my words. "I mean . . . I didn't mean . . ."

Natalie laughs, weary and genuine. "I'm glad you're okay. Redding, too."

"Fleur?" I cradle my slinged left arm.

"His phone hasn't stopped ringing."

Multiple kidnappings, murder, arson, assault, misappropriation of funds from the son *and* daughter of the governor. Fleur will be talking for the next few weeks, probably months. Redding and I kicked ass and saved the day. Like James Bond. Wait, not like James Bond.

Like Foxy Brown and Cleopatra Jones!

Rotating blue light dances up and down East 53rd Street. Clustered together at the end of the block, onlookers try to get a peek, reporters near television vans with erect satellite antennas try to get the story, and cops keep them all from possibly contaminating the crime scene.

In the back of an ambulance, Redding talks to French. She clutches an oxygen mask she's barely used. She puts it down as he hugs her in a wrinkled blue shirt and khaki pants. Three people shake Redding's hand before she crosses the street. I'd bet $100 that a week ago she couldn't have got those people to look her way.

"They picked up Julien an hour ago at his Gold Coast condo. He cried like a baby but went quietly."

"How does it feel to be popular, Detective Stark?"

Redding smirks, then glances down at my arm. "You going to the hospital?"

"Not with my insurance. Plus, EMTs say it's just a bad sprain and a mild concussion. Nothing some ibuprofen and a few days' rest won't fix."

Redding's phone pings. She checks it and a mix of joy and terror crosses her face. "Emmett and Hudson are heading home sometime tomorrow."

I wiggle my toes. Momma would kill me if she saw my bare feet on the curb. "That's good."

Redding looks down the street. "Emmett suggested counseling."

"And?"

"And nothing. He's right. We need it. Hudson, too. We'll find someone good."

"So how much paperwork is this gonna be?"

"I'm taking the win for today. I'll worry about that later." Redding scoots closer and whispers, "Look, I'm going to a safe house until all this dies down." She gestures at the end of the block. "You should come with me."

"Nah, I'm good." My wrist pulses.

"Giovan—"

"I'm good, Redding. Promise."

"I'm gonna have a unit at your house 'til I think you're safe."

"Okay." My phone buzzes. I pull it out of my back pocket. My screen has two new cracks.

Mecca: U ok?

Mecca: Gio???

Mecca: pls let me know ur good!

Mecca: ????

Mecca: N told me ur ok but call me

Mecca is the closest thing I have to family now. I yearn to say the same thing about Redding, but if this past week has taught me anything, it's that I jump into relationships, friendships, too quickly. I'm too eager to be loved, which means I don't love myself enough. Or at all. It destroyed my friendship with Natalie. It almost got me killed with Zanthe. And I want to be different with Redding.

She's not the only one who needs therapy.

"You wanna sit here for a bit?" she asks.

I rise slowly. Every muscle rebels and screams at me, but dammit if I'm not happy I'm alive to feel pain. "I'll call you soon."

"Yeah, I know this isn't the last I'll hear from Giovanni Mason."

I smile at Redding. "You don't get off the hook that easy."

5:02 p.m.
June 21, 2025

"Can you please turn the channel?"

I only need the weather for Mom's service next week, but I can't escape the coverage on the L'Atelier Rouge Disappearances. Mecca grabs her office remote and turns to CNN. It's there, too. The media has already crafted their narrative. At least it involves hero detective Redding Stark, and a "brave" witness who fought for their lives as they confronted Zanthe Yaeger-Gates about the disappearances of missing Black women from Chicago's South Side.

Zanthe got her wish.

Black women are national news and all it took was for almost half a dozen of us to go missing, murder, financial fraud, and political corruption before people paid attention.

Mecca switches again to a station playing smooth R&B. George Benson. "This Masquerade." One of Momma's favorite musicians. Buttery soft vocals envelop us as we select pictures for the obituary. Images of Momma youthful, strong, full-cheeked, laughing out loud. Hugging me. I wipe away tears with my right hand.

"We can do this some other time, Gio."

"I wanna do it now." I adjust my left arm; the sling rubs against my jeans.

Willa knocks on the door and walks into Mecca's office. "I thought I saw you in here." She plasters on a look of sorrow. "First, I want to say how crushed I am about the loss of your mom. She was part of The Ivory family and will be dearly missed."

What was my momma's name, Willa?

"Thank you." I don't look up from the pictures.

She clears her throat. "I also want to apologize for that mix-up with your badge. Don't know what happened there."

"Okay." I stare at another picture of Momma in the Museum of Science and Industry in December. *Christmas Around the World*. She loved that place.

"Well, you can return to The Ivory and resume your duties when you're ready. I've spoken to the Board."

I finally look up and give Willa my attention. "Thanks."

She straightens her tailored tan suit and leaves Mecca's office.

"Humph," says Mecca. "Word through The Ivory is the Board isn't too happy with her performance. *Especially* after the Whitlock fiasco."

"The Board isn't gonna want to replace Willa with me. Besides, I'm done with this place."

I'm no longer dedicating myself to a job or a mission or a person when reciprocity is off the table. I tied myself to The Ivory the way I did because I thought it was the only thing Momma and I still shared, but we shared so much more than that.

My stomach grumbles. Loudly.

Mecca chuckles. "Tootchie's?"

"Hell yes, Auntie!"

Mecca heads toward the back entrance but I loop my right arm with her left. "The Help is gonna leave through the front today."

As Mecca and I exit the elevator, we stroll past the History Wall. Mecca stops. I want to keep going. Memories are too fresh. I still feel the fire. I still see Zanthe's gun pointed at my face. I'm still fighting for my life back there. I should've gone another way.

"The maintenance department already has an order to remove all the pictures of the Whitlock family. Take a good look and say goodbye," says Mecca.

I study the pictures, images I've stared at a thousand times before. R.I. Willowbrook, Board members past and present, one of a young Hartwell Whitlock with Julien and a group of young men.

And one of them looks really familiar.

I gotta call Redding.

CHAPTER 62

Redding

June 21, 2025

I wanted peace, but peace is scary. Not scary like guns and fire and psychopaths. It's the stillness that's haunting. It's the not hopping from one crisis to another that's maddening. Peace means I must be alone with myself and my thoughts.

I walk to the front window and peek outside as Frenchie talks on his phone in the nineties–time capsule kitchen. The drone of another news story about the L'Atelier Rouge Disappearances fills the silence in the cabin. But they aren't disappearances. If Zanthe is forced into a corner, to save herself, she might reveal where she hid their bodies.

Nivea, Stacey, Annette, Olivia, and Mia.

"Get away from the window," orders Frenchie. "Wouldn't be surprised if a reporter followed us down here."

"I'll leave Suits to speak with the press," I say.

Frenchie nods. "He'll be here in ten minutes. Wants to talk about media strategy." Frenchie air quotes the term *media strat-*

egy. "Amazing how he lost your suspension paperwork. Guess all's forgiven now you're Chicago's new superhero cop."

"How many superheroes hide out in a house near Avant, Illinois?"

Frenchie sets down a bowl of popcorn on the scratched living room table near his glasses. "Clark Kent hid in Smallville, Kansas."

The perfume of the overly buttered snack lures me away from the brown-and-black-patterned curtains. I sit on a lumpy couch years past its prime.

Frenchie turns to another channel. "You give Emmett and Hudson the directions?"

"Yep." I check my cell phone for the third time in forty-five minutes and read the same text from Emmett.

E: Should be there in 2 hours.

Then what? What happens when they walk through the door? Should I hug Hudson? Will Emmett and I sleep in the same bed? With Cormac it was a solid month of news vans camped in front of our home. How long will it be now?

"You been on the phone a lot." I snatch the remote from Frenchie.

"Like I said, Suits was just giving me the rundown," he says with his mouth almost full. "Zanthe isn't saying a word. Governor Whitlock's already bought her some fancy-pants lawyer. Don't know how much good it'll do though. Rumor is the state's attorney is already looking to strike a deal with Fleur and that guy Teddy in exchange for a reduced sentence or possible immunity."

Frenchie leans forward and squints.

"You might need those to see." I gesture to his glasses, then grab some popcorn. I try to focus on something else besides the earth-shattering work it'll take to rebuild my family. I settle on one of my favorite movies. *Tombstone.* Val Kilmer's Doc Holliday emerges from the shadows and surprises Johnny Ringo. My phone buzzes. It's Giovanni.

"Hey, what's—"

Giovanni takes a breath. "It's French. French is Governor Whitlock's inside man."

"I, uh . . ." I swallow the rest of my popcorn. "What'd you just say?"

"There's an old picture on the History Wall. He's thinner with more hair, but it's French. He's standing behind Whitlock and Julien."

It's not Frenchie. We're eating popcorn and watching a movie like when I was nine and he let me watch *Terminator 2: Judgment Day* even though Dad said it was too violent. Frenchie danced with me at my wedding. He was front row at Hudson's christening. I babysat Anya. Frenchie was my *first* call after Dad died.

"You there?" asks Giovanni.

"Mmm-hmm."

"He's there?" asks Giovanni.

French casts a look my way and I etch an easy smile on my face. "Yeah, girl. We're cool."

It has to be Markham. Markham ordered me to stay away from the case. But French found the evidence of Giovanni on North Michigan Avenue. That was him being a good cop. Hunting down evidence.

Frenchie's phone pings. He stops eating and stands up. "It's Markham. Wants me to meet him outside so he knows where we are. Be right back, Red."

Markham worked in Avant, Illinois. He told me I wouldn't even be able to get a job here if I crossed him and kept investigating. Markham wouldn't need directions to this house. He'd know how to find this place.

I wait ten seconds and inch up to the window and ease the curtain back. "He's gone. For now." French stands at the head of the driveway.

"I'm calling the police," says Giovanni.

"Call Detective Elliott. He's the only other cop I trust." I text his number to Giovanni. Crunching gravel pulls my attention. A black SUV, like the one I saw at David's apartment, cruises up and stops. Two men exit from the back. One of them, Dagget, checks his weapon, next to a guy with light brown hair. The other man remains behind the wheel. Three assailants.

Four including French.

"Shouldn't I—"

"Do what I said. Please, Giovanni."

I end the call, put my phone on silent. Emmett and Hudson will be here in an hour. Less. French knows they're coming. So, if they kill me, their plan is to wait for my husband and child, and then . . .

No time to run upstairs, grab my gun from my room at the end of the hall, load it, and make it back downstairs. I'd probably reach the top landing before I'd have to start shooting. Fish in a barrel and I'm the fish. I bolt to the kitchen, ransacking the mostly empty drawers for weapons, finding two options: a stainless steel meat tenderizer and a paring knife. I tuck the meat tenderizer between my jeans and belt like I'm Doc Holliday. Ready for a quick draw, I don't want to start a gunfight here. A poorly timed ricochet would kill me faster than the thugs about to come inside. I unlock and open the back door. If I'm lucky, they'll think I ran toward the woods.

The tenderizer digs into my ribs as I crouch behind the kitchen island. The front door eases open. Wary footsteps can't avoid all the weak portions of the living room floor. Each creak alerts me to how close they're getting. I grip the paring knife. I pray. I wait for the change from wood to tile, when a creak becomes a dull tap.

"Yeah, back door's open. Check the property. I'll sweep the rest of the house," someone says.

One. Inhale.

Two. Exhale.

A foot appears to my right.

Three. *Stab!*

A strangled growl erupts from his throat. As he falls to the ground, Dagget aims at me. Unsteady. I rush him, clutching his wrist with both hands. Our bodies bang against the cabinets.

"Always gotta be a sneaky little bitch, huh?" Dagget bends his arm, trying to wedge his Smith & Wesson M&P22 between our bodies. He yanks my ponytail with his other hand.

He fights dirty, but I fight dirtier.

As Dagget tries to tear the hair from my scalp, I lean in as far as I can against his sweaty skin and bite his ear like it's a pork-chop sandwich from Jim's Original. He howls again releasing my ponytail. His other arm slackens, and I bang it against the floor. The gun clatters out of his hand to a dark corner near the dishwasher. I whip out the meat tenderizer and swing toward Dagget's left temple with everything I've got. He's dazed but still reaches for the gun. I pull back and hit him again. Harder. I tug the tenderizer from his skin. Dagget no longer reaches for anything. I pull back for a third strike, but I see another familiar face holding a Heckler & Koch.

Raspy Voice has me dead to rights.

I let Dagget fall to the floor. I can't grab his gun ten feet away. I'm gonna die. So will Hudson and Emmett.

But Raspy Voice holsters his weapon and unsheathes a double-edged hunting knife. "You killed my cousin. My blood. So, I'ma kill you. Then your man." He admires the sharpness and shine of the four-inch blade. "Gonna save your boy for last."

I have no time to process my rage and fear, but I have time to kill. I stand, gripping the bloody tenderizer. "Come get me."

Raspy Voice steps over Dagget's body and lunges forward with the knife, gauging the distance and my reflexes. There's a rush of wind near my stomach. I gotta move faster. He advances a half step and jabs again with the knife as I move counterclockwise, retreating to the head of the kitchen island near the living room.

"You keep backin' up, girl. This not going how you pictured it?" He theatrically tosses the knife to his left hand. Gripping the blade tighter, he takes another half step and sweeps toward my throat. "Pays to be ambidextrous."

"Most men talk this much come up short in a lot of areas." My gaze darts below his belt, quickly returning to his face.

Raspy Voice's smile morphs into a snarl.

"Did I hit a sensitive spot? I'm sure you're not used to that."

I need big, sloppy movements. I rear back again, keeping weight on my right leg though a searing throb revisits every few seconds reminding me it's not healed. But I can't care about my pain right now. Only stopping Raspy Voice from inflicting more of it.

His shoulders give him away. They tense before he attacks. Raspy Voice raises his arm and angles the blade toward my neck again in a fluid motion. As I swing, the tenderizer catches and tears the flesh of his forearm. Raspy Voice hollers as his knife drops to the ground. I kick it out of reach, and it lands underneath a nicked dining room table.

But there are bursts of light. My right jaw doesn't feel anchored to my face as I fall.

Don't pass out, Red. Keep your eyes open or else you'll die. Your family will die.

I crawl to the corner near the dishwasher. Sitting up, I face Raspy Voice and reach behind me. I'm where I need to be. He plays checkers. I play chess.

Raspy Voice flexes his bruised left hand a few times. "One good punch is all it took to lay you out, girl?" He reaches for his gun. "Thought you was tougher than that."

Raspy Voice hears the click, the smile vanishing from his lips.

But I smile though it hurts like hell. "I am tough."

I pull the trigger. Once. Twice. Three. Four times.

He drops to the ground. His eyes wide. Mouth open.

I'm not sorry. I'm in pain, but I'm not sorry.

I keep Dagget's gun and confiscate Raspy Voice's, tucking it into the back of my jeans and under my shirt. I stuff the magazines in my pockets, then pick up the tenderizer, sliding it back in my belt. I push around a loosened back left molar with my tongue. My cheek is on fire.

I ease out of the door. There are voices in the woods. Someone unfamiliar and French. I circle so I can hear in front of me and not behind. Soft grass and unpruned branches conceal me as I sneak up behind a man with moussed honey-brown hair. I put my gun to the back of his neck.

"You wanna die?"

"No," he answers.

"Put your gun down," I order.

He obeys, placing the gun on the grass, and eases back up. I whack him with the tenderizer in my other hand, and he crumples to the earth. I tuck the makeshift weapon into my belt. The guy's still breathing.

If I don't have to kill, I won't. I toss his gun into overgrown brush. I hear French's voice ahead. I follow it past maple and oak trees. I don't see him, but I travel a path of broken branches to a small clearing ahead near a lone spruce.

A gun presses into my right temple.

"I clocked you when you took out the jackass behind me. Always make your enemy think you went left when you went right." He takes Dagget's gun from my grip. My backup remains hidden from his sight.

"I'm your enemy?" I face French. My voice hitches, but there's very little I control now.

"'*We gotta make it okay before we lose everything.*' Remember, Red? I didn't say 'you.' I said '*we*'!" French sniffles. A haze comes over his eyes. "I owed Whitlock from day one. I had a juvie record and a misdemeanor, and he got the charge dropped." Frenchie circles me and settles in a spot just before the clearing. "It wasn't always dirty work like this. Or that punk with the tattoo on his cheek."

Emmett and Hudson will be here in half an hour. Maybe more. Maybe less. No matter how broken my family is, it is still my family. French was part of that.

And now . . .

"I made my choice. Whitlock told me to put the heat on Giovanni, and I did. She even did some of the work for me. But you still cleared her, then you took down Julien and Zanthe. *Both* of his kids. Damn! I'd be so proud of you, if you didn't screw me over by being just like your dad. Whitlock says you gotta pay. So, you gotta pay. I fail this time, and he's gonna kill my Anya, my baby. I choose her. Every fucking time. Sorry, Red. I'm really fucking sorry, but I'ma make you look like a hero."

French holsters his gun and keeps his grip on Dagget's. "I won't hurt Emmett or Hudson. I—I love them, too. I swear."

He aims at my chest. His hand holds a slight tremor as he pulls the trigger, but I don't flinch. And the bullet doesn't fire. I engaged the safety when French's gun barrel pressed against my head. French doesn't have his glasses. He's in a rush. All these things made him sloppy.

Always make your enemy think you went left when you went right."

I retrieve the gun from my back. French drops the Smith & Wesson and reaches for his Glock. I fire first. One to his stomach. One to his chest. I don't see French until he staggers a few feet forward then collapses to the ground.

Kinda like Doc Holliday and Johnny Ringo. I don't think I'll ever watch that movie again.

I inch toward French, kicking his gun away. Two crimson circles quickly bloom. I kneel next to him. I can't hear French, but I can hear the dull screech of police sirens. His lips still move. Maybe he's asking forgiveness. Maybe it's a prayer. Maybe it's gibberish. He grips my hand tighter. I let him. French did what he did, but I won't let him die alone in the woods.

Even if he tried to kill me.

Even if I killed him.

"I'm here, Frenchie. I know you're sorry. I'm sorry, too."

CHAPTER 63

Redding

Six Months Later
December 22, 2025

"Dr. Pynriser says it's all about acknowledgment." I stuff another forkful of Tootchie's fried catfish in my mouth.

She sounds like an evil character from one of those Marvel shows Hudson watches, but I like her. Dr. Pynriser gives me the space to reveal things without pushing.

"What about Detective Elliott?" asks Giovanni.

I grin. "You mean Sergeant Elliot? He's good. Asked if I wanted to transfer to Area One, but I'm riding the hero detective angle, so I still have leverage. Plus, it feels . . . safer working alone. For now."

If I drive by a place with more than six trees, I think of French. I remember his grip on my hand. How it went slack after two minutes. I haven't seen Anya. I don't know if she'll get French's pension.

"My therapist has me working on self-worth," says Giovanni.

I swallow the last of my catfish. "And?"

"Without getting all preachy . . . it's a lifelong journey, I guess." Giovanni shrugs. "Least I'm starting. It'd be a shame to die not knowing truly how awesome as hell I am. You?"

"Well, I already knew I was good as hell." I start laughing.

Giovanni doesn't.

"Okay. I—uh, I think things are better."

I drum my fingers on the table for a minute before I start up again. "Hudson did some sketching in the living room last week. Emmett isn't so pressed when I leave or when I come home late. I don't . . . doubt myself as much."

Frost settles on the edges of the Tootchie's picture window. Servers dodge Christmas shopping bags on the floor near tables. The clatter of dishes and the hum of conversation add to the curated chaos of the holiday. I didn't get Giovanni anything. She didn't get me anything either.

Being alive is all we need.

Giovanni pulls out her phone and shows me a picture of Natalie. Very pregnant. Smiling. "It's still arm's length, but it's healthier than what we had."

I nod and study the people who've just walked through the door. Two men. Late forties. One Caucasian. One Black. Construction gear.

Giovanni glances over her shoulder then back at me. "We're good. No one's tried *anything* since your time in the woods. Plus, Whitlock's got his hands full. He wouldn't come for you."

"I'm not worried about myself."

"He won't come for Hudson or Emmett or me." Giovanni grips my hand.

"Shouldn't I be comforting you?"

"Ah, another word I've learned in therapy . . . reciprocity." Giovanni lets go of my hand. "She talk yet? About Nivea, Stacey, Annette, Olivia, and Mia?"

"No." I sip my lemonade. "Julien'll be pleading guilty next

month. State's attorney offered him thirty years with a chance of parole after fifteen years. That's the best deal he's gonna get after his fancy lawyers abandoned him when Whitlock up and disappeared along with his money."

"You see that press conference?" Giovanni shakes her head in disgust.

It reminded me of those clips I watched of Nixon when he resigned from the presidency. Whitlock opined on what he accomplished. Claimed he didn't know what either of his kids was doing nor would he continue to help with their legal bills. Then he asked for privacy. Then he disappeared.

The scariest and most unnerving realization is the complicity it took for him to reach that level of evil. People stood by or helped him do it. What chance do I have standing up against an institution calcified in the fetid belief that Black bodies can be disappeared for perverseness or pleasure or some warped purpose?

What chance do we have in this world?

Dr. Pynriser would pull me back from the edge. Ask me to focus on something else.

I take a deep breath. "What're you doing after this?"

"Girl, going to sleep. I thought I had my hands full as a head concierge at The Ivory. General manager at The Lavigne Resort is stretching me to my limits, but in the best way. It also helps that the director of operations is nothing like Willa. I can take up space. I can do my job, and they pay me what I'm worth." Giovanni beams ear to ear. "Dinner's on me, I guess."

"Proud of you. Your mom would be, too, Giovanni."

She bites her bottom lip for a few seconds, then says, "Call me Gio."

CHAPTER 64

Redding

December 22, 2025

My back finally cracks as I walk through the door. I welcome the stillness of the house because it's not just the absence of noise. It's the baked-in feeling of comfort along with it.

I have peace when I'm home.

Hudson's sketch pad is lying on the living room table. A partial portrait of Buckingham Fountain decorated in holiday lights. They twinkle from red to green to blue, the skyline beyond; and . . .

My phone rings, the annoying mechanical chiming blares from my back pocket. I wanna sleep next to Emmett. Hog the covers.

"This is Detective Stark."

Static.

"Hello?" I stifle a yawn as I put down Hudson's drawing.

A voice is buried underneath the interference. Clipped words. I can only decipher half syllables.

"Can't hear you. Please call back."

A voice comes through. It's clear. Eerily.

"I'm not dead. Don't stop looking. We're not dead. It's Niv—"

The call ends.

I call back. Nothing.

I call back again. Nothing.

I call back again and again and again.

Denial is a natural human reaction, but Ms. Charlotte played videos of Nivea too many times. I know her voice. This is not a joke.

It's not . . .

It's . . .

I run to the kitchen and vomit in the sink. I heave until there's nothing more my body can give, then slump to the floor.

Acknowledgment.

I lied to myself. Hartwell Whitlock remains on the run and apparently the ghosts I wanted to exorcise aren't ghosts at all.

Nivea, Stacey, Annette, Olivia, and Mia are alive.

★★★★★

ACKNOWLEDGMENTS

I could write a book naming every person who has loved me, encouraged me, and prayed for me, but it would take a lifetime to express how much these acts have guided me, carried me, and sustained me. And I only have these few pages, so I'll try my damnedest.

Thanks to my father, who drove me all around Chicago as I mapped out where Giovanni and Redding would meet, investigate, fight, and triumph. Thanks for the history lessons, the bad jokes, and the trip to that Maxwell Polish joint at midnight that I can't tell Mom about. Your secret's safe with me.

Endless gratitude to my fantastic Momma. I based certain aspects of Redding on you. Her tenacity, her strength, her unwavering desire to do right, and her ability to kick all the booty. She's one of the heroes in this book and you're my hero in real life.

To the best little-big brother I could ask for and you know it. However, what kind of big sister would I be if I didn't tell you that I'm blessed to have you in my life? Thanks for keeping me grounded, sane, and laughing—even when we really shouldn't be laughing.

Eternal thanks to Desi, a beauty-influencing boss. I appreciate you answering all my questions, giving me a glimpse into all the pretty and ugly of your world. And oh Lawd, the tea!

Redding wouldn't be nearly as authentic without CPD Detective Jennifer Elliot. For all of the calls, texts, and emails, I owe you about twenty steak dinners. Thank you for your patience and thoughtfully detailed answers. I truly hope you enjoy this book. And to my cousin Carisa for putting me in touch with Detective Elliot, thank you and love you, cuz.

To Kristen Klus, thank you for taking time out of your schedule to answer questions about the world of hospitality and luxury hotels. It allowed me to craft Giovanni's world in a truly believable way.

The publishing industry can be an unforgiving, all-consuming beast. And I wouldn't have survived without Annie Chagnot of Park Row Books. You took 122,455 words and helped me to create a story that is one of my best yet! Your dedication and understanding of storytelling combined is a thing of beauty. To Beth Marshea of Ladderbird Literary, it's been a pleasure working with you these past seven years. I don't have the words, but I know you'll always be there for me. Same goes here. To my agent, Taj McCoy of Laura Dail Literary Agency, your love, camaraderie, and support are precious jewels that I will hoard like all my pictures of Aldis Hodge.

To my extended family and friends, you all play an important role in who I am now and the journey of who I will become. I love you.

Lastly, I wrote this book not as an indictment against this country and its apathy when Black women or women of color—or anyone not fitting a certain narrative—go missing. *Strangers Behind Closed Doors* is a mirror. It's a reflection of our current world, but we can change what we see. We can reform our actions. We can take the time and the effort to change our beliefs, redefine our priorities, and call out injustice when we see it. And whatever that journey looks like for you, just take those steps.

Keep fighting. Keep loving. Keep living.

Hugs and tacos,
Cathy